"Tara's sh[...] to life u[...]

"Readers will find themselves laughing out loud."
—*Romance Reviews Today on*
DEATH, TAXES, AND SILVER SPURS

"[A] sure shot success!"   —*Fresh Fiction*

"Witty, remarkable, and ever so entertaining."
—*Affaire de Coeur* on DEATH,
TAXES, AND GREEN TEA ICE CREAM

"Be prepared for periodic unpredictable, uncontrollable laughing fits. Wonderful scenarios abound when it comes to Tara going undercover in this novel about tax evasion, drugs and (of course) guns. Good depth of characters and well-developed chapters are essential when casting a humorous series and Ms. Kelly excels in both departments."
—*Night Owl Reviews* on DEATH, TAXES,
AND HOT PINK LEG WARMERS

"Plenty of action and romantic drama round out this laugh-out-loud novel. Fans of Evanovich's Stephanie Plum series or Pollero's Finley Tanner series will enjoy the fast-paced antics and fruity cocktails of Tara Holloway."
—*RT Book Reviews*

Death, Taxes,
and a Shotgun Wedding

DIANE KELLY

St. Martin's Paperbacks

This is a work of fiction. All of the characters, organizations, and events portrayed in this novel are either products of the author's imagination or are used fictitiously.

DEATH, TAXES, AND A SHOTGUN WEDDING

For information address St. Martin's Press, 175 Fifth Avenue, New York, NY 10010.

ISBN: 978-1-250-09490-2

Our books may be purchased in bulk for promotional, educational, or business use. Please contact your local bookseller or the Macmillan Corporate and Premium Sales Department at 1-800-221-7945, ext. 5442, or by e-mail at MacmillanSpecialMarkets@macmillan.com.

Printed in the United States of America

St. Martin's Paperbacks edition / November 2017

St. Martin's Paperbacks are published by St. Martin's Press, 175 Fifth Avenue, New York, NY 10010.

10 9 8 7 6 5 4 3 2 1

To Jana Upton, who wrote as Trinity Blake.
Your life story ended much too soon, with chapters left
unwritten. But it featured a strong, beautiful, smart,
and creative heroine I am glad to have had
the chance to know. See you at The End.

$\mathcal{A}$cknowledgments

As always, lots of people played a role in getting this book out into the world, and I'm grateful for all of their help and support.

Thanks to the IRS special agents who graciously granted me an interview all those years ago. You shared some invaluable information about your intriguing work and impressed me so much with your knowledge, skills, and drive. It's good to know the American coffers are in such capable hands, and that you are fighting on behalf of us all to ensure fair and honest tax administration. Though I've stretched reality in these books for the sake of humor or efficiency and Tara is hardly a model agent, I hope that my books reflect the respect I have for the agency and your profession. Thanks for all you do, and keep up the good fight.

Thanks to my wonderful daughter Lindsay—a talented writer, dancer, actress, playwright, screenwriter, and all-around person. Thanks for not only giving me the idea of the rental scam while you were apartment hunting months ago, but for also schooling me on the ins and outs of Lyft and Uber.

Thanks to my editor, Holly Ingraham, for taking a chance on an aspiring writer seven years ago and helping me hone my skills since. I couldn't ask for a better editor.

Thanks to Sarah Melnyck, Paul Hochman, Allison Ziegler, Jennie Conway, and the others at St. Martin's who worked to get this book to readers. Y'all make a great team.

Thanks to Danielle Christopher and Monika Roe for creating such fun book covers for this series.

Thanks to my agent, Helen Breitwieser, for all you do in furthering my career.

Thanks to Liz Bemis and the staff of Bemis Promotions for my great Web site and newsletters.

Many other writers helped me develop this series or gave me encouragement along the way. Thanks to the members of the Kick-Ass Writers Group—Urania Fung, Simon Rex-Lear, Gay Downs, Vannetta Chapman, Charles McMillen, Celya Bowers, and Kennedy Shaw. Wow, we were just kids when we met, huh? Big thanks to the Killer Fiction Writers—Christie Craig, Jana DeLeon, Leslie Langtry, Gemma Halliday, Kyra Davis, Angie Fox, Amanda Brice, Kathleen Bacus, and Robin Kaye. You invited me to join your blog even though I was still unpublished at the time. Your belief in me meant more than I could ever say. Thanks to Angela Cavener, Angela Hicks, Jana Upton, Michella Chappell, DD Ayres, Candace Havens, Kristan Higgins, Tina Ferraro, Cindy Kirk, Lorraine Heath, Molly Cannon, Andi King, and the other untold members of the Dallas Area Romance Authors, Romance Writers of America, and Mystery Writers of America who have served as my support system all these years and whose critique, suggestions, and/or volunteer efforts have furthered my career and made our industry what it is today.

A debt of gratitude is also owed to Allison Kelley, Executive Director of Romance Writers of America, as well as the entire RWA staff. They work hard to protect the interests of authors, to facilitate the relationships between authors and publishers, and to make sure readers get quality books from well-educated writers.

Thanks to my friends who have cheered me on along the way and shared my books with their friends and book clubs. I'm so lucky to have a great group of friends like you in my life.

Thanks to my husband, kids, and extended family, who have been supportive and encouraging, and at times even unwittingly lent their names to my characters. You are my rocks.

Now for some especially sappy stuff . . .

Though IRS Special Agent Tara Holloway and the other characters in this series are fictional, they have become like friends and family to me. This is the final book in the series, and it's hard to say goodbye to them even though I know it's time and I'm sending them off to live long and happy lives off the page. These characters would not have enjoyed all of these fun adventures if it weren't for you wonderful readers who have bought my books and made my writing career possible. Thank you, THANK YOU, THANK YOU for giving me my dream job! There's nothing as wonderful as connecting with readers through my stories. I'm happy knowing the books in this series have made you feel, think, and laugh. I hope you'll venture into the worlds of the other fictional friends I'll create for you in the future.

I wish all of you big tax refunds, freedom from audits, and many happy returns.

chapter one

*B*ride to Be . . . *Killed?*

Early on a Sunday morning in mid-August, I sat at my fiancé's kitchen table and placed a stamp on the last of our one hundred and thirty-eight wedding invitations. *Done! Yay!*

In a few short weeks, Nick and I would be tying the knot. *Woot-woot!* But until then, we'd be busy with our jobs as special agents for the Internal Revenue Service, fighting tax evasion and white-collar crime. Criminals don't take a day off, and neither would we—at least not until after the wedding when we planned to spend a romantic week in Cancún, Mexico. *Margaritas. Cabana boys with sexy Spanish accents. Beautiful Mexican beaches. Life doesn't get any better than that.*

Even though the invitations wouldn't be picked up until tomorrow, I figured I might as well get them in the mail. There was a blue collection box only a quarter mile away, at the entrance to the neighborhood. Besides, Nick's Australian shepherd mix, Daffodil, had been dropping not-so-subtle hints that she wanted to go for a walk. She'd pawed the inside of his front door, nudged my leg, and when that failed, she'd retrieved her leash and brought it to me in her mouth, dropping it at my feet as if to say *Hey, dummy. Am I making myself clear now?*

I reached out and ruffled her head. "Okay, girl. I give in. We'll go for a walk."

After clipping the leash to her collar, I stashed the invitations in my tote bag and slung the straps over my shoulder. Nick was still asleep in his bed upstairs. He'd had a tough week, learning the ropes as he prepared to move up the ladder at the IRS, taking on his new position as codirector of the IRS Criminal Investigations Division in Dallas. I let him continue snoozing. He'd earned it. Besides, he'd need to be well rested for later. We planned to spend the day packing for our upcoming move, and he'd be the one doing the heavy lifting.

Daffodil dragged me to the door, prancing happily on the floor, her nails clicking on the tile and her fluffy tail whipping back and forth. We eased past the stack of empty boxes in the foyer, headed out onto the porch, and made our way down to the sidewalk. When she stopped to sniff the tree out front, she took advantage of the opportunity to multitask and simultaneously crouched to relieve herself.

We continued down the sidewalk, pausing on occasion so she could smell a bush here, a curb there. It wasn't unusual for cars to be parked on the street in our neighborhood of town houses, so I paid little attention to the white pickup sitting halfway between Nick's town house and mine down the block. It looked just the same as thousands of other trucks in the Dallas–Fort Worth metroplex.

We continued on, passing my place across the street. In the yard was a recently erected FOR SALE sign with the phone number of my Realtor, whose tax returns I'd prepared while working my former job at the CPA firm of Martin & McGee. Nick and I were in the process of buying the house next door to his mother in another part of town, so I hoped my place would sell quickly. Couldn't hurt to get my equity out of my current home and put more down on the new place, lower our monthly payments.

We also planned to hold a garage sale at my place next Saturday to get rid of the things we'd no longer need once we were married. Given that we'd both lived on our own for several years, we had duplicates of some items. Two living room sets. Two sets of pots and pans. Two gun cabinets. We'd begun sorting through our things and separating them into piles of stuff to keep and stuff to put out at the garage sale.

While we hadn't yet agreed whose living room furniture or pans we'd be selling off, there was no doubt we'd be keeping my gun cabinet. Nick had bought mine for me for Valentine's Day. It was painted a glossy red and held my extensive collection of handguns and rifles, even a sawed-off shotgun. But there would be room for Nick's guns in it, too. He had fewer than I did. He'd grown up in the country where he might need a rifle to shoot into the air to scare off a wandering coyote before it went for the chicken coop. I, on the other hand, grew up in a family of gun nuts who liked to hunt. While I'd inherited their affinity for the sport of shooting, I had no killer instinct and couldn't imagine taking aim at an innocent deer or bird. I preferred target practice only, putting a bullet through a paper target or a root beer can. That's not to say I'd never shot anyone. I'd put bullets in the legs of suspects after they'd first shot at me, and I'd even put a bullet through the brain of a member of a dangerous drug cartel. My one and only kill. I hoped it would stay that way. I derived no pleasure from having to use my weapon against people. I hoped I would never have to do it again.

"This way, girl," I told the dog as I rounded the corner. Daffodil turned up the street too, trotting a few feet ahead of me as we made our way onto the main road.

We reached the mailbox and I circled around to the front of it, grabbing stacks of invitations out of my bag and slipping them through the slot, where they plunked to the metal floor inside. Finished, we began to head back down the sidewalk.

We'd taken only a few steps when my ears picked up the sound of a big automobile engine coming up the street in front of us. Daffodil heard it, too. I looked up to see the white truck heading our way. Still, I would have paid it no mind had the dog not pricked up her ears and stopped dead in her tracks, staring at it, as if she sensed something was amiss.

"Everything okay, Daffy?"

VROOOOOM! The driver floored the engine and swerved right at us.

What the—?!?

Luckily for us both, Daffodil's canine instincts were quicker than my inferior human ones, and she darted behind a mature oak tree, yanking me after her. Not a second too soon, either. As I fell to the grass behind the tree, the truck came up the curb, ran over the sidewalk where we'd just been standing, and hit the mailbox with a resounding *BAM!*

The four legs of the box had been bolted to the concrete. But not anymore. The force of the impact ripped them from their moorings. The box flew up in the air and performed a back flip, its door opening and showering out wedding invitations in every direction before the box came down in the center of the main road. *CLANG!* The white pickup never even braked, careening back onto the street and roaring off before I could catch its license-plate number.

SCREEEEEEEECH! An oncoming red Ford Fiesta braked hard but couldn't stop before crashing into the mailbox. *CRASH!* An instant later there was a *poom* as the airbags inflated, followed by *tinkle-tinkle-tinkle* as the Fiesta became a metal piñata, raining parts onto the asphalt. Meanwhile, the mailbox spun like a top down the street, finally coming to rest against the curb.

As I levered myself up from the ground, the airbag deflated to reveal a teenaged girl at the wheel. Heck, the ink was probably still wet on her license. Her eyes bugged wide and her mouth hung open in shock.

I ran to the curb, holding Daffodil's leash tight. "Are you okay?" I hollered to the girl.

She looked at me through the window and burst into tears but nonetheless managed to nod, her dark curls bobbing about her face.

I whipped my cell phone from my pocket and dialed 911.

"Dallas 911," came a male voice. "What's your emergency?"

"A driver in a white pickup nearly ran over me and my dog, and hit a mail collection box. The mailbox ended up in the road and a car crashed into it." I gave him the names of the streets at the intersection. "Last I saw the truck it was heading east."

"Did you get a license-plate number?"

"No. It all happened too fast. But there's got to be front end damage to the truck."

"Anyone injured?"

"No." *Thank goodness!*

"I'll get law enforcement en route."

By this time, traffic had slowed to a crawl as cars backed up behind the stationary Ford and rubberneckers inched around it, gawking as they rolled over the invitations we'd paid a pretty penny for and spent untold hours addressing and stamping. But there was nothing I could do about that now. Holding Daffodil's leash tight, I stepped up to the curb and motioned for the girl to unroll the passenger window. "The police are on their way."

She held out her phone to me. "Can you call my parents?" she blubbered. "They're going to be so mad!"

"Not at you," I assured her. "I'll let them know this wasn't your fault."

I took the phone, found "Mom" on her list of contacts, and dialed the number. "Hello," I said. "My name is Tara Holloway. Your daughter is fine but she's been in an accident."

"WHAT?!?" shrieked her mother.

"She's okay," I repeated to calm the woman. "The accident wasn't her fault. A truck hit a mailbox and it flew out into the street right in front of her car. She's not hurt. She's just scared."

I gave the woman our location.

"I'll be right there!" she cried.

I ended the call and handed the phone back to the girl. "Your mom's on her way."

Sobbing, she nodded and took her phone.

The girl taken care of, I phoned Nick. "Put on some pants," I told him. "Daffy and I need you." I gave him a quick rundown. *Truck. Mailbox. Crash.*

"Holy shit!" he hollered into the phone. "I'll be right there!"

We ended the call and I slid the phone into my pocket. In mere seconds, Nick came running around the corner in sneakers, a rumpled pair of shorts and nothing else.

"Are you all right?" he shouted as he ran toward us.

"We're fine." Well, other than my shoulder having been pulled out of the socket. But I wasn't about to complain.

Nick grabbed me in a bear hug and pulled me to him, holding me so tight I could barely breathe.

When he finally released me, I told him about his hero dog. "Daffodil yanked me to safety. No telling what would have happened if she hadn't clued in and pulled me out of the way." Actually, that was a lie. I knew exactly what would have happened. I would've been plowed down, that's what. I owed her my life.

Nick crouched next to me and cradled Daffodil's face in his hands, looking into her eyes. "You okay, baby girl?"

She trembled in fear, but nonetheless gave him a lick on the cheek. He returned the gesture by kissing her snout. "I can't believe someone tried to run over an innocent dog." He stood and turned to me. "Unfortunately, I have no trouble believing someone would want to run *you* over."

I frowned and put my hands on my hips. "Thanks a lot!"

"You know what I mean." Nick's eyes darkened with concern. "You've made a lot of enemies."

I certainly had. Trouble just seemed to find me. Since joining the IRS, I'd put dozens of people behind bars. Far as I knew, though, all of them were still behind those bars. "Maybe this was just a freak thing," I said. "Maybe the driver wasn't aiming for me. Maybe the driver just lost control of the truck."

"I suppose that's possible. But until we know for sure this was an accident we'd better keep our guard up." Nick turned to the crumpled car and eyed the sobbing girl behind the wheel. "Let's get her out of there."

"Good idea."

Putting up a hand to halt the traffic, he circled around the car and opened her door. "Why don't you come wait with us?"

She swiped her tears away and nodded. She tried to climb out, realized her seat belt was still on, and reached down to release it. Nick held out a hand to help her out of the car.

After leading her over to the oak tree where I waited with Daffodil, Nick glanced back at the envelopes strewn all over the road. "Tell me those aren't our wedding invitations all over the street."

I sighed. "Wish I could."

chapter two

$\mathcal{S}$pecial Delivery

Sirens sounded in the distance, drawing closer. A minute later, a fortyish female police officer pulled up behind the Fiesta, the lights flashing on her cruiser. She climbed out and came over to speak with us. Her gaze went to Nick, and she eyed his biceps appreciatively. I used to get jealous when this type of thing happened, but by now I'd gotten used to it. Female attention was a given when you were dating a hottie. Fortunately, Nick didn't let it go to his head.

After obtaining our names, she said, "All units are keeping an eye out for a damaged white pickup in the vicinity. Nothing so far." She turned to the girl, angling her head to indicate the crumpled Fiesta. "That your car, hon?"

"Yes," the girl said. "My mom and dad bought it for me for my birthday last week."

"It doesn't look safe to drive. I'll get a tow truck out here." With that, she squeezed the button on her shoulder-mounted radio to contact the Dallas PD dispatcher.

Being the sweet dog that she was, Daffodil seemed to realize that the girl, too, was rattled. She looked up at her and wagged her tail, giving a soft *woof?* of concern. The girl crouched down and ran her hands over the dog, the effect seeming to soothe them both.

The officer pulled a notepad and pen from her pocket. "Either of you ladies get a look at the person driving the truck?"

"I didn't," the girl said. "I didn't even see the truck. All I saw was the mailbox flying out into the street and the airbag coming at me."

The cop shifted her gaze to me.

I raised my palms. "Sorry. It all happened so fast and there was a glare on the windshield from the morning sun."

"Can you at least tell me whether there was anyone in the truck besides the driver?"

I shook my head, knowing my responses had to be frustrating her. I felt the same way when a witness was unable to provide helpful information in my cases.

"Did you recognize the truck?" she asked.

"No. It was just a typical white pickup."

"Make or model?"

"Couldn't tell ya." *I should've paid more attention.*

"Anybody got a reason to try to run you down?"

I issued an involuntary snort in response.

She arched an intrigued brow.

"I'm a special agent for IRS Criminal Investigations," I explained. "Since I joined the agency last year, I've arrested an ice-cream-truck driver, several businessmen and tax preparers, a televangelist, the leader of a secessionist group, members of a terrorist operation, a drug-dealing pimp, a country-western singer, members of a drug cartel, a mafia boss, a guy who'd catfished women online, a local talk radio personality, and a human smuggler."

"Among others," Nick added.

The woman looked up and down my relatively scrawny

five-feet-two-inch frame. "Never would've taken you for such a badass."

"Most people don't," I acknowledged. "Sometimes that works to my advantage." I told her that despite my numerous arrests, I wasn't aware of anyone in particular being after me. "This whole thing could have been nothing more than an accident." Maybe the driver had been using a cell phone and accidentally hit the gas and swerved our way. Or maybe the driver panicked after hitting the mailbox and had driven off to avoid the repercussions. After all, distracted drivers and hit-and-runs were not uncommon.

"Maybe." She wrote down my contact information as well as the girl's. "If anything comes up, I'll be in touch." She slid her pen and notepad back into her pocket. "In the meantime, let's see about getting that mail rounded up. Sure seems to be a lot of it."

"I'd just mailed our wedding invitations."

She cut me a look. "Seriously?"

"Seriously."

She shook her head. "I hope you don't believe in bad omens."

While the police officer held traffic at bay with a raised palm, Nick and I scurried about, collecting the envelopes and stuffing them back into my bag. I found three in a storm drain. Some of the invitations had ended up lodged in the branches of nearby trees. Fortunately, Nick was able to reach those or get them down by shaking the branches until they fell. Many of those that had landed on the road bore telltale tire marks. But at least the addresses on all of them were still legible.

After we finished collecting the envelopes, Nick grabbed the dented mailbox and dragged it up onto the curb. He looked inside and found a couple more invitations lodged between the frame and the damaged door.

The tow truck arrived, followed by the girl's mom. The anxious mother eyed the squashed front of the Fiesta, leaped from her car, and ran over to wrap her arms around her daughter. "I'm so glad you're okay!"

Cocooned in her mother's embrace, the girl burst into fresh sobs.

Her mother eyed me over her daughter's shoulder. "What happened?"

"A truck came out of nowhere and hit the mailbox. It flew into the street. Your daughter was coming up the road and had no time to stop."

Her eyes narrowed and her jaw flexed. "Was it a drunk driver?"

"Could be," I said, though it seemed too early for anyone to be drunk. Then again, maybe the driver had gone to brunch and downed a few too many mimosas. "Or it could have been someone on a cell phone who accidentally hit the gas pedal. There's no way of knowing."

Nick, Daffy, and I parted ways with the two. "Take care."

When we returned to Nick's town house, I overturned my bag on Nick's kitchen table.

He took one look at the dirty envelopes and groaned. "This sucks. I know how much time you spent on those."

Money, too. The invitations hadn't come cheap. Neither had the postage. "Besides the time it would take to readdress the invitations," I said, "we'd have to pay a rush fee if we reorder. I say we send them as is. They don't look pretty, but at least they're intact."

He stepped over and pulled me into another hug. "That's one of the many things I love about you."

"What is?"

"You don't sweat the small stuff."

We sat down at the table and compared the names on

the envelopes to the guest list, making sure we had them all. We did. *Phew.*

The crisis now contained, I fixed Daffodil four of my world-famous fried baloney sandwiches and hand-fed them to her, all the while singing her praises. It was the least I could do for the dog who'd saved my life. "You're a good girl, Daffy. My hero!"

She wagged her tail in appreciation and wolfed the food down.

Little did I know that outgoing mail wasn't going to be my only problem. Turned out a certain piece of *incoming* mail would bear a surprise for me, too.

At work on Monday afternoon, my ears picked up the *squeak-squeak-squeak* of the mail cart as it rolled up the hall. *Someone should oil that darn wheel.* The young clerk stepped into my office with a small stack of envelopes and paperwork and slid it into my inbox.

I was on my phone, arguing with an attorney who'd been hired to defend a target in one of my tax cases. I gave the mail clerk a smile and a thumbs-up in appreciation for his delivery services as I reamed the lawyer. "The records your client sent over are incomplete. There were none of the invoices we asked for. Either you send the rest of the documentation over by one o'clock on Friday or I'll be out to arrest your client that afternoon." With that I hung up the phone. I'd had enough of his and his client's bullshit.

I reached over and pulled the stack of mail from the tray. At the top was a postcard advertising a continuing education workshop on the finer points of oil and gas law. *No, thanks.*

Next was an envelope containing a check for $47,368.92 made out to the U.S. Treasury, payment of a settlement

I'd negotiated. *Good job, Tara,* I mentally told myself.
You're a superstar! Okay, maybe that was a bit too self-
congratulatory, but it's not like the American public ever
thanked us for doing our jobs. Heck, most people didn't
even know there was such a thing as the IRS Criminal
Investigations Division or a special agent who carried
both decimals and weapons. I can't tell you how many
times someone saw the holstered Glock at my waist,
gasped, and exclaimed, "Auditors carry guns?" We IRS
special agents worked in the shadows, like Batman. Of
course some might say that cockroaches also worked in
the shadows and liken us agents to the filthy bugs, but
those people would be assholes.

The third piece of mail was an interoffice memo from
Viola reminding the staff that any items left in the refrigerator at 4:30 on Friday afternoon would be tossed out.
One too many tuna sandwiches had been left to grow
fuzz over the weekend. While I didn't enjoy the stench
when I went for my coffee creamer in the fridge come
Monday morning, the shades of blue and green mold
could be quite pretty if you didn't think too much about
their source.

My last piece of mail was a pink greeting-card envelope. There was no return address on the front. I turned
the envelope over. None on the back, either. *That's odd.*
Looked like the sender must have forgotten. I checked the
front again. The postmark indicated the piece had been
mailed from somewhere in Dallas last Thursday.

I opened the envelope and pulled out the card. It was a
flowery model, with "You're Engaged" written across the
front in a fancy font. *How nice,* I thought. *Our first formal
well-wisher.*

But when I opened the card, I realized I'd been sorely
mistaken. The preprinted message "Best Wishes for a
Lifetime of Happiness!" had been marked through in thick

red ink. Instead of the sweet sentiment, the sender had instead scrawled a handwritten message. "At Death You Will Part."

Uh-oh.

Remember what I'd said about trouble always finding me? Looked like it had found me again.

chapter three

*B*est Wishes, Death Wishes

While I had eventually written off yesterday's near-miss with the pickup as a random event, this card told me it might not have been. The driver of the pickup could have actually been trying to kill me. Given that the card had been mailed from within the city last Thursday, the sender might have assumed I'd receive the card on Friday, prior to their attempt to run me down. If not for the fact that the mail clerk had taken a vacation day last Friday, I probably would have received it then. Viola had sent an e-mail to the agents telling us to sort through the mail ourselves if we were expecting something important. Given that I hadn't been anticipating anything urgent, I hadn't gone to the mailroom to check. If I had, I might have been more careful yesterday, kept a closer eye on my surroundings. *That's what I get for being lazy.*

I took the card across the hall to Nick's office and held it out to him.

"A wedding card?" He smiled as he took it from me. "I hope it has a big fat check in it."

"Not exactly."

His smile faltered and he looked down at the card.

When he opened it and saw what was written inside, his face tightened and he rose reflexively from his seat. "What the hell?"

When he looked to me, I shrugged. I had no answer to his question.

He came around his desk. "We need to show this to Lu."

He and I hightailed it down the hall to the office of our soon-to-retire boss, Luella "Lu" Lobozinski, otherwise known as the Lobo. Viola, Lu's secretary and gatekeeper, sat at her desk, typing on her keyboard. She eyed us over her bifocals.

"Is Lu available?" Nick asked.

She answered by angling her head toward Lu's door, the gesture indicating we could proceed.

We continued past Viola and Nick rapped on Lu's open door. "Got a second, boss?"

Lu looked up from her desk. Her towering strawberry-blond beehive defied the laws of gravity, while her 1960s-style fringed and beaded pantsuit defied the laws of fashion. She was a very defiant woman. "Come on in, you two lovebirds."

We stepped into the office and Nick handed the card to Lu. "Take a look at this."

The Lobo's expression morphed from mildly curious to deeply concerned as she read it. When she finished, she looked the envelope over. "No return address." She gazed up at me through her false eyelashes, her orange-lipstick lips turned down in a frown. "This isn't good."

"Death threats usually aren't," Nick snapped.

"I had a close call with a pickup truck yesterday," I told her. "I wrote it off afterward, but now I'm thinking it was intentional."

Lu leaned to the right and called out her door. "Viola? Get all my agents in here. Pronto."

"Will do!" Viola called back.

In minutes, the other special agents who weren't out in the field had gathered in Lu's office, forming a semicircle around her desk. Viola had come in, too, surely wondering what the hubbub was all about.

From her chair, Lu held up the card. "Someone wants to kill Tara."

A snicker emanated from Senior Agent Eddie Bardin, a dark-skinned, seasoned agent who'd been my first partner and would be sharing codirector responsibilities with Nick once Lu left the agency. "That's nothing new."

He had a point. In fact, Eddie had taken a bullet to the skull when a target in one of our early cases had taken shots at us. He and I had also nearly been blown up together by an improvised explosive device. *Good times.*

"Yeah," agreed Agent Josh Schmidt, the office tech guru who sported cherubic blond curls. "That crazy woman we arrested a few weeks ago tried to choke Tara and dragged her down a flight of stairs."

All in a day's work.

Our newest agent, Will Dorsey, chimed in now. "First case I worked with Tara we ended up in a shoot-out in a trucking yard."

Not to be left out, Agent Hana Kim said, "Don't forget the mob boss who tried to burn her to death in his restaurant."

Hana had assisted me in that case. I'd nearly been smoked, literally and figuratively.

I raised my hands in surrender. "Okay! Okay! We can all agree that people have tried to kill me in the past. But all of those attempts involved investigations that were ongoing at the time. Nothing I'm working on now strikes me as risky."

My current caseload was heavy but involved run-of-the mill tax evaders. A freelance home health nurse who'd tried to get away with deducting personal expenses on his business return. A nightclub that had failed to report a significant percentage of cash receipts. Ditto for a farmer who ran a horse boarding facility on his acreage. None of them seemed dangerous. Dishonest, sure, but not threatening.

"Maybe it's someone related to an older case," Lu suggested.

Eddie shrugged. "Or maybe it's personal."

All eyes turned to me.

I raised my palms. "I can't think of anyone in my personal life who'd want me dead." I got along well with my family, friends, and neighbors, and had given no one a reason to have a vendetta against me. At least not that I knew of.

Hana turned to Nick. "Got any old girlfriends who might want to kill your fiancée?"

That was an angle I hadn't thought of, but Nick quickly quelled the questioning murmurs. "None of my exes are psychos."

Lu exhaled a sharp breath. "Until we figure out who's trying to kill Tara and get that person under lock and key, I'm assigning each of you to rotating bodyguard shifts."

Josh gasped. "You mean I'd have to take a bullet for her?" He cut his baby-blue eyes my way, his pinched expression saying he didn't like the idea one bit.

"Let's call it security detail instead," Lu said. "I'm not expecting anyone to sacrifice themselves, but there's safety in numbers and she'll need some help keeping an eye out. Everyone wear your vests and holsters and stay on guard." She quickly worked up a rotating schedule and e-mailed a copy of it to everyone. Once the e-mail had set off through cyberspace, she shooed the agents out of her office. "Back to work, everyone."

I was the last to go. As I reached the door Lu sighed from behind me and said, "Tara?"

I turned around and our gazes met. Worry darkened her heavily made-up eyes. "I'm looking forward to the wedding. Don't go getting yourself killed. Okay?"

I swallowed the lump of emotion choking my throat. "I'll do my best, ma'am."

I returned to my office and plunked down in my chair, running my gaze over my files, trying to decide which case to work on next. *Hmm . . .*

My cell phone chirped and I consulted the screen. It was Detective Veronica Booth calling from the Dallas Police Department. Detective Booth and an FBI agent had recently recruited me to assist on a case involving a mobster who'd extorted money from business owners and left a slew of dead bodies around the metroplex. That same mobster was the guy who'd tried to burn me to death in his wife's restaurant, along with his wife and another employee. I wondered why the detective was calling now. *Only one way to find out.*

I tapped the icon to accept the call. "Hello, Detective Booth. How are you?"

"Out of ideas, that's how I am."

Though her words might sound short, those of us in law enforcement were always overworked. We often didn't have time for niceties and had to get straight to the point.

"You're calling me for a fresh perspective?"

"That," she replied, "and maybe some assistance."

"Whatcha got?"

"Rent scam."

Seemed a new financial scam was always popping up, and rental scams had become the crime *du jour.*

"I've got something I want to run by you, too." Namely, the threat I'd received. "How about I pop on over?"

"I'll tell the front desk to send you up."

When I ended the call with Detective Booth, I consulted the schedule Lu had prepared, picked up my desk phone, and dialed Hana Kim's office. "I need to head over to the Dallas Police Department headquarters. Looks like you're on backup for me today."

"Do I get paid extra for babysitting?"

"It's not *babysitting*," I snapped. "And, no, you don't get any extra pay. But if you stop complaining I'll buy you a coffee on the drive over."

"Deal."

I closed my door, slipped my ballistic vest on under my dress shirt, and buttoned it back up.

When I stepped out into the hall to meet up with Hana, Nick stood from his desk across the way. He'd pulled out the blue stress ball he squeezed to relieve tension. I hadn't seen him use the thing in months, but apparently my death threat had pushed him over the edge. "Promise me you'll be extra careful?" he asked, the ball disappearing in his fist as he closed it.

"I promise."

"Don't worry," Hana added, "I'll take care of your bride to be."

I eyed her to ensure she'd also donned her vest. She had. After bidding Nick good-bye, we made our way to the elevators and I punched the down-arrow button.

"Here." Hana held out her hand. "Eat this."

I opened my palm and she dropped three small wrapped candies into it. I'd never seen them before. "What is this?"

"Yeot," she said. "It's a traditional Korean candy. It's like taffy. It's supposed to make good luck stick to you. I figured with someone out to kill you, you might need some good luck."

She'd gotten that right. I unwrapped one of the candies and popped it into my mouth. "Yum!" But she was right. The stuff sure was sticky. I could hardly chew it. It nearly glued my upper and bottom teeth together. She popped one into her mouth, too.

We rode down to the lobby in silence, not so much on purpose but because our mouths were busy working the candy. Outside, we headed to the employee lot and my plain government sedan, what we feds called a G-ride. Not the sexiest cars around by any stretch of the imagination and not nearly as fun to drive as my personal BMW convertible, but you don't exactly get luxury when you're paying for a car with taxpayer dollars.

We climbed in and headed for the Dallas PD headquarters, making a run through a coffee place drive-thru on the way. I opted for a skinny no-whip latte, ordering a second to take to Booth. Hana went all out and got a caramel macchiato with whipped cream. She could afford the calories. She played softball not only on the IRS team—the Tax Maniacs—but also played in a recreational league as well. Volleyball was more my game, but the only chance I'd had to play since college intramurals was an occasional game at a backyard barbecue. I'd recently pudged out a bit while battling a sweet-potato-fry addiction, but I was trying to get back on track so that I'd look my best on my wedding day. In fact, I had a final fitting for my wedding dress two weeks from Wednesday night. Until then, I'd better add an extra hundred sit-ups to my workouts.

"Thanks." I took the drinks from the young man at the window and situated them in the cup holders. Before I could pull out of the drive-thru, the air was pierced with an earsplitting *BANG!*

Hana and I ducked down in our seats and whipped out our guns.

Hana looked at me, her eyes wide and wary. "Was that a gunshot?"

"It sure sounded like one!"

Stuck in the drive-thru with a building to our left and cars to our right side and rear, we were sitting ducks. Still, we hadn't taken a hit as far as I could tell. If someone had fired at us, they weren't a good shot. I poked my head up to see over the steering wheel.

BANG!

"Sheesh." I sat full upright now and slid my gun back into my holster. "It's just an old VW backfiring." *Get a tune-up, you old hippie!*

"Good." Hana sat up and reholstered her gun, too. She reached for her drink, taking a sip and getting whipped cream on the end of her nose. "For a second there, I thought we were goners."

chapter four

*Y*ou Scratch My Back, I'll Scratch Yours

When we arrived at the Dallas PD headquarters building, we parked and made our way into the building, cardboard coffee cups in hand. We checked in with the uniformed Dallas PD officer working the front desk.

"We're here to see Detective Booth," I said.

The muscular guy looked us up and down, his expression skeptical as he took in the two shorter-than-average women in front of him. "You're the special agents from the IRS?"

"Yes," we said in unison. *And don't let our size fool you. We kick ass.* Hana's narrowed eyes told me we'd had that thought in unison, too.

The guy hiked a thumb toward the elevators. "You can go on up."

"Thanks."

Before we stepped away, Hana handed him one of the candies. "Try this. It's good-luck candy."

"Cops can always use some of that." He unwrapped it, popped it in his mouth, and nodded in approval as the sweet taste hit his tongue.

Yep, Dallas PD could definitely use some good luck after the losses it suffered last year. Five officers were gunned down when a sniper ambushed them at what was supposed to be a peaceful protest to bring attention to police shootings of unarmed black men in other cities. Because the protest had been expected to be calm, and as a symbolic gesture of unity rather than divisiveness, the officers had not been wearing protective riot gear. Four of the officers who were killed served with the Dallas Police Department, while one served with Dallas Area Rapid Transit, or DART for short. On top of the deaths, multiple other officers and two civilians had been shot but had luckily survived, including a mother who had used her body to shield her children from the gunfire. It was the deadliest day for law enforcement in the U.S. since 9/11, and a dark day for Dallas. Ironically, then Police Chief David Brown, a black man, had made significant reforms during his six-year tenure, and the number of excessive-force complaints had decreased dramatically prior to the shooting. The department had focused on deescalation and community policing. But it wasn't enough to stop an armed man intent on revenge.

We rode an elevator up to the third floor and I led Hana down to the detective's office at the end of the hall. The door was cracked. A coffee cup in each hand, I rapped on it with the knuckle of my index finger, saying, "It's Agents Holloway and Kim."

"Come on in," called a voice from inside.

I opened the door and we stepped into Detective Booth's office. She was around forty years old, seasoned enough to have learned a thing or two, at or approaching the peak of her career. She wore a pink button-down shirt and navy blue pants. Her pointy features were pixielike, her honey-colored hair slicked back into a ponytail at the nape of her neck. She stood from behind her desk, her gaze going from me to Hana. "Nice to see you again, Agent Holloway. I see you've brought a friend?"

"Boss's orders," I told her. "The reason Special Agent Kim is with me is what I wanted to talk to you about."

Booth extended her hand. "Good to meet you, Agent Kim."

When they'd finished their exchange, I raised the cup in my right hand. "I also brought you a latte."

She took the cup from me and smiled at it as she cradled it in her hands. "Good to meet you, too."

The introductions complete, we took our seats.

After gulping a healthy slug of coffee, the detective tilted her head and eyed me. "You want to go first or should I?"

"Go ahead," I told her. After all, she'd been the one to get the ball rolling by placing the call to me earlier. Her case should get priority.

"Okay." She picked a file folder up from her desk and held it out to me. "Here's a set of documentation for you on the rent scam. More than forty people have filed complaints in the last five months. The MO is the same each time. The victims found a really good deal on a house or condo listed for rent online, filled out a contact form, and received an e-mail in reply from a man purporting to be a leasing agent working on behalf of the owner. The responses were virtually identical. You know, 'there's been a lot of interest, if you want a shot at the place you better move fast.' That kind of thing."

In other words, the e-mail reply contained the standard BS intended to pressure people into making quick decisions rather than smart ones. But how was the con artist able to access the properties? Did he break in? Steal the keys somehow?

Booth continued. "After he shows each victim the place

and they express interest, he gives them an application to fill out. He tells them that the current tenants will be out at the end of the month. He also tells them that there have been other well-qualified applicants but that he'd love to rent to them because he can tell they really like the place. He says that the other applicants have higher income and more money in savings and, because of that, the property owner will probably consider them better risks. But he suggests that if the victim gets a payment to him before the other applicants they'll have a good chance of landing the lease because the owner is leaving for a two-month trip to Europe the next day and wants to get the deal settled beforehand. He suggests the victim immediately get a money order in the amount of the first and last months' rent, plus a security deposit. The total is usually in the range of three to four thousand dollars."

My mind performed some quick mental math, computing the numbers. Forty victims at a minimum of three grand each totaled at least $120,000 in tax-free money. This crook had cleaned up. And who knew how much more he might have earned since the last report?

Booth continued. "He waits at the unit until the victim returns with the money order. He claims that he called the property owner in the meantime and got the go-ahead to offer them a lease. He has them sign a rental agreement, gives them a copy of it and his business card, and arranges an alleged time later when he'll meet them at the unit with the keys. Then he takes off with their money order, cashes it, and never shows up with the keys at the scheduled time."

I finished for her. "And that's when the victims find out the guy isn't a real leasing agent and had no authority to rent the place."

"Exactly," Booth said. "Neither the victims nor the owners of the properties have any clue who the guy is.

He never uses a phone to conduct business. He only uses
e-mail. Clever, huh?"

Clever, indeed. Cell phones were extremely vulnerable.
Their signals could easily be located and traced, acting
like a homing beacon for law enforcement. But without a
phone number to ping, there was nowhere to begin.

"Did the victims give you a good description?" I asked.
"Was it consistent?"

"Yes and yes." She gestured to the file. "When you read
through all the paperwork, you'll see that each victim's description of the leasing agent is virtually identical. He's
Caucasian, thirtyish. Around six feet tall. Beefy build.
Short brown hair. Always wears eyeglasses with thick
frames and a business suit. No scars, moles, tattoos, or
other distinguishing characteristics that anyone can remember."

Typical. White-collar criminals weren't usually the
type to have telltale battle scars on their faces, visible
body piercings, or their names tattooed across their knuck-
les. They tended to look like clean-cut cookie-cutter business types.

Hana leaned forward in her seat beside me. "How does
he find the properties?"

I'd been wondering the same thing. I knew rental scams
had been on the rise, but I hadn't worked on one before
and didn't know the ins and outs of how they operated.

Booth took another gulp of her coffee. "The so-called
leasing agent rents the places for a few weeks or more on
Airbnb or another vacation rental site, and while he's leasing the place himself he runs the scam. Because he's got
keys to the place and unfettered access, it makes him look
legitimate."

So that's how he had done it. "If he rents the places online," I said, "and posts ads of his own on rental sites, he's
got to be using a credit card, right? Is it a prepaid one?"

"No," Booth replied. "This guy is crafty. He's opened at least three credit card accounts in other people's names and used those cards to rent the properties and place the ads."

Interesting. So he'd not only run a rent scam, he'd committed identity theft as well.

"How did he get the names and corresponding social security numbers to open the credit card accounts?" I asked.

From her seat next to me, Hana scoffed. "If Detective Booth knew that, she'd probably have identified the guy already. She wouldn't have called you in to help."

Hana had a point. The point being that I should stop asking stupid questions. But now I had a smart one. "When he applied for the credit cards under the stolen identities, where did he have the cards sent?" Maybe the address he had the cards mailed to would provide a clue as to his identity.

"He had the cards mailed to the houses he was renting," the detective said. "He signed up for paperless billing so that once the card was received nothing else was ever mailed to the addresses. He kept the cards active by sending in a money order for the minimum payment due each month. That way the accounts were never turned over to collections and the people whose identities he'd stolen remained clueless."

Hana chimed in again. "What about e-mails he sent to the victims? Any leads there?"

Booth shifted her gaze to my coworker. "He used a different e-mail address for each property. Random ones with no pattern."

In other words, we couldn't tap into his e-mails to determine where and when he might be meeting up with a potential victim so that we could make an easy arrest.

Booth took another sip from her cup before going on.

"All of the e-mails were sent from public computers at libraries or hotels. He didn't do anything else on the computers when he sent them."

Too bad he hadn't engaged in other activity on the computer, such as checking his personal e-mail account or doing some online shopping that could have helped us identify him. Also, the fact that he changed the e-mail address each time he rented a place made it impossible for us to know what address he was using now.

"What about the money orders?" I asked. "Any leads there? He would have been required to show ID when he cashed them."

She dipped her head in acknowledgment. "He showed a driver's license each time, but he appears to be using several different ones with different names on them. The one he used most often shows an address in Philadelphia. When I contacted the DMV in Philly I learned that the name and driver's license number were phony. The address doesn't exist, either. It was the same story with the other licenses he used. Completely bogus. My best guess is the guy ordered the licenses online. There are Web sites offering good counterfeits for around a hundred bucks. They're made overseas and are often hidden inside a cheap toy or clothing item when they're shipped to the U.S. in case customs decides to inspect the package."

Ugh. No matter how hard law enforcement tried to make it more difficult for official passports, documentation, and licenses to be faked, it seemed counterfeiters worked just as hard to provide passable forgeries. Short of fingerprints, DNA, or implanting microchips into human beings at birth, there was no failsafe method for identifying someone. And while people might not mind having a chip inserted into their cat or dog in case their beloved pet wandered off, it was unlikely the masses would agree to have a chip inserted in themselves.

"I take it you've sent an alert to places in the area that cash money orders?"

She nodded. "Not sure it'll do much good since he seems to have a whole slew of aliases, but it's standard procedure."

"What about security cameras?" I asked. "Was there any footage from these places? Maybe something showing a license plate?"

"We got a partial license plate at one of them," she said. "We were able to use that to identify the vehicle. Turns out the car belonged to a Backseat Driver."

I was familiar with Backseat Driver. It was the latest private ride service, a new competitor for Uber and Lyft.

She went on. "The passenger used a fraudulent credit card to pay for the ride."

"The same card he used to rent the properties online?"

She shook her head. "No. Again, this guy was smart. He used a different card, probably to prevent us from making the connection. We got a subpoena and Backseat Driver provided us a list of rides paid for by the fraudulent credit card. The guy was picked up at various locations, none of them a personal residence. He took Backseats to meet with the prospective tenants and to cash the money orders. He never used his own vehicle. The video clips are on a flash drive in the file. They include clips from the libraries and hotels where he sent the e-mails from."

Good. I'd take a close look at the video footage when I returned to my office, see if my eyes caught something the detective's hadn't. "Is the card still active?"

"No. The person whose name it was in had applied for a car loan and discovered the account on his credit report. He called the bank and had the card canceled before we could get in touch with him."

Darn. So much for putting a hot watch on the card so

that we could track its use and maybe catch the con artist in action.

Hana had a question now. "You said he didn't use phones in the rental-scam business, but he must've used a phone to access the Backseat Driver app to request a ride."

"That's true," Booth acknowledged. "That was the only phone number we were able to get for him. We tried to ping it but got nothing. My guess is it was a burner phone that he ditched. He seems to know that switching things up with the credit cards will throw law enforcement off his trail, so he's probably switching up phones, too."

"He's certainly covered his tracks." Looked like he'd done his homework, too, researching how law enforcement tracked down those committing financial crimes and doing his best to avoid repeating the mistakes of the criminals who'd come before him. His method of constantly changing credit cards and identities and phones was a good one. Trying to catch him would be like trying to hit a moving target.

Booth raised her palms. "I've done everything I can think of. I interviewed the victims of the rental scam, of course. The owners of the properties, too. I also spoke with the people in whose names he opened the accounts. Most of them live out of state, everywhere from Florida to Wyoming to New Hampshire. I dug and dug, but I couldn't find a common thread among them."

Everything she'd done already was exactly what I would have done, too. I exhaled a long breath. "Not sure what more I can do. Sounds like you covered all the bases. But I'll take a second look, see if I can come up with some fresh leads."

The detective thanked me and said, "Your turn now. What did you need my help with?"

I pulled the greeting card out of my purse. "This."

She took the card from me, read it over, and looked up at me. "You're getting married?"

"In just a few weeks." *Assuming I live that long.*

"Congratulations."

"Congratulate me once I've survived to see the day."

She chuckled, but it was mirthless. "Don't IRS agents get death threats all the time?"

"People have tried to kill us," I acknowledged. "But they don't usually warn us first."

"That's because those people had a sincere intent to kill you." She held up the card. "But things like this? Pure bluster. We see it all the time. Heck, I've received a dozen or more death threats myself. They're usually sent by amateurs who have no real plan to do harm. They just want to scare their victims, cause them some distress and inconvenience. It's the same with bomb threats. When there's a threat made in advance, there's rarely, if ever, a bomb."

She had a point. In September 2012, there had been a bomb threat at my alma mater, the University of Texas at Austin. The campus had been evacuated, forcing tens of thousands of students and faculty to seek safety in the neighborhoods and shops nearby. No explosives were found. Not to be outdone, someone called in a bomb threat a month later at rival Texas A&M University. No explosives were found on that campus, either. On the other hand, a series of bombs had exploded recently in Fort Worth, which sat thirty miles east of Dallas. Although the bomber had later issued a manifesto offering his warped reasons for his actions, he'd given no specific warnings about where he planned to strike. These facts supported the detective's conclusion. "So you think I'm worrying over nothing?"

"Probably."

My shoulders relaxed in relief. The detective was right. Chances were nobody was really after me. The truck narrowly missing me yesterday had likely been a fluke and was totally unrelated to the card. My fears had been unfounded, paranoia. "Thanks, Detective. You've made me feel better. I was really worried, especially after a pickup nearly ran me over near my town house yesterday."

"Wait." Her face clouded and she sat up straighter. "Someone tried to run you down?"

I gave her a quick summary of what happened yesterday. "Thank goodness Nick's dog yanked me out of the way just in time."

Booth frowned and glanced down at the card in her hand before looking back up at me. "That changes things, Agent Holloway. This could be serious, after all."

So much for feeling better! Good thing I'd enjoyed those few seconds of peace while they lasted.

"Any suspects?" she asked.

"I can't think of anyone in particular. None of my current cases involve excessive amounts of money and none of the targets seem dangerous." Of course the people who'd attacked me in the past hadn't seemed all that dangerous, either, until they'd come after me with box cutters, guns, baseball bats, and whatnot.

"Whoever sent the card knows you're getting married. Do any of the people you're investigating know you've got a wedding coming up?"

I lifted my once again tense shoulders. "I can't say for sure. I might have mentioned it in passing to their attorneys or CPAs. You know, if they were wanting to schedule a meeting or deposition while I'd be gone on my honeymoon."

Hana cut a glance my way. "Don't forget about the wedding Web site Kira made."

Kira was a Web designer who dated our fellow agent Josh Schmidt. As our wedding gift, she'd designed a personalized wedding site for me and Nick. It included photos, links to our gift registries, and all of the details about our upcoming nuptials. Date. Time. Place. Heck, the site even noted that I'd bought my dress at Neiman Marcus. And the site was on the Web for all the world to see. I slapped a hand to my forehead and groaned.

Booth arched an inquisitive brow, sat forward, and put her fingers to her keyboard. "What's the URL for your wedding site?"

As I rattled it off, she typed it in. After hitting the enter key, she leaned in and took a minute or two to look over the site. Her gaze moved from the screen to my face. "I'd have suggested you make the site private and require a password to view it, but that horse has left the barn."

I was too embarrassed to tell her that Kira had suggested the same thing, that we limit access to the site. Nick and I had thought the measure unnecessary and that it would be an impediment for some of our older relatives who had a hard enough time finding their way around the Internet as it was. A password would be too much for them.

She chewed her lip while she mulled things over. "Tell you what," she said. "I'll pull the police report for the incident yesterday, put a little extra time into it, see if we can ID the truck." She glanced at the envelope again. "This card was postmarked in Dallas. I'll contact the manager of the postal branch and see about getting security-camera footage for the drop boxes. I'll get in touch with the captain of your sector, too, let him know to have patrols drive by your place on a regular basis, keep an eye on things."

"I appreciate that. Thanks."

"In the meantime," she said, giving me a pointed look, "watch your back."

chapter five

Fresh Eyes, Fresh Ideas

On our way out of the Dallas Police Department head-quarters, a male voice called my name. "Special Agent Holloway? Is that you?"

I turned to see a small man not much bigger than my-self heading my way. Anthony Giacomo, the tiny but tough-as-steel criminal defense attorney who'd defended me months ago in an excessive-force trial after I'd shot a target multiple times in the leg. Of course I never would have done it if the target hadn't shot at me first. *Don't dish it out if you can't take it.* As stylish as he was shrewd, Anthony wore a forest green suit along with a golden-yellow tie and pocket square and an emerald stud in his ear. On anyone else, the clothing would look overdone. On him it looked perfect.

He grabbed me affectionately by the shoulders and cocked his head. "How's my all-time favorite client?"

"I'm doing great, Anthony. How about you?"

"Never better. Just convinced a detective not to pursue a case against a guy I'm representing. Of course the evidence was all smoke and mirrors anyway." He waved a dismissive hand, as if to wave away the metaphorical smoke. "My client wasn't trying to rob that deli. He was only using his pocketknife to point to the pastrami."

Riiiight . . .

"Whoa! What's this?" He grabbed my wrist and held up my left hand. "Is this an engagement ring I see?"

"It is. I'm getting married in October."

He released me and stepped back, his eyes narrowed. "I fight for your freedom only to have you throw it away?" He punctuated his jest with a *harrumph*, but negated it an instant later by leaning in and whispering, "Please tell me you're marrying that big, brawny Nick. No one else would be man enough for you."

"Yep. It's Nick. There's an invitation on its way to you."

Anthony had not only successfully defended me in court, he'd also later sprung me from the local lockup after I'd been swept up in a mass arrest at a frat party on a university campus. If not for him, I could be in prison right now and this wedding might not be taking place—at least not for another three to five years, with time off for good behavior. Given this fact, I hoped he'd be able to join in the festivities.

"The wedding's going to be held in Nacogdoches," I added. "That's my hometown. We've made arrangements for a party bus to drive out there from Dallas if you're interested."

"Party bus? How fun! Save me a seat." He angled his head to indicate Hana, who'd been standing quietly during the exchange. "Is she one of your people?" he said in a stage whisper, as if she couldn't overhear.

"She is." I introduced the two of them.

As Hana shook Anthony's hand, she said, "Your reputation precedes you, Mr. Giacomo."

"You do flatter me so." He reached into his pocket and pulled out a business card, handing it to her. "If you ever find yourself in trouble, give me a call."

With that, he waggled his fingers in good-bye and headed off. While his reputation might precede him, his cologne lingered behind, making the air smell spicy and crisp.

Our business there finished, Hana and I returned to the IRS office, parting ways at the elevators.

"Thanks for coming with me!" I called after her.

She spun around, raised her right hand to offer a two-finger salute, and spun back around to continue in the way she'd been going.

Back in my office, I plunked my butt down in my rolling chair and opened the rental-scam file Detective Booth had given me. In a small plastic sleeve affixed to the inside cover was the flash drive that contained the security-camera clips. Though I was anxious to take a look, it would be best to read the paperwork first, to see if there was a clue in there somewhere that might tell me something to look for as I watched the video.

A variety of documents occupied the file.

First were printouts of the fraudulent rental listings with photos of spacious kitchens, cozy fireplaces, ample closets, and sparkling swimming pools, all offered at rates significantly below market. In fact, some of the ads touted this fact.

Motivated landlord does not want vacancy. Offered at $200 per month less than comparable units in same complex.

Below-market rent. Hurry! Won't last long!

Exceptional deal on a beautiful home.

Next were the actual listings for the properties on Airbnb and other rental sites. I noted that the con artist did not use the same photos of the properties that had appeared on the legitimate sites. Too bad. In a previous case against a criminal who'd lured women via online dating sites, our office tech guru had been able to track the guy down by searching for the culprit's headshots on the Net. But this method only worked when the pictures were identical, or at least shot with the same camera. In this case, the bad guy had taken snapshots of his own to post, probably in an attempt to prevent tech-savvy tenants from realizing he wasn't on the up-and-up.

Underneath the Web site printouts were receipts for money orders made out to various aliases and in varying amounts. As Detective Booth had noted, most of them were in the $3,000 to $4,000 range. Judging from the dates written on the money orders, the guy had hit hard and fast. In fact, he had received five money orders for $3,600 each in a single day, all relating to the purported rental of the same condominium. He must've spaced out the appointments with the prospective tenants so that they wouldn't cross paths with each other. Or perhaps he'd stacked them one after the other so that they would, in fact, cross paths, and realize others were interested in the property as well. Seeing other potential tenants at the property would only increase the sense of urgency to seal a deal.

The next thing in the file were the initial reports filed by the victims, as well as reports prepared by Detective Booth once she'd interviewed them. Each of the reports contained a copy of the e-mail the victim had received from the purported leasing agent after expressing interest in seeing the property. The leasing agent used both Gmail and Yahoo accounts in various names. LeaseDFW. NewHomeNow. PrimePropertyAgent.

A quick glance at the victims' data told me that nearly all of them were relatively young, in their early to mid-twenties. While many con artists specifically targeted the elderly, who tended to be more flush with cash and also more trusting, this guy had realized there was another vulnerable group of potential victims. Young professionals looking for nice places to live, able to scrape together a few thousand dollars yet too inexperienced to have learned that if a deal sounds too good to be true, it probably is. While I certainly felt for these naïve victims, at least they'd have years of employment and earnings ahead of them to make up for this loss. Elderly folks who lost significant sums of money didn't have that option. Their working years behind them, they often ended up destitute, living in a government-subsidized facility or on their children's couches.

According to the reports, all of the rental-scam victims told the same story. They'd seen a listing for a surprisingly affordable rental house or apartment online, went to view the property, and were met there by the man in the suit. He took them on a tour of the property but acted nonchalant, not doing a hard sell at first. Of course he didn't have to, given that the low price for the property already had the victim ready to sign on the bottom line. As Booth had stated during our discussion, when the victim expressed interest, he informed them that he'd received several applications already and that the other tenants appeared to be better qualified financially. But if this particular victim were the first to provide him with the deposit and first and last months' rent, he thought he could convince the landlord to award them the lease because the landlord was eager to get things finalized before leaving on his Caribbean vacation, Hawaiian island tour, or European holiday. The alleged leasing agent suggested that the prospective tenant quickly secure a money order in a specified amount to cover a security deposit plus the first and last months' rent. When the victim returned with the money order, he had them sign a purported one-year lease to begin three to four weeks in the future and arranged a time for him to meet them at the property and turn over the keys once the current tenants moved out.

Much to the victims' surprise, the man never showed up as promised, and the door at the unit was answered either by the property owner or another party who had rented the place on a temporary basis through Airbnb or another short-term rental site, just as the crook had done earlier. When the victims attempted to contact the man at the phone number on the business card he'd given them, they received a prerecorded error message telling them that no such number existed. A glance at the business cards told me the guy had listed a number with a 241 area code. The primary Dallas area code was 214. He'd likely used the same combination of numbers so that people only taking a glance at the card wouldn't immediately spot the discrepancy. A quick Internet search told me that 241 was not in use in the United States. Rather, it was the country code for Gabon, which was located on the central western coast of Africa. A person wouldn't get too far calling there, not unless he or she could speak French, Fang, or Bandjabi.

The victims, who'd given up their leases on their previous residences and had packed all of their belongings into a U-Haul or hired a moving company, found themselves temporarily homeless and in a rush to find somewhere, anywhere to live. Of course they also found themselves short on funds given that the payment they'd made to the con artist had been a significant chunk of change. I felt a kinship to these victims. It hadn't been that long ago that I'd been a fresh-faced young professional, venturing out on my own, learning how the world worked. Of course my job with IRS Criminal Investigations had quickly taught me that not everyone could be trusted and to be extremely careful when it came to financial matters.

I looked over the leases. Other than the address for the rental unit, they were identical, typical leases, containing nothing—other than the low rental prices—that would have raised any red flags.

At the bottom of the file was a document provided by Backseat Driver that listed the times and locations where the con man had been picked up and dropped off. Of course it only listed the locations for rides that had been paid for by the particular credit card Booth had been able to trace after obtaining the Backseat Driver's license plate from the security camera. We had no way of knowing what other accounts he might have opened under other stolen identities.

Booth's handwritten notes next to each entry told me more about the locations where our target had been picked up and dropped off by the rider service. A sandwich shop. A restaurant. A sports bar. Many of the locations were within walking distance of the condominiums and houses he'd rented online, then purportedly leased to the victims of his scam. The guy must've thought that being dropped at places nearby rather than directly at the properties would help cover his tracks. Of course he'd been right. It would have been much easier to backtrack and find out what other credit cards he might be using if he'd been picked up or dropped off directly at the property addresses. The guy we were after was smart, much smarter than many of the tax cheats we dealt with.

I noticed that the addresses that were not located close to the subject properties seemed to loosely cluster around a neighborhood known as the Village, which sat north of downtown and was bordered on the south by Lovers Lane, on the north by Loop 12, on the west by Greenville Avenue, and on the east by Skillman Street. The area contained numerous large apartment complexes with multiple buildings, making it one of the most densely populated neighborhoods in the city. Tens of thousands of people made homes there. I was familiar with the place. My best friend Alicia and I had shared an apartment there when we'd first moved to Dallas after graduating from the University of Texas. It was an enclave for mostly single twenty and

thirtysomethings who worked white-collar jobs, many of them downtown, an easy drive or train ride away.

Interestingly, the information from Backseat Driver indicated that the guy had used the ride service only on evenings and weekends. This data coincided with the victims' reports, all of whom had met with the alleged leasing agent after six on weekdays or on the weekends. This fact told me that the man we sought was gainfully employed elsewhere in a regular nine-to-five job during the workweek. While it might surprise some that a person who essentially robs others has a regular day job too, such was typical for white-collar criminals, who tended to look clean-cut and respectable and legitimate. The problem was, they were never satisfied with what they earned on their day jobs. They were selfish and greedy, always wanting more, not caring who they hurt in the process.

Having looked over all of the paperwork in the file, I inserted the flash drive into my laptop and started up the video. There were a series of security-camera videos from check-cashing places, post offices, and grocery-store customer service desks that offered bill payment and check-cashing services. The clips were spliced together into a long stream. Each showed a tall, broad-shouldered man dressed in a business suit entering the buildings and approaching the counters. He wore eyeglasses with thick frames and had his head ducked, a cell phone pressed against the side of his face. Though his lips were moving, I'd bet my left ovary that he was only pretending to be engaged in conversation, using the ploy as a means of hiding his face and avoiding in-depth discussions with the person at the counter. In more than one clip, he shifted the phone to his other ear to better hide his face after spotting the security camera aimed at him from the other direction.

At each location, he smiled at the clerk and happily produced the money order and a counterfeit driver's license, receiving cash in return. At one location, a female clerk shot him an annoyed look and said something while gesturing to his phone. Probably a politer version of *"How about you stop being so rude and hang up your damn phone while I'm assisting you, jackass?"* The clerk examined the ID, returned the license to the man, and cashed the money order, counting out the bills on the counter. As soon as the clerk finished, the man scooped up the bills, slid them into his wallet, and tucked the wallet into the inside breast pocket of his suit jacket. Out the door he went, his movements now recorded by an outdoor camera that picked up where the indoor camera left off. In most instances he simply walked out of camera range. Where he went from there was anyone's guess.

I continued watching the footage until the end, seeing the man exit door after door after door. In the second-to-last video, an outdoor camera picked up the man darting through the rain to climb into the backseat of a red GMC Acadia. A soccer mom turned part-time entrepreneur sat at the wheel, a bright yellow placard hanging from her rearview mirror identifying her as a Backseat Driver. Just as Detective Booth had told me, the camera picked up a partial license plate, enough for Dallas PD to figure out the rest of it.

When the screen went blank, I removed the flash drive, slid it back into the protective sleeve, and closed the file. I sat back to think.

Is there any clue that has been overlooked?

Any angle that hasn't been considered?

Is there anything I can do that Detective Booth hasn't already done?

Given that she'd offered the police patrols to help keep

me safe, I really wanted to help her out. If I couldn't figure out a new angle, it wasn't due to a lack of drive.

Drive . . .

That's it!

I could sign up to be a Backseat Driver to try to nab the
guy! After all, I had a pretty good inkling that he lived
somewhere in the Village. Many of his rides began or
ended within a short walking distance of the neighborhood. He'd been picked up and dropped off in other locations, too. One in Plano. Two in Richardson. Another near
the DFW Airport. But all of the locations were only a hop,
skip, and a jump from a DART rail station. He could've
easily climbed aboard a train on either the red line or orange line and ridden back to the Village.

I picked up my phone and dialed Detective Booth to
share my thoughts. "Take a look at the map you gave me,
the one that shows where Backseat Driver picked him up
and dropped him off. Several of the spots are within an
easy walk of the Village. Some of the others are near the
DART red and orange lines, which stop at the Village.
Seems possible he lives in that area." I pointed out that all
of his victims had met with him outside standard business
hours, and all of his rides with Backseat Driver had also
been on weeknights or weekends. "I've got an alias I've
used in several previous investigations. Sara Galloway. I
could sign up with the service under my alias and take
calls for evening or weekend rides that originate in or near
the Village. What do you think?"

"I think I'm glad I called you, Agent Holloway."

chapter six

$\mathcal{R}$.I.P.

I signed up on the Backseat Driver site to work as a driver. Of course I'd only accept ride requests that began in or close to the Village. I had to keep the scope narrow to increase my chances of nabbing the rent scammer. Besides, the last thing I needed was to waste a bunch of time driving people all over town and sitting in Dallas traffic, sucking in exhaust and killing my brain cells.

It would take a day or two for the service to process my background check and look over the required documentation to make sure my registration, vehicle inspection, and auto insurance were current. I planned to use my G-ride when I drove for Backseat. Because we agents ran undercover gigs in them, our vehicles were registered and insured in fictitious names so bad guys couldn't trace them to the federal government. The fact that mine was a plain, four-door sedan could possibly give me away. It looked like a typical government vehicle. But maybe people would just think I'd gotten the car as a hand-me-down from my grandmother. Perhaps I should drape crocheted doilies over the headrests or put a Wayne Newton bobblehead doll on the dash, affix a bumper sticker to the back that read WORLD'S BEST MAW-MAW.

I met Eddie, Nick, and Hana at the downtown YMCA at five-thirty to work out. I wanted to be in good shape for my wedding day. Also for the honeymoon in Cancún afterward, which I planned to spend mostly wearing my bikini.

Hana and I lay down side by side on blue mats to perform crunches. She did three for every two I managed. I cut a glance her way. "Show-off."

She responded by grinning and picking up the pace even more, putting me to shame. No doubt about it. My recent sweet-potato-fry addiction had set me back. I'd also been a bit lax about getting my workouts in. I was paying for that now.

A couple minutes later, Hana counted down to the end of her routine. "Four hundred and ninety-eight. Four hundred and ninety-nine. Five hundred." She sprang up from her mat and grabbed her towel and water bottle. "See you later, lazybones."

"I'm not lazy!" I called after her. "I've just been busy!" It was a lame excuse, and we both knew it. But now, in addition to wanting to look good for my wedding, I had a special incentive to get in shape. Someone might be after me, might make another attempt on my life. I needed to be in peak physical form to increase my chances of survival.

When I finished my crunches, I flipped over onto my belly for some push-ups. Upper-body strength had always been an issue for me, as it was for a lot of women. Better work on it in case I found myself engaged in hand-to-hand combat. *One. Two. Three. Ugh . . .*

A few minutes later, I wrapped things up on the mat and headed for the treadmill. I slid my earbuds into my ears and ran three miles to some classic Emmylou Harris country tunes before moving on to the weight machines.

Nick was in the free-weight area nearby, performing bicep curls. He slid a look my way. "You're really pushing yourself today."

"That near-death experience yesterday gave me an incentive."

"Don't overdo it," he warned. "It could be counterproductive. You'll end up stiff and sore."

"Not even married yet and you're already telling me what to do." I was teasing. I knew he was only trying to look out for my best interests and I loved him for it.

An hour later, my muscles strained and my energy depleted, Nick and I left the Y. He positioned himself between me and the parking lot like a human shield as we walked to our cars. It was a loving gesture, but one that made me feel guilty, too. I didn't want him getting hurt trying to keep me safe. But when I told him as much he said, "It's a man's job to keep his woman safe."

"That's both the sweetest and most sexist thing you've ever said to me."

I drove my red BMW convertible, while he followed closely in his truck. Lest someone attempt to run me off an overpass, I stayed on high alert, fully aware of my surroundings. Fortunately, there was no sign of the truck that had nearly plowed me down yesterday. With any luck, an auto body shop would phone the Dallas PD soon and tell them someone had brought the truck in for repairs. We'd nab the driver, put him in the klink, and I could put this ugliness behind me.

At home, I pulled my car in the driveway, keeping careful watch on my rearview and side mirrors to make sure nobody snuck into the bay with me. Nick parked his truck in the drive. He wasn't about to let me go into my town house alone. He'd come in and help me make a sweep to make sure no boogeyman was hiding under my bed or in my closets.

He came into the garage and I pushed the button on the wall to shut the door. We waited until it had rolled fully down before stepping into the house. My white cat Anne trotted daintily up to us, greeting us with a soft *mew*. Henry, my huge and haughty Maine coon, stood in the doorway to the kitchen, issuing a guttural growl that said *If my dinner isn't served in the next two minutes I'm peeing in your closet.*

"Okay, boy," I said. "I'll get your dinner."

While I went to the kitchen and rounded up a can of food for Henry and Anne to share, Nick checked the hall closet. Pointless, really, given that it was so packed with coats and jackets and umbrellas and scarves and mittens that a mouse couldn't squeeze into the space, let alone a full-sized human being. He peeked under and behind the furniture and curtains before heading upstairs. Having fed the cats, I ventured up behind him.

We checked the guest room first. Nothing under the bed or in the closet. Ditto for the guest bath. Nobody in the cabinet or hiding in the shower. My room was clean, too. Well, clean of killers. There were the usual shoes strewn about the floor, clothes hanging from every doorknob, and dog-eared novels on every flat surface. Nobody was in my bathroom, either. If they had ventured in here, they would've been disgusted by the dried-up turd Henry had kicked out of the litter box. Seriously, that cat had no manners.

"I'm going to run down to my place, gather up some clothes and stuff, and round up Daffodil," Nick said. "We're staying with you tonight."

He wouldn't get any argument from me. Not only did I appreciate the extra safety they'd provide, what woman in her right mind wouldn't want to spend her night spooning with a guy like Nick?

I walked him down the stairs and to the front door.

When he opened it, a paper pamphlet fell to the ground. It was nothing unusual. The neighborhood pizza and take-out places were always leaving menus and coupons tucked into the doorjamb. But when I bent over to pick this one up, I gasped. It was a brochure for a coffin, the Peaceful Pine model with a champagne velvet interior that promised "soft slumber at rock-bottom prices." Words were scrawled along the edge of the brochure in the same red ink that had appeared on the card that had been sent to my office. *Plan ahead, Tara. You'll need one of these very soon.*

Nick took one look at my face and knew something was wrong. "What is it?"

I handed him the brochure and he looked it over, both his jaw and fists flexing with rage. "Whoever sent this has a death wish. I'm gonna rip the motherfu—"

"It's probably a meaningless threat. Detective Booth said that people who really intend to hurt someone don't usually give them advance warning." It made sense, of course. Giving a victim warning would only lead the victim to take protective measures, thus making it harder for the killer to achieve their aim. Still, Booth had been concerned when I mentioned the truck. I had no idea what to think at this point. *Am I really in danger? Or is someone just screwing with me, trying to make me go crazy with worry?* If the latter was their plan, they were doing a darn good job.

Nick handed the brochure back to me. "I hope the detective is right and that this is nothing more than an empty threat. But until we figure out who's doing this, you're not staying here."

Again, no complaints on my part. As rattled as I felt, there was no way I'd be able to sleep a wink here tonight. My ears would be pricked until sunrise, listening for things that go bump in the night. "Where should we go?"

Nick ran a hand over his head, as if trying to warm up his brain so that it could produce an idea. "We'll stay at my mother's."

"You sure she won't mind?"

"Mind?" he scoffed. "She'll be thrilled."

He had a point. Bonnie always enjoyed our visits. My mother was the same way. She considered any time with her daughter a treat. Seems she'd forgotten what a pain in the butt I'd been during my teen years.

Nick gestured down the street. "I'm going to leave my truck in your driveway and walk down to my place. That way it won't look like you're alone."

"Good idea."

As I walked him out onto the porch, a Dallas PD cruiser rolled slowly up, easing over to my curb. Booth had been true to her word and sent a patrol.

The male Latino officer at the wheel unrolled his window. "Are you Tara Holloway?" he called.

"Yes, that's me," I called back. I headed over to his squad car with the brochure. "Thanks for keeping an eye on things."

He raised a nonchalant shoulder. "It's what we do."

"I assume Detective Booth filled you in?"

"She says you're a federal agent with more enemies than you can count. Had a near-miss with a truck. Got a written death threat. That sum things up?"

"It did until a minute ago." I handed him the brochure. "Here's the latest development."

He looked over the pamphlet. "Only eight hundred dollars for this casket? That's not a bad deal."

Economical or not, I had no interest in taking a dirt nap any time soon. Nor did I want to push up any daisies, kick any buckets, or serve as worm food. I was happy with my feet on the earth rather than six feet under it. "Can you pass that on to the detective?"

"No problem." He slipped the coffin ad into an evidence bag before looking back up at me. "I'll swing by here every half hour or so. If I see anything out of the ordinary, I'll get right on it."

"Thanks. I'm planning to go stay with my future mother-in-law. I figure I might be safer there."

"What's her address?" he asked, whipping out a pen and notepad. "We'll send extra patrols by there, too."

As I recited her address, he jotted it down. I thanked him a final time and stepped away from the cruiser.

On my way back inside, I passed the FOR SALE sign in my yard. I should probably call my Realtor and warn her of my death threats. Didn't want her taking a client into my place for a showing only to get their heads blown off by a killer lying in wait. As much as I didn't want to die, I'd feel even worse if an innocent person were killed on my account.

I dialed her number. After we exchanged the usual greetings, I said, "Be careful when you show my town house. Someone might be trying to kill me."

There was a long pause before she said, "Did you say someone is trying to *kill* you?"

"I said 'might be.'"

"That doesn't make me feel any better, Tara."

Me, neither. "I've received death threats," I told her. "One at work and one was left on my door today. I also had a near-miss with a truck on Sunday near my place. I've spoken with the police. The truck incident could just be a coincidence. We're not sure. The detective says most people who truly intend to kill someone don't give their victims advance notice that they're coming, but I figured I better warn you, just in case."

"Are you still planning to stay at your town house?"

"No. I'm moving into an extended-stay hotel." It was a lie, of course, but I wasn't sure what the wannabe killer might do to try to off me. If he or she called the Realtor's office under some guise and tried to wheedle information out of the staff, I didn't want them to know my actual whereabouts and inadvertently spill the beans. The fewer people who knew where I'd be, the better.

"If it was obvious you'd moved out, do you think that would reduce the risk of someone trying to get into your place? You know, to kill you?"

"Probably." After all, whoever was after me had shown no interest in damaging my property. He or she could have smashed the windows at my place or scratched up my front door when they'd brought the coffin brochure by today. Maybe even spray-painted the brick. But they hadn't.

"Why don't you move your things into storage?" she suggested. "I can leave the curtains open so everyone will be able to see the place is vacant. It might even make the unit sell faster. Someone looking to make a quick move will know they can get in right away."

"Good idea." I could call my brothers. Under the circumstances, they'd be more than willing to help move my stuff this weekend. We gave each other a lot of crap—that's what siblings do—but we were always there for each other. "I'll get everything out this weekend."

We ended the call and I set to work, packing up a few days' worth of clothes and grooming essentials. With a heavy sigh and a heavy heart, I unlocked my gun cabinet and packed the weapons to take with me. Among them was my long-range rifle. The cherry red Cobra CA380 pistol I'd bought at a pawnshop during an investigation that had put me in the hospital with a major head injury. My shiny shotgun. Hard to miss with that one, the way the shot sprayed all around when the gun was fired. Not that a sharpshooter like me needed an easy weapon like that, but if nothing else the shotgun rounded out my collection.

When Henry and Anne saw me dragging their plastic

pet carriers inside from the garage, they scattered like cockroaches when the light comes on. To them, the carriers meant terrifying car rides followed by poking and prodding by a veterinarian, maybe even a shot or two. They didn't realize there'd be no pokes, prods, or needles tonight, just a warm bed at Bonnie's. Heck, she'd probably greet them with a saucer of warm milk or a can of tuna.

I was still trying to coax Anne out from under the couch when Nick arrived with both Daffodil and a duffel bag in tow.

"C'mon, girl," I said softly, making another futile attempt to lure her out. "Come to Mommy."

Nick had a more efficient method for rounding up the cat. "Get ready," he told me, bending down in front of the couch and sliding his fingers under it. "One. Two. Three."

On "three," he raised the front end of the couch two feet off the floor. Anne looked up in shock. Where had her safe haven disappeared to? What powerful god was this who had opened the heavens?

I took advantage of her split second of surprise to grab her and shove her into the carrier. I slammed the door shut and locked her inside. She came to the metal bars and looked out at me, mewing pathetically. *How could you do this to me, Mommy? Don't you love me?*

I stuck a finger through the bars and scratched her under the chin. *Yes, Mommy loves you. This is for your own good, baby.*

Nick glanced around. "Where's Henry?"

I looked around but saw no sign of the furry beast, either. "Your guess is as good as mine."

Henry was much craftier than Anne. He knew not to hide in the same place twice. We peeked under and behind every piece of furniture but saw no sign of the cat. We pulled back the shower curtains and draperies for the second time that night. *No Henry.* We even peered into every cabinet and closet, though how he would have opened the doors and closed them again behind him was beyond my imagination.

Nick frowned. "He didn't disappear into thin air. He's not David Copperfield."

Time to bring out the big guns. Or, in this case, cat treats. I retrieved a canister of his favorite Salmon Surprise treats from the pantry. "Here, Henry!" I shook the can. *Cha-cha-cha-cha-cha.* "Here, boy! I've got your treats!"

Nick and I stood stock-still in silence, listening for any sign of life coming from anywhere in the town house. All we could hear were Anne's pathetic mews.

I tried the can again. *Cha-cha-cha.*

Nothing.

Nick's patience had run out. "If he doesn't show his furry face in ten seconds, I'm going to start ripping out the walls."

"Let's make one more round." What else could we do?

I circled around the kitchen once more, this time trying things I hadn't before. I opened the refrigerator. *Nope, no Henry in here.* I opened the cabinet under the sink and moved the cleaning supplies around to see if he was hiding in the darkness behind them. *Nope.* Finally, I approached the trash can. It was one of those tall models with a swing top that closed on its own. *Could he have jumped inside?*

I pushed the door open to peer inside. The darn cat cowered on top of food wrappers and scraps and wads of used aluminum foil.

HISSSSSS! Henry whipped out a paw and went for my eye.

Instinctively, I jerked my head back. Just in time, too. His claw raked across my jaw. "Jesus, cat!" I cried, letting go, the lid swinging closed again.

Nick marched over, yanked off the lid, and grabbed

Henry by the scruff of his neck. He held the cat up in front of his face and looked him in the eye. "Cut the crap, cat!"

Henry hung there helplessly, doing his best to swipe at Nick with his paws but unable to get into proper position.

Nick took the cat over to his carrier and stuffed him inside. Henry turned around and yowled. *Yowwwwl! I want a lawyer! We'll file a writ of habeas corpus!* If he'd had a tin can, he would've dragged it back and forth across the bars.

Henry kept up the ruckus all the way to Bonnie's house, while Annie finally gave up her mewing and lay quietly at the back of her carrier, waiting to see what fate awaited her.

I had to wonder, too, what fate awaited me. Would I make it to my wedding day and live happily ever after? Or would Nick and our guests be attending my funeral instead?

chapter seven

$\mathcal{B}$edtime Story

The sun was setting when we arrived at Bonnie's house. While my cats and I waited in my car, Daffodil trotted along after Nick as he hurried inside to let his mother know she had unannounced houseguests. A minute or so later, the garage door rolled up. Nick backed his mother's car out and I pulled mine in. After maneuvering her car onto the other side of the driveway, he pulled his pickup into the garage next to me and jabbed the button to close the garage door. We'd been extremely careful on the way over and were virtually certain we hadn't been trailed, but just in case anyone came looking for us we wanted our vehicles hidden so it wouldn't be obvious we were here.

As the door came down, I saw the bottom half of a black-and-white Dallas PD squad car roll by. Looked like they'd already gotten the message about our new hideout and were keeping an eye on things. *Good.*

Nick and I each grabbed a cat carrier.

Bonnie stepped out into the garage, her forehead furrowed in fear. "Hey, Tara. How you holding up?"

"**I**'ll feel better when we catch whoever it is that's sending me the death threats."

"Got any suspects?" she asked.

Nick snorted. "A dozen or more."

Bonnie gasped. "Good Lord! That many?"

I shrugged. "I've managed to piss off a lot of people since I joined the IRS."

"I suppose that means you've been doing your job."

She got that right. Seizing people's assets and bank accounts doesn't exactly endear you to them.

She reached for the clothes I'd draped over my backseat and the small suitcase containing my makeup, hair dryer, and rollers. "I'll get your clothes and overnight bag."

"Thanks, Bonnie." I went to the trunk and retrieved the oversized suitcase in which I'd stashed my guns.

Inside, she showed me to one of her two spare rooms. "I thought this room would be the best for you. Your cats can watch the birds in the backyard from the window."

"They'll enjoy that." How sweet of her to think of them. She'd be a doting grandmother someday.

"Nick," she said, turning to her son, "you and Daffodil can take the room across the hall."

While Bonnie opened the closet and set about hanging my clothes on the rod inside, I plopped the big suitcase on the bed, unzipped it, and pulled out the guns, laying them on the bedspread.

When Bonnie turned around, she gasped for a second time. "My goodness! I've never seen so many guns!"

Heck, this was nothing. When my dad and brothers got together to go hunting, they carried a virtual arsenal. If there was ever a zombie apocalypse, they'd be prepared. "You know how to handle a gun, right?" I asked Bonnie.

"I do," she replied. "My husband made sure of it when we lived out in the country. We didn't get much crime out there, but every once in a while someone would come around looking for trouble. Being that far out, it could take the sheriff some time to get to you if you needed help."

She let the rest remain unsaid, the rest being that people out in the country had to be prepared to defend themselves.

I picked up the shotgun and held it out to her. "Keep this handy. Just in case."

She took it from me, as well the box of shells I handed her next. She raised the gun. "Do you really think I'll need this?"

"Honestly, Bonnie. I don't know what to think. Nobody followed us here, but if whoever wants me dead is determined to find me they might come here looking for me." A twinge of guilt puckered my gut. "I don't want to put you at risk. Nick, either. Tomorrow night I'll go stay at a hotel."

"You'll do no such thing!" she said with more force than I would have thought her capable of. "It would be too easy for someone to get to you there. Besides, I'd like to help. This house?" She gestured around. "I can turn it into a fortress."

Tears welled up in my eyes. What had I done to deserve a future mother-in-law like her? One who would risk her own life to keep me safe? I reached out and took hold of her hand, giving it an affectionate and appreciative squeeze. "You're the best, Bonnie. I feel lucky to have you in my life."

She offered a soft smile. "Right back at ya', hon."

With that, she left the room to let me finish unpacking.

Once Nick and I both unpacked and settled in, I left the cats sniffing their way around the bedroom and joined Nick and his mother at the kitchen table. One glance at the front windows told me Nick had made sure the curtains were closed so nobody could get a glimpse of us inside.

Bonnie poured me a glass of her homemade peach sangria. She seemed to know without asking that I needed one desperately right now. She set the glass in front of me, slid into the adjacent chair, and shook her head. "I can't believe someone would threaten a bride. Don't they know a girl who's about to get married is nervous enough already?"

Nick grunted. "I don't think they took Tara's feelings into account, Mom."

She ignored his barb, realizing he was on edge, too, and was taking it out on her. "You two are welcome to stay here as long as you like. I'm glad to have the company." Daffodil stepped over and laid her head on Bonnie's thigh. Bonnie ruffled her ears. "You can help me in the garden, pretty girl," she told the dog. "It's time to plant the winter vegetables."

Daffy wagged her tail. She'd be happy to help, especially with the digging.

After the ten o'clock news, we headed off to bed. Bonnie turned down the hall to the right, while Nick and I turned left. "First dibs on the bathroom!" I called, elbowing him aside and scurrying down the hall.

"Is this what it's like to have siblings?" Nick called after me.

"Yep! You gotta move fast!"

When I finished in the bathroom a few minutes later, I stepped to the open door of Nick's bedroom. He lay on the bed wearing a pair of lounge pants and nothing else. Tamping down the desire he always seemed to spark in me, I rapped on the door frame. "Bathroom's all yours."

I returned to my bedroom and changed into my pajamas. Flopping down on the bed, I retrieved my phone and ran through my contacts until I came to the listing for my brother Trace. I jabbed the button to call him.

"Hey, Terror," he said when he answered, using one of many nicknames he had for me, all insulting and derogatory. *Tarable. Tarantula. Taradactyl.*

I responded in kind. "Hey, Trace-Trace-Stupid-Face." *Can't you just feel the love?*

"What do you want?"

"I can't just call my brother to catch up?"

"We catch up when you come to Mom and Dad's."

It was true. We rarely had direct communication with each other unless I was visiting back home. Instead, each of us provided information to my mother, who acted as an information hub, passing on to each of us what she'd learned from the others. You'd think she might tire of this task, but she liked knowing what was going on in our lives. Of course I didn't really want her to know what was going on in my life right now. It would only cause her worry, and I'd caused her enough of that already.

"Want to help me move this weekend?" I asked Trace.

He grunted. "No."

Brothers. Sheesh. "Okay, let me rephrase. *Will* you help me move this weekend?"

"Mom said you weren't moving into the new house for another three weeks." Though he made a direct statement, his tone was questioning.

"That was the original plan. But I need to get out of my current place earlier than expected."

"It's only been on the market a few days," he pointed out. "Did it sell already?"

"No. Not yet. But my Realtor and I agreed that it's best if I vacate." I exhaled a long breath. "I've received death threats."

"Death threats?" He paused a moment. "You shitting me, sis?"

"I shit you not, bro." I gave him the details. "Someone tried to run me down with their pickup. If not for Daffodil pulling me out of the way I'd be roadkill. Then I got a wedding card at work that said 'at death you will part.' Someone left a brochure for a coffin at my front door today and wrote a note on it saying I should buy one because I'd need it soon."

"Whoa."

Whoa, indeed.

"Moving out's a good idea, then," he agreed. "If you got murdered in your town house, it would negatively affect its value."

"If I got murdered, it would negatively affect *my life*."

"Yeah. That, too. But your town house is worth at least a hundred and fifty grand. Your life? I'd estimate it at three bucks and change."

Despite his jests, I knew Trace was worried about me and would come out to help. Still, he wasn't about to miss an opportunity to get something out of me in return. "What's in this for me?"

"What do you want?"

"The Cowboys have a preseason game on Sunday. Get us tickets."

The tickets would cost me an arm and a leg, but better a limb or two than my life, right? "Consider it done."

He agreed to come out on Saturday with both a flat-bed trailer and our other brother. With that much muscle, they'd have me moved out in no time.

"We need to get our story straight." He asked the million-dollar question next. "You know Mom and Dad will insist on coming out to help, too. What are you going to tell them?"

How much to tell my parents about the dangers of my job was an ongoing problem. While I didn't like to lie to them or keep them in the dark, I didn't like to worry them unnecessarily, either. "How about we say the Realtor thought the place would show better if it was vacant? After all, the smell of a cat box isn't exactly conducive to a sale." It wasn't a lie. Both things were true. They just didn't tell the whole story.

"Works for me." Before hanging up, he showed a rare

emotion. "Be careful, little sister. If you were gone—" his voice broke just a bit—"I might miss you a little."

Emotion closed my throat. Before I could reply, my brother had hung up. Looked like he wanted to avoid a sappy exchange. It was just as well. I felt tears welling up in my eyes and blinked hard to force them back. I had to remain fearless and strong if I had any chance of getting through this.

When Nick finished brushing his teeth in the bathroom, he poked his head through the door to my temporary quarters. Daffodil poked her head down below, too. "Good night, Tara."

"Aren't you going to tell me a bedtime story?"

"You want security services *and* entertainment?"

I cocked my head, playing coy. "I'm willing to pay extra."

"It'll cost you two kisses."

"Deal." I puckered my lips.

He came into the room, walked over, and took two kisses from me before sitting on the bed. Daffodil hopped up onto the bed, too. I cradled her furry face in my hands and gave her a kiss on the snout before running my hand down her back. I'd be forever in the dog's debt. There weren't enough fried baloney sandwiches in the world to repay her for saving me.

"Let's see." Nick looked up in thought, trying to come up with a plot, before turning his gaze back on me. "It was a dark and stormy night. Two knights fought each other for the hand of a pretty princess who worked as a tax collector for the king. The more handsome, smarter knight won, and the other one went back to his life of bushes and composted cow poop."

I rolled my eyes at his not-so-veiled reference to Brett, the landscape architect I'd been dating when I first met Nick.

He chuckled and continued. "The knight and the princess got hitched and lived happily ever after. The end."

I harrumphed. "That story stunk. It lacked character development and plot twists. Besides, there wasn't a single heaving bosom or throbbing loin."

Nick leaned in and nuzzled my neck, whispering, "I got your throbbing loin right here."

I pushed him back. "Your mom's right down the hall."

He grunted and pulled back, frowning. "You don't have to remind me."

chapter eight

$\mathscr{P}$issed List

With a final good-night kiss, Nick ventured back across the hall to his room, his dog in tow. I snuggled down into the bed and tried to settle my mind. Not easy to do with a death threat looming over me. I felt frustrated and fearful, like things were out of my control. I wasn't a control freak, but I didn't like this uncertainty, either. I didn't like being forced out of my home. But there was nothing I could do about it. Not until—and unless—I figured out who was behind the threats.

Yep, like I'd told the cop and Booth, I'd made quite a few enemies during my year-and-a-half tenure with the IRS. I had a propensity for pissing people off.

My first big case had involved a man named Michael Gryder who'd operated a foreign-currency exchange scam. He'd duped investors out of their hard-earned savings with the help of a banker named Stan Shelton. Eddie and I had ended up in a shoot-out with Gryder at Shelton's lake house. Both of them were behind bars now. Their young trophy wives, however, were not.

Could Chelsea Gryder or Britney Shelton be the one threatening me? Maybe the two of them were even working together. They'd become close friends after they'd met through their husbands. Of course those husbands were now *ex*-husbands. Maybe Chelsea and/or Britney was so angry that I'd put their sugar daddy behind bars, that I'd put an end to their charmed lives, they decided to put an end to my life, or at least to make me sweat. It was worth looking into.

I'd also arrested a guy named Joe who'd been dealing drugs from his ice-cream truck. Was it possible someone related to him was after me? I had my doubts. Joe was not endearing in the least. I couldn't imagine anyone caring enough about him to want to seek revenge against the woman who'd gotten him convicted. Still, I couldn't rule him out.

Another potential lead was Marcos Mendoza, a man who ran a cross-border crime ring. Nick had investigated the guy three years before I arrived at Criminal Investigations. While Nick had been working undercover in Mendoza's business, he realized he'd been made. Mendoza had figured out that Nick was a fed. Before Mendoza could end his life, as he'd done with so many others, Nick made him a deal. He'd told Mendoza that he was for sale, that if the man paid him off Nick wouldn't share the information he'd learned with the federal government and would instead take the payoff and flee to Mexico. Of course it had been a ruse Nick devised to save his own life. Nonetheless, Nick had been forced to live for three years in exile until, when I came along, the case was resurrected, and the two of us took Mendoza down together.

Could Mendoza be behind this? Maybe his wife? She lived down in Mexico, though, with the couple's daughter. Would she go to the trouble of coming to the U.S. to kill me? Or could the person who was after me be someone in the man's extensive criminal network? It was possible. I'd not only put Mendoza in prison, but I'd also put away two of his goons who'd beaten up a man and his wife who operated a Czech bakery. The couple had been in debt to Mendoza's loan-shark business. But if my would-be killer was related to the Mendoza case, why would the person wait over a year to come after me? Would the person delay all this time in order to avoid suspicion? Again, it was possible. Still, I didn't think it was likely. Anger could fester and explode, sure. But grudges fizzled out quite often, too. Then again, Mendoza's henchman had been linked to a former butcher at a slaughterhouse who was also a suspected hit man. There'd never been enough evidence to arrest the butcher. He might be wanting to skin me and hang me from a meat hook. But if so, I doubt he'd let me know beforehand. I'd put any Mendoza connection down as a loose "maybe."

Another possibility was that the person making the threats was associated with the Lone Star Nation, a secessionist group. I'd had a run-in last year with their elderly, gun-happy leader, August Buchmeyer, and his wife, Betty. Our interaction involved an exchange of gunfire and resulted in the man enjoying several months' stay at a psychiatric facility. I'd also had a slew of the members arrested when they'd held a cockfight on the purported sovereign property of the Nation. Could one of them be after me? Again, maybe. Hard to say for sure. But without their fearless leader, the group had dissipated after Buchmeyer's arrest, and my gut told me they'd moved on to other things. Still, the Buchmeyers weren't in jail, and August had already proven he had both a short fuse and some loose screws. Better give them a visit, huh?

In another major investigation, I'd taken down Noah Fischer, a popular pastor and televangelist who led the Ark church. The congregation worshipped in a huge building shaped like a ship, complete with a gangplank at the entry. Not only had Pastor Fischer cheated the IRS out of thousands upon thousands of tax dollars, he'd fleeced his flock as well, using their tithes for personal gain. And that was only the beginning of his sins. He'd also committed adultery, with both a pole dancer and a parishioner, the latter of whom bore him a child. As if that didn't break enough of God's commandments, he'd even tried to kill me in my own town house. I was certainly not sinless, but this guy took the cake.

While Noah Fischer had ended up in prison, his wife Marissa got off scot-free. Though she'd also benefitted from the improperly used funds, she had not been directly involved in the financial shenanigans. The Fischers' assets had been seized and the two divorced, but neither the financial nor emotional toll had likely hurt Marissa much. She'd gone on to give a series of paid interviews on TV talk shows and in tell-all tabloids, but her crocodile tears didn't fool me. She loved the attention much more than she'd ever loved her husband. He'd been a means to an end.

She'd gone on to star in the debut season of the program *Do Over*, which was essentially *The Bachelorette* but for divorced women to find a second chance at love. I hadn't watched the show, finding much of "reality TV" to be too contrived to be believable. But according to the magazines I'd perused while waiting in the grocery-store checkout line last fall, Marissa, after much angst and deliberation, as well as many suggestive backrubs from the other contestants, had awarded her mended-heart medallion to a guy from her home state of Iowa. He owned a chain of farm-equipment dealerships and no doubt earned a nice living. I heard they'd gone on to get married. Being married to a tractor dealer was not as glamorous as being the wife of a celebrity, but no doubt the guy earned a pretty penny given all the farmland in Middle America.

When the show's season ended, Marissa had faded from the limelight. Presumably she was living large in Des

Moines, enjoying her new life brought to you courtesy of Joove, the wrinkle-fighting face cream that rejuvenates skin and "gives women a second chance to enjoy their younger years."

Given that things had turned out well for Marissa, as well as the fact that she was living three states and seven hundred miles away, it seemed doubtful she'd come after me, even if she was angry at me for putting an end to the life she'd lived here in Dallas. But maybe Noah's stripper girlfriend had decided to seek revenge. Surely Leah Dodd missed the luxuries Noah had been able to provide her. Then again, she'd had her time in the limelight, too, landing gigs on *60 Minutes*, *The View*, and *The Jerry Springer Show*, not to mention interviews with *People* magazine and the *National Enquirer*. She'd earned a pretty penny for sharing her story.

Like Marissa, Leah lived out of state, a three-hour drive away in Shreveport, Louisiana. Would she go to the trouble of coming all this way to try to run me down and personally deliver the coffin brochure to my door? Again, I had my doubts. I couldn't imagine her relationship with Fischer really meant much to her. And weren't sugar daddies readily available to attractive young women? She could have replaced him in a heartbeat. Still, given her line of work, she might have access to the type of unsavory characters who'd be willing to off a federal agent for a small fee. And I supposed it could be possible that she'd been genuinely in love with the fallen pastor. *Hmm . . .*

The IRS had made a concerted effort to curb the number of abusive tax preparers in recent years, and the Dallas Criminal Investigations team had arrested a number of unscrupulous practitioners who'd helped their clients defraud the IRS. The Deduction Diva. The Tax Wizard. A guy who dressed like Elvis and operated his tax business under the name Refund-a-Rama. Heck, Nick and I had ended up in a Mexican standoff with the owner of Bulls-Eye Taxidermy and Tax Processing. I wouldn't put it past Jimmy John McClure to come after me again, to try to even the score. But as far as I knew, the guy was still doing time. Did he have someone else doing his dirty work? Maybe one of his taxidermy clients? The thought was unnerving. I'd hate for my head to end up mounted on someone's wall or my hide to end up as a rug lying in front of someone's fireplace.

In addition to the fraudulent preparers, I'd gone after men who'd been funneling funds to terrorist groups, as well as the woman who'd unwittingly helped them. But all of them were still in jail, too. As was Donald Geils, the owner of a strip club called Guys & Dolls. He'd taken a shot at me once. He took four bullets in his leg in return. The incident had led to that excessive-force trial I'd mentioned, starring yours truly as the defendant. While waiting for the hearing, I'd worked audits and reconnected with a frenemy from college, Chloe Aberdeen-Jennings, whose family owned and operated a candy business. She hadn't appreciated me showing up to audit the company. The two of us had taken a header off a catwalk and ended up in a vat of chocolate together, but she'd been contrite afterward. Or at least she'd seemed to be. Could she be the one who was after me now? She'd had a lot of personal problems, including marital ones, though I thought she'd worked through them. Did she begrudge me my impending wedded bliss? It was certainly possible. It couldn't hurt to check in with both Don Geils and Chloe.

Of course Brazos Rivers and his parents weren't happy with me, either. The young country-western superstar had skyrocketed to fame and fortune, and it had gone to his head. He thought he was above the law, didn't take care of his business. He'd forced me to take care of it for him. He, too, was in prison, singing the blues. Could his parents be behind the threats? I'd met them once and they'd made it clear they had no love and just as little respect for me. While hell hath no fury like a woman scorned, in my experience a parent could be even more hellacious and ferocious when someone attacked their precious baby. *Hmm* . . .

I'd put members of a cartel behind bars, too, and one in the ground. My father had dispatched another member of the cartel. We'd had no choice. They'd had guns at the heads of Nick and Christina. Could one of their family members be after me? Or maybe El Cuchillo—the Knife— was still running the cartel from prison. Maybe he'd ordered someone to toy with and torture me.

Unfortunately, El Cuchillo wasn't the only violent offender I'd put away who potentially had a network of killers at his disposal. Guistino "Tino" Fabrizio, the Godfather of a local mob syndicate, had several enforcers in his group. In fact, we never tracked down an unknown man who'd come to Tino's wife's restaurant, posing as a safety inspector from the fire department checking on the fire extinguishers. When the building was later set on fire with Tino's wife, me, and a chef inside, we discovered the fire extinguisher was empty and useless. Could that unidentified man be the one who was after me now? Was he angry that I'd foiled Tino's plot to kill his wife for the life insurance money? Had he been in line to be paid some of those proceeds?

My most recent cases had involved a crafty talk-radio-show host who'd formed her own bartering network, a guy who'd catfished women online and ripped them off, a human smuggler, and a young woman obsessed with a *telenovela* and seeking revenge on anyone who'd slighted her, just as the heroine of her favorite show did. While members of the bartering network might have been upset that I'd put an end to the exchange program when they had unspent credits, I doubted any of them would be so upset as to risk jail time for threatening a federal law enforcement officer. As far as the smuggler's group went, I was fairly certain we'd nabbed all the major players. But they hadn't exactly been forthcoming with information. *Hmm* . . .

I had a lot of possible suspects, but no sure answers. I also had a full caseload at work and not enough time to chase all of these leads. I supposed I'd have to go after the suspects that seemed the most likely, or the ones that I could pursue with the least amount of time and effort.

I closed my eyes and rolled onto my side. Anne curled up against my chest, purring. Henry refused to join us on the bed, furious that he'd not only been forced to move without his consent but that he was also now forced to share his digs with an inferior species. He opted to sleep atop the dresser. I could only hope he'd be a little more receptive in a few weeks when Nick and I officially blended our two fur families in our new home next door.

While I was grateful to have Nick with me tonight, if pressed I'd have to say I was even more grateful Daffodil was here. If anyone snooped around Bonnie's house tonight, her sensitive ears would pick it up and she'd alert us to the intruders. I'd always been more of a cat person, but dogs certainly did more to earn their keep. No doubt about it.

chapter nine

*H*ard Lessons

Other than me tossing and turning nonstop, the rest of Monday night was uneventful. Honestly, I wasn't sure whether to be grateful for that fact or not. I was glad to be alive when I woke Tuesday morning, but I'd have been even more glad if the Dallas PD had apprehended my would-be killer sneaking up the driveway with clear evidence of murderous intent that would put the creep away for years to come.

Judging from the sound of water running in the shower, Nick had beat me into the bathroom this morning. But it was just as well. The siren scent of coffee lured me toward the kitchen, Anne trotting after me.

Bonnie had risen with the sun and fixed a full breakfast. Scrambled eggs. Blueberry pancakes with maple syrup. Biscuits and gravy. Fresh-squeezed orange juice and fresh-brewed coffee. *Yum!* Daffodil sat at Bonnie's feet, looking up hopefully while she watched Bonnie flip a pancake. Henry, meanwhile, lounged on the countertop a few feet away, unceremoniously cleaning between his spread toes. The cat had no manners whatsoever. Fortunately, Bonnie didn't seem to mind.

"There you are," I said to Henry. "I was wondering where you'd been all night."

"He was with me," Bonnie said. "He climbed up on my bed and slept right next to me the whole time."

Ungrateful brat. I pampered the spoiled beast yet he rarely gave me the time of day, let alone willingly cuddled with me. I had to force my love on him, giving him kisses while he stiff-armed me, trying to keep me at a distance.

Bonnie waved the spatula at the spread of food. "Help yourself, hon."

"This looks delicious, Bonnie. Thanks."

I retrieved a plate from the cabinet and a fork from the drawer and proceeded to fill the plate with food. She did the same. We'd just taken seats at the table when Nick wandered in, dressed in work clothes but his hair still damp from the shower. With my soon-to-be mother-in-law sitting next to me, I tried not to think of how sexy he looked.

Nick cut me a glance and gestured to the breakfast. "Is this the kind of morning meal I can expect you to cook once we get married?"

I shot him a pointed look in return. "This is the twenty-first century. I could ask you the same thing."

Bonnie silenced us with a *pshaw*. "Any time either of you want some home cooking, all you'll have to do is come next door."

I saluted her with a gooey, syrup-covered forkful of pancake. "Good to know."

As we headed to the garage after breakfast to retrieve our cars, I noticed my shotgun leaning against the wall next to the front door. If anyone came looking for me here today, Bonnie would give them a double-barreled greeting.

Will was my safety buddy on Tuesday. He walked with me to the courthouse, where I planned to seek a search warrant for the financial records of Teacher's Pet Tutoring Center.

On the steps of the courthouse stood reporter Trish LeGrande, her microphone at her glossy pink lips, her oversized breasts pulling her pink dress taut across her chest, her butterscotch hair pulled up into a pile of loose curls on top of her head. She looked down at her cameraman two steps below her as she spoke about the ongoing trial of a former county commissioner on racketeering charges. Seemed there was always some elected official getting themselves in hot water in Dallas. A former police chief. School board members. Heck, I'd recently arrested a judge who was on the take from a gas company. She'd accidentally shot her innocent husband in the melee at their home. Fortunately, he'd survived.

Will and I made a wide circle around the reporter, walking up the far edge of the steps so that we wouldn't be visible in the background of the recording.

When Trish finished speaking, she snapped her fingers in our direction. We kept going because, hey, we weren't dogs about to pee on a rug. If she wanted our attention, she could be more professional about it, at least treat us like human beings.

"You!" She waved her hand now and trotted toward us, teetering on her heels. "Wait!"

Given that we were the only people on the steps other than her and her cameraman, it was clear she was speaking to us. While we might have ignored her had we not worked for the federal government, we knew as feds we had to play nice with the media as much as possible.

"You're from the IRS, right?" she asked when she reached us. "Criminal cases? Agent . . ."

She waited for me to fill in the blank, but I didn't. She should know damn good and well who I was and where I was from by now. The woman had interviewed me more than once before, reported on several of my cases. She'd even house-sat for my previous boyfriend. She and Brett met when he was doing some free landscaping work for Habitat for Humanity and Trish had come by to interview the volunteers and work on the project. Needless to say, their cozy little arrangement hadn't sat well with me. She'd later flirted with Nick, too, when she'd interviewed him regarding a tax investigation. I didn't trust the woman as far as I could throw her. *I wonder if I could throw her all the way to the curb? Maybe in front of that oncoming bus?*

She stared at me, blinking, still waiting for me to fill in the blank.

Though I'd been the one to attend Miss Cecily's charm school as a girl, Will had more manners than I. "She's Special Agent Tara Holloway," he said. "I'm Special Agent William Dorsey."

She shook his hand. I extended my right hand as well, simultaneously raising my left to push back my hair in a veiled attempt to make her notice my beautiful engagement ring. I'd like to say I was above such petty acts, but obviously I was not. *I got him. You didn't. Neener-neener!* I angled my hand one way, then the other, hoping the ring would sparkle in the morning sun and catch her eye. It didn't. Or at least she pretended not to see it. Either way, I had to put my hand down now or it would just look weird.

"What are you two doing here?" she asked. "Working a big case?"

While some of our cases became matters of public record, the instant case was not yet at the public stage. Still, it couldn't hurt to take advantage of this opportunity to make a public-service announcement about the rental scam, warn tenants to beware when they handed over deposits. Who knows? Maybe someone watching would call in with a clue as to the identity of the man we were after. Of course I didn't want to show my face on camera or the guy I was after might recognize me.

"We're here on a minor matter this morning," I told her, "but we do have a bigger case brewing. A widespread rental real estate scam."

At the word "scam," her face brightened. Someone else's misery was her breaking news, the story that would get her face in front of hundreds of thousands of people in north Texas.

She turned to her cameraman, who'd followed her over. "Start rolling."

"Wait!" I threw up a hand. "Let Agent Dorsey fill you in. I'm working undercover and need to keep my face off television screens."

Will looked to me. "What should I say?"

I gave him the basic facts of how the rental scam worked so he could relay them on tape. "There's been about forty victims in the scam I'm looking into. Over a hundred grand stolen."

He nodded. "Got it."

As soon as Will was ready, the cameraman got his equipment going and Trish cast the lens a serious look. "This is Trish LeGrande with Special Agent William Dorsey from the IRS Criminal Division. I hear there's a real estate rental scam hitting unsuspecting people in our area. Could you give us the details?"

She shoved the mic into Will's face.

"The IRS has partnered with Dallas PD," he said, looking into the camera, "to pursue a person operating a fraudulent leasing scam. In a typical situation, the culprit posts a rental listing online for significantly less than market value. When he meets with the prospective tenants at the property, he poses as a rental agent. He tells them that there has been interest from other parties and that if they want to lease the place they need to move fast and get him

a deposit right away. He suggests they obtain a money order and offers them a written lease when they return with
the deposit. It's not until weeks later when the tenants
attempt to move in that they discover the man had no
authority to lease the property."

Trish put the mic back to her mouth now. "How many
victims have there been and how much money is involved?"

"There have been dozens of victims," Will said, "and
over a hundred thousand dollars wrongfully taken. Of
course the man we are after is only one of many people
running this type of scam."

Trish shook her head in feigned empathy with the victims. "So the things our viewers should look out for when
renting a place are unusually low rent and pressure to provide a deposit quickly?"

"Exactly."

At that, she turned back to the camera. "This has been
Trish LeGrande reporting from the federal courthouse in
Dallas." She held her phony smile for three seconds and
then motioned for her cameraman to head back to the van,
not bothering to thank me or Will for the information or
our time, or even bidding us farewell. *Typical.* Oh well.
At least we'd gotten some important words in.

Will and I headed into the courthouse. Ross O'Donnell,
an attorney from the Department of Justice who represented the IRS in many of our matters, led me through
my arguments in front of Judge Alice Trumbull, a left-
leaning judge who tended to be more of a thorn in our
side than the wind beneath our wings. But while I sometimes wished she'd be a little more loose with her inter-
pretation of the Fourth Amendment, I also respected her
for not rubber-stamping every government request for a
search warrant. She kept things in check as intended.

Ross looked up at the heavyset, gray-haired judge.

"We're here seeking a search warrant, Your Honor." He explained that I suspected Teacher's Pet had cheated Uncle Sam.

The judge turned to me, her jowls jiggling. "What makes you think the owner of this tutoring business isn't paying the taxes owed?"

"These, Your Honor." I held out the teacher's personal tax returns for the past few years as well as the ones for the corporation through which the business was run.

The tutoring center was owned by a former high school teacher whose certificate was revoked after it was discovered she'd helped students in her class cheat on standardized tests. Private tutoring companies, however, were held to no such ethical or professional standards, and it was doubtful any of the clients realized their tutoring dollars were lining the pockets of an unscrupulous teacher who had also refused to remit any of those dollars to the U.S. Treasury as required. Rather, she'd claimed that the business had incurred a loss each year since its inception. I wasn't buying it.

"Her ads offer both package discounts and cash discounts. Suspiciously, any cash income she's received has gone unreported. Only the check and credit card payments, which leave a paper trail, have been accounted for on her return. She's also claimed inordinate supplies and repairs expenses." These costs seemed less legitimate and more an attempt to zero out her taxable income. "She's claimed a net loss each year." I held up the paperwork. "You'll notice there's also documentation showing that the Texas Education Agency revoked the suspect's teaching license for unethical behavior related to standardized tests."

"Uh-oh," Judge Trumbull said. "This woman's been in trouble before, has she?"

"Yep. She also has no apparent means of support," I told

the judge. "Unless she has some source of nontaxable income, things don't add up. She's also failed to respond to
the multiple notices we've sent to her, both at her place of
business and her residence."

"All righty," Judge Trumbull said, picking up her pen
to sign the order. "You've got me convinced."

After signing the order, she handed it down to me.

"Thanks, Your Honor." I turned and thanked Ross for
his help, too.

"Anytime," he said.

On our walk back to the IRS office, I asked Will
whether he'd mind if I tacked another stop or two onto
our trip out to Teacher's Pet. "I'd like to visit a couple of
the rental-scam victims. See if I can glean anything from
them that the detective didn't."

"No problem."

After I phoned the victims to let them know I'd be stopping by later, Will and I headed out to Teacher's Pet.

Will drove while I kept a keen eye out for any killers
on our tail. Several white pickups caught my eye, but none
had damage on the front.

Will cut his eyes from his side mirror to me. "See anybody coming after us?"

"Nope. Looks like we're in the clear."

"Good."

Will pulled into a spot directly in front of the tutoring
center. The other spots were empty. No surprise there. It
was early in the day and most kids were still in school.
Other than homeschooled children who could attend tutoring at any time of day, kids who attended public and
private schools would need tutoring later in the afternoon
and early evening, after school hours.

We climbed out of the car and approached the door.
While nobody was in the waiting area that was visible

through the glass window, the lights were on inside. We tried the door and found it locked, so I pushed the buzzer next to it.

A few seconds later, a woman poked her head out of a room down a narrow hallway. I recognized her as the disgraced teacher who ran the place. She approached the door with a smile. To her, Will and I probably looked like a professional married couple seeking help for their young child who was struggling with remainders or long division. We'd let her think that. If she realized we were from the IRS, she might not unlock the door.

She put a hand on the knob, but before she turned the lock, she spotted Will's car. The plain four-door sedan had government vehicle written all over it. Her smile faltered. "Are you here about tutoring services?"

"Yes, ma'am," I said. *I'm here to learn why your numbers don't add up. Teach me how that math works.*

Despite my words, she appeared unsure.

Will improvised. "I noticed you looking at our car. Ugly, isn't it? We had to take our Lexus to the shop and this was the only loaner they had available."

"Good one," I whispered through unmoving lips, knowing the woman wouldn't be able to hear me through the glass.

His explanation seemed to satisfy the woman and she turned the knob. *Click.*

We stepped inside and I handed her the search warrant. "I'm IRS Special Agent Tara Holloway." I held out a hand to indicate my partner for the day. "This is Special Agent William Dorsey. We're here to seize your computers and records."

"What?!?" She looked from the two of us, down to the document in her hand, and back again. "Why?"

Why do guilty people always feign innocence? Just for

once, I'd like a suspect to say, *"You're here to collect some of that money I didn't report, ain't ya?"*

"Why?" I repeated. "Because you failed to voluntarily respond to our requests for information." Never a wise thing to do. Ignoring us only pissed us off and made us more determined to nail a tax cheat.

"But I-I . . ." she stammered. "I never got any notices!"

Liar, liar, pants on fire. Multiple notices had been sent to both her business and personal addresses. "Be that as it may," I said, knowing there was no point in arguing the issue, "we're authorized to do a search and seizure. Where are your computers and hard-copy files?"

Her initial shock over now, her face hardened. "I don't have to tell you where anything is."

"Okeydokey," I replied. "We'll just find it ourselves. Of course that will take longer. We could be here all day. Heck, it might take us until your students arrive this afternoon. I'm sure their parents will wonder who we are. It would be rude for us not to introduce ourselves and tell them why we're here."

Her face remained hardened, but her eyes told me she realized she was in big trouble here and that she would be a fool to make things worse for herself. The bad publicity could ruin her business and put the other educators who moonlighted for her out of business. If she had any hope of coming out of this situation with her business and what little remained of her dignity intact, she'd be best off cooperating.

She waved a hand, motioning for us to follow her. "The administrative office is back here."

An hour later, Will and I left Teacher's Pet lugging a couple of desktop computers and a slew of paperwork with us.

The woman fumed as we carried the stuff out the door.

"I don't know how you expect me to run my business without my computers!"

"We left your backup drive," I retorted. "All your data is on it. Go buy yourself a new computer and you'll be up and running again in no time."

With that we placed the computers on the back floorboards, climbed into the car, and took off. *Neener-neener.*

chapter ten

*H*omeless

I plugged the address for one of the rental-scam victims into my phone and the voice guided us to an apartment complex. It was in Farmers Branch, a suburb to the north and slightly west of Dallas. We pulled into the development and circled until we saw a building marked with the letter *K*.

We parked, walked up two flights of stairs to the third-floor apartment, and knocked. A few seconds later a woman in her mid-twenties answered the door, a tiny baby strapped to her chest like it was wearing its mother as a gargantuan backpack.

"I'm IRS Special Agent Tara Holloway," I told her. I angled my head to indicate Will. "My partner, Agent Dorsey."

While its mother greeted us, the baby drooled and babbled, flailing its arms and legs and burping a green-bean-scented belch in our general direction. *Brrup.* Despite the drool and belching, the baby managed to be absolutely adorable. My uterus sat up and took notice. "Your baby's a cutie."

"She's my whole world," the young mother said, gazing lovingly down at the baby's bald head for a moment before stepping back to allow us inside.

We followed her into the apartment. It was much too small for their oversized contemporary furniture, leaving little walking space. But it would make a fun and easy maze for the kid once she started pulling herself up and along the furniture.

Will dropped onto the first chair he came to, while I perched on the love seat. The woman sat down on the couch, taking her baby's hands in her own, the baby wrapping its tiny fists around her index fingers and gurgling. Seriously, this kid made an excess of saliva somehow look adorable. *Is that my biological clock I hear ticking?* Or maybe the death threats had caused my subconscious to put things in perspective. As much as I loved my job, I didn't want to die for it, especially when I had so many exciting things ahead of me. Becoming Nick's wife. Becoming a mother. PTA meetings and family camping trips and evenings on the couch snuggled up with my husband and kids, a bucket of popcorn, and a movie. *I'll be damned if I'd let some angry tax cheat take that away from me.*

But for now, I needed to deal with the matter at hand. I turned to the woman. "I know you gave a complete statement to Detective Booth, but I'm hoping maybe there's something new we can glean, something that might help us track down the guy who's running the scam."

"I hope you lock him up," she snapped, "and throw away the key. My husband and I gave him a four-thousand-dollar deposit on a three-bedroom house. We were so excited that we'd have more space and a room for the baby and a yard for her to play in. Now, thanks to him, we're crammed into this one tiny bedroom. It's half the size of the place we moved out of, and I've got to lug my baby stroller and groceries and laundry up two flights of stairs.

This was the only place we could find that was available on short notice."

"I'm sorry for all you've gone through."

"It sucks," she said. "Big-time."

I pulled a legal pad and pen from my briefcase to take notes and turned my attention back to her. "Can you run through everything again for us? Start at the beginning, when you first saw the ad."

"Okay."

She proceeded to tell us the same story she'd told the detective, provided the same information that was in the written statement she'd given the police. Nothing new popped out at me. I hadn't taken a single note. I glanced over at Will. His expression told me he hadn't gleaned anything new, either. *Darn.*

I had no idea what to ask, but it couldn't hurt to spitball. "Did it surprise you that the leasing agent didn't provide a phone number when he responded to you?"

"No," she said. "Nobody talks on the phone anymore."

It was true. Most communication these days was electronic or in person.

"Did you see him use a phone?" Maybe she'd have noticed a clue among his apps, one for his bank for instance. *Yep, I'm definitely grasping at straws here.*

"No. He claimed he called the owner of the house while my husband and I had gone to get the money order, but I never actually saw him use a phone."

So much for that. "Did he say or do anything that would give you any clue as to his identity? Maybe have an unusual accent?"

She shook her head.

"Did you notice a class ring, maybe, or did he make small talk about sports with you or your husband, maybe mention where he'd gone to college or high school?"

She shook her head again. "He only talked about

the house. Showed us around, pointed out some of the good things about it and the neighborhood, and then mentioned that two other couples had applied to lease it already. He said that since we had a baby he could see that the house would be a good move for us. We had told him we were really wanting to get out of an apartment. He said if we got him a money order he'd work on the landlord and suggest she rent to us instead of the others."

"When you left, did you notice if he got into a car?"

"No," she said. "He just gave us a date and time when he was supposed to meet us there again to give us the keys, and then he went back into the house. He said he was going to make sure everything was turned off and locked up before he left."

Nothing she'd said had been helpful, but knowing the rat had caused new, young parents so much inconvenience and grief only strengthened my resolve to nab the guy. This should be one of the happiest times of their lives, and he'd screwed it up.

I stood and extended my hand to shake hers. She wriggled her finger out of her baby's grasp and shook my hand first, then Will's.

She looked into my eyes, her face cautiously hopeful. "You think you'll be able to find the guy? Get our money back so we can get another house?"

"I'll do my best," I told her. "And if we find him, you'll be the first to know."

I hated to mislead the woman, get her hopes up. Even if we found the guy, he'd likely spent the funds he'd duped his victims out of. But I had been honest when I'd told her I'd do my best. And given that the guy seemed to have a day job, maybe he had some savings or assets we could snatch to repay his victims at least part of their losses.

We climbed back into Will's car and drove to the office-supply store where the other victim worked as an assistant manager. After checking in at the customer service desk, we were directed to the office-furniture display at the back of the store, where Cory was overseeing the assembly of a cushy, high-back reclining desk chair.

"I could use one of those," Will said.

"You and me both."

The furniture Uncle Sam had provided for us might be economical, but it was far from ergonomic. Mine wobbled, having seen much better days and too many bureaucratic butts over the years.

"Cory?" I said, extending my hand. "I'm Special Agent Tara Holloway with the IRS."

"Agent Will Dorsey," my partner said, extending his hand, too.

He shook my hand and Will's.

Our introductions complete, I asked him to tell me about his experience with the bogus leasing agent.

"He seemed like a good guy," Cory said after he'd run through the facts. "I didn't get a single bad vibe. He made me feel like he was on my side, you know? That he was looking out for me."

"Con artists are great pretenders." They knew all kinds of tricks to gain a person's confidence and throw off suspicion. They excelled at reading people, figuring out their desires and weaknesses and pretending to empathize with them.

"I was really bummed not to get the condo," Cory said. "I've been wanting to get a dog. Saw one at the shelter I fell in love with. A border collie." He pulled his cell phone from his pocket and showed us a photo of a furry, black-and-white dog with a hopeful expression on its face as if asking *Will you please take me home with you?* "I was going to name him Chaplin. You know, since he's black-and-white and Charlie Chaplin starred in all those black-and-white movies? The place I thought I was getting had a small patio and a patch of grass out back that would have been perfect."

"So you didn't get the dog?"

"Couldn't," he said. "The apartment I'm in now doesn't allow pets."

My resolve renewed itself. Not only had the con artist cost Cory a new home, he'd cost a homeless dog one as well. Still, while I appreciated Cory speaking with me and Will, again I had learned nothing new. Looked like I'd wasted everyone's time here.

"Thanks," I said, holding out my hand. "If we find this guy, we'll be in touch."

After driving to a taco stand to pick up lunch, Will and I returned to the office. I carried my bag of food into Nick's office, set it down on his desk, and plunked down in one of his chairs.

"Are those tacos I smell?"

"*Sí, señor.*" I gestured to the bag. "Help yourself. I bought extra."

"Did you get the extraspicy salsa?"

"Of course."

"That's my *chica.*"

While we ate, I told Nick more about the case, about my fruitless visits to the victims that morning, about Chaplin, too. "Cory showed me a picture of the dog. He was really cute." Yep, the dog gave the adorable baby we'd seen earlier a run for her money.

Nick poured salsa over the top of his taco. "Maybe the Backseat Driver thing will work out," he said to encourage me. "Maybe you'll catch the guy when he goes for a ride."

"Or maybe you could come with me to look at some properties," I suggested back, raising hopeful brows. After all, the culprit only seemed to show properties in the evenings and weekends. I wouldn't mind putting in some overtime if it would help me catch the guy, but I didn't want it cutting into my personal time with Nick.

He held up his taco. "I should've known this food was a bribe." He proceeded to implicitly accept my bribe by taking a big, crunchy bite.

"You're about to become codirector of Criminal Investigations," I reminded him. "You should feel lucky you have an agent under you who works hard and is so dedicated to her job."

A wicked grin tugged at his lips. "Oh, I feel lucky to have you under me, all right, especially when you're working hard."

I rolled my eyes. "I should file a sexual harassment complaint against you."

"You started it," he said. "Coming in here, offering me your taco."

Sheesh.

Having secured Nick's promise of assistance, as well as endured his sexual innuendo, I took my tacos back to my office to eat while perusing the online rental listings. Five minutes in, I realized what a daunting task it would be. Given that Dallas was one of the largest metropolitan areas in the United States, including the sprawling suburbs, there were thousands of properties listed for rent. But I could narrow it down a little based on the scammer's typical MO.

First, the con artist never provided an address online, offering only the name of the neighborhood or area. *Oak Cliff. Inwood. Ridgewood Park.* He provided a specific address to the victims only after he scheduled their appointment, and he never scheduled the appointments far in advance. Most were within a mere day or two of his response, probably to keep the victim from having time to do research on the property. Given this practice, I knew not to respond to any listings that provided an address for the property.

Second, the guy only rented properties in desirable areas. I bypassed all rentals in the sketchier parts of the city.

Third, the rental rate would be below market for the area. Unfortunately, not being a real estate expert, I wasn't familiar with the going rates in the various neighborhoods and could not immediately tell whether a rental price was exceptionally low. I decided to respond only to those listings that specifically mentioned that the rental price was a good deal. Although not all of the con artist's ads had pointed out what a deal the tenants would be getting, many of them had.

I crunched my way through a couple of tacos as I scrolled my way through the listings. An hour later, I had a salsa stain on my shirt. *Mild* salsa. Unlike Nick, I preferred not to set my insides on fire when I ate. But I'd also responded to fifteen rental ads using my alias Sara Galloway. Now, I just had to wait for the responses and hope that one of them would lead me to the con artist.

chapter eleven

*H*appily Never After

I spent the first part of Tuesday afternoon working on my other cases.

Detective Booth called at two-thirty. "I checked with the post office. They've sent me the footage from their security cameras. I'll send you a link. Take a run through it. See if you recognize any people or vehicles."

"Will do." With any luck, one of the cameras would have gotten a clear picture of the person who mailed the card to me and we could put this case to rest right away.

"I also got a response from the profiler on your death threats."

"And?"

"She can't be sure given what little we have to go on, but she thinks the timing could be significant, that your upcoming wedding might have been what made whoever is after you come out of the woodwork now. The person targeting you may be trying to screw up your romantic relationship because you did the same to them."

So much for happily ever after. Whoever was after me might want me to live happily *never* after.

Booth continued. "She also thinks the suspect is likely to be female."

"Why's that?"

"Because the suspect sent a card. How many men do you know who send greeting cards?"

She had a point.

"Men are more likely to vandalize property or ambush their targets. And if they're going to contact a victim, they tend to use the phone or go online."

My mind instantly went back to the list of potential suspects I'd come up with last night. If what the profiler said was correct, the most likely candidates were Chelsea Gryder, Britney Shelton, Marissa Fischer, Fischer's pole dancer girlfriend, or Chloe Aberdeen-Jennings. I supposed Amber Hansen, the parishioner who was raising Fischer's love child, could also be a suspect, but I had my doubts. After we'd sent her anonymous photos of the pastor coming out of the pole dancer's apartment, she'd gone on TV and spilled the beans about their relationship. She seemed more than happy to take the cheating creep down.

I told Booth about these potential suspects, mentioning Marcos Mendoza as well. "He's in prison. His wife lives in Mexico."

"Hmm. Let's focus on the others, then. They seem to be the more likely suspects. Do any of them have a history of violence?"

"Not that I'm aware of," I said. "Chloe and I had a wrestling match in a vat of melted chocolate, but that was more of an impulse thing." In other words, it was unlike a premeditated assault with a motor vehicle.

"If you don't find anything on the security tape," she said, "let's pay the four locals a visit. We've got nothing to lose. I'm swamped tomorrow, but how's your Thursday morning look?"

Though I had a heavy workload, I had no meetings or appointments scheduled for Thursday. "I'm open."

"Good."

We arranged to meet up then to visit the suspects and ended our call. I logged into my e-mail, pulled up the link Booth had sent, and clicked on the arrow to start the show. A date and time stamp in the bottom corner told me the recording had started at 5:03 on the date before the card had been postmarked.

The footage began with a male postal employee emptying the contents of the outdoor mailbox. Three cars backed up in the lane as they waited for the man to finish loading the various-sized envelopes into a rolling canvas bag that was open on top. Unfortunately, the footage was recorded by a camera mounted on the building and the mailbox was positioned so that the passenger side of the vehicles faced the building as patrons drove through. This meant I would neither see the drivers' faces as they rolled down their windows to drop their mail nor the particular piece of mail they placed in the bin. *Ugh.*

When the postal worker was done unloading the mailbox, he stepped back next to it and positioned the bag so the waiting patrons could drop their outgoing mail into it. Once the three cars had moved on, the postal employee did the same, rolling the box toward the building and out of camera range.

Presumably, anyone who mailed something from this point until the mailbox was emptied the final time the next day could potentially be the person who'd sent the death threat. My eyes remained glued to my screen for the next hour. It seemed to be feast or famine as far as the mail drop was concerned. No cars would appear for minutes at a time, allowing me to forward quickly through the footage. Then a line of cars would back up in the lane, several customers arriving in quick succession.

I slowed the tape each time a vehicle pulled into the lane and gave the car a quick once-over to see if the vehicle struck a chord. A red BMW caught my eye, but that was because it was similar to my personal vehicle. Same with a truck that looked similar to Nick's. The rest was a parade of sedans, coupes, minivans, SUVs, pickups, and motorcycles, with one guy wheeling through the mail-drop lane on a skateboard. None of them gave me pause. I tried to take a look at the drivers, too, but given the resolution of the footage, the frequent glare from the sun reflecting off the windshields, and the fact that most cars had tinted glass, it was difficult to see who was inside them. The first driver through had short dark hair, but the gender was impossible to determine. The second was a bushy-bearded man in sunglasses. Or was the beard actually a scarf instead? Hard to say. The third was either Big Bird or a woman with lots of feathered, golden-blond hair. Identifying the drivers appeared to be a hopeless pursuit.

When the footage switched to the camera mounted over the mail drop in the lobby of the post office, I performed the same routine, slowing the video down as patrons approached the box, speeding it up when there was no action, such as in the wee hours of the night. Unfortunately, nobody who dropped mail in the box looked familiar and, as far as I could tell, the only one who'd dropped off a pink envelope was a blond woman about my age. She didn't look familiar.

The footage from the retail area was likewise unhelpful. A few people bought postage and three of them applied stamps to pink envelopes at the counter, handing the mail over to the clerk. But none raised my suspicions. The first was an elderly woman. The second was a teenaged girl. I knew neither of them. The third was a thirtyish woman who also mailed a couple of small packages. She paid for her postage with a traceable debit card. Whoever threatened me would likely have been smart enough to pay in cash to avoid leaving a paper trail.

When I reached the end of the tape, I sighed in frustration and replied via e-mail to the detective. *Thanks for sending the footage. Nothing stood out but I'll run the license plates and see if that gets me anywhere.* Of course I'd have to run the plates later. It was already after five and Nick had turned off the lights in his office and come to my door. "Ready to head out?"

"Yep." I logged out of my computer, gathered my things, and flipped the light switch off.

After another workout at the Y, we aimed for his mother's house, stopping for gas on the way. As Nick filled our tanks, I glanced around, keeping an eye out for would-be assassins. A silver coupe with tinted windows had pulled into the frozen yogurt shop on the other side of the divided, four-lane street. I'd been keeping a close eye on my side and rearview mirrors on the drive to the gas station, and I was pretty sure this was the same car that had been a few lengths behind us on the freeway. A little niggle in my mind told me this car might have been one I'd seen in the security-camera footage I'd watched earlier. Then again, like the white truck that had nearly run me down, two-door silver cars were quite common.

As the digits on the pump counted up and the gasoline flowed through the hose, I continued to watch the car. Oddly, nobody climbed out of the vehicle after it parked. Looked like they might not truly be after a frozen treat, after all. Looked like they might be after me, instead.

Uh-oh.

I rolled down my passenger window to speak to Nick, the acrid odor of gasoline drifting in on the breeze. "Hey!" I called to get his attention. When he stepped up to the window, I said, "We might have a tail." I discreetly gestured to the car across the road. "See that silver car?"

He didn't turn his head, but cut his eyes in that direction, trying to discern what he could in his peripheral vision. "Yeah. I see it."

"It pulled in a couple of minutes ago, but nobody has gotten out. It's just sitting there."

"That's odd. Glad you noticed."

"How should we handle this?" As much as I wanted to go over there and confront the person myself, why should I make myself such an easy target? As far as I was concerned, if someone wanted me dead, they should have to put in the effort to come after me.

"Call 911," Nick said. "Let's get Dallas PD out here to question them."

"Good idea." While he returned to the pump to finish the transaction, I whipped out my phone and spoke with dispatch. "I'm a federal agent," I told the woman. "I've received multiple death threats and was nearly run down by a pickup. I'm virtually certain someone just tailed me to a gas station." I provided her with the closest intersection so that the responding officer would be able to find us.

"Got a make, model, and plate number for the car?" the dispatcher asked.

"No, but I can get it." I reached under my seat and pulled out the enormous field glasses my father had given me. They'd come in handy on several occasions. I held them to my eyes and peered at the car. *Holy shit!* I saw two pairs of binoculars looking right back at me. "Oh, my gosh!"

"You okay?" the dispatcher asked.

Before I could explain or catch the license-plate number, white reverse lights came on at the back of the vehicle and it rocketed out of the lot. With a screech of tires, it took off, turning left out of the far end of the parking lot and roaring out of sight.

"They're taking off!" I told the dispatcher the direction they'd headed in.

"I'll get an officer en route."

Nick stepped back up to the window. "Hurry!" I told him. "Get in!"

Leaving his car at the other pump, he hopped into mine. I, too, screeched my tires as I took off after the silver coupe. Unfortunately, a red light caught me at the turn. I would've run it if not for the fact that there was another car in front of me and one blocking me in to the side. Swerving into the oncoming lanes to get around the cars would have been too risky.

By the time I was able to turn a minute later, there was no sign of the silver coupe. We drove down the road for a couple of miles, passing a Dallas PD cruiser coming from the other direction. Evidently the female officer at the wheel hadn't spotted the car, either. *Dammit!*

We returned to the gas station, rounded up Nick's truck, and headed to Bonnie's place. He'd called ahead and she'd already backed her car into the street so that we could easily and quickly pull into her garage and out of sight.

As I zipped into the driveway, I noticed a moving truck next door and a crew carrying furniture out of the house Nick and I planned to buy. *I wonder if they'd let us move our stuff in early?* I hadn't yet made arrangements for a storage facility, and it would be much easier to move my furniture just one time rather than moving it into storage only to have to move it again a few weeks from now.

When we came inside, we noticed that Bonnie had a pile of security items from Home Depot in the living room. Interior security bars for the windows. Bars for the doors that slid up under the door handles to prevent someone from opening them from the outside. Reflective window film that would allow those inside the house to see out, but would prevent anyone on the outside from seeing in. My gut twisted. She'd had to go through all of this trouble and expense because of me. I'd reimburse her every penny.

Before I could raise the issue, Bonnie took one look at us and said, "You two look frazzled. What happened?"

Nick and I exchanged glances, knowing we'd only worry her with the news. But while we didn't want to upset her, we didn't want to lie to her, either.

"Someone followed us to a gas station," I said. "When they realized we'd spotted them, they drove off. We called the police and looked for them ourselves, too, but we had no luck."

She closed her eyes as if in silent prayer before opening them again. "You're both wearing your bulletproof vests, right?"

"Yes." Not that the vest would do much good if the people who were after me decided to go for a headshot. But no sense in pointing that fact out to Bonnie and making her worry more. "I noticed the neighbors are moving out next door. Think they'd let us move my furniture in this weekend?"

"Let's find out." She picked up her phone and dialed. When the phone began to ring on the other end, she handed the receiver to me.

"Hi," I said when a woman answered. "It's Tara Holloway."

"Hello, Tara," the woman said. "How are you?"

Nervous? Anxious? Wondering whether I'll live until my wedding day? "Fine," I lied. I was in no mood to rehash the worry gnawing at my gut. "How are you?"

After exchanging pleasantries with the wife, I said, "We noticed you were already moving your things out." I explained that I'd have to vacate my town house on short notice. "My Realtor thinks it will sell faster if it's vacant." And free of my bloodstains and gore. "Any chance Nick and I could move our furniture in this Saturday?" As long as my brothers were driving all this way, I figured we might as well move Nick's stuff, too.

"Of course!" the woman said. "Anything we can do to make things easier is fine with us. We're tickled to death that Bonnie's son will be moving in next door to her."

Tickled to death. That might not be such a bad way to go. Unfortunately, I doubted tickling is what my would-be killers had in store for me.

"Bonnie missed Nick terribly when he was stuck down in Mexico," the woman added. "I can't tell you how many times I peeked over the fence and saw her sitting on the rocking chair on her back porch with tears streaming down her face. Thank goodness he made it back. I heard you had something to do with that?"

"I did what I could." I'd smuggled a wrongly accused fugitive over the border without informing my boss about my plans. It was a good thing it had all worked out or I could have ended up in deep doo-doo—or, if I'd been apprehended south of the border, deep *caca.*

The woman's comments made me wonder, once again, whether Marcos Mendoza could be behind the threats. After all, it was my pursuit of the cold case that had led to his downfall. Or maybe he harbored fury at Nick and knew the best way to get to him was to threaten the thing Nick loved most. *Me.* That was an angle I hadn't considered before. *Hmm.*

"We were planning to have a cleaning service come out and give the place a thorough once-over before you two moved in," she said. "I'll get that scheduled right away. I'll have the carpets shampooed, too."

"I can't thank you enough."

"It's nothing," she said. "I hope the two of you have as much fun raising a family here as we did."

I hoped we would, too.

An hour later, as Nick was installing the new security bars and I was helping Bonnie clean up the dinner dishes, Detective Booth called me. "The officers on patrol haven't seen a silver coupe with two occupants in the vicinity of the yogurt shop. I ran out there myself to see if I could get anything from security tapes. A camera at the yogurt place picked up a license plate."

My spirits lifted and I reflexively stood taller. *We have a plate number! We can get them now!* It would be so nice to be able to relax again.

But my spirits were not destined to remain lifted for long.

Booth continued. "The plates belonged to an SUV. A Kia Sorrento. It was wrecked and sold as salvage to one of those auto graveyards where people go to pick spare parts. Those places aren't supposed to sell the plates, but they do it all the time. That, or people just remove them from the wrecked cars and steal them."

"Any chance they've got security cameras there? At the auto parts place?"

"I checked," she said. "They don't."

Frustration flooded through me. "Dang it!"

"If nothing else," Booth said, "at least we know that there are two people involved. Could you tell anything about them? Were they male? Female?"

All I'd been able to make out through the darkly tinted windows were the four circles of the two sets of binoculars looking back at me. "I didn't get a good enough look. The security camera footage didn't show them?"

"No," she said. "It wasn't at the right angle to pick up the occupants of the vehicle."

Ughhhh.

"Can you tell me the license plate number?" I asked. "I'll run back through the footage from the post office, see if the car drove through the drop-off lane."

She rattled it off and I thanked her.

"Stay in touch," she advised.

"Will do."

With that, we ended the call.

"No luck?" Bonnie asked, clutching a plate tightly, her face drawn in worry.

I shook my head.

She angled her head to indicate the shotgun, which she'd brought into the kitchen and leaned against the cabinet in easy reach. "If the people in the silver car are stupid enough to come after you here, we'll be ready for 'em."

That evening, I ran through the video footage from the outdoor camera at the post office again, looking to see if the silver car with the stolen plates appeared. Sure enough, around 8:05 in the morning on the day the engagement card had been postmarked, the car rolled through the lane, stopping for a second or two so that the driver could place my death threat in the box. Unfortunately, it was impossible to see through the windshield. A newspaper had been spread inside the glass to block the view into the car, leaving only three or four inches along the driver's side so he or she could see to maneuver through the lane. *Dammit!*

While I was frustrated that we weren't able to identify the person or people in the car, at least I hadn't wasted my time searching hundreds of license-plate numbers, trying to find one registered to a familiar name. I supposed I should be grateful for small favors, huh?

When I arrived at work Wednesday morning, the light

was blinking on my desk phone, indicating a voice mail awaited me. I dialed into the system to listen, expecting it to be a taxpayer who'd received a notice or maybe their accountant or attorney responding on their behalf. Instead, a man snarled, "How does it feel to be pursued, Agent Holloway? Hope you enjoyed a taste of your own medicine."

The call ended with a loud *click* as the receiver was slammed down. That told me the call had come from a traditional phone rather than a cell. Probably a pay phone, if the caller had been able to find one. At any rate, while law enforcement could tap into a call in progress and trace it, tracing a landline call was impossible after it was completed. Still, while we couldn't trace the call, I found it interesting that the voice belonged to a man given that the profiler had suggested the person after me was more likely to be a woman. Had the profiler been wrong? Or was this man in cahoots with a woman?

I went down the hall to Lu's office where I dialed into my system once again and let her hear the call. "That's not all," I told her. "Someone followed me and Nick from the Y last night, too."

Her lips puckered into a tight little ball of orange lipstick. "I've had just about enough of this!"

Yeah. Me, too. The question was, *What can we do about it?*

Lu grabbed her phone from her desk and jabbed some buttons. "Josh!" she barked. "Get down to my office."

He arrived half a minute later.

She gestured for him to take a seat and filled him in on the latest developments. "I want you to wire Tara's G-ride and her personal vehicle with both a dash cam and a rear-view camera that will record while she's driving. I also want you to install security cameras at her town house and her mother-in-law's place."

"Got it," Josh said, his eyes gleaming. He loved any opportunity to work with gadgets.

Lu let out a long, loud breath. "I've only got a few more days in this job and I'll be damned if I'll lose an agent right before my retirement. I want to go out on a high note."

I forced a smile. "I'll do my best not to get killed, ma'am."

"You do that. But for now, get out of here." She wiggled her fingers in the direction of the door. "I've still got things to do before I turn over the reins to Nick and Eddie."

I returned to my office and called Detective Booth from my cell phone. After telling her about the security camera footage from the post office, I said, "Listen to the message that I found on my voice mail this morning." I played it for her, holding my cell phone microphone to the earpiece of my desk phone. When the message ended, I returned to the line. "What do you think?"

She paused for a moment, apparently pondering the message. "I'm not sure," she finally admitted. "It could be that the primary suspect is male after all. The only thing I feel certain about is that this situation is serious."

Not exactly what I wanted to hear, but an honest answer.

"Keep your head down," she added.

Earlier she'd told me to watch my back. The only way I could both watch my back and keep my head down is if I stood up, bent over, and stuck my head between my legs. But I knew she was speaking metaphorically, so I let the conversation end there.

After ending my call with the detective, I checked my e-mails. At the top of the queue was a message from Backseat Driver. My application to become an evening and weekend ride-service provider had been approved. *Hooray!* The message directed me where to go to pick up my official bright yellow plastic placard to hang from my rearview mirror. Finally, it reminded me of their policies and procedures, most of which were common sense.

Treat passengers with respect.

Never comment on a passenger's appearance or ask about their relationship status, as such comments could be construed as sexual harassment.

Never touch a passenger.

Do not use abusive language or gestures.

Riders under the age of eighteen must be accompanied by an adult.

Drivers must obey posted speed limits and all traffic laws.

No texting while driving. Hands-free calls only.

Driver may not carry a firearm in the vehicle while providing services as a Backseat Driver.

I'd do my best to obey the rules, but I'd be breaking that last one for sure. Given that whoever was after me knew I'd spotted them last night, they wouldn't be likely to try to follow me again. Still, I couldn't put an unsuspecting rider at risk without having adequate protection. Besides, I'd still be on official IRS undercover business while driving for Backseat. Federal law trumped their policies.

I moved on to my other e-mails, excited to see several responses relating to the rental properties I'd inquired about yesterday.

The first e-mail provided a name and phone number for me to call for more information. I dialed the number to confirm that it was a working number. "Dallas Palace Properties," came a woman's voice. "How may I help you?"

"Sorry," I replied. "Wrong number."

After hanging up the phone, I responded to the e-mail. *Thanks for getting back in touch, but I've decided not to move after all.*

The next e-mail provided an address for the rental property and suggested I drive by to take a look at the outside before arranging an appointment. It warned me not to disturb the current tenants. This message wasn't from the crook, either. I replied with the same response. *I've decided not to move after all.*

While I also dismissed the ones in which a person with a female name had responded, a couple of the others looked promising. One was sent from a Yahoo account and was signed by a man allegedly named Johnny Brewster with the title "Independent Property Manager." No business name was listed. He asked if I had any questions about the property and wanted to know if I could meet him there Thursday evening at seven-thirty. No address for the property was provided, nor was any phone number given. His suggested time for viewing the property was outside of normal work hours, which also fit into the con artist's usual routine. *Could this be the guy I was looking for?* Everything so far fit his MO.

I pondered how best to reply and eventually came up with, *Yes, I can meet you at seven-thirty Thursday. What's the address? May I have your phone number in the event I get stuck in traffic?*

Another response came in from a Gmail account. The sender identified himself only as Shane, no last name. He said he had availability on Saturday after four to show the property. He'd supposedly be tied up before then with the three other showings he had scheduled. *Hmm.* Was he trying to create a sense of urgency on my part by mentioning the other showings?

I replied to him with, *How about four-thirty? What's the address? Also, can I have your full name and phone number to call you with questions?*

Their responses would tell me whether I might be on the right track.

I spent the next few hours working on some other

matters, occasionally bringing up my e-mail to see if Johnny Brewster or Shane no-last-name had responded.

Brewster responded around two-thirty with the address of the subject property, but no phone number. *Yep, definitely a possibility.* Of course I could rule him in or out for sure by putting in a call to the property owner and finding out whether they'd hired Brewster to rent the property for them.

I logged into the Dallas County Appraisal District's Web site and entered the address in the search box to determine who owned the property. It was a married couple who'd owned the property for decades. Next, I ran a search by their names. Another property popped up, this second one listed as their homestead. Given the relative sizes of the two properties, and the fact that the rental was a three-bedroom two-bath house and their current residence was a two-bedroom one-bath condominium, I surmised that the couple had probably once lived in the larger home but decided to rent it out when they downsized to the lower-maintenance condo.

I found their home phone number and placed a call. Unfortunately, I got an answering machine. *Darn.* They'd recorded a cheerful outgoing message together: *Sorry we can't get the phone right now. If you leave us a message, we'll call you back as soon as we can. Bye-bye!*

I left a quick message. "Hello. This is Special Agent Tara Holloway from the Internal Revenue Service. I need to speak with you about an urgent legal matter." I left both my office and cell numbers for them to call, crossing my fingers they'd call me back soon. My time was valuable. I'd hate to waste it by going out to the property if nothing was amiss.

Given that I couldn't reach the owners right away, I decided to do a little digging into Johnny Brewster, see if he was legit. A search of the Texas driver's license records told me that, though there was no Johnny Brewster with an address in the Dallas area, there were both a Jonathan Vincent Brewster and a John Everett Brewster. Could one of them be the Johnny Brewster who'd responded to my e-mail?

The first was forty-one, older than the age estimate the victims had given. But maybe he looked young for his age. John Everett Brewster was thirty-three. Both were tall, five feet eleven and six feet two inches respectively. That jibed with the description. Both had brown hair, but the first had green eyes and the latter had brown eyes. While John Everett Brewster had no restrictions on his license, Jonathan Vincent Brewster's license reflected restriction code A, meaning he had to wear corrective lenses while driving. The crook, too, wore eyeglasses.

I input the addresses from their licenses into the map app on my phone. Neither one was in the Village, though one was in Richardson, only half a mile from a DART rail station. Maybe he was the guy I was after and he'd taken the train north to get home after the Backseat Drivers dropped him off near the Village. I looked at their tax returns next. Both had W-2 income from employment, Jonathan Vincent Brewster at the city's parks and recreation department and John Everett Brewster with a general contractor operating under the name Renaissance Renovations, Inc. *Hmm.* Neither appeared to work for a property-leasing company, which told me one of three things. One, the Johnny Brewster I was looking for might not be either of these men. Two, one of these men might have started leasing properties on the side during the current tax year, which would explain why income from the leasing activity wasn't included on his preceding year's tax return. Or three, the Johnny Brewster who'd responded to me was a fraudulent alias being used by the con artist.

In other words, I still had no definitive answer whether Johnny Brewster was legit or bogus.

I moved on to Shane's response. It didn't rule him out, either. *I'll e-mail you with the address an hour in advance of our meeting. Sorry to be so secretive but when I've given out addresses before, prospective tenants have showed up during other appointments and it's very awkward. Can you send me your questions? It's easier for me to respond via e-mail.*

This second response only heightened my suspicions. Despite my explicit request, he'd provided neither his full name nor phone number. Had he intentionally ignored my requests, or was it an unintentional oversight? I wrote back with a couple of simple questions. *Is there an extra pet deposit? Is the heat gas or electric?* I didn't care about the answers, of course, but felt the need to ask something given that I'd said I had questions.

Shane's reply came back just before I left the office for the day. His answers were terse. *$250 add'l pet dep. Heat is gas.*

Okeydokey, then.

chapter twelve

$\mathcal{B}$ackseat Boys

Despite the fact that my car now had both dash and rear cameras, Nick insisted on following me that evening. He trailed me as I swung by the small storefront office from which Backseat Driver's local administrator operated. When I gave the fiftyish dark-skinned man my alias, he flipped through a stack of placards until he found one with the name Sara G printed on it. "Here you go," he said as he handed it to me. "Happy driving."

We were on our way to Bonnie's house when a push notification came up on my phone alerting me that a ride had been requested from an address associated with a Potbelly Sandwich Shop location on Central Expressway just south of Southwestern Boulevard. The place was only a mile from our current location and within walking distance of the Village.

Bingo!

I jabbed the button to accept the gig, made a quick U-turn, and passed Nick, who had unrolled his window and raised a palm in a "what's going on?" gesture.

I flicked the placard hanging from my rearview mirror and he nodded, turning around to follow me. A couple of minutes later, I pulled up to Potbelly's, my gaze roaming the patrons on the sidewalk outside, hoping to spot a tall, beefy man in eyeglasses and a business suit. Instead, the next thing I knew, three teenaged boys in jeans, T-shirts, and tennis shoes were banging on the back windows. *Bam-bam-bam.*

"Sara!" the one who appeared to be the oldest hollered. "Let us in!"

"Sa-ra! Sa-ra!" chanted the others, pumping their fists.

Crap. I had not anticipated playing chauffeur for a bunch of kids. In fact, wasn't it against the rules for me to transport unaccompanied minors?

I unrolled the back window but didn't unlock the doors. "Is one of you eighteen? If not, I can't pick you up. It's against the rules."

"I'm eighteen," said the first one.

"Can you prove it?"

He pulled out a state ID card and handed it to me. Sure enough, he'd turned eighteen three months earlier. I was surprised he didn't have a driver's license yet. He'd been eligible for over two years. Then again, it was probably just as well this punk wasn't on the roads.

I returned the card to him and pushed the button to unlock the back doors. The boys climbed in, pushing and shoving each other all the while.

One of the younger ones cut me a look with a quirked lip. "This car is ugly as shit."

While I had to agree with his opinion of the car, I felt the need to let him know I wasn't going to listen to a string of profanities during the ride. "Watch your language," I snapped back.

He rolled his eyes and spoke in an exaggerated tone. "Well, *excuuuuse* me. This car is ugly as doo-doo. Is that better?"

I didn't bother giving him a reply. Once they were

seated, I waited for them to fasten their seat belts. They didn't.

"Buckle up," I told them.

"The other drivers don't make us do it."

"Well, *this* driver does." I turned off the engine. "If you want to go anywhere, you buckle up."

They groaned and grumbled but eventually clicked their belts into place. I tapped the icon so that the app would navigate to their destination, restarted the engine, and pulled out of the parking lot.

"Hey!" the oldest boy yelled in my ear as he leaned forward between the front seats. "If we give you twenty bucks will you buy us some beer?"

"No."

"Pleeeeeease!"

If he was trying to endear himself to me, he needed to stop shouting in my ear. "No means no."

"Thirty bucks?"

"What part of 'no' do you not understand?"

"Forty?"

"Absolutely not." I wasn't supposed to touch passengers, but this kid was in my personal space and about to burst my eardrum. I retrieved my briefcase from the passenger seat and positioned it between the seats, forcing him back. I hadn't touched the kid. My briefcase had.

"Fifty?"

I met his eyes in the rearview mirror. "It doesn't matter how much money you offer me. I'm not going to buy beer for children."

He slumped back against the seat muttering something. It was probably just as well I didn't hear.

As soon as he'd vacated the space between the seats, the middle boy insinuated himself in the space. "What snacks do you have?"

"Snacks?" Was I not only supposed to drive people around, but feed them, too? Seemed like a lot to ask for the amount of money I was being paid.

"Yeah," he said. "Drivers usually have cookies or chips or crackers or something."

I moved my briefcase and opened the console. Inside were a handful of cellophane-wrapped fortune cookies that had been sitting there for months. I grabbed three of the cookies and tossed them back to the boys. "There you go."

There was an inordinate amount of crinkling and crackling as they unwrapped the cookies and broke them into pieces to eat.

"Ew! This is stale!" The kid tossed the cookie in the air. Half of it landed in the front passenger seat, the paper fortune sticking out of it.

"Mine's stale, too!" cried another boy. "It's chewy! It's not supposed to be chewy!"

The other made a gagging noise as he spat the chewed-up cookie into his hand. "How old are those fortune cookies?"

I shrugged. "Six months. A year, tops."

More gagging noises ensued.

"I need some water," one insisted. "Now!"

I glanced at the GPS readout. We were only ten minutes from their destination. They'd survive. "You can get some water when you arrive at wherever you're going."

"It's our dad's house," the oldest one said. "It's his visitation night."

"Yeah," said another. "Mom makes us take Backseat Driver because she can't stand the sight of his face."

Despite their bratty attitude, I felt a small twinge of pity for them on hearing that. The pity was soon forgotten when the middle boy said, "I can't stand the sight of his face, either!"

The boys shared a laugh that led to a shoving match with them repeatedly kicking the back of my seat. One of them even managed to land a kick on the ceiling.

"Cut it out!" I demanded. "Now!"

But they didn't stop. Instead, one of them yelled, "He's touching me!"

Another replied back, "He touched me first!"

For the love of God. I was tempted to pull out my pepper spray and douse the trio. Seriously, did they have no manners at all?

My phone rang with an incoming call from Nick. "What's going on up there?" he asked from his car behind me. "It looks like World War III is taking place in the backseat."

"That's about the gist of it."

"Hey!" the oldest boy yelled. "You're not supposed to be on the phone while you're driving."

"And you're too old to be acting this way!" I said before returning to the call. "We're almost there," I told Nick. "Seven more minutes."

I hung up the call and turned on the radio to drown out the noise. It was tuned to my favorite country station. One of the boys reached across the seat in an attempt to change the station. I blocked his reach with my forearm. "My car, my music."

The three continued to argue and fight and pummel each other.

"Don't make me pull this car over!" I shouted, only to be ignored. I was within a block of their father's house when my patience officially ran out. I pulled over to the curb and turned the radio off. "Get out."

The three looked out the window, then at each other in stunned silence.

"But we're not there yet," the youngest one said meekly.

"Tough toenails. You can walk from here. Get out."

When they made no move to get out, I turned off the engine. "I can sit here all night. I've got nothing better to do."

"Obviously." The oldest one snickered. "Or you wouldn't be a Backseat Driver."

The other two snickered, too. *Turds.*

Nick pulled up behind me, climbed out of his truck, and came over. When I unrolled the window, he stuck his head in and looked from me to the boys. "What's the problem?"

"Who are you?" asked the middle boy.

I turned around. "He's the one who's going to drag your bratty butts out of this car if you don't get out voluntarily."

The oldest one threw up his hands. "Geez! Okay!" He opened the door and climbed out. His brothers followed suit.

As they headed to their father's place down the block, I called after them. "Don't forget to add a tip!"

We were pulling into Bonnie's garage when the app sent me another push notification. A REVIEW HAS BEEN POSTED FOR SARA G. I tapped the screen. The three little pigs had reamed me. *Sara G is rude and gave us old cookies and made us listen to crappy country music. Worst driver ever!*

Oh, yeah? Well, I could review them right back, give a warning to the other Backseat Drivers. *Boys fought constantly and tried to get me to buy them beer. Worst passengers ever!*

Take that, you little shits. Next time you'll be riding with mommy or daddy.

I reached over to grab the half-eaten fortune cookie from the passenger seat. Might as well see what the fortune said, right? Maybe it would say something profound and positive that would make up for the last half hour. I yanked on the paper strip and read it.

Live like you're dying.

So much for positive messages, huh? I mean, the advice was good but, really, *live like you're dying?* Was this an omen? A warning from the fates?

Would I soon be dying?

chapter thirteen

$\mathcal{A}$re You My Murderer?

The couple who owned the house Johnny Brewster planned to show me hadn't called me back. I left another message on their answering machine first thing Thursday morning. I hoped I'd hear from them today so I'd know for certain whether Johnny Brewster was on the up-and-up or whether he was a lying lowlife. I'd just as soon not have to traipse halfway across town to meet with him and see the property if I could clear this matter up quicker and easier with a simple return phone call.

I met Detective Booth in the parking lot at the Dallas PD headquarters at eight-thirty. While Nick had followed me on the drive over, there was no need for him to remain with me since I'd be teaming up with the detective today. Nick could go to the office and get his work done, and I could feel like less of a burden on everyone.

He gave me one last, anxious look. "You ladies be careful, okay?"

"We will," I promised.

Booth patted the gun at her hip. "Anyone tries any funny business, we'll be ready for 'em."

Once Nick had rolled up his window and driven off, she

gestured to a squad car parked nearby. "Let's take a cruiser. It'll come in handy if we make an arrest and need to transport a suspect."

"Good idea." Neither of our usual vehicles were equipped for transport.

Our first stop would be Amber Hansen's home. I looked up her address in the driver's license records and we drove to the house. But rather than a redhead, an Asian woman with glossy black hair came to the door. She looked from me to the detective, a wary expression on her face. "Can I help you?"

"We're looking for Amber Hansen," Booth said. "Is she home?"

"She doesn't live here," the woman said. "I guess she's the one who lived here before me. I get mail for her occasionally, but I don't know where she lives now."

"So you're a tenant?" I asked.

The woman nodded.

Booth pulled out her notepad. "What's your landlord's name and phone number?"

The woman pulled up her contacts list on her cell phone and rattled off the information. We returned to the car where Booth placed a call to the landlord. Though I could hear only her half of the conversation, I got the gist.

"When did she move out?" Booth asked. After a short pause, she eyed me. "Four months ago, huh? What forwarding address did she provide?" She jotted it down as she recited it out loud. The address was in Houston, a four-hour drive to the south. "Got a phone number for her?" Booth jotted the number down, too. "Thanks," the detective said before ending the call. Booth immediately dialed Amber's phone number. Apparently she reached a voice mail. "Miss Hansen, this is Detective Booth with the Dallas Police Department. Give me a call as soon as you can." She left her number.

Once she was off the phone, I thought things over out loud. "The fact that Amber's moved away plus the fact that she's got a kid tells me she's not the one behind the death threats. She'd have to be stupid or crazy to risk losing her child and going to jail just to seek revenge on the woman who brought down her boyfriend, especially when that boyfriend had been untrue to her."

Booth offered an ironic smile. "Agent Holloway, if people weren't stupid or crazy, you and I would be out of work."

I dipped my head in acknowledgment. "Point taken."

We aimed for Chelsea Gryder's new address next. On our way, we passed Pokorny's Korner Kitchen, a Czech bakery and café. It was located in a red brick building, with white eyelet curtains at the windows. I'd interviewed Mr. and Mrs. Pokorny last year as part of my investigation into Marcos Mendoza. The couple had taken out a high-interest loan from Mendoza, not realizing he was a heartless loan shark. When they'd been late with a payment, he'd sent two goons out to trash their business and beat them senseless. A third young man, who'd avoided jail time by turning state's witness, had stood watch at the door while the other two did their dirty work.

"Turn in here," I told Booth as we approached their lot. "You have to try the Pokornys' pastries. They're incredible."

We went inside to find Darina Pokorny behind the counter. Darina was an attractive woman in her early fifties, short and pleasantly plump with a round face and pink cheeks. Her hair was blond with white undertones, and it sprang from her head in tight ringlets, as if her head were covered in curling ribbon. She was dressed in white cotton pants, a white shirt, and a red-and-white-checked apron spotted with smudges of chocolate, lemon, blueberry, and cherry, as well as a healthy dusting of confectioner's sugar.

She eyed me a moment, her gaze narrowing as she tried to place me. But then her eyes and mouth went wide with recognition. "Agent Holloway! So good to see you!" She came around the counter and took my hand in both of hers. "How have you been?"

"Busy," I told her.

She nodded, giving me a knowing look and pointing into my face. "Busy catching crooks, I bet."

"Yep." I introduced her to Detective Booth and the two shook hands.

She circled to the back of a glass case. "You can't fight crime if you're hungry. I'm sending a dozen kolaches with you." She proceeded to fill a box with the fruit-filled pastries. When she finished, she called back to her husband Jakub, who was busy in the kitchen. "Jakub! Come say hello."

He poked his head out of the curtains. Like his wife, he was dressed in white. He had a sturdy build and fair features, along with a thick mustache and short hair. The Saint Christopher medallion I'd noticed when I'd first met him still hung around his neck. "Agent Holloway!" He stepped out from behind the curtain. "We are not in trouble with the IRS, I hope?"

"The only trouble I've brought is a big appetite," I replied with a smile. "But your wife is taking care of that."

Darina held up the box of kolaches to punctuate my point. When she went to hand them to me, she noticed my ring. "You're getting married? How wonderful!"

I told her that Nick and I planned to tie the knot in early October.

"Be sure to come by afterward," Darina said. "I want to see pictures."

"I can do you one better, if you're interested." I reached into my purse and pulled out one of the extra invitations

I'd tucked inside. I handed it to her. "We'd love to have you come if you're able."

Darina smiled. "Of course! We owe you our lives. We'd love to celebrate with you."

Booth and I left with a dozen kolaches. Of course I'd insisted on paying for them. We IRS agents were not allowed to take anything of value from a taxpayer, even if the gift was their idea. We'd eaten half of them by the time we arrived at Chelsea's new home in Allen.

"You weren't kidding," Booth said, licking apricot filling from her finger. "These are delicious."

They were probably fattening as heck, too, but we'd ignore that little fact.

My research had told me that Chelsea had already remarried, once again choosing a much older man. Her new husband was an oil-industry executive named Howard Capps who'd had three wives and five children before hooking up with the former Mrs. Gryder. Yep, Chelsea was the consummate gold digger and Capps seemed to be the consummate dirty old man.

I hadn't warned Chelsea that we were coming, figuring it would be best to catch her off guard. Maybe she'd do something stupid, like leave the red marker she'd used to pen my death threats lying in plain sight on her coffee table. It sure would be nice to find some obvious clue that would lead to an immediate arrest and resolution of this matter.

Her new home was beautiful, a recently built two-story custom model of gray stone. A pavestone pathway lined with azalea bushes led from the sidewalk to the front porch. The double doors had oval glass insets with fancy scrolled ironwork over them for both appearance and safety.

There were no cars in the drive, but I'd bet dollars to

doughnuts—or quarters to kolaches—that she had a new sports car parked in one of the bays and herself parked in a king-sized bed. Kept women had no reason to get up before noon.

We stepped up to the door and rang the bell. A few seconds later, a woman in her sixties answered the door. She was dressed all in black, a feather duster in her hand.

"Hi," I said, handing the woman my business card. "I'm Special Agent Tara Holloway with the IRS." I held out a hand to indicate Booth. "Detective Booth with the Dallas Police Department."

The woman looked down at my card before speaking. "I'm Edna, the housekeeper. Nanny, too, when the kids are here." She cocked her head. "Can I help you with something?"

"We need to speak with Chelsea."

A look flitted across Edna's face, one that told me she found some delight in Chelsea's potential troubles. She stepped back to allow us into the spacious foyer. "Come on in. I'll go wake her."

As we waited by the door, Edna disappeared down a hallway to the right. We heard her knock on a door. "Mrs. Capps? You have visitors." There was a brief pause, followed by more knocking. "Mrs. Capps?" she repeated, louder this time. "You have visitors waiting for you out here."

I was glad she didn't tell Chelsea exactly who was waiting for her. If the young woman knew it was two members of law enforcement, she might have tried to make a break for it, sneak out a back window.

Edna returned a moment later. "She'll be right with you."

A minute later, Chelsea careened down the hall in a loosely tied red satin bathrobe that revealed more of her cleavage and thighs than I'd ever want to see. Her blond hair sat like a tangled tumbleweed atop her scalp. She had a hand on her head as if trying to keep it from rolling off her neck. Her eyes were bloodshot and she reeked of booze. She wasn't just hungover. She was still drunk.

She looked at me, squinting as if trying to identify me, then unsquinting when doing so evidently exacerbated her headache. "You're that lady from the IRS, aren't you? The one who arrested Michael?"

I know who I am, thank you very much. "Special Agent Holloway," I reminded her.

She looked from me to Booth. "Are you from the IRS, too?"

"No," Booth replied. "Dallas PD."

Chelsea's bloodshot gaze ping-ponged back and forth between us. "Why are you here?"

No point in beating around the bush. "We came to find out if you've been trying to kill me."

She snorted a laugh. "Kill you? Are you serious?"

"Perfectly serious," I said back.

A variety of emotions crossed her face in quick succession. Confusion. Then back to amusement. Then alarm. But, yeah, mostly confusion.

She's not the one. Even if this young woman had wanted me dead, it seemed clear she lacked the initiative to make it happen. Booth seemed to sense the same thing. She let out a slow, soft breath.

Chelsea narrowed her eyes at me again, but this time it seemed as if she were trying to see why I'd consider her a suspect. "Why would I want to kill you?"

"Because I ruined your marriage to Michael Gryder."

She shrugged, the movement of her shoulders causing her robe to shift, giving us an unfettered view of a nipple now. "It was probably for the best. We'd gotten bored with each other already. Besides—" She gestured around the foyer and thankfully the robe shifted again, covering things back up. "Look where I landed. Five bedrooms, four baths, a swimming pool, hot tub. We've got a game room with a huge TV and a wet bar, too. No more traveling to stupid places like Tulsa or Boise, either."

Sheesh. I'd bet Tulsa and Boise would have some unflattering things to say about her, too.

"Where were you early Tuesday evening?" I asked. Might as well find out where she was when the silver coupe had followed me.

"Tuesday?" She looked up in thought before returning her eyes to me. "I was here," she said. "At home."

Edna, who'd been pretending to dust nearby but had actually been eavesdropping, concurred. "I can vouch for her. From three in the afternoon until at least ten that night she was lying on the couch binge-watching those housewives shows. She had me bring her potato chips and wine." She cut Chelsea a disapproving look. "*Lots* of wine."

Chelsea looked from Edna back to me. "See? Told you."

Behind her, Edna rolled her eyes.

I exchanged glances with the detective. She was already backing toward the door. In other words, *this is fruitless, so let's move on.*

"All right," I told Chelsea. "Thanks for speaking with us."

She shrugged once more and this time the whole boob slipped out before she turned to head back to her bedroom.

Edna saw us to the door. Before closing it on us, she whispered, "I'll keep an eye and ear out. If I hear anything strange, I'll call you."

"Thanks."

We climbed back into the Dallas PD squad car and aimed for Britney Shelton's new home in the prestigious Bluffview neighborhood, which lay to the east of the city's smaller Love Field Airport. We pulled up to the house on Elsby Avenue. The residence was a contemporary

L-shaped model with gray paint, futuristic outdoor light fixtures, and rows of solar panels on the roof. Fitting, given that Britney's new husband, like Chelsea's, worked in the energy industry. Malcolm Bybee, however, seemed to realize that petroleum had seen better days and that newer, cleaner energy sources were the future. He ran a growing company called Star Power Solar Systems that specialized in harnessing the power of sunshine, which we had plenty of in Texas. Too much, really. Our summers here felt as if we were living in a broiler.

We parked at the curb and stepped up to the intercom system attached to the iron security gate that enclosed their driveway and the front of the house. Booth jabbed the button and we watched the house expectantly. There was movement at one of the tall, narrow windows that flanked the front door. A moment later, a man's voice answered, "May I help you?"

Booth leaned in toward the speaker. "Detective Veronica Booth from Dallas PD and Special Agent Tara Holloway from the IRS here. We need to speak with Britney Bybee."

The man hesitated a short moment. "May I ask what this is regarding?"

"It's a private matter," Booth replied.

"I'm her husband," the man said, as if that automatically gave him a right to know. It didn't. This wasn't 1920.

Booth didn't miss a beat. "If she wants you to know her business, she can tell you all about our conversation after we talk to her."

He paused a moment before speaking again. "Do you have a search warrant?" he demanded.

"Do you have something to hide?" the detective demanded right back.

Wow. Booth was quick and relentless. *I like that in a partner.*

The man hesitated again. "Just a moment, please. Let me see if she's home."

Yeah, right. We already knew she was home. The bright yellow Porsche 911 Turbo S in the driveway told us that. The personalized license plate read BRIT'S!

We stood there for several minutes. Keeping people waiting was a typical power play, both in business and law enforcement. But it was also a waste of my precious time. I stared at the door, willing it to open. *Hurry up, you jerks. I've got a busy schedule.*

Finally, the door swung open and Britney emerged. Like Chelsea, she was dressed in sleepwear, though Britney's at least covered all her naughty bits. She still sported the augmented breasts and frosted blond hair I remembered, but her skin was no longer Oompa-Loompa orange. She'd either stopped using self-tanning cream or found a product that didn't look so hideous.

Her husband, who had gray streaks in his hair and was at least twice her age, followed her to the gate. Neither made any move to open it, looking at us through the bars. I seared Britney with my gaze. *If you're the one who threatened me, I'm going to put you behind another set of bars.*

"Y'all wanted to see me?" Britney asked. She looked from the detective to me, but there was no flicker of recognition. Of course I'd only met her once, at a Texas Rangers baseball game. We'd sat in the private box suite owned by the bank where Britney's then-husband worked. She'd hardly given me the time of day, though, content to get drunk and dish with Chelsea rather than serve as a hostess.

I figured I might as well dive right in. "Did you send me a death threat?"

Her waxed brows drew together. "Send you a *what*?"

"A death threat."

She scoffed. "Why would I do that? I don't even know who the hell you are."

Dammit, she looked sincere. "I'm the agent who got your former husband thrown in jail."

She was as concerned about the end of her earlier marriage as Chelsea had been. She shrugged. "Things weren't really that great between us. His trial gave me a good excuse to end things." She looked up at her new husband with adoration. "Then I met Malcolm." She turned back to us. "We're soul mates."

They were something, all right, but I doubted it was soul mates.

Booth chimed in now. "So you're denying you mailed a death threat to Agent Holloway?"

She looked the detective right in the eye. "The last thing I mailed was my high school graduation announcements. That was five years ago. I couldn't find a post office if you offered me a million dollars."

A true gold digger, always thinking in terms of money. Still, what she'd said was probably true. Snail mail had become nearly obsolete, used only for wedding invitations, announcements, greeting cards, and, of course, death threats against federal law enforcement. Looked like we'd struck out again.

"That'll be it for now," Booth said. "If we need anything else, we'll be back in touch."

As we headed back to the cruiser, the couple headed back to their house.

From behind us, Malcolm snapped, "What was that about?"

"Hell if I know," Britney said.

"A police car out here?" he said. "The neighbors are going to talk."

"Hell if I care," Britney said before slamming the door behind them.

As we returned to the car, I felt a bit like the baby bird in the classic children's book *Are You My Mother?* But instead of searching for my mom, I was searching for my would-be murderer. Like the little bird, though, I seemed to be asking the wrong people and getting nowhere. But like the little bird, I wouldn't stop until I found who I was looking for.

chapter fourteen

Sweet Spot

Our next stop was Cowtown Candy Company. The operation sat on a twenty-acre tract north of Fort Worth. The two-story administrative building and manufacturing facility had been painted in a black-and white-cowhide pattern, as had the company's delivery trucks, which also featured brown eyes, pink noses, and smiling lips. Cowmobiles. The Cowtown Candy Company logo spanned the side of the trucks, the company's name spelled in script designed to resemble rope. An old-fashioned red barn sat to the rear of the main building, surrounded by a small, scattered herd of Holsteins snacking on grass in the sunshine, a few of them napping in the shade of the trees.

As Booth pulled the squad car into the lot, I pointed to a bluish-silver Town & Country Limited minivan. "That's Chloe's car."

"Good. She's here."

We checked in with the receptionist who called up to Chloe's office. After speaking with Chloe, the receptionist addressed me. "You can go on up. She said you know the way."

I certainly did. It was up some stairs and across the very

catwalk from which Chloe and I had fallen while engaged in a catfight. That's how we'd ended up in the vat of warm chocolate below. *Ah, sweet memories.*

I led the detective upstairs to Chloe's office. She met us at the door, looking as darn dazzling as ever, a real-life Anne Hathaway. Her dark hair hung like silk to her shoulders, her fair skin glistened, and her eyes glimmered as if filled with stardust. She looked like Snow White, come to life. But I knew the woman had another side to her, one that was less princess and more narcissist. I'd seen that stardust glow like heated embers of hate when I'd confronted her about the company's accounting records.

Chloe and I had lived in the same dorm our freshman year of college. I'd lent her my class notes, helped her move her heavy boxes in and out of the building, lent her quarters for the washing machines and clothes dryers. But had she ever returned the favors? Nope. Never.

Still, she'd purportedly turned over a new leaf last year after I'd audited the company and discovered some major screwups and bad behavior on her part. She and her husband had been having trouble at the time, and she'd done some unscrupulous things in a desperate attempt to maintain her aura of perfection. I'd pitied her for all the pressure she'd put on herself to achieve an unattainable human standard, and we'd worked things out without her going to jail. She should be grateful I hadn't gone after her with guns blazing.

"Tara!" came a cheerful male voice from down the hall before I could introduce the detective to Chloe.

I turned to see Chloe's older brother Jeremy, whom I'd also met at the university, swinging toward us in his loose-limbed way. He flashed his adorable dimple and gave me a hug. "Good to see you! What brings you by?"

No point in beating around the bush. I gestured into

Chloe's office. "I'm here to find out if your sister is trying to kill me."

"Again?" He chuckled, clearly assuming I was joking. "I think she learned her lesson last time. She had chocolate in her ear canal for a month."

Chloe, on the other hand, took my statement at face value, her mouth gaping. "You think I'm trying to kill you?" she said on a breath, wrapping her arms around herself in an act of self-consolation. "*Why* would you think that?" She swallowed hard. "*How* could you think that?" Her gaze held disbelief, but it held a lot more hurt.

My intestines wriggled inside me. I felt like an absolute shit. Clearly, Chloe was not my would-be killer. She was a hardworking woman who'd once been a self-centered girl intent on achieving perfection at any price. But she'd learned her lesson. Despite the glamour she maintained, she was someone else now.

Booth came to my rescue. "Agent Holloway has received multiple death threats. I insisted she take me to meet anyone with whom she'd had a physical altercation while working at the IRS. We're simply trying to eliminate all of the possible suspects, however unlikely they may be."

The hurt subsided in Chloe's eyes. "Oh. Okay."

Booth held out her hand for a conciliatory shake. "I can see I'm clearly on the wrong path here. We'll cross you off our list."

Chloe dipped her shiny, silky head. "Thanks."

Jeremy snorted. "Sure you can't take my little sister off to jail for just a little bit? It would serve her right for all those times she hid the cookies when we were kids."

I laughed and waved my left hand dismissively. "The statute of limitations has run out on those offenses."

"Hey!" Jeremy grabbed my wrist. "You've got a ring!"

"I do."

"You'll be saying those words again sometime soon, then, huh?"

"October second," I told him.

"What kind of wedding are you having?"

"Traditional," I said. "A ceremony at the Baptist church I grew up attending, followed by a barn dance."

"A barn dance? You mean a real, honest-to-God, gen-u-ine hootenanny?" He leaped into the air and kicked his heels together. "Sounds like fun!" Jeremy's goofy, funny nature is part of what made him so popular in college. "It's probably rude to ask," he said, "but can you put me on the guest list? Chloe, too? I always like a good party and Chloe needs to have some fun. She works too hard."

"I'd be glad to," I told him. "We've got a party bus coming out, too, if you'd like to ride out on it."

"Heck," Jeremy said. "I'd like to drive it!"

After I shook Chloe's hand, Jeremy walked the detective and me back downstairs and handed both of us an extralarge bag of assorted western-themed candy. *Just what we need. More sugar.* But I wasn't about to pass up a bag of candy. Once again, I insisted on paying, even though Jeremy argued with me.

He raised a hand in good-bye as we headed out the door. "Y'all take care now!"

Back in the cruiser, Booth reached into her bag and fished out a Cowtown Cow Patty, a fudge dome shaped irregularly, just like the bovine dropping it was named after. I, on the other hand, went for a Licorice Lasso.

"What now?" Booth asked as she removed the wrapper. "Who else's marriages have you ruined?"

"Marcos Mendoza's and Marissa Fischer's."

I gave Booth some quick details about the cases, how

I'd put Marissa's lying, cheating husband in jail and relieved Mendoza of his left nut with a strategically aimed shot from my Glock. "That feat earned me the nickname The Sperminator."

She issued a soft snort. "Good one."

"The problem is Marissa lives in Iowa and Mendoza's in jail." Neither one seemed a viable suspect. The postmark on the card I'd received had been a local postmark. It was unlikely Marissa would drive all the way down to Dallas to send it. Mendoza could have had someone on the outside doing his dirty work for him, but who?

"Taking out Mendoza's nut had to leave him feeling emasculated," she said. "He could be our guy."

"He's in the federal correctional institute in Seagoville," I told her. "So are Joe Cullen, Noah Fischer, Don Geils, and Giustino Fabrizio."

The detective had been the one who'd first put two and two together months ago and realized Tino Fabrizio could be behind some unsolved murders in the Dallas area. When she realized the guy had mob connections in Chicago, she'd pulled the FBI into the case, and the FBI had later pulled in the IRS.

"I know you didn't end Fabrizio's marriage," she said. "He did that himself when he trapped his wife in her restaurant and set it on fire to cash in on the life insurance policy he'd taken out on her."

The bastard had trapped me inside the burning restaurant, as well. A chef, too. Fortunately, we'd managed to escape. It hadn't been easy.

"But what about the other two?" Booth asked. "The Joe guy and Geils. Did you screw up their relationships?"

"As far as I know, neither of the others was in a relationship when I busted them. But as long as we're going out to the prison, we might as well talk to them, too." Heck, for

all I knew these inmates had become BFFs and had plot-
ted together to scare the pants off me. I visualized the four
of them showering next to each other and striking up a
conversation.

> Joe: Hey, guys. What are you in for?
> Mendoza: Tax evasion.
> Geils: Me, too!
> Fabrizio: Same for me. Who put you here?
> Mendoza: A little bitch named Tara Holloway.
> Geils: That's the one. I tried to shoot her but I
>   missed.
> Joe: I had a loaded shotgun under the freezer in my
>   ice-cream truck, but I didn't think to use it. I'm
>   such a dumbass!
> Fabrizio: It's not too late to finish the job. I got guys
>   on the outside. What say we kill her?
> Mendoza: Sure. But first, could you soap my back?

It would be an hour-long drive out to the facility south-
east of Dallas, but Booth wanted to make the drive. "Might
as well exhaust all potential leads," she said.

We headed out, making small talk along the way. She
regaled me with tales of her exploits as a beat cop when
she was younger. "I chased a burglary suspect into the
woods once. He disappeared into thin air. Couldn't find
him anywhere. Then I hear a couple of angry squirrels
chattering and look up to find him in a tree. He refused to
come down on his own, but eventually the limb broke and
down he came anyway."

As her story illustrated, most criminals weren't all that
smart. Unfortunately, though, some were. The guy running
the rental scam was one of the latter types. He'd carefully
planned his scheme, making it difficult for law enforce-

ment to get a bead on him. But sooner or later he had to slip up, didn't he?

As we parked and climbed out of the cruiser, a few men in the yard came to the fence, curious. I could feel their gazes boring into me. Even though I had a gun on my hip, it was unsettling.

One of the men put a hand to his mouth and blew us a loud kiss. *SMOOOOCH*. I pretended to catch it in the air and applied it to my ass. The others laughed.

Booth and I checked in at the front desk and provided the clerk with our badges and driver's licenses. It took twenty minutes after we arrived to get cleared.

The clerk read over the list of inmates I'd requested to see before looking back up at me. "You put all of these guys behind bars?"

"Yep."

"Impressive. You should join our frequent felons program. Three more convictions and you'll win a refrigerator." He cast me a roguish grin before hitting a button and buzzing us through a secure door.

On the other side, we found a black, brawny warden. As he held out our visitor badges he said, "Got some bad news for you. Mendoza, Geils, and Cullen are here, but Giustino Fabrizio's been transferred to a facility in Illinois. The Chicago PD's putting him on trial for a series of murders."

Fabrizio had already been sentenced to a fifty-year term for attempting to kill his wife, me, and the chef who'd been in the restaurant. That should keep him in the klink until he passed on to the great hereafter. But convictions occasionally were overturned. Prosecutors knew it couldn't hurt to go ahead and try the heartless creep for other crimes, obtain additional convictions. Besides, members of his mob network had turned on him in exchange for lighter sentences for their misdeeds. The new evidence they'd provided had led to many a cold case up in Chicago being reheated. Nonetheless, I was disappointed we wouldn't be able to confront the guy face-to-face.

The warden led us down an empty hall to a series of rooms with glass panels in the doors. Through the first two windows, we could see inmates meeting with people in business suits, probably their attorneys. The warden stopped at room number three and typed in a code to unlock the door. The lock released with a loud *click*. "There you go."

After the detective and I seated ourselves in the interrogation room, Marcos Mendoza was led into the small, stale space in handcuffs. Though he had the same dark hair and widow's peak, he seemed much smaller than I remembered him, now reduced from the dangerous, violent, and powerful international business tycoon he'd once been to a mere jailbird. Or perhaps he really was smaller. Maybe that nut I'd taken out had reduced his testosterone levels and caused him to shrink and shrivel.

Any reduction in testosterone clearly hadn't reduced his hate for me, however. He sat down and glared at me, his eyes narrowed into little dark beams, as if he were trying to bore holes into my head with his gaze. I stared right back. *You don't scare me, you one-nut nincompoop.*

After introducing herself, Booth leaned casually back in her chair, her eyes on the inmate. "Agent Holloway received the card you sent." She let that soak in for a moment. "Who mailed it for you? One of your former business associates?"

Mendoza said nothing, though his gaze shifted from Booth to me and back again. He didn't even bother to deny her accusation. "You want to speak with me," he said, "you get my lawyer."

"We're not charging you," she said. "We're just asking you some questions."

"You'll get no answers," he said, "unless you get my lawyer."

Booth and I exchanged glances. We both knew if his attorney were present we'd have even less chance of getting answers. She leaned forward across the table, getting in his face, knowing if he touched a hair on her head the guard standing outside the glass watching would be on him in an instant. "Know this," she said. "If you've threatened a member of law enforcement, we will make sure you never get out of this place."

He sneered and leaned in, too, leaving only an inch between their faces. "I'm serving a life sentence," he hissed back. "No matter what I do I'm never getting out of here."

Undaunted, Booth laughed and sat back. "Sucks to be you, huh?"

He sat back, too, looking small again, his posture speaking for him. *Little bit. Yeah.*

Mendoza was taken away and, minutes later, the warden returned with Don Geils. Geils stood only five feet five inches. His rounded belly, upturned nose, and body covered in coarse black hair made him look like an oversized potbellied pig. He took one step through the doorway, met my gaze, and stopped in his tracks. *"You?"* he spat. He turned back to the warden. "You only said I had a visitor. You didn't tell me it was this bitch!"

The warden shrugged and slammed the door in Geils's face just as he tried to exit. Geils's forehead smacked against the glass, leaving a greasy smudge. He rubbed his head and turned around, skewering me with his look. "What the fuck do you want?"

Before I could answer, Detective Booth gestured to the chair on the other side of the table. "Take a seat."

He scowled at her. "If you think I'm going to let some pussy cop tell me what to do, you've got another think coming."

"Fine," she said. "I'll allow you to stand."

His eyes narrowed, as if he weren't sure whether standing would now mean he was complying with her orders or not. Being the obstinate ass that he was, he decided to neither stand nor sit, but instead put a foot on the seat of the chair and rested his arms on his crooked leg. *Sheesh*.

Booth stared at him for a long moment, assessing him before speaking. "Agent Holloway received an interesting greeting card recently."

Befuddlement flickered across his face before he marshaled his features and treated us to a smirk. "Oh, yeah?" Don Geils was a disgusting, vile man, but he wasn't entirely stupid. He could read between the lines and tell that the card had upset me, crossed a legal line. "The card contained a threat, huh?" He looked from Booth to me. "A death threat, maybe?" Though I tried not to react, he seemed to sense he'd hit the nail on the head. He let loose a vicious laugh. "So you two came here hoping I'd confess? Maybe slip up and say something to incriminate myself?"

"Sure," Booth replied, matter-of-factly. "How about it? Did you do it? Have someone on the outside mail it for you?"

Though his brief confusion earlier had me doubting his guilt, he wasn't above wanting to cause us trouble, have us waste our precious time chasing down rabbit trails. "I'll admit this," he said, leaning toward us and doubling down on the smirk. "Maybe I did, and maybe I didn't."

Booth pondered things for a moment before turning to me. "He didn't do it."

"Nah," I agreed. "Not him."

He stood up straight, the smirk morphing into a pout. "I said 'maybe I did.'"

"We heard you." I waved a dismissive hand. "But you're just being a jackass. You didn't have anything to do with it."

"You don't know that!"

"Yeah," Booth said. "We do." She stood and summoned the warden. "You can take Mr. Geils back to his cell."

The warden took Geils by the arm. As he was led out, Geils turned and looked back at me over his shoulder. "I hope whoever sent that card follows through!"

Yep, he'd definitely just admitted something—*his innocence.*

As the door swung closed, I turned to Booth. "We've got another shot here." That shot was Joseph "Joe Cool" Cullen, the ice-cream-truck driver I'd arrested for selling drugs.

"I hope he's the one behind the threats," she said. "I'd like to make some arrests and get this behind you. Mostly for your sake, but also so you can focus on the rental-fraud case."

"Me, too." I couldn't blame her for acknowledging the stake she had in solving the threats. So long as I was looking over my shoulder and spending time following leads on the death threats, I couldn't be fully devoting my attention and time to tracking down the con artist who'd duped dozens of Dallas residents. How many more people might fall victim in the meantime?

A few minutes later, the door opened and Joe walked in. Like Geils, Joe was a short man, standing only five feet six. But while Geils was a porker, Joe was a string bean. He had the same acne-pocked face I remembered, the same goofy grin. But the outdated mullet had been replaced by a buzz cut, his swagger with a stoic stroll. He gave me a polite nod. "Hello, Agent Holloway." He turned to Booth and gave her a nod, too. "Ma'am."

Booth cut a look my way, a look that said *This is the cocky twerp you described on the drive over?*

I eyed him closely. "How have you been, Joe?"

"Never better."

I found that hard to believe. I mean, living in a cage? Shared showers? No privacy when you pooped? "Really?"

He smiled patiently. "You did me a favor, sending me here. I'm on the straight-and-narrow path now. I've turned my life over to a higher power." He raised his palms and looked up at the ceiling.

My thoughts slipped out. "Oh, Lord."

Joe turned a beatific gaze back on me. "Exactly."

"Are you for real?" the detective asked. "Or are you blowing smoke?"

"No smoke," Joe said. "'Lying lips are an abomination to the Lord, but those who act faithfully are his delight.' That's Proverbs chapter twelve, verse twenty-two."

"Okay, Mister Delightful," Booth retorted. "Tell me this. Did you have anything to do with a card that was sent to Agent Holloway recently? A brochure that was left on her door?"

"No," he said. "Someone looks over all of our mail before it's sent out."

"What about someone on the outside?" she asked. "Did you have a friend or family member do it for you?"

"No. The only person on the outside I keep up with is my mother, and she's got no reason to send anything. Last time she came for a visit, she told me that for the first time in her life . . ." He paused for a moment, choking up. "She's proud of me." Tears welled up in his eyes.

Oh, for goodness' sake! I reached into my purse, pulled out a small packet of tissues, and slid them across the table.

"Thanks." He wrangled one from the package and dabbed his eyes.

Booth summoned the warden again. "We're done with him."

As Joe was led away, he, too, looked over his shoulder. "Have a blessed day!"

Once they'd gone, Booth turned to me. "Any point in speaking with the pastor?"

"Might as well," I said. "We've come all this way."

When the warden returned, I asked if he could bring Noah Fischer to the room. "This will be our last request."

"I hope so," the warden replied good-naturedly. "I'm wearing out my shoes going up and down these hallways."

He left, returning soon thereafter with the disgraced pastor in tow.

Fischer's face bore the burn scars he earned the night he'd broke into my place and I'd been forced to use a can of flammable extra-hold hair spray as a weapon. His skin appeared sallow, the lack of access to expensive skin-care products and a day spa having also taken its toll. He had the same fair hair that I remembered, though much less of it, his hair halo shrinking to accommodate an expanding bald spot. He dropped into the seat across the table, locked his livid gaze on me, and spewed forth. "Go to hell!"

While Joe had purportedly found God in prison, it looked like Noah Fischer had lost Him here. Then again, Fischer had never been a true believer. He'd used God for his own gain, executing a religious ruse that had fooled many, but not me.

"Good to see you, too," I replied.

His eyes were lakes of fire, flickering with flames of fury.

Booth launched right in. "We know you've sicced your girlfriend on Agent Holloway."

"I have no idea what you're talking about," he snarled. "Besides, I don't have a girlfriend."

"Sure you do," I said. "The pole dancer from Shreveport."

The hot fury in his eyes seemed to cool and he shifted his gaze away from us, as if he didn't want us to see the emotion there. "We're no longer in contact," he said, his voice quieter now.

"I don't believe you," Booth said.

His gaze moved back to us. "Check the visitors' log. You'll see. She hasn't come to see me in months."

"What about Amber Hansen?" I asked.

He scoffed. "You're kidding, right? We're not on speaking terms. She had the nerve to go on TV, publicly shaming me. Like she was so innocent, screwing around with a married man."

"What about Marissa?" I asked. "Are you two still in touch?"

"No," he said, his voice softer now. "My wife has never come here."

"Marissa's your *ex*-wife," I reminded him. *Sheesh.* Did he really expect Marissa to come for a visit after she'd learned that he'd not only had an affair with a stripper, but also secretly fathered a child with one of the parishioners?

My words seemed to stoke the fire again. "Marissa should be in jail, too!" he snapped. "She spent as much money as I did. Maybe even more!"

"That's true," I agreed. During Fischer's reign as head pastor of the Ark, his wife amassed an extensive jewelry and shoe collection. "But she wasn't responsible for the fraudulent tax reporting and she didn't break into my house and try to shoot me. That was all your doing, buddy."

Rather than treating me to a smart-assed comeback, he simply stared straight ahead for a long moment before issuing a choking sound and breaking down completely. He put his head in his hands and sobbed uncontrollably, his shoulders shaking. Looked like life in prison didn't agree with him. He should've thought about that before he ripped people off and tried to end my life.

Booth and I stood, leaving Fischer behind.

As we stepped out of the room, the warden heard the sobbing and peeked inside. "Is he crying?"

Booth nodded. "You might want to give him a moment to compose himself before you take him back to his cell."

"Yeah. I take him back there with tears on his face and the other inmates will rip him to pieces."

chapter fifteen

Such a *Stronzo*

Before leaving the prison, I turned to the warden. "Can we take a look at the visitors' log?"

"Sure." The log was kept digitally. He stepped over to the computer on the countertop and typed in Noah Fischer's name and inmate number. When he finished, he turned the monitor toward me and the detective so we could take a look. We leaned in and looked over the information.

Booth pointed to a line on the screen and turned to me. "Leah Dodd was here in early August."

In other words, Fischer's claim that his former girlfriend hadn't been to see him in months was untrue. "Do you think he intentionally lied?" I asked. "Or do you think it just seemed like a long time to him?" After all, according to the lyrics of "Unchained Melody," time passes slowly in jail.

She shrugged. "Hard to say. But I'd keep Leah Dodd on your radar."

With a good-bye to the warden, Detective Booth and I headed out of the prison. As we walked to the car, she asked more about Fischer's former wife, Marissa. "So she didn't know what was going on at the church? The financial improprieties?"

"She must have known her husband was paying their personal expenses with church funds," I said, "and she certainly benefitted from the arrangement." Besides filling the closets of their luxurious parsonage with designer clothing and their bellies with meals at the area's most expensive restaurants, the couple had taken vacations all over the world under the specious guise of mission work. "Problem was, she had no responsibilities for the church's accounting or tax reporting. Noah Fischer handled their personal finances and taxes, too. We'd have had a hell of a time trying to pin anything on her."

It was frustrating to see the beneficiaries of crime profit from someone else's dirty deeds, but often the best law enforcement could do was catch the big fish and hope the smaller ones would learn their lesson about swimming with sharks.

We climbed into the car and set course for Dallas. It was half past one when we passed the city limits sign. *Home again, home again, jiggity-jig.* The kolaches we'd picked up early that morning at Pokorny's Korner Kitchen had long since been digested, as had the candy we'd eaten. Our vacant stomachs grumbled and groaned and growled.

"We didn't get to speak with Tino Fabrizio," I said, "but we could go visit his wife at her restaurant, see what she might have heard, and get some lunch. Kill two birds with one stone." *Or one stromboli.*

"Works for me."

Booth drove to the restaurant. Given that she'd looked into Tino Fabrizio's security business, which had been located right next door to the bistro, she knew exactly where it was located. As we turned into the lot, it gave me no small pleasure to see that all evidence of Tino's former business was gone. His wife had expanded her restaurant and taken over the space.

When we entered Benedetta's Bistro, Luisa, Stella, and

Elena looked up from their various places around the room. The three sisters were all dark-haired, dark-eyed, and olive-skinned young Italian beauties. *Bellas.*

"Tori!" cried Stella, the youngest, using the alias I'd gone by when I worked at the restaurant. That's how she'd known me for weeks. It was probably hard for her to think of me as someone else.

She rushed over and gave me a hug. We'd grown close when I worked at the restaurant, but the fact that I'd saved their mother's life would forever brand me as a hero in her eyes.

I hugged her back. "It's good to see you, Stella."

The others came over and we exchanged smiles and hugs, too. I held out a hand to indicate Booth. "You remember Detective Booth, right?"

They nodded. After Tino Fabrizio had been arrested, Booth and the FBI agent working the murder cases had interviewed the women to see if they knew anything that could prove helpful. They hadn't. Tino had done a good job of keeping his wife and daughters in the dark where his dirty dealings were concerned.

The girls shook Booth's hand and murmured greetings.

When they were done, I said, "I told Detective Booth about the chocolate cannoli here and said she had to try it."

"It *is* the best in all of Dallas," Elena said, extending a hand to show us to a table.

As I took my seat, I looked up at her. "Is your mother around? I'd like to say hi." No sense telling them I wanted to discuss the death threats with their mom, see if their father might be behind them. It would be hard enough to come to terms with the fact that your father was a killer. They didn't need another reminder from me.

"She's in her office," Elena said. "I'll go get her."

Booth picked up the menu and perused it. "What's good here?"

"Everything," I told her. I spoke the truth. God would be as delighted in me as he'd been in Joe earlier. "I gained ten pounds when I worked here. But I'd recommend Tara's Mushroom Pasta."

She raised a brow. "Is that named after you?"

I nodded. "I tossed a few fried mushrooms on top of my pasta one day and realized how good it was. Bendetta liked it, too, and added it to the lineup."

She closed her menu. "I'll give it a try."

Benedetta, the parent from whom her girls had gotten their dark beauty, stepped up to the table. "Tara, how are you?"

I stood and gave the woman a hug. "I'm good." Okay, so saying I was good wasn't entirely true. But God would just have to forgive me, and we'd get to that subject in a minute. I held out a hand. "You remember Detective Veronica Booth from the Dallas Police Department?"

"Wonderful to see you again," Benedetta said, taking her hand.

"Can you sit with us?" I asked, keeping my voice low so her daughters wouldn't overhear. "I have something I wanted to talk to you about."

"Of course." She dropped gracefully into the seat next to me.

Elena returned. "Have y'all decided what you'd like?"

"We'll both have Tara's Mushroom Pasta," I told her.

"Excellent choice," she said with a grin. "Iced tea? Sparkling water?"

We opted for tea.

Once Elena had left the table, I turned back toward her mother. "I've received death threats, Benedetta. Someone tried to run me down in the street, too."

"Che cavolo!" Her hand went reflexively to her chest as if to slow the beat of her heart. "Who would do such a thing?"

The detective flicked her cloth napkin to open it and settled it on her lap. "That's what we're trying to find out."

Benedetta's eyes ran between us, narrowing. Her mouth became a grim line, too. "You're thinking it could be Tino, aren't you? That stupid, evil, nasty—" Her eyes popped wide and her mouth curved up as her daughter stepped up to the table with our drinks.

"Thanks, Elena," I said after she'd set my tea in front of me.

Once she'd gone, so did Benedetta's smile. She resumed her tirade against the girls' father. "Awful, horrible, disgusting *stronzo!*"

I wasn't sure of the exact translation of that last word, but I could hazard a guess. "Do you think he could be still running his mob network from prison? I've heard he's in jail in Chicago now. Maybe that cousin of his that you didn't like has been helping him out."

She bit her lip and slowly lifted her shoulders. "It's possible," she said. "That side of the family was no good. But last I heard they were trying to distance themselves from Tino. They don't like snitches, and when one of them gets arrested, they're treated like a snitch. They assume that whoever got picked up might turn on them. At the very least, the person who gets taken in makes the organization vulnerable. Mobsters don't like feeling vulnerable." She gave me a pointed look. "If you ask me, Tino's days on earth are numbered. The guys in Chicago? They got other guys on the inside, ones who didn't roll over, ones they still trust. They could have someone shank Tino in the shower. *Uno, due, tre.*" She picked up a knife in one hand and raised the other, snapping her fingers once, but unlike

Trish LeGrande's earlier snaps, this one was meant for emphasis and thus didn't offend me.

Luisa ventured over to the table, apparently responding to the snap. "Did you need me, Mom?"

Rather than telling her daughter the real reason she'd snapped her fingers, Benedetta said, "Bring Tara and her friend a couple bottles of the new Lambrusco to take home with them."

"Thanks," I told her. "But I'm not allowed to accept anything of value from a taxpayer."

She laughed. "How many free meals did you eat when you were working here?"

"Too many," I said, laughing in return. "But that was different. I was undercover."

"Do what she says, Ma," Luisa said with a smile. "She has a gun."

I nodded and smiled back. "You're a smart girl."

As Luisa topped off my tea glass, she noticed my hand. "You have a ring on your finger! You're getting married? To Nico?"

Nico had been Nick's alias. He and Josh had opened an art gallery in the same strip center as the restaurant so that they could keep a close eye on both me and Tino's security business.

"Yep," I said. "Nico and I are getting married in October."

Benedetta clapped her hands three times in glee. "I'm so happy for you! Will the ceremony be here in Dallas?"

"No. We're getting married in my hometown in east Texas. Nacogdoches."

"Ah," she said. "It's beautiful there. So many trees."

"Would you and the girls like to come?"

"Of course!" She tossed her hands in the air. "We'd love to!"

"And we'd love to have you." I realized the party bus could be getting awfully crowded. We might have to arrange for a second bus to ensure everyone got a seat. "I'll get an invitation in the mail to you."

"Grazie," she said. "I am so happy for you. I know your marriage will be much better than mine." She rolled her eyes and waved her daughter away. "Bring them each a chocolate cannoli, too." She turned to Booth. "It's to die for."

Given the recent threats on my life, I preferred to think of the cannoli as worth *living* for.

Our meals arrived and we dug in, topping the pasta off with the delicious chocolate cannoli.

When we returned to the cruiser, we both unbuttoned our pants to let our full stomachs have more room.

"You weren't kidding about that food," Booth said as she started the car. "It was delicious."

chapter sixteen

House Hunting

Amber Hansen hadn't returned Detective Booth's call by the end of the workday. The property owners hadn't returned my call, either. *Darn.* Looked like I'd have to go out to the house, after all.

Eddie was on duty to be my backup tonight. I felt bad that I was taking his time away from his wife and daughters, so I treated him to an early dinner, his choice of places. He picked a Mexican restaurant called El Loro Loco, which translated as the Crazy Parrot. We'd picked up breakfast tacos there while working a recent human smuggling case.

As we walked in the door, we were greeted by the irritating screech of a mechanical parrot. *"SQUAWK! Welcome to El Loro Loco!"*

Eddie cringed. "I'd forgotten about that damn bird."

I hadn't. That's why I'd put my fingers in my ears when we'd walked through the door.

A young Latina woman stepped up to the hostess stand. "Table for two?"

When Eddie answered in the affirmative, she led us to a booth. We passed several customers enjoying frozen margaritas. Too bad I was still technically on the job, even though it was after normal working hours. A margarita sounded pretty darn good about then.

We enjoyed a nice meal of enchiladas and headed out to the property. On the drive over, I silently implored the Almighty to let Johnny Brewster be the guy we were seeking. I wanted the crook caught before some other young person got duped out of their hard-earned dollars.

We pulled up to the house. It was a modest brown brick ranch-style home, with minimal landscaping. It sat on a busy, relatively noisy street. That could explain why the rent was below market for the neighborhood. With real estate, whether buying or renting, it was all about location, location, location.

A sleek and sporty blue Honda Civic sat in the drive. *Hmm.* When the con man had shown the other victims the various properties, none had seen a car. He'd presumably taken a Backseat Driver to and from the property. Had he grown lax now? Had he gotten away with the scheme for months now and was no longer being as cautious? Or did this car belong to someone else he was showing the property to?

As we climbed out of our car, a man climbed out of the Civic. I recognized him from his driver's license photo as John Everett Brewster, the guy who worked for the building contractor. He wore khaki pants and a short-sleeved plaid shirt. No business suit. *Hmm.* This guy was tall, which matched the description of the suspect we sought, but he was not what I'd consider beefy. Just average. But maybe he'd dropped a few pounds since the security footage I'd seen.

At that point, taking everything into account, I was ninety percent sure he wasn't the guy we were after. While his physical features loosely fit the description, he wasn't wearing a suit. Plus, the other guy used fake names, not his real one. Still, maybe he'd changed his MO, decided to go legit. If anything, criminals could be unpredictable.

Brewster met us on the driveway. "Hi, Sara." He extended his hand for a shake before turning to Eddie. "Are you her husband?"

"I am," Eddie said. "God help me."

I elbowed him in the ribs.

"Follow me," the guy said, turning and leading us up to the porch. "I'll show you around." He put a key in the lock, turned it, and opened what had to be the portal to hell.

"My God!" I cried, reflexively taking a step back and covering my nose and mouth. "What's that smell?" It was as if every tomcat who'd ever lived had raised his tail and doused the place with all the spray they could muster.

Eddie turned his head away and coughed, fanning his watering eyes. "Did a skunk get trapped inside?"

Brewster grimaced. "Sorry. The former tenants used this place as a meth lab until they were arrested last month. The owners are planning to replace the carpets and repaint the walls before a new tenant moves in. They're going to have the ductwork cleaned, too." He scurried inside and began throwing windows open. "Come on in and take a look around," he choked out.

Eddie took three more steps back and shook his head. "I'm not going in there without a hazmat suit."

I blinked back involuntary tears and stepped away, too. "I'm with you, buddy."

My doubt that the guy inside was our suspect had increased from ninety to ninety-five percent. I wanted to get this farce over with so I could go home to Bonnie's and relax in front of the television with Nick and a big, cold glass of peach sangria.

Brewster came back to the door and wheezed out, "Aren't you coming in?"

"We'll pass," I said.

He nodded in acquiescence, stepped back out onto the porch, and closed the door behind him. "I probably shouldn't show this place again until we get the work done."

You think? "That would be a wise decision."

"Y'all could come back then," he suggested, hope in his voice. "Take another look?"

No way, José. "Maybe."

"Do you have any questions?" he asked, looking from me to Eddie and back again.

The only question I had pertained to him rather than to the house. I was curious why the money he made as a leasing agent hadn't been reported on his tax return. Was he paid in cash that he neglected to report? "How long have you been doing this?" I asked. "Leasing houses?"

"Only a few weeks," he said. "I work for a general contractor who does a lot of remodels on older homes and rental properties. I prepare estimates for the clients, none of the actual labor. I'm not that handy with a hammer." He offered a self-deprecating smile. "A lot of the homeowners complain about what a hassle it is to deal with their properties. One of them actually asked whether he could hire me to manage it. I realized it would be a great side job, a chance to make some extra money. The whole thing happened organically. I've always wanted to own my own business. I'm hoping this will take off so I can quit the contracting job and manage properties full-time."

My meter of doubt had now reached one hundred percent. I knew with full certainty he wasn't the man running the real estate scam. Plus, the fact that he'd only recently started this side business explained why there'd been no income reported for it on his return the year before.

I stuck out my hand again. "Thanks for your time."

With that, Eddie and I left and returned to the office to round up his car. He followed me down the highway until

I took the exit that led to the Village. I needed to put in some time with Backseat Driver tonight. With any luck, maybe I'd find the con artist tonight and put the case to rest once and for all.

I parked in a visitor spot of one of the apartment complexes and activated my app to accept notifications from Backseat. A few minutes later, my phone pinged with a message from Backseat Driver. A passenger needed a ride from the Tom Thumb grocery store near Lovers Lane and Greenville Avenue.

Could this be the guy? It sure would be great if it were. It would make up for striking out earlier.

I quickly pulled up the information about the rider on the app. He was an infrequent passenger, only using the service once every couple of months. I checked the reviews to see how other Backseat Drivers had described him. *Polite. Doesn't annoy you with small talk.* One even said, *The man sure knows how to wear a suit!*

Bingo! Or at least the possibility of bingo.

I jabbed the icon to accept the ride. A minute or so later, I pulled up in front of the grocery store, Eddie trailing behind. A man in a business suit with a cart of groceries in front of him waved to get my attention. While he was dressed like the con man we were after, his skin color didn't match. This guy was dark-skinned. This trip had been a waste of my time. Still, I owed it to this guy to see it through. It would be rude to leave him stranded.

I got out and helped the guy load his groceries into the trunk. When we finished, he climbed into the backseat. I closed the trunk and turned around. *Holy shit!* Two men in Halloween masks were only ten feet away and headed directly toward me. One was Darth Vader, the other a Storm Trooper. *Are they going to kill me?*

My heart and mind reeled. My gun was in my purse in my car. So was my pepper spray. *Dammit!* I did the only thing I could think of. I crouched and assumed a karate stance. Or at least what I assumed was a karate stance.

Darth Vader stopped walking and slid his mask up, exposing his face.

I didn't recognize him. Nor did I recognize the Storm Trooper when he did the same. "You okay?" he asked.

Jeez. I'd totally overreacted, hadn't I? These were just two guys who'd bought costumes at the pop-up Halloween store next to the supermarket. I could see the store's big orange banner behind them. GET YOUR COSTUMES HERE!

"Ha-ha," I said, my laugh sounding as forced as it was. "Just joking."

"Ohhh-kay," Darth Vader said, exchanging a look with his friend. The look said *This chick's unstable. Let's get out of here.* And get out of there they did, hurrying off at twice the pace they'd been walking earlier.

From his car down the curb, Eddie raised his hands from the wheel as if to ask *What the hell?* Apparently he'd seen them come out of the store and realized they hadn't posed a threat. Easy for him. He hadn't had his back turned.

I climbed into the driver's seat, fastened my seat belt, and started the engine.

"Thanks for the ride," my passenger said. "My car's been in the shop all week. The alternator went out."

I groaned in sympathy. "That's going to cost you."

"Tell me about it."

I held up a bottle of water. "Water?"

"No, thanks."

I decided to open it for myself, unscrewing the top and taking a swig. With the hot temperatures we'd had lately, it couldn't hurt to stay hydrated.

We rode in companionable silence while I drove the short distance to his apartment, only a mile away.

He pointed out the window. "That's my reserved spot there. You can pull into it."

I parked and helped him carry his groceries to his door. He gave me a smile, a "thanks," and a three-dollar cash tip before closing it. Though I appreciated his generosity, it wouldn't be a good idea for me to retain the cash. Federal employee rules and whatnot. I'd contribute it to the coffee fund at work tomorrow.

Eddie followed me as I drove to Bonnie's. Once I'd pulled into the garage, he lowered the window of his car on the street and raised a hand in good-bye. I raised one in return.

When I climbed out of my car, I heard the telltale sounds of Nick's truck engine cooling off. Looked like he'd put in a late night, too.

He met me at the door, a full glass of his mom's sangria in his hand.

"For me?"

"You know it."

I gave him a smile and accepted the glass. "You sure know how to greet a lady."

He cut me a mischievous grin. "That's not all I know how to do to a lady."

Unfortunately, he couldn't show me any of those other things while we were living under his mother's roof. *Ugh.*

I changed out of my suit and into my pajamas, sighing as I flopped down on the couch next to my fiancé. Somewhere out there was both a con artist and my aspiring killer. But for now, I was going to relax and enjoy me some Nick time.

chapter seventeen

Moving Day

Friday passed without incident. Nobody tried to run me over, stab me, or otherwise put an end to my life. I supposed I should be happy about that. But it was hard to be happy knowing that someone might be holed up somewhere, plotting to run me over, stab me, or otherwise put an end to my life at some later point. The uncertainty, the constantly looking over my shoulder, was eating away at me.

But in addition to those awful feelings, I felt something else as well. *Curiosity.* My visit to the prison and Booth's subsequent question about Marissa Fischer's involvement in the financial indiscretions at the Ark church had me wondering. Was Marissa staying on a straight-and-narrow path now? Had she learned from her experience that honesty was the best policy?

I typed her name into my search browser. While a multitude of articles detailing the downfall of Noah Fischer mentioned Marissa, all of that was old news to me. There were several articles from celebrity gossip sites detailing her marriage to Darryl Lundgren, the guy who ran the chain of tractor dealerships, as well as some photos of the two cheek to cheek, looking as happy as two people could be. But her fifteen minutes of fame had run out last year, and the gossip columnists seemed to have lost interest in her.

I logged into the social media sites to see if she had active accounts. Boy, did she ever. Her Facebook page contained numerous photos, mostly pictures of herself, either alone or with her new husband. Marissa was on the tall side, her brown hair, highlighted with copper and bronze streaks, hanging down to her chest. Her most recent pics featured the two standing on what appeared to be the deck of a cruise ship. According to her posts, she and Darryl had left over a week ago to embark on a four-week grand Mediterranean cruise. The ship would make stops at no less than twenty-six ports, among them Barcelona, Naples, Venice, Malta, Athens, and Monte Carlo. She'd posted the same pics on her Instagram, Twitter, and Pinterest accounts.

Though I'd searched the sites primarily out of curiosity, the pics also told me that I could cross Marissa off my list of suspects. She couldn't very well come after me when she was halfway around the world having the time of her life, could she? But maybe Fischer's pole-dancer girlfriend could.

I logged onto Leah Dodd's Facebook page. Like Marissa and the parishioner Fischer had knocked up, Leah had long, reddish hair. Pastor Fischer certainly had a type. Both Leah's last name and her chest sported double-Ds. Her lip bore a small mole, à la Cindy Crawford. While Leah had thousands of male "friends" when I'd checked her Facebook page last year, she had even more now. Heck, she'd even started her own fan page. She had over ten thousand likes. No wonder, given the suggestive pics she posted of herself on the page. One showed her riding her pole, her auburn hair tossed back. Another depicted her crawling toward the camera, her cleavage dangling below her. A third photo showed her on a beach wearing only a pair of bikini bottoms, her hands covering her breasts, her mouth spread in a playfully naughty smile.

The page noted the name of the club in Shreveport where she danced. It also noted that she was available to dance at "private parties" for "negotiable rates."

I sat back in my chair and pondered things for a moment. Had losing Noah Fischer's consistent patronage been an issue for her? The woman oozed sex and was surely a favorite at the club where she danced. But strippers had a short shelf life. Dancing topless was for the young and nubile. Maybe she'd hoped to get more money out of Fischer and get out of the game. Maybe I'd ruined her plans by throwing her benefactor in the klink. And maybe now she sought to ruin my plans, too. Then again, maybe this was too many maybes.

I logged out of the social media sites and finished looking over the records in Teacher's Pet's computer files. By matching the tutoring schedule to the payment records, I discerned that the owner had received at least twenty grand in unreported cash income each year she'd been in business. I calculated the taxes due, tacked on interest and penalties, and prepared a formal notice demanding payment. I phoned her to let her know the assessment was on its way. If she failed to comply, we'd seize her other assets and carry her cheating ass off to jail. Of course I worded that information much more professionally.

"We expect you to promptly arrange to make payment," I said. "If you fail to do so, the next step is incarceration. Your personal and business assets would also be forfeited."

"What about my computers?" she demanded.

"You can also come by our office any weekday between eight-thirty and five o'clock to pick them up."

She scoffed and snapped, "You took them out of my office. You should bring them back."

"And you should've paid your taxes," I snapped right back. So much for trying to maintain my professionalism. This woman was getting on my last nerve. "If you don't pick them up in thirty days, we'll turn them over to impound. Your choice." I hung up the phone before she could respond. *Neener-neener.*

Nick looked up from behind his desk across the hall, his brows drawn. I suppose I had sounded a little testy, hadn't I? But I couldn't help it. I had a death threat hanging over me, a rental-fraud case I couldn't seem to solve, and no nookie to relieve my stress.

"Want to drive out to August Buchmeyer's place with me?" I called to Nick. His court case had concluded. Luckily, the jury had come back with a quick conviction.

"Buchmeyer?" Nick said. "That kook?"

"Yeah. He's my last suspect in the area."

Nick stood from his desk. "I suppose we might as well. I have my doubts he's behind the death threats, but you never know."

I had my doubts, too. But I couldn't just sit here and do nothing. It wasn't in my nature. Besides, the Buchmeyers lived out in the boonies. It would give me and Nick a chance to spend some time together.

We chatted and sang along to the radio as we maneuvered out of downtown, through the suburbs, and ventured into the countryside.

"Here it is," I said as we approached the gate that led onto the Buchmeyers' property.

Nick slowed again. A plywood sign lay in the shallow ditch next to the gravel drive. The sign, which had once proudly graced the barbed-wire fence, read PROPERTY OF THE LONE STAR NATION. TRESPASSERS WILL BE VIOLATED. A cockeyed, weather-beaten blue trailer rested in a thick patch of weeds inside the gate, an enormous, outdated satellite dish standing between it and a half-dead mesquite tree. Buchmeyer's ancient two-tone brown pickup was parked on the packed-dirt driveway. The rusted tractors, horse trailer, and trampoline that had littered the yard when we came out before were now gone, as were the sounds of clucking chickens and the stench of bird poop from the long metal buildings farther back on the property. Looked like they'd shut down their chicken operation. The Burnet flag remained, though its azure-blue background and single gold star were faded now. The flag, the last one flown over Texas when it was still an independent country, hung limp and lifeless as if it had accepted its defeat, the breeze not even bothering to pick it up. The two coonhounds we'd seen here last year were still around, lounging in the shade under the pickup.

The cheap metal gate had a chain on it to keep it closed, but no lock this time. I hopped out and opened the gate, closing it again after Nick had driven through. I climbed back in the car and rode the short distance to the trailer.

Betty Buchmeyer, August's wife, met us at the door. "What are you two doing back here? Didn't you cause us enough problems last year?"

When we'd come out before, we'd found a stockpile of Spam, canned beans, toilet paper, and guns and ammo in one of the barns on-site. Tents and survival gear as well. The stash had been seized to cover taxes due on the couple's chicken-ranching operations. Needless to say, the Buchmeyers had been none too happy to see the government take off with their supplies and weapons. But, heck. They'd left us no choice. They'd not only failed to file or pay their taxes for years on end, but they'd also refused to respond to the many notices they'd been sent. Had they been reasonable, they could have worked something out. Besides, there was no telling what they'd planned to do with all those guns. They'd stockpiled enough weaponry and ammunition to fight the Civil War all over again.

I looked up at the woman. "I got your card."

She frowned. "What card?"

"The one you sent to my office."

"Why on earth would I send you a card?"

I decided not to beat around the bush. "To threaten my life."

She rolled her rheumy eyes. "Don't flatter yourself. You're not worth the trouble."

"Oh, yeah?" I went up the steps. "Your husband got anything to say about that?"

She snorted. "Why don't you come in and ask him?" She opened the door wide and stepped back to allow us inside.

We walked in to find August on the couch. He looked up at me and Nick. "Why, hello there!" he said happily. "Grab a beer and join me. Can you believe what they're saying about Nixon? Think he'll get the boot?"

It was clear that even though August Buchmeyer was still here, he was no longer *all there*. Heck, I was pretty sure he hadn't been *all there* last year, either.

I turned to Betty. "We'll go now. Sorry to have bothered you."

Her face and voice softened. "Sure you can't stay for a few minutes? Sometimes, when he's talking to people, he . . ." She seemed to be searching for the right word. "He *comes back*."

No matter how loony her husband had been, it was clear she missed the man he once was. While I couldn't understand the life choices the Buchmeyers had made, I could understand that kind of love and devotion.

Nick and I grabbed chairs from the kitchen table and pulled them over. Nick turned to August. "My guess is that

Nixon will resign before they impeach him. That would be the smart thing to do, wouldn't you say?"

"I suppose so," August said. "If it were me, though, I'd put up a fight."

I fought a smile. "I have no doubt you would."

August waved a gnarled hand and started to say something, but he eyed us again, his gaze narrowed. "Hold on. Ain't you two from the government?"

"He's back," Betty said, a smile on her face. "You better get on out of here."

Nick and I bade them good-bye and hightailed it out the door.

"You're lucky I ain't got my gun on me!" August shouted after us. "I'd put some buckshot in your ass!"

I had no doubt about that, either.

A little after four, the woman who owned the property Johnny Brewster had shown me finally called me back. She and her husband had been out of town visiting their grandchildren and had just received my message.

"Nothing to worry about," I told her. "I'm investigating a rental scam but I was able to discern that your leasing agent isn't involved."

"Thank goodness!" she said. "When I got your message, I was worried."

I could only hope that renters in the Dallas area had seen Will's report on the news and knew to be wary of sign-now situations.

Detective Booth phoned me a few minutes later. "I heard from Amber. She says she's innocent."

No surprise there. "Were you able to verify her whereabouts the night the silver car followed me?"

"Not definitively. She works from home and claims she was home all day with her car in the garage."

In other words, she may or may not be telling the truth. Still, I was inclined to believe her. She'd seemed far more upset at Noah Fischer for his betrayal than she'd been at law enforcement for taking him down.

"Thanks for letting me know," I told the detective.

"Sure. Stay safe now."

"I'll try my damnedest."

While Will and Eddie stood guard outside our town houses that evening, Nick and I hustled about, packing up the rest of our things for the garage sale and move the next day.

My nightstand drawer was full of miscellaneous chargers and plugs, but I had no idea what devices they belonged to. *Keep or toss?* I decided to keep them. We'd have more space in the new house and, with my luck, as soon as I tossed them, I'd come across the appliance or electronic gadget they paired with.

I stripped the bed and stuffed the sheets, pillows, and spread into a large box, secured it with strapping tape, and scribbled "bedroom #2" on the box. Nick's bed was bigger and more comfortable, so we planned to use it in the master. I grabbed the clothes from the rack in my closet and carried them out to my car in the garage, draping them across the back seat and, once the seat was loaded, filling the trunk. My shoes tumbled into another box, my towels into another. I would've liked to take more time with the packing, but I simply didn't have it. I'd have to spend more time on the back end, when we unpacked at the new place, but so be it.

Being less of a pack rat, Nick finished his place before I was through with mine, and he came down to help me. He bent down to clear the cabinet in my bathroom. He took one look inside, grunted, and turned to me. "There's a dozen half-empty bottles of lotion in here."

"I know." I tended to tire of the same scent and often moved on to a new bottle before finishing an older one.

He took another look. "You've got three different types of lavender."

"Yep." It was my right as a woman.

"Should I throw them out?"

"No," I said. "That would be wasteful."

"Do you plan to use them all?" His voice and face were skeptical.

"Eventually." I made a rotating motion with my finger. "I'll circle back to them."

"Maybe we should just get rid of them."

I cut him a look. "And maybe we should get rid of those fishing lures you haven't used in a while."

Without another word he swept the bottles up in his arm and scooped them into a box.

When we finished upstairs, we moved on to the kitchen. He picked up my toaster, cleared it of crumbs, and put it in one of the boxes on the counter. He pulled out my pasta maker, which I'd bought on a whim one day when I'd been feeling uncharacteristically domestic. Of course the machine was still in the box, the urge to make noodles from scratch having passed on my drive home from the store when I remembered I had no talent for cooking but great skill at ordering takeout.

"Should I put this with the stuff for the garage sale?" Nick asked, holding up the box.

"No. I want to keep it."

"You're never going to use it."

This again? "You're never going to use that home beer-brewing system you bought, either."

He raised a shoulder in a one-sided shrug. "Can't argue with that logic."

We finally finished around eleven and sent Will and Eddie home with sincere expressions of gratitude. "I can't thank you enough."

"That's right," Eddie agreed, sliding me a sly smile. "But you can babysit for me and Sandra once this whole ordeal is over."

"It's a deal."

"Me, too!" Will insisted.

"You got it." It was the least I could do.

On Saturday, Nick, Bonnie, and I rose before the sun and drove to my town house to get ready for the garage sale and move. Both Hana and Josh had agreed to be lookouts for us this morning so that Eddie and Will could spend time with their families.

Hana positioned herself at one end of the block, while Josh parked at the other. Both had their guns at the ready. They had radios, too, so that they could give us a quick warning if need be. Chances were whoever was after me would see the G-rides and realize we had protection, but you never knew what someone might do, especially someone crazy and violent enough to want to kill a person. Bonnie sat sentry at my town house, positioning herself in a lawn chair on my porch, my shotgun discreetly hidden behind the bush but within easy reach. With this many eyes on the area, the event should be safe.

After we arranged the items in the driveway, we put a sign out on the main thoroughfare just outside the neighborhood, next to the new mailbox that had been installed to replace the one in which I'd deposited our wedding invitations, the one that had been damaged by the pickup. The sun had barely begun to light the morning sky when a car pulled to the curb. It was the first of many, the die-hard yard-sale pros who knew you had to arrive early to have the best selection.

Nick was dickering with a man over the price of a lawn-mower when Hana came over the radio. "Two rough-looking women just passed in a Subaru Forester. They slowed when they saw me and seemed to be checking out my car. They're on their way. I'll come down, too."

"I'll be in the garage."

I used the remote to open the garage door and scurried inside, closing it after me. When the door lacked only a couple of inches from the concrete, I pushed the button again to halt its descent. I crouched down and peered under the door. Close to me were several pairs of feet milling around, but farther back I saw the Subaru. The driver pulled to the curb across the street and two women climbed out. One was tall, thin, and dark-headed. The other was thin, but short, about my height. She had white-blond hair styled in a buzz cut with bangs. They both wore ripped jeans, ankle boots, and tight black T-shirts.

I pushed the talk button on my radio to get in touch with Hana and Josh. "I see the women. I don't recognize them. But if they've been hired to kill me, I wouldn't, anyway."

Hiring a female hit man would be a smart thing to do. People tended to be much less suspicious of women. In fact, was there even a term "hit woman?" I'd never heard it used. In this day and age of feminism, it seemed like there should be, though. *Now that's an odd thought to have, isn't it?*

"I'll hang around until they go," Hana replied.

Through the gap, I saw Hana approach on foot. Her Glock was hidden under her loose cotton shirt. She stopped at the edge of the drive and feigned interest in a clock radio.

The dark-haired woman examined a nightstand that had been passed down from my brother Trace to me years ago when he married and he and his wife bought a new bedroom set. She pulled the drawers in and out to test them. Satisfied that they didn't stick too badly, she called out to Nick. "Will you take five bucks for this?"

"How about ten?" Nick said as he stepped over.

She came back with, "Seven."

He replied with, "Sold."

He took her cash, tucked it into his pocket, and carried the nightstand to the back of the Subaru, stashing it in the cargo bay for her.

The other woman negotiated with Bonnie over a couple of DVDs. One minute and three dollars later, she returned to the Subaru, too.

Once they drove off, I came back out of hiding. Looked like it had been a false alarm. Then again, maybe they realized I wasn't accessible and simply improvised. I made a mental note to keep an eye out for the two.

We'd gotten rid of nearly everything by the time my brothers arrived at noon. My parents were with them.

My mother hopped out of my father's truck the instant it stopped moving and stormed over to me. "Tara!" she scolded. "Why didn't you tell me someone's been trying to kill you?"

I cut my eyes to Trace, who was climbing out of his truck. "You weren't supposed to tell her."

"I didn't," he said. "I told my wife and she told Mom."

"Thank goodness she did!" Mom put her hands on her hips. "Don't you ever keep something like this from me and your father again! I have half a mind to put you in time out."

"I'm a little too old for time out, Mom."

"Maybe so," my mom retorted. "But if you ever want to taste another one of my pecan pralines you will not keep secrets from me."

The mere thought of being deprived of the yummy treats for the rest of my life made my heart sink. "But that would be cruel and unusual punishment!"

Still scowling, she nonetheless gave me a kiss on the cheek and a tight, warm hug. She gestured around at the few remaining items. A chipped souvenir coffee mug from a long-ago trip to Port Aransas for spring break during college. A pole lamp that refused to stand up straight. A pair of striped kitchen curtains that had faded in the relentless Texas sun. All of which would go into the trash. "How'd y'all do?"

As Bonnie came over, Nick pulled the wad of cash and coins from his pocket and counted them out. "One hundred thirty-seven dollars and seventy-five cents."

"Not bad," Bonnie said before giving both my mother and father a hug.

My dad pointed to the house. "We best get busy if we're going to get everything moved today. It won't all fit on the trailer at once."

While Hana and Josh stayed on lookout duty, the rest of us went inside. While the men took out the large pieces of furniture, we women packed boxes with kitchenware, books, clothing, shoes, and framed pictures, as well as various and sundry knickknacks, tchotchkes, gewgaws, and bric-a-brac. In other words, miscellaneous junk I'd managed to collect over the years.

We spent the rest of the day moving everything from Nick's place down the street and my town house to our new home next to Bonnie's, carefully watching for a tail. Fortunately, we saw none. Whoever was after me appeared to have taken the day off. Or perhaps they were holed up somewhere, planning some particularly heinous and painful way of dispatching me once they had the opportunity. *Ugh. There's a happy thought, huh?*

The house Nick and I would soon own was a one-story Tudor-style model with a two-car, front-entry garage. Mature Bradford pear trees flanked the drive. A row of yellow rosebushes ran along the front and sides, their blooms not only providing a nice splash of color but a pleasant scent as well.

Before we brought anything in, Nick and I took my family on the grand tour. The cleaning crew had left everything spotless and gleaming, the freshly shampooed carpets looking as good as new.

I led my parents and brothers into the living room.

"This is good-sized," Mom said, stepping over to the windows along the rear wall that looked out onto the covered back patio and shady yard. She took a peek outside. "That yard will be great for the dog and kids, too, once you have 'em."

We went to the kitchen next. My mother, who loved to cook, inspected the pantry, dishwasher, and oven. "Self-cleaning," she noted. "That'll come in handy."

We proceeded to the dining room. "We're planning to replace the wallpaper," I told them. The current paper was out of date.

My mother glanced around. "You know what else would look nice in here? A big, wide mirror in a gold frame. It would make the room look even bigger and reflect the light from the windows."

"Good idea."

Mom had always had a knack for decorating.

We headed down the hallway.

"This is the home office," I said, leading them through the French doors. "Don't you just love the built-in bookshelves and cabinets?"

Mom dipped her head in agreement. "Sure is nice."

In the master bedroom, I threw open the doors to the enormous walk-in closet.

"Holy cow!" Mom said. "That closet's nearly as big as a bedroom itself."

Finally, my clothes wouldn't be crammed up against each other anymore. They'd have room to breathe. The built-in shoe racks would also be a plus.

She glanced into the bathroom. "Is that a whirlpool bathtub?"

"It is." The bubbling tub had been one of my favorite features. I couldn't wait to relax in it with a good book after a hard day at work.

"You'll enjoy that," Mom said.

"I sure will." Maybe Nick and I would enjoy it together. *Hee-hee!*

After showing them the other two bedrooms and the second bath, I turned to my parents. "What do you think?"

My mother took one of my hands and one of Nick's in hers. "I think you two are going to make a lovely home here." She gave our hands an affectionate squeeze before releasing them.

As the men unloaded the furniture and boxes from the truck, my mother, Bonnie, and I directed them where to deposit the boxes and place the furniture. We had a hard time deciding on the arrangement in the living room.

"Should the TV go on this wall?" I asked, pointing to one of the walls. "Or should we put it on an angle in the corner and put the couch over there?" I pointed to another spot.

Naturally, we forced the men to try every possible way of arranging the furniture before deciding we liked it best the very first way they'd placed it.

The men exchanged glances and shook their heads. "Women," Trace muttered.

Soon, they had the trailer emptied and were ready to go back for a second load.

I checked the time on my phone. It was a quarter to four. Shane should have e-mailed me the address of the rental property by now.

I pulled up my e-mails. Sure enough, there it was. I quickly checked the location on my maps app to see how long it would take me to get there. The two-bedroom condo was located right outside the 635 loop near Richland College, part of the Dallas Community College system. I could be there in half an hour. Of course I might not need to go to the appointment if I could speak with the owner first and determine whether Shane was authorized to rent the place on his or her behalf.

I searched the appraisal district listings. The condo was owned by a real estate investment partnership called Prairieland Rental Properties, Ltd. Though I found a phone number for the partnership online, my call to the number went instantly to voice mail, the outgoing message telling me I had reached them outside of normal business hours and to leave my name and number if I would like a call back. I didn't bother leaving the information. I'd soon know for myself whether Shane was the man Detective Booth and I were hoping to take down.

I explained to Bonnie and my family that I'd need to beg off for just a bit to go to the appointment. "I should be back in a couple of hours at the latest," I told them.

"Be careful, hon," Dad said, his eyes dark with concern.

"Don't worry," I told him. "Josh will be going with me."

"I will?" Josh called from the open window of his car nearby.

"Yep." I walked over and climbed into his passenger seat.

Josh and I headed north on Central Expressway and arrived at the condominium development with ten minutes to spare. The parking lot of the complex was half full with cars. We took a spot in the visitor section, climbed out, and strolled around until we found the unit. We stood on the porch, waiting and watching.

We continued waiting and watching until 4:35. Then 4:40. Then 4:45.

Without Shane's phone number, I had no way to call him to determine if he were merely running late or if he didn't plan to show up at all. Maybe he was the con artist, had gotten an inkling that I was in law enforcement, and decided not to come. Or maybe he was the con artist but had been visited by the ghosts of leases past, present, and future last night and decided to change his ways, go straight. Or maybe he'd simply gotten stuck in Dallas's unpredictable traffic.

As it turned out, it was the latter.

When Shane careened into the lot at 4:50 in a sporty red Nissan 370Z, he raised a hand to let us know it was him. But that raised hand, along with the sandy blond hair and beard, told me he wasn't our guy.

"It's not him," I told Josh with a sigh.

Shane hopped out of his car and strode rapidly in our direction. "Sorry I'm late. There was a wreck on the tollway."

"No problem," I said, though frankly, I was pissed. If the guy had given me his damn phone number, I would've been able to figure out that he wasn't the target I was looking for. I wouldn't have wasted both his time and my own.

He took us inside, where we glanced around, pretending to be evaluating the place.

I pointed to the ceiling in the kitchen. "Am I the only one who sees the Virgin Mary in that water stain?"

Before either of the men could respond, an earsplitting sound came from the unit next door. *SKREEEEEEEE! BUH-BUH-BUH-BUH-BUH!* The wall between the units vibrated, the cabinet doors quivering on their hinges.

I covered my ears and hollered, "What the heck is that?"

Josh, who'd also covered his ears, shouted, "Air in the water pipes!"

Clearly, this place had some major plumbing issues.

When the sound quieted down to a soft sputter, I removed my hands from my ears, quickly paced the condominium, and declared it "not what we're looking for."

"What *are* you looking for?" Shane asked. "Maybe one of the other properties I manage would work for you."

"That's okay," I told Shane before turning to Josh. "I think we should go with the duplex we saw this morning, don't you?"

Josh played along. "I agree, sugar pie."

Sugar pie? He didn't have to play along *that* well.

We thanked Shane for his time and returned to my town house. The men were able to fit the rest of the stuff from my house on the flatbed and in the bed of my brothers' pickups. They drove down the street and loaded the remaining space on the trailer with Nick's furniture, putting his smaller items and boxes in the back of his and Dad's trucks.

As we started off down the street, I saw my Realtor pull up to my place with a potential buyer. I hopped out of the car to speak with her.

"Quick question," I said, taking her aside as the middle-aged woman who'd come to see my place headed on to the porch. "Do you know if there are any special financing programs for first-time homeowners that wouldn't require a big down payment?"

"There sure are," she replied. "I've got mortgage people who can finagle all kinds of financing. You might have to cover more of the closing costs, but the details can be worked out so that the overall deal is fair to everyone." She cocked her head. "Why? You know someone who might be interested in the place?"

My mind went back to Cory, the assistant manager of the office-supply store, the one who'd lost several thousand dollars in the rental scam, the one who'd planned to adopt the border collie and call him Chaplin. The address of the place he'd thought he was leasing wasn't too far from my town house. My place was affordable and had a small backyard that could comfortably accommodate a dog. The neighborhood was nice for walking a dog, too. Lots of trees shading the sidewalks. "I might know someone," I told my Realtor. "I'll give him your number."

"Great."

As soon as we returned to my and Nick's new place, I took a brief moment to call Cory. "Any chance you might be interested in buying a place in Uptown?" I told him about my town house and pointed out that buying a place provided tax benefits that renting did not. "And besides the tax benefits, you'd be building equity."

"Your place sounds exactly like what I'd be looking for," he said. "But I don't know if I can afford it."

"Talk to my Realtor," I told him. "She said there's financing programs for first-time homeowners who don't have a lot of savings. I think you'd like the place. I have. And you could adopt Chaplin if he's still available."

"He is," Cory said. "He's big and hyper and that turns a lot of people off. But I'm a runner. He'd love putting in three or four miles with me every day."

"No pressure, of course," I said. "If you're interested in the place, that's great. But if not, that's fine, too." I gave him the phone number for my Realtor's office.

"I'll give her a call," he said.

When we ended the call, I resumed lugging boxes inside.

By the end of the day, all of us were pooped, but the house was beginning to take shape. I could almost visualize the life Nick and I would have there—assuming I survived to move into the place. *Ugh.*

We had enough beds for my brothers and parents to

sleep in the new house, while Nick and I returned to Bonnie's. Tomorrow we'd all attend the Cowboys' preseason game together. With all of the overtime I'd been putting in lately, I was looking forward to taking a day off and just having some fun.

chapter eighteen

*J*ust Because You're Paranoid . . .

Sunday morning, we all enjoyed a wonderful breakfast at Bonnie's, prepared by both my mother and soon-to-be mother-in-law with only a little help from me. They made the eggs, biscuits, gravy, and home fries. The only thing either one of them trusted me with was using the electric juicer to juice the oranges. Pretty hard to screw that up.

After breakfast, we got ready for the game. We packed our coolers with food and drinks, donned our blue and silver Cowboys gear, and drove out to the enormous stadium in Arlington at eleven. The game didn't start until one, but my father and brothers had brought a grill and charcoal and insisted on tailgating beforehand. As if we hadn't had enough to eat only a couple of hours earlier. Still, it was nice for us women to be waited on by the men for a change. We hung out under a shady tarp in lawn chairs with our feet up while the men grilled burgers and bratwurst in the hot sun.

Though today's game was only a preseason match, it had nonetheless sold out. Scalpers meandered through the crowd, holding up tickets and calling out to those nearby, "Anybody need tickets for the game?"

Not us. I'd bought ours earlier in the week, right after speaking with my brother. They were crappy seats, near the top of the stadium, but that's all that had been left at the time. No one in our group would complain. We always managed to have fun at sporting events, even if we were stuck in the nosebleed section. Besides, a massive, two-sided screen hung over the football field. The thing was 160 feet wide and 72 feet tall. It had enjoyed the title of largest TV screen in the world until an even more gargantuan one was erected at Texas Motor Speedway in Fort Worth not long ago. They'd even named that one. Big Hoss. Yep, it really is true that everything's bigger in Texas. At any rate, while we might not be able to make out the details on the field with our naked eyes, the big screen would more than make up for the less-than-stellar seats.

Dad stepped up to the grill and tossed in some wood chips to add extra flavor. The smoke wafted across the parking lot, mingling with the smoke from other grills.

He waved his big metal spatula as five men in Green Bay Packers jerseys wandered by. "You cheese-heads sure came a long way just to lose a football game." His jovial smile let them know he was only razzing them.

The men stopped by the grill.

"You don't know what you're talking about," said one. "Your 'boys are going down."

Trace opened the cooler and gestured inside. "The only thing going down today are these beers. Help yourself."

One of them looked at the others. "This must be that Southern hospitality we've heard so much about."

The men reached down into the ice and grabbed bottles of beer, shaking the cold water from their hands.

A dark-haired man in a number 12 Aaron Rodgers jersey read the label on the bottle and scrunched up his nose. "This stuff was made in Texas. Got anything brewed in Milwaukee? You know, where God intended?"

His group laughed, twisted the tops off their bottles, and took long pulls on their beers.

Dad took a sip from his bottle and pointed to the 12 on the man's jersey. "Your number twelve can't hold a candle to our number twelve." He was referring to Cowboys legend Roger Staubach, whose number had been retired along with the quarterback.

"We'll see about that," the guy retorted.

Dad offered the group brats as willingly as he'd offered his jovial jeers and beers. They hung around for a while, talking field strategies with Nick, my father, and brothers, all of whom were not only fans of the game, but former players. Of course the men seized the opportunity to relive their glory days, even if they weren't all that glorious. Trace was better known for tripping over his own feet than moving the ball. But no sense reminding him of that fact when he'd spent the entire day yesterday helping me out.

"You should've seen me," Dad said. "I wasn't even supposed to receive the ball, but a big ol' gust of wind picked it up and carried it right into my hands. I ran that thing for seventy-six yards before the other team took me down. Took three guys to do it, too. Earned myself the MVP award."

The Packers fan had to one-up Dad, of course. "Oh, yeah? Well, I once ran a ball for seventy-nine yards."

"In the wrong direction!" his friend said.

The Packers fan raised his beer in a self-salute. "It was still seventy-nine yards."

They all shared a laugh.

As I sat, I noticed a tall man and a woman walking down the next row of cars, appearing for a split second, then another, as they passed behind the vehicles. During one of those split-seconds both of their heads turned to look in our direction, their noses probably detecting the delicious scent coming from my father's grill. Like many coming to today's game, they were dressed head to toe in Cowboys gear. Both wore hats. His was a ball cap. Hers was a visor style with her hair pulled up inside and out of sight. The couple had even painted their faces silver and blue. Yep, the Cowboys sure had some die-hard fans.

Die.

Hard.

Anxiety slithered up my spine, and I sat up straight. When the couple reappeared again between the next two cars, they were looking ahead of them. *Hmm.* Something about the two seemed vaguely familiar. *What is it?* It was impossible to tell what they looked like with their hair hidden under their hats and makeup covering their features.

I was about to say something to Nick when the men burst out laughing. They were having a good time. Why ruin it with what was more than likely a case of paranoia? After all, we hadn't noticed anyone following us here. Then again, if the two had worked as a tag team, we might not have noticed.

Before I could think any more about it, Bonnie held out a plastic cup. "Here you go, Tara."

"Thanks." I took the cup from her. Beer was not our favorite, so we women had brought a thermos of Bonnie's peach sangria to share instead. It was a light, refreshing drink and, truth be told, the alcohol helped me forget my troubles. At least it did until we packed things up to go inside with the rest of the crowd.

Suddenly, things felt claustrophobic. Dozens upon dozens of people milled all around me, coming too close, some even bumping into me. What if one of them had a knife? The metal detectors at the entry should have caught any steel knives, but manufacturers made nylon ones now. Heck, I'd registered for a set of nylon knives for our wedding. Some were as large as twelve inches and had a serrated edge that could rip right through human skin and organs. The security screeners wouldn't pick those up.

My fight-or-flight instinct kicked in. With so many people boxing me in, I wouldn't be able to flee if someone came after me. It would also be easy for an assailant to disappear into the crowd. My eyes darted around and my heart pumped so fast it was a wonder blood didn't spurt out of my ears.

As if he could hear my heart pounding, Nick glanced down at me. My mother, who had a sixth sense when it came to her children, also turned my way.

Nick draped an arm over my shoulders. "You all right?"

My mother read my face and knew immediately that I was freaked out. "Did you see something?"

I shook my head. The fact that I hadn't seen someone wasn't really the issue. It was what I felt. And what I felt was an eerie sense that whoever was after me was *here*. The Joseph Heller quote from *Catch-22* popped into my mind. "Just because you're paranoid doesn't mean they aren't after you." "I just feel it," I said. "I think they're close."

"Harlan!" my mom barked. "Boys! Y'all form a circle around Tara. Keep her in the middle."

Next thing I knew, I was enclosed in a shield of humans, my mother leading the way and Bonnie taking up a lookout position at the rear. Now I knew how celebrities felt when they were surrounded by their bodyguards to keep them safe from overzealous fans, or how politicians felt when they were surrounded by Secret Service to shield them from the angry constituents they'd disappointed or lied to.

We shuffled along, en masse, to our seats. Mom and Nick insisted I take the seat in the center. She and Bonnie took the ones at either end of our row, while my two brothers were the next ones in. Dad and Nick sat on either side of me. With this human barrier around me, my safety was virtually ensured. But was theirs now at risk? I'd feel terrible if one of them got hurt defending me. *Ugh*.

A few minutes later, the action began down on the field. Green Bay won the coin toss and decided to receive. Within the first seven minutes, both teams had scored touchdowns, and the stadium filled with the roar of the crowd.

As the end of the first quarter neared, my fears had mostly dissipated. Really, what were the odds of whoever was after me coming to the game? They'd have had to follow me here, and then they'd have had to spend big bucks on tickets from a scalper. They'd also risk getting caught on one of the many security cameras scattered around the stadium. Chances were slim to none they were actually here, right? But while my fear had drained away, my bladder, on the other hand, had filled up.

"I need to go to the ladies' room," I told Nick.

"I'll come with you," he said.

I put a hand on his shoulder to keep him from rising. "I'll be fine. I was being paranoid earlier. We didn't notice a tail this morning. Besides, what are the chances that whoever is after me would pay hundreds of dollars for scalped tickets? Coming after me in a place this crowded would be a huge mistake."

Nick's eyes narrowed as he thought things over.

"I don't want you to miss any of the game," I said. "Mom will come with me. She can keep a lookout."

Nick looked unsure, but when the Cowboys got within three yards of scoring again, he made the decision to let me go without him. Still, he admonished me to "be extra careful."

Mom stood as I passed her and squeezed down the row with me. Finally, we emerged onto the main walkway. Mom and I stopped and glanced left and right, looking for the closest ladies' room.

She pointed across the hall and down a ways. "There's one."

We headed to the restroom, carefully eyeing those who approached or who were gaining on us from the rear. None looked like the two suspicious women who'd come to the garage sale or the couple I'd seen in the parking lot earlier, and none raised any red flags.

Mom and I hurriedly relieved ourselves and washed our hands. As we exited the ladies' room, a fresh roar came from the crowd.

"The Cowboys must've scored," Mom said.

I was glad Nick had stayed in his seat. I wouldn't have wanted him to miss the touchdown.

We aimed for the entry to our section. As we approached, I noticed the couple from the parking lot. Or at least it looked like the same couple. With so many people here dressed in similar clothing and wearing face paint, I couldn't be certain. Given that I couldn't see the woman's hair or face, my eyes went to her chest. The loose jersey and the fact that she was moving made it impossible for me to tell whether she sported Leah Dodd's double-Ds.

When both of them locked their eyes on me, I stopped in my tracks and reached out a hand to my mother. "I'm getting that feeling again. See those two people by the entrance?"

She looked their way, but by then they'd turned their attention away from me. "The ones putting mustard on their pretzels?"

"Yeah. I'm getting a weird vibe from them. I think I might have seen them in the parking lot, watching us when we were tailgating."

Her maternal instincts kicking in, Mom stepped in front of me. "What should we do?"

I wished I had my gun with me. I hadn't brought it. It was a hassle to go through the clearances. Ironically, the Cowboys stadium and the stadium in Houston were the only two in the NFL where off-duty police officers were permitted to carry their weapons. Though the NFL had a rule against it, Texas law trumped NFL policy. The theory was that cops were responsible for maintaining law and order 24/7, even if they were technically not on the job at the time.

"I'll call Nick." I whipped out my phone as I backed up against a stand selling fan gear. Maybe I should buy one of those big foam fingers. If the two in the face paint were truly out to get me, I could give them a nice big poke in the eye.

I dialed Nick's number. As I put the phone to my ear, the man looked my way again and said something to the woman.

"Tara?" came Nick's voice through the phone.

The two were headed our way now, their strides long and purposeful. The man's hand eased into the front pocket of his pants. *Holy shit! Is he going for a weapon?* By the time Nick could get to us, we could be dead. I grabbed my mother's hand, turned, and yanked her after me. "Run!"

I sprinted as fast as I could, dragging my mother along with me. When we reached the next entrance, I pulled her back into the stadium and down a flight of steps. If that couple was going to try to kill me, they'd have to do it here, in front of eighty-thousand witnesses. Maybe the scene would be replayed on the huge screen hanging over the field. A halftime horror show.

A voice came from my hand. Nick's. "Tara?" he hollered. "Tara?"

I put the phone back to my ear. "We're one section over."

My eyes scanned the seats until I found him. I waved my arm to get his attention. "Down in front!" someone yelled.

Mom and I crouched down so as not to block the view of the field. "I saw a suspicious couple coming at us."

"Stay where you are. Your dad and I will come get you."

I jabbed the button to end the call and looked up to the entrance. The couple was nowhere to be seen. My cheeks heated. I felt like an idiot. I guess they weren't after me after all. That, or they'd changed their minds when they realized I'd seen them. Kind of hard to take someone by surprise once they'd seen you. But yeah, the more likely conclusion was that I'd simply gotten spooked over nothing.

My father and Nick appeared in the entrance. Mom and I climbed the stairs to join them and we returned to our seats.

Once I'd settled in, I reached over and took my father's binoculars from his knee. I put them to my eyes and scanned each of the next three entrances to our right several times, looking to see if the two had reentered the stadium. After all, there were multiple pretzel stands spread about the circular walkway. They wouldn't have had to walk more than one or two sections over to get to the stand I'd seen them at.

Ten minutes later, the two still hadn't come back into the stadium. Even if they'd stopped to use the facilities or check out the foam fingers and pom-poms-on-a-stick, they should have been back by now, shouldn't they?

Still, I supposed there could have been reasonable explanations. Maybe the pretzel stand closer to their seats had a long line of customers or had run out of pretzels, and they'd walked much farther than I assumed. Maybe they'd bought the less expensive standing-room-only passes. Of course, the standing-room level was below the one we were on. Would someone come up here to get food?

Hmm.

I didn't know anything for sure, other than the fact that I wanted to smack Nick upside the head with my program when he borrowed my dad's binoculars to get a closer look at the cheerleaders during their halftime dance routine.

"You're about to be a married man," I told him. "You shouldn't be ogling other women."

"I'm not ogling," he said. "I'm appreciating their art form. Dance is one of the humanities. I'm trying to become more cultured."

I snorted. "Yeah, right."

He lowered the binoculars and cut me a pointed look. "Don't think I didn't notice you checking out the butts and biceps on the players."

He had me there. I blame the tight pants.

The game ended with a score of 34 to 31 in favor of the Packers. But while the Cowboys had lost the game, at least I hadn't lost my life.

I'd take that as a win.

chapter nineteen

$\mathcal{B}$ackseat Blues

The following week, I provided five more rides to men who were not the purported leasing agent. While four were perfectly pleasant and polite, one of them asked whether I provided other services.

"What do you mean?" I asked.

He formed a fist with his hand and pumped it up and down.

Once again I found myself pulling over and demanding my rider get out of my car. "Out. Now."

He sneered. "Make me."

When he refused, I phoned Nick, who'd pulled over right behind us. "This perv in my car just asked for a hand job and is now refusing to get out."

Nick didn't waste time on a reply. He ejected from his car, stormed up to back door, and ripped it open.

"Who the fuck are you?" the man cried, looking up at Nick.

Nick didn't bother responding to him, either. He grabbed the man by the shirt, yanked him out of the car, and tossed him headfirst into an oleander bush. "Don't you ever talk to a woman like that again. You hear me?"

"I hear you," the man said meekly, lying facedown among the limbs, afraid to move for fear Nick would kick his ass.

I promptly reported the rider to Backseat Driver so he would be banned from using the service again.

I also looked through dozens more rental listings online that week, responding to several of them. While a few seemed suspicious at first, I was able to rule them out by contacting the property owners and verifying that the leasing agent who'd responded to me was legitimate. While I'd gotten nowhere, at least I hadn't wasted precious time trekking all over Dallas to determine whether the agent was bogus or not.

Detective Booth called on Thursday with some new information. "We received another complaint against that so-called leasing agent. The victim wasn't able to tell me anything new, but I got the name on the credit card the leasing agent used to rent the place. I was thinking maybe you should call this one. See if you discover a link between the con man and the person whose identity he stole."

"I'd be glad to."

She gave me the man's name and contact information. "He's in his forties, lives in Madison, Wisconsin. That's all I know."

It was enough for me to get started. As soon as we ended our conversation, I placed a call to Tyrone Robinson. After identifying myself, I gave him the bad news. "I'm working a case with a detective from the Dallas Police Department. A rental-fraud case. Unfortunately, the guy we're after obtained a credit card in your name that he's been using to lease properties."

"Well, hell! I have a credit score of over eight hundred. This better not screw it up!"

I couldn't blame the guy for getting upset. I'd be angry,

too, if I'd found out someone had put my good credit and good name at risk. "As of now, he's been making the minimum payments to keep it active, but his typical routine is to hit one card hard for a short period of time, then move on to a new one. When he moves on, he'll default. But I can tell you how to take care of it so that you don't end up with a ding on your credit report when that happens."

"I'd appreciate it. I always pay my bills on time and other than my mortgage I have no debt. My car's been paid off for two years."

"All we know about this guy is that he's Caucasian, looks to be around thirty, stands around six feet tall, and has a beefy build and brown hair. He wears business suits and eyeglasses when he meets with the prospective tenants. Sound like anybody you know?"

"The only person I know in Dallas is my uncle. He moved down there a few years ago. Got tired of the winters up here and met himself a woman online who convinced him to come down there and give Texas a try. I haven't gotten down there to visit him yet, but I've been meaning to. We were really close when I was younger."

"So you've never been to Dallas?"

"No. Lived in Madison all my life."

Hmm. Tyrone had no connection to Dallas other than an uncle who lived here. Could the con artist have somehow obtained Tyrone's personal information through the uncle? It seemed to be a stretch. Besides, Booth had told me that most of the other identity-theft victims had lived out of state, too. She'd mentioned Florida. Wyoming. New Hampshire. It seemed more likely that the leasing agent had hacked into a database containing personal information for people all over the U.S. Still, the Dallas connection could be worth pursuing. "Can you give me your uncle's phone number?"

"You think he can help?"

"Honestly, Mr. Robinson? I have no idea. But it's worth a shot."

After Tyrone gave me his uncle's number, I gave him a rundown on how to file a fraud alert on his credit report and an identify-theft affidavit with the credit card company. It would be a hassle, but it would protect his stellar credit score. "Thanks for speaking with me."

When we hung up, I phoned Tyrone's uncle and identified myself. I explained the situation and the reason for my call. "So what I'm trying to do is to figure out whether there might be a connection between you and the man posing as the leasing agent. He seems to have had access to your nephew's name and social security number. Do you know where you might have provided that information?"

"I can't think of anywhere off the top of my head," he said. "But let me give it some thought. If something comes to me, I'll give you a call back."

"Thanks."

While he thought things over, I decided to pull out the file and call the other people in whose names the fraudulent credit card accounts had been opened, see if they had a Dallas connection.

The first one I called worked for an awning company called A-1 Awnings that was based in Dallas, though he'd been employed at its regional office in North Carolina. "I've never even been to Dallas," he said.

I jotted a note on my legal pad. *A-1 Awnings.* "Thanks for the information."

My next call was to Sebastian Rivera. He'd never lived in Dallas, either. "Any chance you ever worked for a company called A-1 Awnings?"

"Never heard of it," he said. "The only connection I have to the state of Texas is a sister who worked at an advertising agency in Fort Worth. Bloomfield and Associates. She moved back here to Florida last year."

When we ended our call, I jotted another note. *Bloom-field & Assocs.* While the ad agency wasn't located in Dallas, the city of Fort Worth was only thirty miles or so to the west.

The third person told me that he'd grown up in Dallas and worked in the city for a few years when he'd become an adult, but that he'd moved to New Orleans when he decided to pursue a career as a jazz musician. "Life's too short to spend it hawking overpriced used cars to people who can't afford them."

I made another note. *EZ Autos.* "Any chance you know someone at A-1 Awnings or the Bloomfield and Associates advertising agency?"

"Never heard of either one."

I called Tyrone's uncle and the man from A-1 Awnings back. The uncle had never heard of A-1 Awnings and knew nobody associated with EZ Autos or the ad agency. The man who worked at A-1 Awnings knew nobody who worked for Bloomfield and Associates or EZ Autos, though he recalled seeing the used-car dealer's ads on TV.

I'd reached a dead end. *Dang.* Unless I could make a connection between everyone whose identity had been stolen for the fraudulent credit cards, the only options I had left were to keep trying to suss out one of the properties listed by the con artist and to keep driving for Backseat. It was a tedious, time-consuming process.

On a bright note, I received no further death threats during the week. On a second bright note, my Realtor called me on Friday.

"I've got good news," she said.

"You do?" *Thank goodness.* I sure could use some.

"Cory liked your town house and made an offer. It's within your acceptable range, and he's been approved for financing."

"Fantastic!" At least my home sale was moving along, even if the real estate investigation wasn't.

Cory sent me a text shortly afterward. All it said was *Me and my new roommate*, but the selfie he'd sent told the rest of the story. It was a pic of him with a black-and-white dog who looked thrilled to be getting out of the shelter. The dog's eyes were bright, and his tail, a bushy blur in the shot, was clearly wagging in joy. I was happy things had worked out for the two of them. I sent him a text in reply. *Congratulations! I hope you both enjoy the place as much as my cats and I did.*

Friday evening, shortly after Nick, Bonnie, and I finished eating supper, I drove over to the grocery store in the Village to wait for ride requests. Nick had followed me. I was getting really tired of having a babysitter every time I left the office or Bonnie's house, and I hated to be continually inconveniencing my coworkers and my future husband. Nick had endured a tough week, spending his days in court testifying in a major tax-evasion trial. Attempting to explain the intricacies of corporate tax law and how the company's chief executive officer and chief financial officer had manipulated the company's data was difficult and daunting. He was doing his best, but he said the jurors looked either confused or bored out of their minds. He feared they might not get a conviction. I knew he'd love nothing better than to sit on his ass on the couch with a beer in one hand and the television remote in the other, but here he was, stuck playing my knight in tired armor. I couldn't even make it up to him in the bedroom, not with us stuck living in separate rooms at Bonnie's. But I supposed nothing could be done about the situation until we caught whoever had made the death threats against me.

I took a space at the edge of the parking lot, backing into the spot so I could pull out quickly and easily if I needed to. Nick did the same, reversing into a spot nearby.

In almost no time my phone pinged with a ride request from Backseat Driver. Someone named Cameron G needed a lift. Both the pickup and drop-off addresses were in the Village, only a couple of miles apart at most. I wouldn't be earning much on this job. Then again, I wasn't in this for the paycheck. I thumbed the app to accept the job.

I headed out with Nick trailing behind. Three minutes later, I pulled up in front of an apartment building. A woman in her mid-twenties came out. She had hair the color of caramel. She wore strappy heels and a sleeveless dress tight enough to show off her goods but in a tasteful floral print that kept things reasonably classy. As she tottered over, I rolled the window down. "Are you Cameron?"

"That's me," she said as she reached for the back door handle.

I'd assumed Cameron would be a dude. *Damn these unisex names!* Looked like I'd wasted my time again.

After she climbed in and buckled her belt, I eased away from the curb.

She virtually bounced in the backseat. "I'm so excited! I met this really great guy at a coffee place earlier in the week and he's taking me out to dinner tonight."

I remembered my dating days, how excited I'd get about a guy only to realize two or three months later that he had an unacceptable flaw. He was skipping classes and flunking out of school. He had no sense of humor, or didn't understand mine. He'd lied about where he'd been the night before and seemed to think I was too stupid to realize it. Yep, a girl's gotta kiss a hell of a lot of frogs to find her prince. Still, for Cameron's sake, I tried to muster some enthusiasm. After all, I'd eventually found Nick, and his flaws were few and manageable. "First dates can be a lot of fun," I said in reply. "I hope it goes well."

"He's a programmer," she gushed. "He must make pretty good money because he dresses really well. He drives a nice car, too. I saw it when we walked out to the parking lot together. It's a black Fiat Spider. You know, the two-seater convertible?"

Oh, to be so young and easily impressed.

"Sweet ride," I said. I fought the urge to ask why he hadn't picked her up in the car. If he was such a great guy, why was he expecting her to come to him, especially on the first date when he'd presumably be on his best behavior, trying to make a good impression? I'd never even met the guy and had already pegged him as a shallow, self-centered jerk.

We were halfway to the programmer's apartment when another ride request came in via the Backseat Driver app on my phone. Coincidentally, this request came from the same address we were on our way to. I figured it must be someone else in the same apartment complex. The rider was identified as Casey B. Like Cameron, Casey could be either a male or female name, though the first Caseys that came to my mind were Casey Jones, the legendary railroad engineer who sacrificed himself to save the lives of others, and Casey at the Bat, featured in the classic poem. I tapped the button to accept this second job, too. *In for a penny, in for a pound, right?*

The closer we drew to the guy's apartment, the less confident Cameron G became. She pulled out a mirrored compact and powdered her nose. She pulled out the compact again seconds later to apply another coat of lip gloss. She'd barely returned it to her purse when she yanked it out again to check her hair. *Sheesh.* Sometimes I missed those wild and crazy single days. But at times like this I was darn glad they were over. The dating game could be exhausting!

My GPS told me to turn into a complex, so I did. It was a huge place, with half a dozen buildings in sight and more around the bend. "Do you know which building he's in?"

"Thirteen." She craned her neck to check the numbers as we rolled farther into the lot. As we rounded the bend, she said, "There it is. The one up ahead with the girl standing out in front of it."

"Okey doke."

We passed the black Spider, which was parked in a reserved, covered spot to our left, and rolled on a few more feet. As I pulled over to the curb, I got a better look at the girl standing outside. She wore a light green retrostyle dress and had cinnamon-colored hair that hung in a straight sheath to her chin. Her cheeks were tear-streaked, her eyes pink and puffy from crying. She looked pale, frail, feeble, and heartbroken. She held a tissue to her runny nose as she hobbled forward in stiletto pumps that looked sexy but painfully uncomfortable. She took note of my yellow placard and went to open the back door of my car. *This must be Casey B. I've struck out again.*

As Casey teetered to the back door, Cameron opened it to get out.

"Thanks for the ride!" Cameron called over her shoulder as she stepped past Casey.

Casey put her hand on the top of the door, but didn't get into the car. Instead, she turned to watch as Cameron walked up to an apartment on the first floor and knocked.

A screech came out of Casey like none I'd heard before. If I hadn't known it came from a young woman, I would've thought it had come from a velociraptor. "You bitch!"

The next thing I knew, Casey kicked off her heels and launched herself at Cameron like a human missile. Cameron cowered in the alcove, throwing up her hands to protect her face as Casey came rocketing in her direction.

Sheesh, again. Looked like we were going to have a catfight.

I shoved the gearshift into park, leaped from the car, and ran toward the two as Casey started clawing at Cameron and yanking her hair and clothing. Cameron used the only weapon she had to defend herself, her clutch purse. She swung it at Casey's face in a desperate and futile attempt to make Casey back off, whapping her repeatedly on the forehead and cheeks. *Whap-whap-whap!*

"Get away from me, you crazy freak!" Cameron cried, landing a solid *whap* with her purse on Casey's tearstained cheek. "Get away!"

She landed another *whap* on Casey's nose and blood spurted out of it, staining the front of her dress and the concrete with red spots. *Ew.*

"Break it up!" As I ran up and threw my shoulder into the fray, trying to insinuate myself between the two, the apartment door opened. A good-looking guy in his mid-twenties stood there, looking both astonished and amused. I took it that he was the programmer.

I put a hand on each of the girls' shoulders and tried to push them back, but with my strength split between the two of them I only managed to separate them by a few inches. The guy made no move to help me, to clean up this mess of his making. Luckily for me, Nick ran up, grabbed Casey around the waist, and pulled her backward. Her arms reached out in a final yet futile attempt to grab Cameron, her bare heels dragging across the concrete.

Now that her attacker had been subdued and she knew she was safe, Cameron burst into tears, too, clearly not accustomed to being physically attacked. "Why?" she cried. "Why?"

I turned to the guy standing in the doorway. "What's going on?"

He pointed to Casey. "I broke up with her"—he turned his finger to point to Cameron now—"so I could go out with her."

"You jerk!" Casey shrieked, squirming in Nick's arms. He might've stopped her physical assault, but short of sticking her stiletto in her mouth he couldn't stop her verbal one. "You asshole!"

"She's right, you know," I told the guy. "A gentleman would have made sure his ex was gone before his date arrived." I turned to Cameron. "He couldn't even be bothered to come pick you up or protect you from being attacked. Why are you wasting your time with this guy?"

She turned from me to him, swiping at her tears with her hand, a frown taking over her face.

Casey stopped struggling, turned around in Nick's arms, and, realizing he had nice, strong shoulders, proceeded to lay her head on them and bawl. Nick cut his eyes to me and raised his palms in a "what the hell do I do now?" gesture.

If Cameron decided to call the police, Casey could end up facing assault charges. The longer she stuck around, the more likely that was to happen. Though she was the one who'd started the fight, she'd gotten the worst of the deal. Not only had her nose been bloodied, but her dress was ruined. Those stains weren't likely to come out. Add in the abject humiliation, and I felt sort of sorry for the girl. Her hurt had been fresh and raw and she'd lost it. It could have happened to anyone.

As I headed back his way, Nick scooped the girl up in his arms and carried her to my car, putting her in the back and buckling her in. He moved his vehicle to an unreserved parking spot and climbed into my passenger seat. "Let's get her home."

chapter twenty

The End of an Era

Despite my having saved Casey from an assault charge and attempting to console her on the way home with platitudes about how there were "many other fish in the sea," that "a pretty girl like her was sure to find someone better soon," she had the nerve to slap me with a negative review. *Driver should mind her own business!*

Oh, yeah? Well, two could play that game. I reviewed her as well, so that all of the other Backseat Drivers would be forewarned. *This woman be cray-cray. The only vehicle she should be riding in is the crazy train.*

On Saturday afternoon, Nick came with me to look at an underpriced property near the Galleria mall in north Dallas. The leasing agent had been spotty with his information, fully failing to respond when I asked questions. He texted me the address a mere half hour before he expected me to meet him at the condo.

I pulled out my laptop, determined who owned the property, and attempted to find a phone number for the woman. Unfortunately, she had a common name and there were several people in the Dallas area who shared it. I didn't have time to work my way through them before I'd have to head over to the property, so I didn't bother.

The condo was on the second story of a three-story building. Seeing no one waiting outside, we stepped up to the door and knocked. The instant the door was answered I learned two things. One, this guy was not the purported leasing agent who'd been ripping people off. This guy was short, with light brown hair that looked as if it hadn't even been combed. Second, the reason he hadn't been more forthcoming with answers to my questions was because he was a disorganized mess. The portfolio he clutched against his chest had papers sticking out of it in every direction, as well as a purple Skittle smashed on the back of it.

"Mrs. . . . ?" he asked.

"Galloway," I replied.

He looked down at a sticky note he'd stuck to the front of his portfolio. "Galloway. Right. Sorry." He held out a hand to invite us inside.

We'd taken only a couple steps into the place when a thunderous sound overhead instinctively caused us to duck and cover our heads. *BOOM-BOOM-BOOM-BOOM*. The pattern of the sound told me it was footsteps.

Nick straightened up. "Who lives upstairs, a herd of buffalo?"

The guy forced a laugh. "Communal living, eh?"

BOOM-BOOM-BOOM. A moment later, the footsteps were drowned out by rock music being played at approximately eight million decibels. Whoever moved in here better invest in a good pair of earplugs.

We made a quick round of the unit before returning to the door.

"This doesn't work for us," I said. "We need a place on the first floor. We've got an old dog who can't manage stairs."

"Oh. Okay. I might have one I could show you." He

opened his portfolio and a cascade of paperwork fluttered to the ground. He bent down to scoop the sheets up, glancing over each one as he retrieved them. "Let me just see here . . ."

"Don't bother on our account," I told him. "I think we'll go ahead and renew at our current place. Thanks anyway."

With that, Nick and I left.

On the drive back to Bonnie's, I groaned. "This rental-scam case is busting my chops."

"It's definitely taken up a lot of your time."

"Yeah, my *personal* time."

"You don't have to tell me." He cut a look my way. "I can't even remember the last time we—"

"Itemized each other's deductions? Claimed each other's personal exemptions?"

"That's one way to put it."

"Me, neither. As long as it's been I'm pretty sure we qualify as virgins again." I exhaled a sharp breath. "Should I give up and tell Detective Booth that I couldn't make any headway? Put the ball back in her court?"

"I'm sure she'd understand," Nick said as he eased into the exit lane. "She couldn't figure out who the guy was, either. He seems to be extra crafty."

He was, which had made me want to bring him down all the more. Some of our targets were stupid and easy, posing little or no challenge. This guy, on the other hand, seemed to pose *too much* of a challenge. He wasn't the average crook, that was certain. He was much smarter, covered his tracks much better.

Still, I was IRS Special Agent Tara Holloway, dammit! I didn't bow down and I didn't give up. No matter how much I might want to. No, I'd see this thing through to the end, no matter how long it took. I was nothing if not dedicated. On the contrary, maybe I was just too stubborn to know when to call it a day. "I'll give it one more week."

Nick chuckled. "I knew you couldn't give up. It's not who you are."

"It's not who you are, either."

"That's why we make such a good team."

My resolve renewed, I returned to my bedroom when we arrived at Bonnie's house and got myself ready for Lu's retirement party. We'd already held one last year, shortly after I'd joined Criminal Investigations, when Lu had said she'd planned to leave the agency. But she'd rethought things and decided she wasn't quite ready to be a lady of leisure, after all. Because we agents had put down nonrefundable deposits, and because we were always looking for any excuse to have a good time, we'd held a party anyway. It had been a lot of fun.

But things had changed since then. Lu had met Carl, a fellow sexagenarian who, like Lu, dressed like he lived in another era. They'd had some ups and downs but weathered them well, their feelings for each other only growing stronger. They'd moved in together not long ago. With a boyfriend at home to keep her company and do things with, Lu now had the incentive she needed to actually retire for good.

I dressed in a slinky, strapless red dress. It was covered in sequins and had a slit that stopped at my upper thigh. It was the dress I'd been wearing the night I met Brett, the guy I'd dated before Nick. Not that I'd ever tell Nick that. As far as he knew, this dress had no history. No sense getting him riled up over nothing. Besides, I loved the thing and hadn't had another opportunity to wear it.

Nick put on his fanciest suit and, after allowing his mother to exclaim over us for a moment or two, we headed out the door.

When we arrived at Guys & Dolls, Maddie, one of the young ladies who used to dance topless at the place when it was a strip club, greeted us at the door. Her boyfriend had abandoned her and their two-year-old daughter, and she'd been forced to strip to make ends meet. Exhaustion led her to try the drugs her boss, Don Geils, was dealing behind the scenes. Fortunately, after I'd arrested her boss, she'd turned her life around and now worked as a hostess and waitress, her tips added to her customers' credit card slips rather than tucked into her G-string.

She gave me a hug. "You busting Don Geils was the best thing that ever happened to me."

While busting the guy might have been the best thing that ever happened for her, it was one of the worst things that had ever happened for me. I'd ended up on trial for shooting him in the leg and thought I might be forced out of the job I loved, the job I lived for. Thankfully everything had turned out okay. But I didn't want to burden her with the reminder. Instead, I forced a smile and said, "I'm happy for you. How's your little girl?"

Maddie beamed. "As cute as ever!"

"Glad to hear it."

We walked into the club as if we were walking back in time. The interior featured the Art Deco décor that was popular decades ago, all done up in black and gold. A number of wide mirror panels hung behind the stage and along the walls. Elevated booths upholstered in black vinyl were positioned around the perimeter, with black-topped tables on the floor in the center.

Maddie led us to our reserved table right up front. Lu and Carl had already arrived and stood as we approached. Lu wore a glamorous gown in a shade of green that looked lovely in contrast to her pinkish-orange hair. She'd doubled her usual makeup and had on an especially glam pair of false eyelashes for the occasion, too. Carl had worn his best polyester leisure suit, black with contrasting white thread around the lapel, along with his shiny white bucks. We greeted each other with hugs.

As we sat, Carl draped an arm over the back of Lu's chair. "It's going to be nice having Lu all to myself every day now."

I wagged a finger at him. "We've got dibs on her for at least one lunch a month."

He smiled. "I'll give you the third Thursday."

I smiled back. "We'll take it."

The other agents and their wives or partners filtered in. Eddie and Sandra, who took seats directly across from me and Nick. Josh and Kira, the latter having worn her sapphire nose ring and an intact pair of fishnet hose rather than her usual hole-filled ones for this special occasion. Will and his wife. Hana and her girlfriend. Viola came with the mail clerk, who'd offered to give the older woman a ride. Her night vision could be problematic.

We ordered wine and cocktails, poured and prepared by Angelique, one of the other former dancers who tended bar, her tips now tucked into a jar. She looked much happier, too, going about her business with the efficient, certain movements of a woman with recently acquired dignity.

The club's owners, Merle and Bernice, came over to our table. A former Vegas showgirl and dancer, Bernice had been cosmetically enhanced in as many ways as possible, yet her personality was sincere. She was a graceful, ageless woman, with champagne-hued hair swept up into a French twist. She was the informant who'd first contacted the police when she'd suspected Don Geils was running prostitution and drug rings from the club. The information she provided was instrumental in bringing Geils and the criminal enterprises down. While Bernice was the epitome of elegance, Merle looked like a grandfatherly version of Charlie Brown, short and boxy with a total of three hairs curling across his scalp. But unlike the sad sack he resembled, Merle was a creative genius, a playwright who'd spent far too many years with his talents and love for Bernice hidden away. When I'd arrested Don Geils, I'd not only given Maddie and Angelique a new lease on life, but I'd spurred Merle and Bernice to finally get together.

Nick had worked the investigation at Guys & Dolls with me, taking a job as a bouncer at the strip club. It hadn't been easy for me to play the role of squirrelly bookkeeper amidst all the exposed, curvy flesh Nick had a front-row seat for, but we'd managed to get through it. Nick and I stood to greet Merle and Bernice.

"So wonderful to see you two!" Bernice exclaimed, her hands on my bare shoulders. She ran her gaze over me. "Tara, you look absolutely gorgeous!" She'd only seen me in my boring business suits before. She probably hadn't realized I had it in me to be girlie, too.

"Thanks, Bernice. So do you."

Merle turned to Nick and shook his hand. "Congratulations. You've got yourself one hell of a lady." He should know. He'd been my supervisor at the club and gotten to know me better than any of them. He'd even figured out I was a member of law enforcement working undercover, but instead of blowing our case he'd kept that fact to himself. He was a good guy at heart. He'd been the one to summon me back to the club when the poop had hit the fan inside, posing risks to Nick and my friend Christina Marquez from the DEA, who'd been working the sting with us.

Bernice draped her hand over Merle's shoulder. "Merle and I were so pleased to receive the invitation to your wedding. Y'all brought us together and we'd love to see you get married, too."

Aww . . .

She went on. "I'm surprised the invitation made it to us. The envelope looked like it had been put through the wringer."

"We had a little trouble when I went to mail them," I

explained. "Someone in a pickup tried to run down me and Nick's dog, instead hit the mailbox I'd just put the invitations in, and sent it flying into the road. The invitations ended up all over the place. By the time we could collect them, some of them had been run over."

She put a hand to her chest. "My goodness! I'm glad you and the dog are okay!"

"It gets better," I told her, though the story getting better meant things had gotten worse for me. "I've since received death threats."

Merle eyed me, fury flaring in his eyes. "You think Don Geils could be behind all of it?"

"It's possible," I acknowledged. "But I went to see him in prison. Both the detective from Dallas PD and I sensed he wasn't involved."

Bernice offered a soft, but concerned, smile. "Well, I hope you figure it out and make an arrest soon. The last thing a bride needs is more to worry about."

She could say that again.

Merle spotted the time on the clock over the bar and turned to his wife. "Time to get the show on the road."

They said good-bye for now, telling us they'd see us again at the private afterparty I'd arranged in the club for those of us from the IRS.

Our drinks and food arrived, and we dug in, chatting while we ate. The show began right as they brought dessert, a lemon sorbet adorned with fresh strawberries and blueberries.

Tonight's performance was a variety show, including everything from a stand-up comedian who did a ten-minute shtick about local politicians, shticking it to the mayor, but all relatively benign and in good fun. He was followed by a team of male tap dancers who nearly stomped the stage into splinters. The next act involved a young woman dressed in a hayseed cowgirl costume. She sang lonesome love ballads, accented at just the right moments by the mournful howl of her bandana-wearing hound dog, who sat at her feet. *What a riot!* With the variety of talent, the show was a huge hit with the audience, earning the performers a well deserved standing ovation and shouts of "Bravo!"

When the last bow had been taken, the performers left the stage, and the house lights were brought up, the other customers filed out, leaving only those of us with the IRS to end the evening with a more intimate gathering.

Angelique brought three bottles of champagne to the table and popped the corks. *Pop! Pop! Pop!* She and Maddie proceeded to fill glass flutes for each of us.

"I'm so jealous," Maddie said as she filled Lu's glass with the bubbling beverage. "I'd give anything to be able to sleep in every day and relax."

"It certainly will be nice," Lu agreed. "After forty-plus years at the IRS, I suppose I've earned it. Of course it'll probably take me a week or two to remember that I don't have to get up and go to work in the mornings."

Once Maddie left the table, I stood and raised my glass. "To the one and only Lu," I said, turning to her. "When I interviewed with you, you mentioned your plans to retire, and I told you that if you hired me, you'd be sitting around in your bathrobe watching soap operas and sucking down bonbons before you knew it." I reached down, retrieved the large gift bag I'd brought, and handed it to her. "Here's everything you need to make that happen."

She took the bag and pulled out the contents, a plush robe in the same pinkish-orange shade as her hair, a pair of matching slippers, and an extra-large box of assorted bonbons.

She laughed, exclaimed how soft the robe and slippers were, then looked up at me, her eyes growing wet and her lip quivering with emotion.

My eyes became misty, too. Lu's departure from Criminal Investigations marked the end of a long and successful era.

I waved my hand at her in a futile attempt to stop her tears. "Don't cry or it'll make me cry, too!"

But it was too late. As tears ran down her cheeks, a drop escaped my eye and ran down mine, also. One glance around the table told me everyone else was likewise feeling woeful and wistful. I grabbed a napkin and fanned my eyes to dry them. Once I had my tear ducts under control, I raised my glass even higher. "Cheers!"

Others called out, "Hear, hear!" We clinked our glasses and sipped our champagne.

Nick followed me, standing with his glass raised. "Lu, you're leaving me and Eddie with some big shoes to fill. Of course in your case those shoes are fringed go-go boots. But you've taught us well, and if the two of us can do half the job you did, we'll be proud. Enjoy your retirement."

His words were followed by more clinks and more sips.

Each of the other agents made toasts in turn. Eddie took the opportunity to tell Lu that when he'd first met me he'd thought she'd been crazy to hire the scrawny country girl. "But you had an uncanny ability to see diamonds in the rough."

"Hey!" I dipped my fingers in my champagne and flicked it at him in revenge.

He ducked to avoid the spray and laughed, raising his glass. "To Lu!"

Josh noted that Lu knew how to use the unique abilities of her agents to the fullest. "You always let me go into full-on geek mode when it would help with a case. You've helped each of us grow into the best agents we can be."

It was true. She'd assigned me to some of the more violent cases, knowing my superior gun skills might be needed. But she'd also made sure we each received a variety of assignments so that we wouldn't become bored and so our skills and knowledge could continue to grow.

Hana stood next, turning to our boss. "Lu, you opened the doors for female agents like me and Tara by proving that women are smart, strong, and capable."

It was true. Lu and the other ballsy women who'd come before us had broken down barriers, blazed a trail, and shattered glass ceilings. Lu had managed to do it in her own fashion, too, both literally and figuratively. Nope, there'd never be another Lu.

"To Lu!" Hana cried, and we all drank again.

Will, who'd been the last to join the division, was also the last to toast Lu. "Thank you for taking a bored collections officer and giving him a chance to see how exciting tax evasion could be."

When we finished toasting Lu, she stood and raised her glass, gazing around at her former employees. She wagged an accusing finger at us. "Y'all challenged me at every turn, often didn't do as you were told, and caused me all sorts of grief with the big boys up the chain." She stopped wagging her finger. "Yet somehow I love every one of you for it."

She smiled for a brief instant before dissolving into sobs. Carl stood to finish the toast for her. He raised his near-empty glass. "To all of you agents!"

We drank together one last time. By that point, Lu was crying so hard one of her false eyelashes broke free and ran down her cheek, dropping to her ample bosom. I was sniffling and sobbing, too. I was going to miss the heck out of her. But we all knew it was time. Time for her to relax and turn the reins over to the next generation of directors.

We thanked Merle, Bernice, and the Guys & Dolls staff, and moved out to the parking lot. We exchanged final hugs there, we agents waving as Lu and Carl drove off. "Bye!" "Enjoy your retirement!" "We'll miss you!"

I turned to Nick and Eddie. "Looks like you two are officially the bosses now."

Nick stood tall. "That's right. And none of you better forget it."

Eddie said, "We want all of you at your desks by eight o'clock Monday morning."

Hana waved a dismissive hand as she headed to her car. "I'll get there when I get there."

Josh said, "Expect a big budget request from me. There are some new surveillance tools I want to buy."

"My G-ride needs a new transmission," Will added. "Put that in the budget, too."

As the other agents walked off, leaving just me, Nick, Eddie, and Sandra, Eddie put a hand to his head. "I've already got a headache."

Nick chuckled. "You and me both, buddy."

chapter twenty-one

A Fitting End

Early Sunday afternoon, as I waited in the grocery-store parking lot, my phone came alive with a ride request from a Michael S who needed a pickup at a café nearby and a drop-off in Plano. Though I was hesitant to accept another job given the catfight I'd had to break up on Friday, I remembered my resolution to keep working on this rental-scam investigation until the job was done. *Ugh.* I hated myself about then. *Why do I have to be so darn dedicated?* But a quick check told me no Backseat Drivers had posted negative reviews of the guy. In fact, they'd posted no reviews at all. But maybe that was to be expected. The account had only been opened three days prior.

Nick didn't seem all that thrilled to be spending his Sunday on a wild-goose chase, either, but he wanted me hurt or dead even less. He followed me to the restaurant, the two of us in touch by speakerphone. I could tell immediately when the rider raised his hand to flag me that he wasn't the criminal we were after. This guy stood only around five feet nine inches and, though not thin, he wasn't what anyone could rightfully call beefy. Besides, he wasn't wearing a suit and tie. He was dressed in jeans,

sneakers, and a Dallas Mavericks tee. "It's not him," I told
Nick.

"Damn!"

I punched the button to end our call and unlocked the
doors.

The rider had his phone pressed to his ear when he
climbed into my backseat and continued the conversation
the entire way, staring out the window with his head down,
his uncovered cheek facing away from me, only the back
of his hand and small swaths of chin and forehead visible
to me. Though he spoke quietly, I listened in. Call me nosy,
but what else did I have to do at the moment? With him
on his phone, I couldn't even turn on the radio.

It seemed to be a very one-sided conversation, Michael
S offering only the occasional *mm-hm, yeah, okay, all
right*, or *that'll work*. To entertain myself, I mentally filled
in what the other party might be saying, my imagination
identifying the person on the other end of the phone as
myself.

> *Me:* "Hey, dude. You're wearing Superman under-
> wear, aren't you?"
> Rider: "Mm-hm."
> *Me:* "I bet you suck in your stomach and flex your
> muscles in front of the mirror, too."
> Rider: "Yeah."
> *Me:* "Will you give me a big tip when this ride is
> over?"
> Rider: "All right."

Fighting a smile, I eyed him in the rearview mirror.
Hmm. The more I looked at what little I could see of
him, the more something about him seemed oddly familiar.
Maybe we'd had a class together back in college. Some of

the lower-level business courses had hundreds of students. He could have been among the throng and my mind might have subconsciously filed away the memory. Or maybe he worked somewhere I frequented. A coffee place or a sushi restaurant or one of the firing ranges where I practiced. Or maybe he just had one of those everyday faces that everyone kept mistaking for someone else. If he hadn't been on the phone, I would've asked him whether I looked familiar, too. If he'd answered in the affirmative, I'd have tried to figure out the connection. But as it was, with him fully engaged in a phone conversation, all I could do was speculate.

Oddly, I couldn't hear the other half of the conversation. While I wouldn't necessarily expect to make out every word, it seemed I'd hear something, an especially loud word here or there, an unintelligible stream of sound, maybe a laugh or cough. But when he paused after speaking, there was no audible response. The person on the other end of the call must be speaking very softly, maybe even whispering. Given this fact, my imagination took me in another direction now.

> *Other person: When we meet with the Russian spies,*
>   *bring a duffel bag full of cash.*
> Rider: Okay.
> *Other person: Don't forget to ask for their piroshki*
>   *recipe.*
> Rider: All right.

As I exited onto the service road in Plano, a Dart rail train zipped up along the tracks behind the businesses. Though this line was identified as the Red Line, the train was nonetheless painted the DART system's signature bright yellow, the colors sometimes causing confusion to those not familiar with the system. Flashes of yellow came between the restaurants and shops as I drove along, inadvertently racing the train. When we reached our destination, I pulled into the restaurant while the train continued on to the downtown Plano station a quarter mile north.

The guy opened the back door of my car, swiveled his phone upward to mumble a quick thanks to me, and walked off, still with the phone at his ear. If nothing else, I had to give the guy credit for being a good listener. That wasn't a trait too many men could claim. But though he seemed willing to lend an ear, that's evidently where his generosity ended. One look at the rider service app told me he hadn't tipped.

Cheapskate.

On Wednesday evening, I had my final dress fitting at the Neiman Marcus flagship store downtown. It was the last time I'd try the dress on before my wedding day. *Weeeee!*

I kept a close eye on my rearview mirror as we drove over, but saw no one tailing us. I found a parking spot on the street, only half a block from the store. It was my lucky day!

Eddie was on backup duty for me again, so he had been forced to come along. He let me know he was none too happy about it, either.

"It's bad enough my wife and girls make me go shopping with them," he griped as we entered the store. "Now I've got to go shopping with you, too."

"Suck it up, buttercup."

He scowled. "If you talk to me like that when I'm officially your boss, I'm going to write you up."

"No you won't."

He grunted. He knew I was right, and I knew he knew it. We'd grown close during our investigations. Neither of us would do anything to hurt the other in any way.

"Besides," I continued, "this isn't really shopping. I'm just going to try on my dress really quick and then we'll go."

He grunted again. "There's no such thing as 'really quick' when it comes to a wedding dress. It took three people half an hour to get Sandra out of hers after our wedding."

He had a point. Most wedding dresses were complicated contraptions, with lace-up backs and bustles and tiny buttons by the billions. Mine, however, was relatively simple.

We made our way through the shoes and purses and passed through cosmetics, where small bottles of foundation and nail polish were lined up inside the glass shelves. On top of the counters were samples of blush and eye shadow in every shade imaginable for customers to try. Padded chrome stools with low back supports sat sideways next to the counters, where makeup artists could work their magic while the customer could check out the progress in the lighted oval mirrors. A woman in her fifties sat on one of the stools, a saleswoman applying powdered blush to her cheeks.

Eddie and I circled around the displays and climbed onto the escalator, which carried us up and above the first-floor cosmetics counter, the scent of competing brands of perfumes and lotions hanging in the air like an invisible, cloying cloud.

Eddie waved his hand. "I hope this smell doesn't stick to my clothes. If I go home smelling like some other woman's perfume, Sandra might take a rolling pin to me."

"Don't worry," I said. "I'll vouch for you."

Once we'd reached the top, I wound my way to the bridal salon, Eddie following in my wake.

He stopped to check the tags on a couple of dresses. "Good God, these things cost a fortune!" Eddie had twin girls and some very expensive days ahead of him.

"Better start saving now, buddy."

"Maybe I'll get lucky and my girls will elope." When we reached the fitting area, he flopped down in a chair positioned outside. "I'll wait here." He stretched his long legs out in front of him. If anyone came for me, they might find Eddie asleep in the chair. But with any luck, they'd trip over his feet.

I checked in with the pretty, honey-haired clerk and she retrieved my dress, which was zipped up inside a fancy vinyl bag for protection. She led me to a sizable dressing room and stepped inside with me. I felt like a classy woman from the Elizabethan era, with a lady-in-waiting to tighten my corset and tell me how beautiful I looked.

As the clerk hung the dress on a hook and unzipped the bag, I removed my blazer and draped it over the back of a chair. When the young woman turned around, she gasped and her hands instinctively went up.

I followed her wide-eyed gaze to the holster at my waist. As a fed, I was around guns all the time and I'd forgotten how disconcerting they could be to civilians, especially when they were brandished unexpectedly. I raised my hands, too, in a calming gesture. "It's okay. I'm in federal law enforcement."

She put a hand to her chest. "I didn't mean to overreact. It just surprised me is all."

Still, I could tell the sight of the gun was making her uncomfortable. I removed the gun from the holster, unzipped my purse, and slipped it into the special concealed-carry compartment inside. *Out of sight, out of mind, right?* Maybe now she could relax and focus on me instead of my weapon.

I removed the rest of my clothing, draping it over the chair. Once I'd stripped down to my bra and underwear, the clerk held the dress up for me to wriggle into. I fought a sigh. The dress was so pretty, so perfect. I couldn't wait for Nick to see me in it!

As she carefully slid the wedding gown over my head, she asked, "What did you decide about the lace gloves?"

I eased my head out of the neck hole. "Gloves?" I had absolutely no idea what she was talking about.

"The lace gloves," she repeated as she gently tugged the dress into place over my hips. "When you called the other day to check on your appointment I suggested that lace gloves might be a nice accessory for this dress." She set my shoes out in front of me and held out a hand to help me balance while I slid my feet into them. "We have some gloves that match the lace on the dress perfectly. You said you'd think about it."

"That wasn't me," I said. "I didn't call." She must've gotten me confused with another bride, maybe one who'd purchased the same dress as me.

The clerk looked befuddled, but she didn't belabor the point. "Well, I can show them to you now, if you're interested. See what you think."

"Why not?"

She opened a small, flat box that had been resting on a side table in the room and showed me the contents. Inside was a pair of lace gloves with ruffles around the wrists. While they'd merely get in the way during the ceremony, when Nick would need to have access to my ring finger to put the wedding ring on it, they would definitely be an unusual and pretty accompaniment for the dress later in the evening at the reception.

I plucked them out of the box one by one, slid my hands into them, and looked into the three-way mirror, turning to and fro to admire myself in the dress and gloves. "They add a nice touch, don't they?"

She smiled at me in the mirror. "Told you so."

I checked the price tag. The gloves weren't cheap, but they weren't outrageous, either. "I'll take them."

"Wonderful."

We carefully checked the hem and the places where the dress had been taken in, namely the bust. Yep, I'm a 32A. Some girls get breasts, others get brains. I was the latter type. Of course some girls got both, but we hate those girls, so let's not talk about them.

The clerk helped me out of the dress and, while she carefully bagged it up again, I changed back into my work clothes. When she carried the dress out of the fitting area for me, Eddie stood. "Can I help with that?"

"That would be great, Eddie. Thanks." As short as I was, I'd have to hold the hanger over my head to keep the dress from dragging on the ground. But as tall as Eddie was, he could easily handle it.

I followed the clerk to the cash register and handed her my Neiman Marcus card to pay for the gloves. My parents had already paid for the dress and shoes, God bless 'em. They'd probably taken out a second mortgage or sold a kidney to do it, but that's the kind of parents they were.

Once I'd signed on the electronic pad, the clerk handed me a bag with my shoes and the boxed gloves tucked inside.

I took the bag from her, as well as the receipt. "Thanks."

"Enjoy your wedding day, and best wishes!" she called after me.

Eddie and I headed back to the escalator to ride down to the first floor. I stepped onto the moving stairs, and he stepped on a second or two later, ending up on the step two back from me. As we rode down, my eyes spotted a tall man standing near the bottom of the escalator. He wore a cowboy hat that shielded his face from view and was looking down at his phone, using a finger to scroll across the screen. While he didn't appear all that unusual, when he glanced up at me and I noticed he was wearing dark sunglasses—*inside*—my nerves went on full alert. *He's the same guy from the stadium, isn't he?* He reached into the front pocket of his jeans and pulled something out. I saw a glint of metal.

Holy crap! Is that a knife in his hand? Or just some spare change?

The escalator continued to carry me toward what felt with each inch to be a more certain doom. My heart thudding in terror, I turned and tried to run up the escalator, but Eddie and my wedding dress blocked my way.

Instinct told me to move and move fast. It told me that by the time I dug my gun out of my purse, the man would have slashed me into bloody, fleshy strips. It also told me to grab the rubber railing in both hands and fling myself over it.

So I did.

Stupid instinct. Didn't it know the cosmetics counters lay below? Surely I'd crash through a glass countertop and be sliced to death with the shards. Either way, it looked like my manner of death would be similar.

I looked down as I plummeted to the first floor. A makeup stool barreled toward me. Or rather, I fell at it. No doubt about it, we were destined to collide. I did the only thing I could think of. I spread my legs.

An instant later I landed backward on the stool, spread-eagled, momentum causing my torso to flop over the low back. *WHOMP!*

Now I know why trapeze artists never work without a net.

The woman standing behind the makeup counter shrieked in surprise and flailed her arms. I shrieked too, though my cry was in pain. I felt like I'd been punched in the gut, like my pelvic bone had shattered.

Eddie hollered from above me, looking over the railing

as the escalator continued to bring him down to the first floor. "What the hell, Tara? Are you okay?"

"No!" I squeaked out. *I think I broke my vagina!*

My wedding dress swinging out behind him, Eddie ran down the rest of the steps and circled around to me. "Are you crazy? Why did you jump?"

I gestured in the direction of the man, though I couldn't see him from where I sat atop my splintered nether regions. All I saw now were sparklers burning at the edge of my vision as if it were the Fourth of July. "There was . . . a man!" I grunted out through the agony. "At the bottom . . . of the escalator!" I gasped again for air. "He had a knife!"

"A knife?" Eddie threw my dress onto the counter and sprinted back in the direction from which he'd come.

At that point, I had no fear. Heck, I almost hoped the man would come and put a quick end to me, put me out of my misery.

Slowly and gingerly, taking a deep breath against the pain, I eased myself back off the stool and stood bent over with my legs wide apart as the cosmetic clerk frantically paged for assistance. "Security to the Lancôme counter! Security to the Lancôme counter!"

chapter twenty-two

*P*rivate Screening

The saleswoman's hysterical voice brought three well-muscled security guards running. When they stormed up, she gestured to me. "This woman just jumped over the side of the escalator!"

The men looked my way and stepped over, forming a ring around me to prevent my escape, questioning looks on their faces. They probably thought I was a shoplifter who'd been spotted and was trying to make a desperate escape.

"I'm federal law enforcement," I spat through teeth gritted against the pain. "I've received death threats recently. There was a suspicious-looking man at the bottom of he escalator." I paused a moment to breathe. "I think he had a knife."

The saleswoman's eyes widened again.

"What did the guy look like?" asked one of the men, a burly guy with a balding head and an electronic earpiece.

"Caucasian," I said. "He was wearing a cowboy hat and sunglasses."

"Clothing?" he asked.

I couldn't remember, dammit! My focus had been on the metal object in his hand. "I don't know."

"Was he alone?"

"As far as I could tell."

Two of the men rushed off to look for the guy, while one stayed with me and the saleswoman.

Eddie returned a few minutes later. "I didn't see anyone in a cowboy hat," he said. "I checked both floors."

"He probably bolted," the security guard said. "Ran out the doors."

Slowly, I straightened up, grimacing against the pain, wooziness causing me to sway. Eddie reached out a hand and grabbed my upper arm, stabilizing me until the sensation passed.

Now that I was upright, I looked up and scanned the ceiling and walls for security cameras. Retail stores, especially upscale ones, tended to have a lot of them. It helped deter shoplifting and provided evidence of the crimes for use in court later. My eyes spotted several cameras that could have picked up the man who'd been waiting at the bottom of the escalator. "Can we see the security-camera footage?" I asked the guard.

"Of course." He jerked his head to indicate the far corner. "Let's go back to my office."

Eddie lifted my wedding dress off the counter as we went to follow the man. The cover was spotted with colored powder from the eye shadow testers displayed underneath.

The saleswoman took one look and said, "I'll call up to the bridal department. They'll get you another bag."

"Thanks." The last thing I wanted was my beautiful dress getting stained with makeup.

We followed the man to the security office in the back corner. Inside, he took a seat behind his desk. Eddie sat in one of the other chairs, while I remained standing. My crotch hurt too much for me to risk putting any pressure on it.

The man worked his computer keyboard and mouse and pulled up video footage. He turned the monitor so that we could all watch it at once and started the feed from one of the cameras.

This particular camera was angled to look down the escalator. As we watched the screen, we saw Eddie and me step onto the moving staircase, our backs to the camera. Down below, the man in the hat sauntered up and stopped, looking down at his phone. We could tell more about him now. He wore jeans and a basic white button-down shirt. Typical attire that would blend in, make him easy to overlook.

He held the phone in his left hand and fingered the screen with his right. As we watched, the hand that had been working the phone's screen went into his pocket. It was clear he clutched something shiny in his hand when he pulled it out of his pocket, but the camera was too far away for us to tell what it was. A tall, thin, dark-haired woman in a salmon-pink dress with a stand-up collar stepped onto the escalator behind me and Eddie, partially blocking the view of the man and me. A couple of seconds later, there I went, up and over the side of the escalator, falling out of sight. The man's head whipped to the side as he watched my improvised acrobatic stunt. But instead of coming to my aid or running over to gawk like most people might do, he instead stalked quickly off.

The security guard was able to track the man's movements through the store by switching to different camera feeds. The guy took long, quick strides out the door, moving fast, but not so fast as to garner attention. On the screen, we saw a security guard bolt past him, no doubt responding to the cosmetic clerk's frantic call for help.

The outside camera showed the man in the cowboy hat hurrying off down the street and out of sight.

"Can you go back earlier?" I asked the guard. "To when the man entered the store?"

"It'll take me a minute or two," he said, "but I can do it." He swiveled the screen back his way and worked his computer, leaning in to consult the screen. When he'd found the footage, he turned the screen in our direction again.

The monitor showed a view of the sidewalk outside. The time stamp in the bottom corner told me the recording had been taken two hours earlier, well before Eddie and I arrived for my appointment. As we watched, the man in the cowboy hat walked up and entered the store, keeping his sunglasses on. He veered toward the men's department, which sat near the bottom of the escalator. After sorting through some shirts on a rack, he pulled his phone from the chest pocket of his shirt, as if he'd received a call. He listened for a moment, then looked up the escalator as if eyeing something at the top. He ended the call shortly thereafter and slid the phone back into his chest pocket.

He spent the next hour and a half meandering around the men's department, not trying anything on and not buying anything. If I hadn't been sure whether he'd been after me before, I was now. He wasn't shopping. He was lying in wait.

To move things along, the security guard sped up the feed so that the picture moved at ten times normal speed. We watched until the camera showed him pulling his phone out of his pocket once again. He didn't put the phone to his ear this time. Rather, he appeared to be reading a text. Phone in hand, he stepped into place near the bottom of the escalator. Once again we saw the footage of him playing with his phone, pulling something shiny from the pocket of his jeans, and stalking off after witnessing my crazy leap over the side of the escalator.

Eddie pointed at the screen. "It seemed like he looked up at someone when he got that first phone call. Can we see the footage from the second floor?"

The guard once again played around until he found what we were looking for. Sure enough, at the same time the man had looked up from downstairs, the woman in the pink dress had stopped at the railing next to the escalator entrance on the second floor. She, too, was on her cell phone. It was difficult to tell much about her face with the phone and upright collar obscuring her cheeks and her long, loose bangs lying low across her brows. But there was one thing we could tell for certain. The woman sported a pair of watermelons on her chest, just like Leah Dodd, the stripper Noah Fischer had an affair with.

She looked down the moving staircase, no doubt at the man, though he was offscreen. She strolled off a few seconds later. *She's the woman I saw at the stadium, isn't she?* Something told me she was.

We watched the rest of the footage. Just as the man had roamed aimlessly around the first floor, she milled about the second, picking up and examining stemware in the china department, checking out the towels, waving off every offer of assistance from the sales staff. *Just browsing.*

As the time for my appointment drew closer, she slunk into the bridal department, positioning herself behind a pillar. No wonder Eddie and I hadn't seen her.

The video showed me and Eddie arriving, my partner flopping down in the chair to wait. The guard sped things up until I exited the fitting area and went to the register to pay for my gloves. On the screen, the woman whipped out her phone and sent a text. It had to be the one the man waiting downstairs had received.

As Eddie and I stepped onto the escalator, she fell in

behind us. When I went up and over the railing a moment later, she gave herself away. She waved her arm, signaling to the man in the cowboy hat to get the hell out of Dodge.

Yep, the two were together and that shiny metal object in the man's hand had to be a knife, just as I'd thought. They must be the same two people who'd been in the silver coupe that had followed me and Nick to the gas station, the same couple I'd seen putting mustard on their pretzels at the Cowboys game.

But who the hell are they?

"Can you zoom in on the woman's face?" I asked the security guard.

When he did, the screen went blurry, her features fuzzy. *Dang it!* Was she Leah Dodd wearing a dark wig to cover her reddish hair? The one time I'd seen the woman in person was a mere glimpse from across a parking lot last year, and it had been nighttime, too dark to tell much. Other than that, I'd only seen her in photographs. If I could have gotten a closer look or if the resolution of the security-camera footage had been better, maybe I could say for sure. But as it was, I was uncertain. After all, she wasn't the only woman with large breasts, and without a clear image of her face I couldn't verify whether this woman had Leah's telltale lip mole.

I turned to Eddie. "Do either of those people look familiar to you?"

He shook his head. "Can't say that they do."

"Can you save those clips to a jump drive for me?" I asked the security guard.

"Sure thing." He seemed happy to oblige, glad to be part of this investigation. An attempted murder in the store had to be much more exciting than the routine shoplifters he usually dealt with.

When he finished, he handed us the drive. "We'll keep

an eye out for those two. I'll let you know if I see them again."

"I'd appreciate that." I handed him my business card.

After rounding up my dress, safely zipped inside a clean bag, we headed outside. Every step was excruciating, sending sharp pains through my midsection. "Ouch! Ouch! Ouch!"

Eddie walked and I *ouch*ed down the sidewalk to the car. We stopped a few feet away.

"You think it's safe to drive?" I asked.

Eddie looked around. While there was still a number of cars and people in the area, it was a much smaller crowd downtown than during the morning and evening commute times. Besides, in my experience, people didn't pay much attention to what anyone else was doing. Humans also had a tendency to normalize things. Even if anyone had noticed someone sliding something under a car, the person's first thought probably wouldn't have been, *He's planting a bomb.* It would have been something like, *He must be checking his tires* or *He must have dropped some loose change.* Heck, normalization was one of the reasons people failed to react immediately in dangerous situations, such as those involving an active shooter. When people heard the *pop-pop-pop*, they convinced themselves the sound couldn't be gunfire, that it must be something else, something benign, like popcorn or fireworks.

Eddie and I had nearly been blown up once before, so we decided to err on the side of caution. I placed a call to 911. "This is Special Agent Tara Holloway with the IRS. Another agent and I were just followed into a store by two people. One of them was armed with a knife. Any chance you can send someone out with an explosive sniffing dog to check out our car?"

"We'll send a K-9 team your way. Sit tight."

The thought of sitting at all, let alone sitting "tight" made my pelvic bones throb worse. As we waited, I took advantage of the time to see if I could verify Leah Dodd's whereabouts. I logged onto her Facebook page, found the name of the club where she danced, and placed a call to it.

"Pleasure Palace," a male voice said.

"Is Leah Dodd working tonight?" I asked.

"I haven't seen her, but I'll check if she's on the schedule." He put me on hold, Donna Summer's sexy classic "Love to Love You Baby" coming through my speaker. He returned a few seconds later. "She starts dancing at nine."

"Thanks." I jabbed the button to end the call.

Eddie crooked a brow in question.

"I can't be sure," I told him, "but it's possible the woman in the store was Leah Dodd, the stripper Pastor Fischer was seeing on the side before Nick and I arrested him. Problem is, she's scheduled to work at nine tonight at the club in Shreveport where she dances."

He consulted his watch. "If that was her in Neiman's, she'll be late for her shift."

Shreveport sat a three-hour drive to the east. Even if she planned to take a flight, by the time she drove to the airport, checked in, flew to Louisiana, and drove to the club, she'd be late for work.

Within minutes, a small fire truck arrived. A female firefighter with curly brown hair climbed down from the truck, a frisky Belgian Malinois hopping down after her. The handler attached a leash to the dog and headed our way. "Are you the IRS agents?" she asked as she walked up.

"That's us," I replied. "Thanks for coming out."

The dog sniffed my shoes as his handler cocked her head. "They said someone pulled a knife on you in Neiman's?"

"Unfortunately, yes. They've been after me for a few

days now. That's why we were nervous about getting in the car without having it checked out first."

"You made the right call," she said. "Better safe than sorry."

Speaking of calls, I'd bet it was the woman who'd been on the escalator behind us who'd phoned Neiman's asking about my appointment for my fitting. She'd probably been the one the clerk had discussed the lace gloves with. I really had been stupid to put so much information on our wedding Web site. I'd made it easy for my would-be killers to plot against me. *Ugh.* I was tempted to flog myself, but decided the pain in my pelvis was enough penance for my stupidity.

The dog's nose moved up to my knee now. Lest he go for my cracked crotch, I took a step back and he turned his attention to Eddie's loafers.

The woman said, "C'mon, boy. Time to earn your keep."

She led him over to my car and issued an order. The dog began to sniff, starting at the wheel wells, slowly and methodically working his way up and down and around the vehicle. *Sniff-sniff-sniff.*

When they'd come full circle, the woman reached down to scratch his ears. "Good job!" The dog wagged his tail and she gave him a treat. She looked up at me and Eddie now. "The car's clear. You're good to go."

"Thanks," I told her. I looked down at the dog. Too bad I didn't have a fried baloney sandwich I could give him. "Thank you, too, boy."

He wagged his tail casually in reply as if to say, *No problem. It's what I do.*

chapter twenty-three

$\mathcal{T}$ime Heals All Wounds

Eddie drove me to the minor emergency clinic.

Kelsey, the red-haired receptionist, glanced up as I walked in. "Uh-oh. What is it this time, Agent Holloway?"

The receptionist knew me by name and vice versa. I was a regular in the place. In the last year and a half, Dr. Ajay Maju had treated me for everything from burns to broken bones to a stab wound inflicted by a rooster. The doc wasn't just my main medical care provider, he was also now the husband of my bridesmaid Christina Marquez, a DEA agent I'd met working the case against the drug-dealing ice-cream man. The two had met when Christina had brought me to the clinic to be treated for an injury. My pain was their gain.

I stepped over to her desk and leaned down to whisper in her ear. "I think I broke my naughty bits."

She held her pen poised. "That's another first." She jotted a note in my file and handed the folder back to a nurse, who waved for me to come in and follow her down the hall.

I was standing next to the exam table a few minutes later when Ajay rapped on the door and entered with my file. He looked up from the paperwork and cast me an incredulous look. "You think you broke your vagina?"

"Yes."

His tone switched from questioning to correcting. "You can't break your vagina."

"How do *you* know?" I snapped, my pain causing me to be short with him. "You don't even have one."

Ajay was the epitome of patience. "I don't have to have one to know they don't break. I know they don't break because I'm a doctor and I've studied human anatomy in critical detail."

I grimaced. "Are you sure? It really feels broken. I fell a good fifteen feet and landed spread-eagled on a stool."

He shook his head. "This could only happen to you, Tara."

He had me there. He laid the file on the counter and came over, gently pressing his hands against my lower abdomen and pelvic bone.

I cringed as he touched the sensitive area. "Going straight for third base, huh?"

"Why beat around the bush?" he said. "Of course that's sort of what I'm doing now."

"Ha-ha," I snapped. "Real funny."

He told me to spread my legs and, once I had, felt along my inner thighs. *Ow!* When I grimaced and grunted in pain, he said, "Maybe you actually do have the first ever broken vagina. Or a fractured pelvis. Let's get an X-ray and find out for sure."

A nurse took me into another room where I gingerly eased out of my pants. A technician took an X-ray of my lower half. Fifteen minutes later, I was back in both my pants and the exam room and Ajay had a picture of my pelvis pulled up on his computer screen.

"How's it look?" I asked.

"The bad news is you have a hairline fracture right

here." He ran his finger along a thin vertical line that began at the bottom and went halfway up the bone. "The good news is that it's not bad enough to require surgery, and if you take it easy you should make a full recovery. In the meantime, I'll get you some painkillers and an ice pack." He whipped out his prescription pad, scribbled on it, then ripped the square sheet from the pad and held it out to me. He reached into a drawer, pulled out one of those instant ice packs, and squeezed it to activate it. After handing it to me, he reached into another drawer and pulled out a foam ring.

"What's this?" I asked as I took it from him.

"Hemorrhoid ring. People usually center them around their bum to keep the pressure off, but in your case you can center it around your broken bits."

"Good idea."

"It goes without saying that you shouldn't be riding horses, pogo sticks, or Nick until the pain is gone."

The mere thought of any of those activities made me groan.

As I turned to go, he said, "See you at your wedding or your next injury, whichever comes first."

At nine-thirty that evening, I phoned the club in Shreveport again. "Can I speak with Leah Dodd?"

"She's not in yet," the guy said. "She phoned to say she'll be late. Car trouble."

Did she really have car trouble? Or did she have *attempted murder* trouble? There was no way to know, but it certainly seemed to be quite a coincidence. When I ended the call with him, I phoned Detective Booth and gave her an update. "The woman at Neiman's had a big bust, like Leah Dodd. The club where she's scheduled to dance tonight says she called in and said she'd be late due to car trouble."

"What's the name of the club?"

I gave Booth the information.

"I'll call Shreveport PD and see if we can get an officer out there to check on things. I'll have them make a run by her apartment, too."

"Thanks."

First thing Thursday morning, Detective Booth called me with an update. The officer from Shreveport PD reported that Leah showed up for work around midnight, late enough that she would have had time to drive back there from Dallas.

"She claimed her battery died while she was on the freeway in town," Booth said. "She said she doesn't have roadside assistance and had to wait until a friend could drive out to give her a jump."

"Any cameras in the area where she was allegedly pulled over?"

"Unfortunately not."

In other words, we couldn't positively verify or refute her story. *Ugh.* I thanked Booth for making the calls and spent the rest of the day wondering whether my headshot would appear in the newspaper next to Leah's someday under the headline "Last Dance—Stripper Murders Federal Agent."

At eight o'clock on Friday evening, I was sitting on my foam donut in the parking lot of an apartment complex in the Village, waiting for ride requests from Backseat Driver. My nether regions still ached, but the prescription pain meds, ice pack, and donut had helped relieve the pain some.

A notification popped up on my screen. A rider needed a pickup at White Rock Lake, which sat only a mile or so to the east of my location. His drop-off destination was an address here in the Village. I tapped the screen to accept the ride.

As I drove over with Nick, once again trailing me, I realized that maybe Joe Cullen had been on to something. He'd turned his life over to a higher power. Maybe I should turn this investigation over to one.

I turned my eyes to the sky. *Okay, God. I know you can see me through the big hole in the ozone layer that all of my driving around town has only helped to enlarge. You know I'm getting married soon. How about you toss me an early gift in the form of an arrest in the rental-scam case? Make this rider be the one? Pretty please? Amen and hallelujah.*

But alas God does not answer all prayers, and he wasn't feeling generous that evening. When I pulled into the parking area at the lakeside park, I was flagged down by a guy with a closely trimmed beard, a sweaty T-shirt glued to his chest, and a bluetick coonhound on a leash. Looked like the two of them had taken a jog around the lake.

When I stopped my car, he opened the back door. "Get in, boy!" he called to his four-footed friend.

The dog jumped into the backseat and the car immediately filled with the musky odor of damp dog. When the man slid in after his pet, eau d'athlete was added to the aromatic milieu—or should I saw mil-*ew*?

I turned and looked over the seat at the man. "Did your dog go for a swim in the lake?"

He nodded. "He likes to cool off after a run."

While I couldn't much blame the dog, I could blame his owner. Either he shouldn't have let the dog cool off in the water, or he should've taken a dip in the lake himself, washed off the sweat. One source of stink I could handle, but two was blatantly unfair. I unrolled my window to grab a breath of fresh air and rolled it back up, holding my breath.

As I started off, the air held in my lungs, a soft jingle of dog tags began behind me. The sound grew louder and louder as the dog worked itself into full-body shake, showering me and the inside of the car with dog-scented droplets. "Hey!"

I ducked in my seat, but it did no good. The dog thoroughly doused me. At the same time, my lungs screamed for fresh oxygen. I fought the burn until I couldn't hold my breath any longer. I gasped in the stench, certain I felt my lungs recoil when the dank air hit them. At that point, the only thing I could do was turn the air conditioner on full blast and hope the air pressure would hold the stink at bay in the backseat.

The guy hardly engaged me on the drive to his apartment, but he spoke continuously to his dog. "What do you want for dinner, boy? Should we grill some steaks? There's some leftover brisket in the fridge. Or maybe we should order a pizza. Does a pepperoni pizza sound good, boy? Does it?"

The dog wagged his tail. Looked like he'd be equally pleased with steak, brisket, or pizza. In my experience, dogs didn't tend to be picky as long as they got some of whatever their humans were having.

Their dinner decided upon, the man asked the dog about his morning plans. "Want to go for another run in the morning? Huh? Do ya?"

The dog glanced his way then turned to look out the window. *I might have other plans. Let me get back to you on that.*

Finally, we arrived at the apartment complex.

The guy pointed to a building. "This is me."

Good. Maybe I could finally breathe again.

As the guy climbed out, he pulled a key ring from the pocket of his running shorts and thumbed the fob. A *dink-dink* sounded and the lights flashed on a Dodge Avenger parked a few feet away.

"Wait. Is that your car?" I asked.

"Yeah."

I asked the obvious question. "Why didn't you drive *your* car to the lake?"

"Because I didn't want to stink it up," he replied with an undertone of *duh*.

So he didn't want to stink up his own car, but believed it was perfectly okay to stink up mine, even though I purportedly needed it to make a living. What a jerk. I mentally rolled my eyes, but gave the dog a nice scratch behind his ears before he hopped down. He might be stinky, but he was just doing what dogs do. And besides, he was kinda cute.

Thanks to the ice pack, painkillers, and foam cushion, my nether regions felt much better by the time Saturday rolled around. Good thing, too. My bridesmaids were throwing me a bridal shower brunch and I wanted to enjoy it.

Alicia had been my best friend since we'd met in college, so of course she was my matron of honor. I'd recently served as maid of honor at her wedding, too. My other bridesmaid, Christina, and I had grown very close in the relatively short time we'd known each other. We'd first met early last year while working the case against Joe, the drug-dealing ice-cream man, but she'd later helped me in the Mendoza investigation and we'd both worked on the undercover sting at Guys & Dolls. Fighting crime together really brings two people close.

They'd rented a private room at the back of the restaurant for the shower. In case the couple who was after me tried to pull something here, Nick took a seat at a table near the front door to play security guard. Bonnie, my mother, and I headed to the back. Though we arrived a half hour before the shower was to begin, we found Alicia and Christina already enjoying mimosas and mini almond croissants.

They stood as we entered. "Hey, y'all!" Alicia said, giving us each a hug. Christina followed suit.

Once they'd released me, I gestured to the drinks. "You got a head start on us, I see."

"We had to make sure everything tasted okay," Christina replied facetiously.

We joined them, taking glasses and loading small plates with pastries.

Christina set up her laptop on a table near the door, and played a continuous loop of pictures of me and others that she'd rounded up from the guests. There were Alicia and me in our dorm room in our pajamas, looking hideous and unkempt as we were three days into hell week, cramming for exams. We'd both put a hand up to block the camera, but to no avail. Our classmate still got the pic.

"Remember those days?" Alicia asked with a smile.

"Like they were yesterday." It was amazing how quickly the time had flown since we graduated from college. We'd been mere kids back then, and now here we were, doing important jobs and paying mortgages and getting married. Before we knew it, we'd probably have kids and PTA meetings and soccer games.

Another shot showed me and Alicia with our fellow female accountants, breaking open a bottle of Fireball whisky at midnight on April 15 after an exhausting tax season. Alicia cut me a knowing look. "Those April fifteenth celebrations were a lot of fun, weren't they?"

"Yep." Still, while I missed the parties that marked the passing of the tax-filing deadline, I didn't miss the eighty-hour workweeks that came along with tax season each

spring. I worked plenty of overtime at the IRS, but only
when I had a particularly intense case and rarely for weeks
at a time. Besides, the hours passed much faster when you
enjoyed your work like I did.

Another photo popped up on the screen. This one featured me and Christina doing yoga. Or, more precisely,
Christina performing a perfect scorpion pose while I
appeared to be trying—and failing—to kick myself in
the back of the head. The next shot was of me and Alicia
on her wedding day as we put on our makeup, rollers in
our hair.

"We've been through a lot together, haven't we?" I asked
the two.

"We sure have," Alicia said.

Christina nodded in assent. "Good times."

The guests filtered in over the next half hour. Women
I'd worked with at Martin & McGee. Lu, Viola, and Hana.
Eddie's and Will's wives. Kira. A few other girls I'd known
from college or high school who now lived in the Dallas
area. Over the next hour, we chatted and laughed and ate
and drank and played silly games, like bridal bingo. The
cards spelled out B-R-I-D-E along the top and featured
pictures of wedding-related things. A chapel. Rings. A
wedding cake. A bottle of champagne.

Christina called the winning square. "B, bouquet."

My mother squealed and clapped her hands. "Bingo!"

Alicia handed my mother a small silver gift bag. "Here's
your prize."

Inside was a bar of artisan lemongrass soap. Mom held
it to her nose. "Mmm. This smells terrific."

Was it wrong of me to hope she'd put it in the guest bath
at their house so I could use it when I visited?

When it was time for me to open my presents, Alicia
pulled a chair over to the gift table for me so the boxes and
bags would be in easy reach. My friends and family had

been exceedingly generous, and many of the items on my gift registry were discovered in the bags. New towels. Place settings. A wine rack that could hold a dozen bottles at once.

I opened a card from Nick's mother to discover a gift certificate to Victoria's Secret. My cheeks heated when I realized what it was.

Bonnie laughed. "Sorry to embarrass you, hon. But your mother and I want some grandbabies while we're still young enough to enjoy them. I thought something from that store might speed up the process."

It might, indeed.

When the shower was over, I thanked all of my guests. "Thanks so much for coming!"

"It was great to see you. It's been way too long!"

"See you at the wedding!" I called as the last of them were leaving.

I turned to find Christina and Alicia cleaning up. "I'll help with that."

"Absolutely not." Alicia waved me off. "You're the guest of honor."

I ignored her. It had been a while since I'd had some girl time with friends and I was in no rush to put an end to our time together.

While we scurried about, collecting errant tissue paper, bingo cards, and tabletop decorations, Christina asked about work. "Have you made an arrest in that rental case?"

"Not yet." I exhaled a sharp breath. "But it's not for lack of trying. I've read over the reports, interviewed some of the victims, racked my brain to try to find a connection between the identities he's assumed. He seems to have access to a never-ending supply of personal data to steal. He changes his alias and the credit cards he uses on a regular basis, so we haven't been able to backtrack our way to him. I haven't managed to peg the right properties online, and everyone I've picked up with Backseat Driver so far was a false lead."

Christina balled up a sheet of wrinkled tissue paper and tossed it in the trash. "You said you have video footage of him, right?"

"Yeah."

"Want me to take a look? See if I spot anything you and the detective didn't?"

"Sure. Another set of eyes can't hurt." It was unlikely she'd notice anything new, but we had nothing to lose, right? Luckily, I had the flash drive in my purse and Alicia's laptop at my disposal. I slid the drive into the USB port and we gathered around the screen. Alicia joined us.

As we watched the video, I noticed once more how the man held his phone to his ear. Just like that passenger I'd picked up at the café recently, the one who'd given me an odd, familiar vibe. *Hmm. Could they be one and the same?*

No, I told myself. *Of course not. The leasing agent is tall and beefy, but the rider was only average-sized.*

Or was he?

I turned to Alicia, who knew not only makeup tricks but also fashion ones. She was always helping me pick out the best clothes to flatter my flat figure, to make me appear curvier than I really was. "This guy on the screen," I said, gesturing at him. "You think he's really as tall and beefy as he looks?"

My bridesmaids leaned in for a closer look.

"Maybe not." Alicia tapped a button to pause the screen. She pointed to his shoes. "See the heel on those shoes? It's unusually high. Add in a pair of lifts inside the shoes and the guy could make himself look three or four inches taller."

Three or four inches could make the difference between average and tall.

My body began to buzz. Maybe I should've given more

credence to that familiar feeling I'd had when I picked the guy up.

Alicia pointed to his suit next. "I can't say for sure, but this jacket could have shoulder pads. That would make a man look broader. Plus, he's wearing a tie with horizontal stripes. People wear vertical stripes to look taller and thinner, but horizontal stripes would make him look wider."

Christina pointed to his hands and chin. "His hands don't look meaty," she said, "and his jawline isn't rounded. You know, like it would probably be if he were truly heavier."

The longer I stared at the screen, the more disproportionate the guy looked, like a businessman in a fun-house mirror. I had to give it to him, he sure knew how to put up a complete ruse.

I phoned Backseat Driver right away. "Get me a supervisor, please." My account had been flagged so that those in managerial positions would know I was law enforcement working undercover and should be given access to information.

When the woman came on the line, I told her my name and driver ID. "I gave a guy a ride recently in Dallas. He went by the name Michael S. Can you give me the full name, address, and credit card number on the account?"

"Of course," she said. There was a short pause as she pulled up the information. The sound of her fingers clicking on a keyboard came through the phone. "Okay. I've got it pulled up. The name on the card is Michael Simpson." She went on to give me an address and account number.

As she recited the information, I wrote it down. The information wouldn't get me anywhere immediately, unfortunately. The con artist used stolen identities and had the credit cards delivered to the rental properties rather than his own home address. He also never used the same credit cards for both renting properties and Backseat Driver services. But with this information I could get in touch with the credit card company, find out which of the many Michael Simpsons in the U.S. the con artist was purporting to be, and see if the real Michael Simpson could tell me what link he had, if any, to the Dallas area. Of course I might be able to catch the guy even sooner if he requested another ride through Backseat.

"If any rides are requested on the Michael S account," I told her, "please notify me immediately."

"All right," she said, the sound of her tapping her keyboard again coming over the line. "It's all set up."

I called the credit card company next. Of course they wanted a search warrant before they'd provide me with information about the alleged account holder, such as the social security number I'd need to determine which of the hundreds, if not thousands, of Michael Simpsons the con artist was pretending to be. I'd expected as much. But at least I was able to obtain the e-mail address for the legal department. I'd send a copy of the warrant there once I had it.

For the first time in days, I found myself feeling buoyed and hopeful. Then again, maybe what felt like hope was just a combination of mimosas and painkillers. Either way, *weee!*

chapter twenty-four

$\mathcal{P}$olicies and Procedures

The hope I'd felt after my bridal shower on Saturday grew even more as the following week progressed.

I went with Ross O'Donnell to the courthouse for a search warrant Monday morning. Judge Trumbull approved my request with little argument. "Get that guy before he hurts anyone else."

"I'll do my best, Your Honor."

I'd e-mailed the order to the credit card company. A legal assistant had given me the social security number for the Michael Simpson in whose name the card had been issued. Armed with that information, I was able to determine that he lived in Las Cruces, New Mexico. I'd found his phone number right away and called him.

After explaining who I was and why I was calling, I said, "The con artist seems to have access to a database with your private information in it. Many of the other victims were also out of state. It's possible that the guy hacked into some kind of nationwide database, but we're exploring the possibility of whether all of you have a common Dallas connection. If so, that might tell us where the guy is getting your information."

"My brother lives in Dallas," he said. "I've been there to visit him once or twice. But other than that, I don't have a connection to the city."

Hmm. Michael Simpson had a brother living here, and Tyrone Robinson's uncle lived in the city, too. Did the brother and the uncle have something in common? Of course I'd already spoken with the uncle and he hadn't been able to provide any clues. Maybe Simpson's brother could.

"Do you mind if I call your brother? See if he might be able to help me out?"

"Feel free," Simpson said.

He gave me the number and I dialed it right away. Again, I got a voice mail. *Ugh.* Nobody seemed to answer their phones these days. I left a message and asked him to call me. "It's urgent."

In the meantime, I figured it couldn't hurt to respond to a few more of the real estate rental listings, continue to fight the battle on multiple fronts. I found four or five listings that seemed to be unusually good deals and filled out the reply forms for more information about the properties.

Simpson's brother returned my call late on Monday. He gave me what could be my first solid lead.

"We get fifty grand of life insurance as an employee benefit at my job," the guy said. "I'm single and I don't have any kids so I listed Michael as my beneficiary. I had to include his social security number on the form. I remember because my mother gave it to me. I'd planned to call Michael for it, but she happened to call me first so I just asked her while we were on the phone."

"So Michael doesn't even know he's the beneficiary?"

"Probably not," the brother said. "It didn't seem like a big deal. I'm only thirty-two and I'm healthy. There's not much chance he'll ever cash in on the policy."

"Good point. Which life insurance company is the policy with?"

"Couldn't even tell ya," he said. "I filled out so much paperwork when I started my job it's all a blur. I'd have to check with human resources."

"Could you do that and call me back?"

"Sure. It's almost five, though. It might be tomorrow before I can get the information."

"No problem," I said, though actually I wanted to scream. I was getting close. I could sense it. Just like I'd sensed the guy in my car with the phone to his ear seemed familiar. "Just to make sure I've covered my bases, do you have any connection to A-1 Awnings, EZ Autos, or an advertising agency called Bloomfield and Associates?"

"No. Why?"

"Just ruling out some other potential leads."

Simpson's brother called me back early Tuesday morning. "The HR department says my life insurance policy is with Metroplex Mutual Life Insurance Company."

I jotted the name down, as well as the name of the company he worked for, Glassen Inc. I phoned the man who worked for the awning company first. "When you worked for A-1 Awnings, were you offered life insurance as part of your benefits package?"

"I believe so," he said. "If I recall correctly, I had a policy that would pay my wife a hundred grand if I died." He chuckled. "Thankfully, she never got the money."

"Do you know if the policy was with Metroplex Mutual Life Insurance Company?"

"I don't recall the name of the company. Sorry."

While he wasn't able to tell me, maybe the administrative offices at A-1 Awnings could.

Yep, they could.

After I'd called, been transferred three times, each of which required me to identify myself and explain my situation, I finally reached someone who had the goods.

"We offer our employees a one-hundred-thousand-dollar life insurance policy with Metroplex Mutual," the woman said. "We've used them for years. They're right here in town and easy to do business with."

"Thanks for the information."

My nerves buzzed. This lead seemed to be getting more and more solid, like pudding as it cooled. Still, it could be coincidence. A look at the insurance company's Web site told me they aggressively targeted employers in the Dallas area and had landed a respectable market share. If Sebastian Rivera also had a link to Metroplex Mutual, I'd feel sure that the insurance company had to be the connection.

I phoned him and explained what I'd found so far. "I'm thinking the insurance company could be the key." I mentally crossed my fingers. "Does the name Metroplex Mutual Life Insurance Company mean anything to you?"

"I've never heard of the company," he said.

Dang it! But then I realized he, like Michael Simpson's brother, might be linked to the company but not even know it. Maybe Rivera's sister, the one who'd worked at the ad agency, had listed Sebastian as a beneficiary on her policy.

"I suppose it's possible," he said when I posited the idea. "She's married now, but she was single when she worked there and our parents had already passed on. But I don't know for sure."

He gave me his sister's number to call. Once again I got a voice mail. *UGH!* But although I'd left her a message, I wasn't going to just sit and wait for her to call me back. I grabbed my keyboard and mouse, pulled up the Bloomfield & Associates Web site, and dialed the phone number for their HR department, crossing my fingers someone would answer the phone. It was straight up 5:00 p.m., quitting time.

The phone rang once.

Come on, my mind pleaded. *Please, somebody, answer.*

The phone rang again.

Somebody! my mind willed. *Anybody!*

The phone rang a third time.

Answer the damn phone right now! my mind screamed.

Luckily for me, Bloomfield & Associates' clocks must run slow and someone was still in the office. "Human Resources Department," said a male voice.

"This is Special Agent Tara Holloway with the IRS. I'm working a fraud case. Your company isn't implicated in any way, but I suspect one of the victims might have been a beneficiary under a life insurance policy provided to an employee. Can you tell me whether Bloomfield and Associates offers life insurance for its staff?"

"We do," the man said. "The amount of the policy varies depending on what job the person has and what their salary is."

"What company are the policies with?"

"Metroplex Mutual Life."

My buzzing nerves buzzed even more. *Bzzzzzz!*

"Thanks." As soon as I was done with the man from the ad agency, I phoned Tyrone Robinson's uncle. "Any chance you've got a life insurance policy with Metroplex Mutual Life that lists Tyrone as a beneficiary?"

"I sure do," he said. "How in the world did you know that?"

Ding-ding-ding! We have a winner!

I leaped out of my seat and threw a happy fist in the air. *This is it! This is the key!* Metroplex Mutual was the link I'd been looking for, the connection that could take me to the con artist. After my impromptu celebration, I sat back down. "All of the other identity-theft victims were

beneficiaries of policies with the company. I figured
Tyrone might be, too."

"Well, don't that beat all," the man said. "You can't trust
anybody these days, can you?"

"Not hardly." Seemed everyone was out to get everyone else. Then again, maybe I had a skewed view of the
world given my job and the constant frauds I dealt with.

As soon as I ended the call with Tyrone's uncle, I called
Metroplex Mutual's legal department. A recorded voice
told me I'd reached them after business hours. *Dammit!*
Lawyers worked long hours, too, didn't they? Probably
someone was in the office, listening to the phone ring and
ring and ring, but refusing to answer it. I'd have to wait
until the following morning to speak with someone there.
But at least the wheels of justice seemed to be in motion.
Finally!

When I phoned Metroplex Mutual Life Insurance Company's legal department back first thing Wednesday
morning, the attorney I spoke with took umbrage with me.
"You're insinuating that someone within the company
might have misused private information."

I wasn't just insinuating it, I was flat-out accusing an
employee of identity theft. But better to play nice or he
could make things more difficult for me. "It's just a theory I'm working," I said. "It would be an unusual and
amazing coincidence for all of the victims to be associated with Metroplex Mutual." In other words, where there's
smoke, there's fire. And this fire was a four-alarm inferno.

"As I'm sure you're aware," he said, "any breach of our
company's security protocols could have devastating con-
sequences to our reputation. Any employee with access to
sensitive data goes through intensive background screen-
ing and training. We have had no reason to distrust our
employees or believe any such breach has taken place."

"All I want to know," I said, "is whether you can identify one or more employees who would have had access to the policy information for employees of A-1 Awnings, Bloomfield and Associates, and Glassen Incorporated."

"I could," he said, "but I won't. Not without a warrant."

In other words, if I wanted information about their policies, I'd have to go through the proper procedures. While I could understand his defensive posture, I knew it meant another trip to the courthouse, another delay. The wheels of justice might finally be in motion, but it was slow motion. Couldn't someone just cut me some slack and do what I wanted them to do without requiring an act of Congress?

"All right," I acquiesced. "I'll get the warrant and get back to you. In the meantime, can you take a look at some security-camera recordings and tell me if you recognize the man in the footage?"

He acquiesced, though the tone of his voice told me he considered me a pain in the ass. That was nothing new for me. "Okay," he said on a huff.

I e-mailed the file to the Metroplex Mutual Life legal department. Maybe the guy running the rental scam really was as big as he looked. If so, it seemed he'd be easier to identify. Maybe they'd take one look, peg him right away, and I could put an end to this seemingly endless investigation.

No such luck.

When the lawyer called back an hour later, he had no answers for me.

"We didn't recognize him," the attorney said. "Of course Metroplex Mutual employs over six hundred people. Those of us in the legal department don't know them all. Besides, the video isn't all that helpful. The phone obscures the man's face in nearly all of the footage."

Argh! "Thanks for trying."

I phoned Ross O'Donnell to see about getting a warrant to send to the insurance company.

"Before Judge Trumbull will issue a warrant," he said, "you'll need to get affidavits from the people who had insurance polices with Metroplex Mutual. They should stipulate that they provided the name and social security number of each person whose identity was later used by the bogus leasing agent. It would be even better if one of them happened to have a copy of the application they filled out when they applied for the policy. You know, so that it would show that they had listed the victim's private information."

In other words, I had a bunch of hoops to jump through today.

But jump through them I did. I made phone calls. Obtained e-mail addresses. Typed my fingers off, chipping a nail in the process. By the end of the day, I'd prepared affidavits and e-mailed them to Sebastian Rivera's sister, Michael Simpson's brother, and Tyrone Robinson's uncle. As soon as they sent the executed affidavits back to me, Ross and I could ask Judge Trumbull for the warrant.

Yippee!

chapter twenty-five

*H*iding Out

As Nick followed me home to Bonnie's that evening, he called my cell. I jabbed the button to put him on speaker.

"We've got a tail," he said without preamble. "A black SUV. It's been behind us for a couple of miles."

My heart did a backflip and my chest tightened in fear. "Are you sure?" I said on a shallow breath.

"I'm not taking chances," Nick said. "Not with your life."

Aww. He really does love me, doesn't he? "What should we do? Evasive maneuvers?"

There was too much traffic for us to use our weapons. I was a sharpshooter, but even with my top-notch gun skills I couldn't guarantee a clean shot out of a moving vehicle, especially when I'd have to keep my other hand on the steering wheel. I might accidentally shoot an innocent person or cause a fatal accident.

"If they make a move," he said, "I'll run interference and you get the hell out of here. But I don't think they know we're on to them. This could be our chance to bust their asses."

If we could nab the culprits right now, heck, I was all for it.

"Skip the exit for my mom's house," Nick directed me, "and keep going straight. I'll call 911 and get Dallas PD out here to pull them over."

"Good idea."

When we ended our call, I checked my rearview and side mirrors. Sure enough, way back, I caught a glimpse of a black SUV that came into view in my side mirror as I rounded a small curve in the freeway.

My heart pulsed at warp speed, my skin vibrating. Steering with my left hand, I reached down and pulled my gun from my holster, holding it at the ready in the unlikely event I'd be able to get a clean shot. Of course even if I could get a clean shot, I couldn't fire until they'd taken a shot at me first. No way could I risk another excessive-force trial. But chances were good that, if they took a shot, they'd shoot me from behind where I wouldn't see it coming. Maybe they had a long-range rifle and a scope, ready to do just that. Maybe my blood and brain matter would end up splattered all over the car just like the water drops from the wet dog.

Yikes.

I slumped down in my seat, doing my best to keep my head low. Of course that also made my eyes too low to see well. Add in the fact that I was trying to watch what little I could see of the road in front of me as well as the SUV behind me, and the situation posed more of a challenge than I was up for. I was no Danica Patrick.

The early evening sun streaming through the windshield glinted off my engagement ring. *Will I live to see my wedding?* Each of these incidents made me less and less certain. Maybe Nick and I should just go to the justice of the peace first thing in the morning and say our I dos. That way, if I were killed, at least I'd have had the privilege of being Nick's wife for a short time.

HOOOOONK!

The driver in the next lane not only laid on his horn but also treated me to a raised middle finger and a mouthed Fuck you! So much for Southern hospitality, huh? I must've accidentally swerved over the line.

"Give me a break!" I hollered back. "Someone's trying to kill me!" There was no possible way he could hear me with my windows up. Heck, he was a good ten yards ahead of me now. Still, if nothing else, the yelling made me feel better.

Nick phoned me back a few seconds later. "The SUV was coming up fast but they exited right after you swerved and that car honked. They must have realized we'd noticed them and that they'd lost the element of surprise."

Dammit! My stupidity had let them get away. On the other hand, if they'd been making a break for me, maybe it was a good thing I'd swerved. They might've gotten a headshot in before I could drive away. I could be dead right now, my brains decorating my dashboard. *There's a happy thought.*

I put Nick on speaker and set the phone in my cup holder. "What now?"

"Take the next exit and loop back."

Keeping in touch by phone, we performed all sorts of evasive maneuvers in case they tried to return to the freeway and catch up with us. But neither Nick nor I noticed a tail any longer. We took surface streets for a couple miles, returned to the freeway, and backtracked. When we pulled into Bonnie's garage, we lowered the door as quickly as we could to hide our vehicles.

Bonnie met us at the door, my shotgun in her hands. Her face was puckered with worry. "I just got a phone call from some woman. She didn't say who she was, but she asked for you, Tara."

Holy shit! The people who are after me know we're staying at Bonnie's! They could be on their way here right now!

"What did you say?" I squeaked, terror clutching my throat.

"I told them I'd never heard of Tara Holloway and they must have the wrong number."

Nick and I exchanged glances. If the caller knew Bonnie was Nick's mother, they'd know she was lying about knowing me. It might have been better if she'd admitted knowing me, but had feigned confusion as to why they'd think I was at her place. But regardless, it was water under the bridge now.

I pulled my phone from my purse. "I'll call Dallas PD."

Nick yanked his phone from his pocket. "I'll call the U.S. Marshal's office."

As we placed our calls, we rushed around the house, turning off all the lights and closing blinds and curtains to make it more difficult for anyone on the outside to see in. Daffodil dashed around after us, seeming to think we were playing a game. *Woof! Woof-woof!*

"I'm IRS Special Agent Tara Holloway," I told dispatch when a male agent answered. "I had a tail and I believe whoever followed me might be on their way to my mother-in-law's house. That's where I'm staying. I need backup here ASAP." I rattled off the address.

"We've got a unit in the area," the dispatcher said. "I'll send it over."

I stood next to the front window, my back flattened against the wall as I peered out around the edge of the curtain to keep an eye on the street. Nick did the same on the other side, while Bonnie peeked out the kitchen window, watching the backyard. Two cars drove past on the street out front, but neither was a black SUV. The next car was a cruiser from Dallas PD. I closed my eyes for a moment and exhaled a long, relieved breath.

Two uniformed officers, one blond and one balding, exited the vehicle, careful to watch their backs as they came up the drive. I hurried over and opened the door as they walked onto the porch. Nick stepped up behind me.

The bald one said, "We understand you're the IRS agent who's being stalked?"

"Yes, that's me." I extended a hand to shake theirs. "IRS Special Agent Tara Holloway."

Nick put out his hand, too. "Senior Special Agent Nick Pratt. I'm Tara's fiancé." He gestured to Bonnie, who'd come over, too. "This is my mother, Bonnie Pratt."

The blond-haired officer glanced down the street as a minivan approached. "I'll keep an eye on things out here."

We thanked him and stepped back to allow his partner inside.

Bonnie held out a hand to indicate the living room. "Please take a seat. Can I get you something?"

"I wouldn't say no to a cup of coffee."

"How do you take it?"

"Black."

While Bonnie prepared a pot of coffee, Nick, the officer, and I sat down in the living room.

He pulled out a pen and notepad to take notes. "You were followed?"

I nodded. "By a black SUV."

"Did you get the make and model? License plate?"

"No. It all happened too fast." I looked to Nick. "Did you?"

"No," he replied, standing. "But maybe your cameras picked it up."

Good thing he could think on his feet. My mind was

still whirling. I'd forgotten all about the dash and rear cameras Josh had installed.

I fished through my purse until I found my keys and handed them to Nick. While he went to the garage to grab the cameras, the officer continued his questions. "Any idea who might be following you?"

"I've made a lot of arrests during my time with the Service, but I've already met with most of the people I considered likely suspects. Nothing panned out. The people who are after me appear to be a couple. A tall man and woman. I've seen them at the Cowboys stadium and at Neiman's. The woman seems vaguely familiar. It's possible she's a stripper from Shreveport named Leah Dodd, but I don't have any concrete evidence to prove it."

The officer nodded slowly, mulling things over before offering a noncommittal shrug. "Sooner or later they're bound to slip up."

I'd had the same thought. But the next thought was always *How much later?* Seriously, how long could this go on?

Nick returned with the cameras and we huddled together on the couch to watch the footage on the small screens. Unfortunately, while the SUV had come briefly into view in my side mirror earlier, the rear camera, which had been centered at the back window, didn't pick it up. Rather, the camera showed a steady view of Nick and his car following me, once in a while picking up the fender of a car to the right or left as we rounded a curve. Likewise, the dash camera showed nothing, no SUV slowing intentionally to let me pass. Evidently, the SUV had never been in front of me.

I closed my eyes in frustration, putting a hand to my forehead. "We've got nothing."

"Dammit!" Nick stood from the couch to walk off his anger.

KNOCK-KNOCK.

I nearly ejected from my skin as someone rapped on the front door. A second later, a male voice called, "U.S. Marshal."

The officer and I stood and went to the door. I opened it and let the marshal inside. "Thanks for coming so quickly."

We held a powwow in the foyer, Nick and his mother joining in, too.

I gave the marshal the details. "Detective Booth has gone with me to interview some of the potential suspects, but we haven't had any luck."

"Too bad," he said. "This kind of thing, with the suspects approaching you in public places, raises the risk of collateral damage."

In other words, innocent people could be hurt by the criminals who were after me. Guilt gripped my gut once more. This situation sucked from so many angles.

He turned to the officer. "Given that it's a federal agent who's the target here, seems best we marshals keep watch, let you all go about your usual business." The marshal turned back to me. "We'll keep a car and agent here round-the-clock for the time being."

Good. Bonnie would have protection while we were gone.

The marshal added, "If the people who are after you think you're staying here, there's a chance they'll come by. Maybe we can catch them then."

If only. I'd been so anxious since the incident at Neiman's it felt as if my stomach were spurting a constant stream of acid. I'd been on a steady diet of Tums.

The police officer made a move for the door.

"Thanks, Officer," I told the cop, shaking his hand as he left.

"Anytime."

Though the open door, I raised a hand to the blond officer outside, calling, "Thank you!" to him, too.

The marshal pulled out his cell phone. "Let me get your numbers."

He added all of us to his contacts list, including Bonnie's landline number. He pulled a handheld radio from a clip on his belt and held it out to me. "Take this. In case we need to reach each other quick."

I took it from him. I wasn't sure whether having the radio made me feel more or less safe. Sure, we could rouse the marshal faster. But—*eek!*—would we need to?

With the radio serving as a centerpiece, Nick, Bonnie, and I ate a quiet dinner. Afterward, we watched a little TV and prepared for bed, doing our best to pretend it was a normal night and that there was nothing unusual about having a marked cruiser from the marshal's office parked like a sentry at the curb out front.

After donning my pj's, I climbed into bed and Annie curled up next to me. Henry, on the other paw, seemed to sense the tension in the air. He hissed and fidgeted for half an hour before finally settling down at the end of the bed, staring at me through the darkness, his eyes reflecting what little light came from the clock.

I don't like it any more than you do, buddy.

On Thursday morning, Bonnie stayed home with the pets and the marshal while Nick and I went to work. I felt guilty that Bonnie would be trapped in her house all day, but she told me not to worry. "I'll catch up on my television," she said. "Read some magazines I haven't had time to get to."

"Do you have plenty of groceries?"

"Of course. With a son like Nick, you know I keep my fridge and freezer stocked. Besides, if I need anything I can get it delivered."

There was something to be said for living in an era when anything you wanted or needed could be brought to your doorstep. A few more years and going out in one's yard would be considered an adventure. I placed a hand on Bonnie's forearm. "I'm sorry about all of this."

"It's not your fault, Tara," she said, patting my hand. "Don't blame yourself. Blame whoever it is who's trying to kill you."

"You'll keep the shotgun handy? Just in case?"

She reached over next to her chair and patted it. "Got it right here."

At the office, Viola looked up as Nick and I stepped off the elevators. "What's going on?" she demanded. The woman seemed to have a sixth sense about us agents, just like a mother has with her children.

I filled her in. "I was followed last night by an SUV."

Her eyes went wide. "That doesn't sound good."

She could say that again.

"Be careful," Nick warned Viola. "The security team downstairs does a good job, but if these people are intent on getting Tara, they might pull a stupid stunt here at the office."

"I'll get you my spare ballistic vest," I told her. "I'd feel better if you were wearing it." She wouldn't feel better, though. Not physically anyway. The darn things were hot and heavy. But better uncomfortable than dead.

I scurried to my office and returned with the vest.

Viola took it from me, her eyes glimmering with excitement. "Can I have a gun, too?"

She wasn't properly trained and qualified, so we couldn't give her a weapon.

"Sorry, but no," I said. "We can give you a quick lesson in close combat, though. How's that?"

"Let's do it!"

With Nick playing the role of the attacker, I showed her

the defensive moves I'd learned. "Go for the eyes, nose, neck, groin, or knees. Those are the vulnerable spots. At least on men. If it's a woman attacking you, skip the groin."

Really, why didn't men have vagina envy? They walked around with that pendulous organ hanging out, making them vulnerable. They should be jealous of what we had. It could be just as fun and didn't pose an easy target. Then again, after landing on that stool and smashing my girlie parts, I knew better than anyone that women weren't entirely safe from crotch-centered catastrophes.

Viola tried the moves out on Nick, being careful to avoid actual contact. She swung the pad of her hand upward toward his nose. "How's that?"

"You got me!" He fell to the floor in mock defeat, spreading his arms wide and letting his tongue loll out as if he were dead.

"Good job," I told her. "I pity the fool who tries to take you on."

Nick and I went to our offices to get to work. I checked my e-mails. While Tyrone Robinson's uncle and Michael Simpson's brother had returned their affidavits, I had not yet received a completed form from Sebastian Rivera's sister. I hoped she'd hop to it. I wanted to get the search warrant, get over to Metroplex Mutual Life Insurance Company, and find out, once and for all, who was the man running the rental scam.

In addition to the two affidavits, my e-mail inbox included four replies regarding the rental ads I'd responded to. One of them gave the property address and noted that he'd be holding an open house on the upcoming Saturday from ten A.M. to noon. An open house was an efficient way to show a place to a lot of people in a short time. But it was not the method normally used by the con artist. I dismissed the reply. I also dismissed two other replies that had been sent by female leasing agents. I told all three of these that I had already decided on a place, but thanked them for getting back to me.

The fourth reply caught my attention. A purported leasing agent named Cliff said he could show me the subject property tonight at seven. *Does that time work for you, Sara?*

I wrote back. *Yes, 7 is good. What's the address?*

His reply came in around three that afternoon. The house was on Peavy Road in a neighborhood known as Casa Linda Estates that sat a couple miles northeast of downtown.

Great! I wrote back. *See you at 7.*

I noticed that Sebastian Rivera's sister had also returned her affidavit in the meantime, along with the application she'd used to apply for the insurance. I printed the documents out to have ready for court and called Ross. "Can you meet me at the courthouse in fifteen minutes to get a search warrant?"

"It's a date."

I shoved the affidavits into my briefcase. Before heading out, I looked up the owner information for the Peavy Road property on the Dallas County Appraisal District Web site. It listed a woman's name. I found a number for her and dialed it as I headed down the hall. If I were working as a private CPA, this type of multitasking would enable me to double bill. But since I worked for Uncle Sam, my efficiency earned me only the usual paycheck.

The phone rang three times before going to voice mail. *Jeez Louise! Does nobody answer their phones these days?* I left a message. After identifying myself, I said, "I'm working an investigation with the Dallas Police Department. We're hoping you might have some information that could help us. Please call me back immediately. It's urgent." I left my cell number so she'd be able to reach me while I was on the go.

Josh was my backup for the day. He and I met Ross at the courthouse with the documentation.

While Josh stood with his back to us, keeping an eye on the people in the gallery and the door to the courtroom, Ross made a plea to the judge on my behalf for the search warrant. "Special Agent Holloway was able to determine that Metroplex Mutual is the common link among the victims. This fact gives us reason to believe the culprit works at the insurance company."

Judge Trumbull looked down at me and raised a gray brow. "This guy's taken unsuspecting young people for over a hundred grand?"

"Yes, he has, Your Honor. Including a young couple with a baby." I was going for sympathy points there. What kind of bastard would leave a little baby homeless?

She signed the order with a flourish and handed it down to me. "Go get 'em, Tara."

chapter twenty-six

*T*emporarily Trans

"Why are you skipping?" Josh asked on the way back to the office.

"I can't help it!" I cried, executing a twirl on the sidewalk. "I might finally solve this case!"

Two men in business suits gave me odd looks as I skipped past them. *Dallas can be such a pretentious place.*

"I'm embarrassed to be seen with you," Josh said.

I skipped in a circle around him. "Get over it."

Back at the federal building, I returned to my office, scanned the search warrant, and sent the file off to Metroplex Mutual's legal department. Now they'd have no choice but to provide me with the names of their employees who'd had access to the subject files. Even if the guy tonight turned out to be legit, at least I was making progress.

Nick had to stay late at the office to finish some administrative paperwork that he, as the new codirector of Criminal Investigations, was now responsible for. He was concerned about me going out to the appointment without him. He frowned when I told him my plans. "You won't just have the potential target to contend with, you might be followed again. What if the two from Neiman's follow you to the rental house and confront you inside?"

"Chances are this will be another dead end," I told him. "I'll be in and out in five minutes tops. Besides, I'll have Josh with me."

Nick's grunt said what his mouth wouldn't. Josh, though brilliant when it came to technical matters, was not the most physically formidable agent in the office. He also wasn't as adept with his weapons as the rest of us. If I were being honest, I'd admit I wasn't thrilled with the arrangement, either. But under the circumstances, we didn't have much choice.

I reached out a hand to squeeze Nick's forearm in reassurance. "I'll watch my back. I'll be fine."

"You better be," Nick said. "Because if you get killed, I'm going to take Trish LeGrande as my date to your funeral."

"That skank?" I put my hands on my hips and glared at him. "Just for that I'm going to be *extra* careful."

He cut me a pointed look. "That was exactly what I was going for."

Josh and I rode in separate cars over to the property. As we drew near, I realized that, on the off chance the guy really was the one I'd given a ride to before, he might look out the window, see me or my car, and put two and two together. If he realized I'd been working undercover to nab him, he might bolt out the back door and disappear into the wind.

I hooked a right onto Inadale Avenue and pulled to the curb at the edge of Ferguson Road park, rolling my window down in the process. Sticking my hand out the window, I signaled Josh to get out.

Josh pulled in after me, climbed out of his vehicle, and walked up to my car, sliding into my passenger seat. His nose twitched and his lip quirked as he glanced around. "What is that godawful smell?"

"Wet dog and runner's sweat."

I'd wiped the seats down and hung a lemon-scented air freshener from the rearview mirror, but the stench remained. On the bright side, once you were in the car awhile, you no longer noticed it.

I shared my concerns with him. "I don't think I should be the one to speak with the leasing agent. If he turns out to be the guy I gave a ride to before, he might recognize me and realize it's too much of a coincidence that his Backseat Driver and the potential tenant are the same person. He might not even open the door."

"But he's expecting a woman," Josh said. "Sara Galloway, your alias."

"That's a problem."

Or is it?

I reached into my purse, whipped out my plum lipstick, and yanked off the cap. When Josh opened his mouth to question me I quickly coated his lips.

"What are you doing?" he shrieked.

"Turning you into a passable Sara. Hold still." I took out my mascara next and gave his lashes a couple of swipes. Finally, I reached out and fluffed his blond curls. Luckily for us, he didn't have a five-o'clock shadow.

He pulled down the visor and eyed himself in the mirror. Even he had to admit he could pass for female. An ugly female, but still passable.

He gestured to his chest. "What about this?"

I wadded up some tissue and stuffed it down his shirt.

He looked down and shimmied his shoulders ever so slightly. The balls of tissue slid down to his belly. "This isn't going to work."

"We'll have to make it work."

"How?"

Yeah, Tara. How? I thought for a moment, my mind going back to the big bazoombas on the woman at Neiman's. Were they real or fakes? I wriggled out of my blazer and tugged at the hem of my shirt, pulling it out of my pants. "Look away," I told Josh, pointing out his side window. Once his head was turned, I reached up under my short-sleeved shirt and unhooked my bra. I wriggled and wrestled and wrangled for a moment or two, and finally got the thing down to my waist. I held it out to him. "Put this on."

He eyed my bra as if he thought it might bite him. "You've got to be kidding me."

I wasn't kidding at all. Fortunately, Josh wasn't much bigger than me. "Do it." I thrust it at him and gave him a pointed look. My newly released nipples pointed at him, too.

He groaned but complied. As he took off his shirt and slid into the bra, I put my blazer back on.

"Yuck." He arched his back to put some distance between the bra and his skin. "It's warm and moist."

"A little boob sweat never killed anyone."

He tried to reach behind himself to fasten the clasps, but had no luck. He turned his back to me. "You're going to have to fasten it."

I pulled the straps, but Josh's chest was bigger than mine after all. I could get the ends within a couple inches of each other, but that's the best I could do. But I was nothing if not resourceful. I wasn't just the Annie Oakley of the IRS, I was the MacGyver, too. "Hold on a second." I fished a paper clip out of my briefcase and used it as an extender, sliding one end through the hook and the other through the eye. "There. That'll work."

Josh stuffed the tissue balls into the cups of the bra. When he finished, he wriggled again. The tissue stayed in place. Josh was now the proud owner of a pair of 32As. "This is uncomfortable," he complained. "It feels itchy and confining."

"That's why women rip their bras off the instant they get home from work. Welcome to our world."

He adjusted his breasts again. "I'll need to work on my voice."

Really, there was no need. He didn't have the most masculine voice to begin with. It was asexual. But no sense insulting the guy. "Let me hear what you've got."

"Hi," he squeaked, sounding like Minnie Mouse. "My name is Sara."

I shook my head. "Too fake. Bring it down a notch."

He tried again. "Hi," he said. "I'm Sara."

The voice still sounded fake, but maybe it's because I knew it was. "Take it down one more notch."

"Hi," he said. "I'm Sara."

"That's perfect," I said.

He scowled. "That's my normal voice."

"Go with the second one, then."

His disguise taken care of, he asked about the plan. "What do I do?"

"Snap a pic of him if you can and send it to me. See if he goes through the usual routine. If he asks for the money order, tell him that you can't do it right away. Tell him you don't have enough in your checking account and that your savings is at a different bank with no debit card linked to the account. Tell him the soonest you can get the money order to him is first thing tomorrow once the banks open. When he leaves the property, we'll nab him."

"Okay. Got it."

Josh returned to his car and we drove on. While I stopped a few houses down from the alleged rental, he continued on, pulling to the curb in front of the house. The driveway was empty.

No car. This fits the con artist's typical MO.

My nerves began to buzz again, my body alive with prebust jitters. I pulled out my phone and turned on my Backseat Driver app, tapping the button to indicate I was available to accept riders. After stashing my phone in my cup holder, I pulled out my field glasses. Through the lenses, I saw Josh knock on the door. With the bay window blocking my view, I couldn't tell who answered, but I'd see soon enough when Josh sent me the pic. Josh—*or should I say Sara?*—disappeared inside.

My cell phone chirped. It was the owner of the house returning my call. *Good.* "You said to call you about an urgent investigation?"

"That's right. I'm working with a detective from the Dallas Police Department on a rental-property scam."

"Rental scam? What do you mean?"

I explained how the scam worked. "I'm wondering about your house on Peavy Road." *The one I've got my eyes on at this very moment.* "Are you trying to find a long-term tenant for the property?"

"No," she said. "I only rent it out online for a few days or weeks at a time. I've got it listed on Airbnb."

"Do you have a property manager?"

"No," she said. "I handle the details myself."

Given that the house was an easy drive to the Cotton Bowl and fairgrounds, I surmised a lot of her business would be from people coming in town for football games, concerts, or the annual state fair.

"So you didn't hire a leasing agent named Cliff to find a tenant?"

"No."

Aha! I'd finally found the elusive guy. *Woo-hoo!* I did a sitting happy dance, rocking the car. Hey, I'd earned the right.

"Is someone renting the house now?" I asked.

"Yes. A man. He's got it for another week."

No doubt the place had been rented under the identity of another poor sucker whose name and social security number had been stolen from Metroplex Mutual's life insurance policy database. I still didn't know the name of the man who'd been stealing the data but, with any luck, in a few minutes I would.

I had to be careful how I handled things from here. The last thing I wanted was this woman driving out to the house to confront the con artist. We were in the middle of a sting and when the guy realized the jig was up, he could get violent. I'd hate for her to end up in the middle of things and get hurt, or worse. "I need you to agree that you will not go the property for any reason until I call you back and tell you it's okay. It could be dangerous for you."

"Okay," she agreed. "I'll wait to hear from you."

A few seconds after we ended our call, a text came in from Josh with a photo of the guy.

Suit? *Check*.

Eyeglasses? *Check*.

Tara Holloway's next bust? *Check, check, check!*

chapter twenty-seven

$\mathscr{H}$e Can Hide but He Can't Run

A few minutes later, Josh came out of the house, walking slowly to his car. He'd just reached it when *ping!* I glanced down at my phone. A notification had come in from Backseat Driver. A pickup was requested at Bishop Lynch High School. The campus sat only a couple of blocks away. The drop-off location was at an International House of Pancakes on Central Expressway, not far from the Village.

It's him!

I couldn't help myself. I giggled in glee. "Hee-hee-hee!"

I jabbed the button to accept the gig, started my car, and headed over to the high school. On the way, I phoned Detective Booth. "That leasing agent we've been after? My partner just met him at a house. He's requested a ride from Backseat. He's about to get into my car."

"Yesss!"

I visualized her pumping her fist.

"Should I drive him to the police headquarters?" I asked.

"He might figure out what you're doing and try to bail out," she said. "I'm still at HQ. I'll get an officer and a cruiser and we'll come after you."

I told her the route we'd be taking and gave her my license-plate number.

"Got it. See you soon!"

I phoned Josh. "Follow me," I said, "but keep some distance so a Dallas PD patrol car can get in between us. They'll pull me over and then we'll make the arrest."

"Got it."

The plan in place, I returned my phone to the cup holder and pulled to the curb in the fire lane in front of the school. As I waited, I kept an eye out for the guy, whose true identity I still didn't know. *Whoever you are, you're about to go down.* Sure enough, he emerged from the end of the block a moment later and began walking over. As before, he had his phone pressed to the side of his face.

I glanced down at his shoes. Yep, even from this distance I could tell the heels were higher than usual. This guy was a fraud in so many ways. I couldn't wait to bust his sorry butt!

He was twenty yards away when he stopped in his shoe-lift-enhanced tracks. *Crap!* Had he recognized my car? Was his con man's intuition telling him something was odd, that the same driver who'd picked him up before across town was picking him up now?

I willed him forward, sending telepathic messages to his brain. *Come on*, my mind said to his. *There's only so many Backseat Drivers in the city. It's not that big of a coincidence that you've taken a ride in this car before.*

The last thing I wanted was for him to bolt and me and Josh to have to chase him through a residential area. There'd been kids playing basketball in a driveway, others hula-hooping in a front yard, an elderly couple rocking on their front porch. I didn't want to put those people at risk.

When the guy made no move, I raised a hand to wave hello and offered what I hoped was a benign smile. Feigning nonchalance, I yawned, fluttering my hand in front of my mouth in a performance worthy of an Emmy. *The award for the best fake yawn goes to IRS Special Agent Tara Holloway!*

When he still made no move, my mind screamed at his. *Get your ass over here, you conniving crook! Now!*

He stepped forward, his mind bending to my will. *Neener-neener.*

He climbed into the backseat and closed the door. His nose wobbled on his face and he swiveled his phone upward, the microphone at eye level. A pointless gesture since nobody was really on the phone with him. "What's that smell?"

"Wet dog," I explained for the second time. "Sorry. I've tried everything I could to get rid of the stench but nothing's worked." I reached over the console and opened it, retrieving a snack and holding it up. "Fortune cookie?"

The guy cast me a strange look. "No, thanks."

As I pulled out of the high school's parking lot, the guy pretended to be engaged in conversation again, reciting the same limited set of conversational snippets as before. Once again, I filled in the other side of the conversation in my head.

Rider: That'll work.
Me: Me and Booth arresting you, you mean?
Rider: Mm-hm.
Me: Are you a total dumb ass?
Rider: Yeah.
Me: Is it okey dokey if we take you to the pokey?
Rider: All right.

As we continued on, my phone pinged. I plucked it from the cup holder and took a look at the screen. The jerk had already reviewed me on the Backseat Driver app. *Car reeks. I'll never use this driver again.*

That's right, you won't, I thought, fighting a smile.

I spotted a Dallas PD cruiser waiting on the shoulder of the freeway as we approached the Mockingbird exit. It took everything in me not to throw my head back and emit an evil laugh. *Mwa-ha-ha-ha!*

The guy must have spotted the cruiser, too. He turned to look at it, turning even more when he saw the cruiser turn on its lights and pull out behind us.

"Are you speeding?" he demanded, leaning forward over the seat to check my speedometer.

I glanced down at my dash as if doing the same. "Little bit. Oops!"

My gaze went to my rearview mirror. He'd lowered his phone, clutching it at his chest. For the first time, I could see the guy's full face, and the look of panic on it was priceless. *Ha!* Why not take advantage of the situation to screw with him a little? "This is my tenth ticket this year. I could lose my license. Hold on tight. I'm going to try to outrun the cop." I punched the gas. *Vroom!*

"No!" the guy shrieked. "You have to stop!"

"Jeez! Don't get your jockeys in a bunch." I eased off the gas pedal and applied the brake. "Think the cop will let me off if I slip him a twenty?"

"Don't do it!" He gripped his phone so tight it was a wonder it didn't break in his grasp. "You'll get arrested!"

"I don't know." I shrugged. "Maybe I'll get lucky and the cop will let me go with a warning."

He sputtered, his eyes wild. "This is going in my review!"

Oh, yeah? Bite me.

I pulled to the side of the road and stopped the car. The squad car pulled in behind us. A few seconds later, Josh eased by in his G-ride. When he glanced my way, I subtly acknowledged him by raising my fingers off the wheel.

A bulky, dark-skinned male officer climbed out of the cruiser and walked up on the driver's side. I unrolled my window. "Hello, Officer Sexy."

My rider unrolled the back window and looked up at the officer, too. "I'm not with her!" he cried. "I'm just a paid rider!"

The cop, who was in on the situation, fought a smile. "I understand, sir." He turned back to me. "You know how fast you were going back there?"

I scratched my head. "I'm guessing it was too fast?"

"You're a good guesser, ma'am." He held out his hand. "I need to see your license and insurance."

I retrieved my insurance card from the glove box and pulled my fictitious Sara Galloway license from my wallet, along with a twenty-dollar bill. I put the bill on top and held them out to the officer.

He eyed the bill before shooting me a wink with his left eye. "Are you trying to bribe me?"

"No, siree," I said. "Just showing my gratitude for your faithful service to the citizens of Dallas."

He took a step back. "I'm going to need you to get out of the car."

"Okay." I took the keys out of the ignition and climbed out of the car, closing my door behind me.

"Put your hands on the hood."

I stepped to the front of the car, turned, and put my hands lightly on the warm hood.

He stepped back to the open window and looked in at my passenger. "I'll need you to exit the vehicle, too, sir."

"Why?" the guy cried. "I didn't do anything! I told you, I'm just a rider! She's a driver with Backseat." He pointed to the yellow placard hanging from my rearview mirror. "See? I don't even know her!"

"No worries," the officer said. "It's standard procedure. Now step out, please."

The guy audibly fumed, but complied.

"Hands on the trunk," the officer said.

"Why?" He threw his hands in the air. "I didn't do anything wrong."

"Standard procedure," the officer repeated. "No worries."

Oh, this guy should be worried, all right. Luckily, he seemed to buy the explanation.

As my rider turned to face the car and put his hands on the trunk, Detective Booth emerged from the squad car and approached from behind.

My passenger must have seen her reflection in the back window. His eyes went wide and he turned his head. "Who are you?"

When she offered only a victorious smile in reply, he seemed to realize the whole thing was a setup. The officer reached for the guy's hand, but before the cop could cuff him, he took off running in the same direction we'd been traveling.

Dang it! We'd been so close to making an easy arrest.

With fruitless shouts of "Stop!" and "Get your ass back here!"—*the latter came from my mouth*—the three of us took off after him, our footsteps pounding on the pavement and competing with the noise of the cars rushing by on our left. One of them honked in encouragement. *Beep-beep!* I wasn't sure if the driver meant to encourage those of us in law enforcement, or the criminal attempting to evade us.

My rider had sprinted only a dozen or so steps when a rubbernecker inadvertently turned his wheel as he turned his head and nearly plowed the con artist down. He shrieked and jumped aside, leaping right out of his left shoe, leaving the loafer behind as if he were Cinderella running away from the prince's ball. He continued to run in a lilting gait, one leg three or four inches longer than the other with the special shoes and lifts. Up-down. Up-down. Up-down.

Though I was giving it my all, Booth and the police officer were both taller than me and had longer legs. They gained on the guy quicker than I could.

Booth grabbed at his jacket, but it was buttoned and there wasn't enough give in the fabric to get a real grip on anything. She went for his arm next, grabbing his elbow as his arm swung back. When he continued to struggle, trying to rip out of her grip, the male officer charged him, body-slamming him against the retaining wall. *Ouch.* That had to hurt.

Pop-pop-pop!

Small chunks of concrete fell from the wall just ahead of me. *What the hell?*

Pop-pop-pop!

YEE-OW! I felt a jab in my shoulder, like someone had stabbed me with an ice pick.

Pop-pop!

"I've been hit!" the cop cried, ducking.

"Me, too!" hollered Booth, putting a hand to her stomach as she fell to a crouch.

Luckily for the alleged leasing agent, the body slam he'd received had shielded him from the gunfire. Nevertheless, he screamed in panic and melted to the ground, his hands over his head to protect himself.

Grimacing in pain, I grabbed the guy off the pavement. "Get in the car!" I shouted. "If you know what's good for you!"

We hustled him back to the cruiser and dove inside, Booth and me in front, the officer and the leasing agent in back, and all of us with our heads down. The DPD officer had been hit in the upper back, right at lung level, and gasped for air. Even so, we'd been incredibly fortunate. All three of us had been hit in the torso, our lives saved by our ballistic vests. The gunshots hurt like hell, but they wouldn't kill us. At least not these gunshots. There was a chance the shooters could circle back and take another go at us.

Booth grabbed the mic for the cruiser's radio. Before pushing the talk button, she asked, "Did any of you see the car where the shots came from?"

"Not me!" I grunted out through the pain.

"Me, neither!" cried my rider.

The officer was in too much agony to speak, but he shook his head.

Booth pressed the talk button and shouted into it. "Shots fired at officers on Central Expressway northbound at Mockingbird exit! Backup needed! Send an ambulance!"

The three of us pulled our weapons and held them at the ready in case the shooters returned.

I also pulled out my phone and called Josh. "Any chance you saw the car the shooters were driving?"

"What shooters?" he asked. In other words, he hadn't seen anything.

"We took fire," I explained. "Someone shot at us while we were making the arrest."

"Holy shit!"

Holy shit, indeed.

We kept our heads down and, while I can't speak for the others, I'm fairly certain we all prayed. Fortunately, no further bullets came our way. The shooter probably realized additional law enforcement would be en route.

Backup arrived in less than two minutes and the officer, Booth, and I climbed out of the car, but not before taking a look around at the elevated overpass and exit ramps to make sure the shooter hadn't set up shop there, hoping to get a head shot in as we exited the cruiser.

When the leasing agent made to get out, too, I put up a

hand to stop him. "Where do you think you're going?" I
reached that same hand out to snag his wallet from his
pocket, then put the hand to his chest and shoved him back
against the seat. "Stay right there!" I hollered, my pain
making me extra hostile. I took advantage of the opportunity to poke the guy in the shoulder. *Yep.* Alicia had been
right. His suit had shoulder pads.

I opened the wallet and thumbed through the contents.
The guy had an assortment of credit cards and driver's
licenses in five different names from just as many states.
None were Texas licenses. I leaned down to the glass.
"Who are you?" I asked.

All I got in reply was a death glare.

He might not be talking, but we'd figure out who he was
sooner or later. I slammed the door in his face.

The officer jabbed his key fob to lock the guy inside.
Click. He tossed the keys to a backup officer.

Though Booth's wounds, like mine, were more super-
ficial, she climbed into the ambulance with the officer
who'd been shot in the back. She took his hand where it
lay on the gurney. "It's going to be okay." With that, she
raised her other hand in good bye to me as the medic closed
the door.

Josh circled back for me in his car, screeching to a stop
where the ambulance had pulled out only seconds before.
"Are you all right?"

"I will be after you get me to the doc."

Leaving my car behind on the shoulder, Josh drove
me to the medical clinic.

Kelsey glanced up as I entered, noting the fresh gri-
mace on my face. The ride over had been nothing short of
torture, my shoulder impacting the seat each time Josh
braked.

"Ooh," Kelsey said. "This one's bad, isn't it?"

"Gunshot," I grunted out.

All heads in the waiting room turned my way.

"It's okay." Kelsey held up a palm to reassure the other patients. "She's in law enforcement."

While Josh took a seat in the lobby, the nurse rushed me back to a room and brought Ajay to me right away. "You were shot?"

I nodded. "I'm wearing a vest, but it still hurts like the dickens."

He helped me out of my clothing. "Nice boobs," he said. "They're perky."

Damn. I'd forgotten that Josh was wearing my bra. "Just make the pain go away!"

"All right. Be forewarned, though. You're going to have a hell of a bruise come tomorrow."

Ajay fixed me up with another ice pack and prescription painkiller, giving me my first dose right there in the exam room. Soon, I was living in la-la land. And, *ahhhh,* what a lovely, wondrous place it was.

chapter twenty-eight

The Big Day

The time between the shooting on Central Expressway and the wedding seemed to pass in an instant.

Booth called me the morning after the shooting. "The guy still won't tell us who he is. His fingerprints were of no help, either. They're not on file." In other words, he had no prior record.

"Leave it to me," I told her.

Nick drove me over to Metroplex Mutual. The insurance company's attorneys hadn't yet had time to respond to the warrant I'd sent over the day before, but now that we'd made an arrest, it was probably a moot point. If we showed his photo around, surely someone here could tell us who the guy was. I'd brought the con artist's mug shot with me. While the HR staff couldn't readily identify the guy, they called in supervisors from each of their departments to take a look.

"I have no idea who that is," said the first.

The second said he looked "vaguely familiar."

The third nailed him instantly. "That's Caleb Beck," she said. "He works in my department. We process new applications for some of our larger clients. You know, major employers."

"Any chance he handles applications for A-1 Awnings, Bloomfield and Associates advertising agency, Glassen Incorporated, and EZ Autos?"

"He does."

Not anymore!

Nick dropped me at the Dallas Police Department, and Booth and I drove over to Beck's house to search it. It was sparsely furnished, making the job easy.

"Check this out," the detective called from his bedroom.

I followed her voice to find her crouched down in his closet, a gym bag in front of her. The zipper was open to reveal stack after stack of twenty-dollar bills, held together with red rubber bands.

"Wow! You found the mother lode."

She carried the bag to his coffee table and we took seats on the couch to count the stash.

When we finished, I pulled out my phone and used the calculator app to add it up. "There's over a hundred grand here."

She raised her hand and we exchanged a high five. The victims had lucked out. Beck had spent only a small fraction of what he'd taken in and saved the rest.

We confiscated Beck's computer and turned it over to Josh. He came to my office later that day with a handful of printouts.

I took the documents from him and quickly perused them. E-mails. Browser history. Bank records. I'd read through it all in more detail later, but for now I wanted the general gist. "What did you find?"

"Lots. Beck was the victim of a rental scam himself last year. He'd made a reservation at a place on the beach for him and his girlfriend. She dumped him by e-mail a day before they were supposed to leave for the trip. If that wasn't bad enough, he'd been turned down the week before for a better-paying job at the insurance company. He drove all the way down to the beach anyway, only to find out the rental listing was a scam."

Under normal circumstances, I'd feel sorry for someone who'd taken so many hits in quick succession. But this guy? Nope.

Josh went on. "He lost twelve hundred dollars in the rental scam and never recovered a cent of it. He filed police reports, did a lot of digging, figured out how the con artist had duped him and executed the scam."

I put two and two together. "So first he was angry, then he realized he'd learned enough to run the same con himself. He got greedy. If he couldn't make more money honestly, he'd make it dishonestly."

"Looks that way. It also looks like Beck planned to buy himself a cabin near a ski resort in Colorado once he'd swindled enough to cover the cost plus living expenses for a few years. He's run a bunch of searches for real estate listings in Vail and Aspen, prime vacation spots."

Between the fraud charges and resisting arrest, the only vacation Caleb Beck would be taking was to state prison. Three to five years, at least.

In addition to pulling evidence from Beck's computer, Josh accompanied me when I went to the young mother's apartment with a check for nearly the full amount of the deposit she and her husband had given the con man. Once again, she was wearing the adorable baby on her chest like a human corsage.

"Surprise!" I held out the check.

She took it from me and looked down at the numbers. "Oh, my gosh! This is amazing!" She pulled me into a hug, her baby squirming between us, happily gurgling and cooing. "We'll be able to get a house now!"

It hurt like heck when her arm pressed on my gunshot wound, but the pain was offset by how good it felt to be a hero.

While we'd wrapped up the rental-scam case, we still hadn't definitively identified the people who were after me. We'd reviewed the dash cam on my G-ride again, as well as the one on the police cruiser. Though we'd determined that the shots had been fired from a white Dodge Dart with two occupants, once again the lawbreakers had changed the license plates to untraceable tags, this set stolen from a Chevy Sonic in a shopping mall parking lot.

The Shreveport police had spoken with Leah Dodd and determined that, once again, she had no ironclad alibi. She claimed to have been at home alone napping around the time of the shooting, alleging that she'd never heard the officers knock on her door until they came back a second time hours later. Leah had voluntarily submitted to a gunshot residue test at that time and passed. But had she scrubbed her hands clean in the interim? We couldn't disprove her claim, and no arrest could be made.

Even with my would-be killer still on the loose, there was no way Nick and I would postpone our wedding. We'd put too much money and time into the event not to go through with it. Besides, who would be stupid enough to try to kill me at an event that would be attended by multiple armed members of law enforcement? In addition to us IRS agents, DEA Agent Christina Marquez-Maju would be at the wedding, serving double duty as a bridesmaid and bodyguard. Detective Booth had also offered to keep watch both at the church and the reception as a security measure.

Nope. No way would we let anyone ruin our big day.

The weekend of our wedding finally arrived. With so many people in town for the event, a good number of them armed federal law enforcement agents, whoever had been after me would have to be a fool to try anything here. Still, there were a lot of fools in this world. Even though we were nearly certain nothing would happen, none of us fully let our guard down.

Detective Booth sat sentry in a Dallas PD cruiser outside the church Friday night, and the rehearsal went off without a hitch. The church didn't catch fire. Nobody tried to knife me on the way down the aisle. Nick's truck didn't explode when he started it to drive the two of us to the rehearsal dinner afterward. I was beginning to think that the couple who'd threatened me had not only lost their minds, but had lost their nerve as well. Or maybe their bloodlust had been satisfied when they'd shot me, even if they hadn't killed me.

Given the large number of people who'd arrived on the party bus, our group packed the patio at the barbecue joint. Heck, nearly everyone who'd be at the wedding the next day was also at the dinner. The food was served, the keg of beer was tapped, and toasts were exchanged, the guests clinking their beer mugs. Tomorrow it would be champagne flutes, but tonight was all about casual fun.

Afterward, while many retired to their hotel rooms, a more intimate group drove out to my parents' place. Since it was a relatively small town, there weren't many venues for holding bachelor and bachelorette parties. Holloway Manor was just as good a place as any, especially now that my parents had put a new floor in the barn that would make it great for dancing, as well as adding a pool table, dart board, and a cornhole set.

While the men hung out in the barn and polished off another keg of beer, the women gathered in the living room with pitchers of Bonnie's peach sangria, bottles of wine, and an assortment of brownies, pies, and, of course, my mother's famous pecan pralines. We shared memories and laughs until well into the evening.

When the grandfather clock in the foyer struck midnight, we called it a day. After exchanging hugs with our guests in the driveway, Mom, Bonnie, and I headed inside to bed. I'd just finished washing my face and brushing my teeth in the bathroom when I heard the men come in downstairs. Looked like they were calling it a day, too.

I slid into the bed in my childhood bedroom, realizing it was the last time I'd sleep there as a single woman. A sense of melancholy covered me like the green and gold afghan my mother and grandmother had crocheted for me. How many nights had I lain in this very bed, dreaming about the man I would one day marry? I'd wondered what he would look like, what his name would be, what about me he would find appealing and what about me he might find irritating but tolerate anyway because he loved me enough to put up with my quirks and imperfections. Now I knew all of those things. His name was Nick. He had dark brown hair, gorgeous amber eyes, and the body of a modern-day warrior. He admired my intelligence, spunk, and tenacity, and he put up with my stubbornness, just as I put up with his in return. And while I was not a supermodel by any stretch of the imagination, he made me feel like the most beautiful woman in the world.

Sigh.

I feel asleep dreaming of tomorrow, of that walk down the aisle to my husband-to-be, of the warm, wonderful kiss that would seal the deal after Nick and I finally said "I do."

I woke on my wedding day to the sounds of birds chirping in the trees outside the window and the smell of coffee brewing and blueberry muffins baking in the kitchen downstairs. *Some things never change.*

I ventured downstairs to find Mom, Dad, and Bonnie already seated around the table, chatting. Mom looked up. "There's the bride!"

I gave her a smile and everyone a "good morning" before aiming for the coffee pot. Once I'd filled my mug and added some creamer, I slid into a seat at the table.

Bonnie gestured at the window over the sink, which framed a cloudless blue sky. "Beautiful day for a wedding."

"It certainly is." The sun was shining bright and nothing would darken my mood today. Not even that little niggle in the back of my mind that said maybe, just maybe, whoever wanted to ruin my big day was somewhere here in Nacogdoches, plotting and planning.

The timer dinged and Mom got up to pull the muffins from the oven. She fanned them with the pot holder to speed up the cooling process, then proceeded to pluck them from the pan to fill a breadbasket. As soon as she'd placed the basket in the center of the table, all of us reached for one.

"Save one for me," Nick said, stepping into the kitchen. He walked over and gave me a kiss on the the cheek, craftily stealing my warm muffin as I looked up at him.

"Sneaky." I wagged a finger at him and grabbed another from the basket as he plunked down into the chair next to me.

When Mom took her seat again, she nudged Bonnie. "You ask 'em."

Bonnie shook her head. "No. You do it."

"What?" Nick said.

Mom and Bonnie exchanged glances and fought grins. "Bonnie and I were talking earlier, and we were just wondering when you two might be giving us a grandchild."

"You already have grandchildren," I reminded my mother.

"I know," she said. "But none of them are *yours*."

Now I was the one fighting a grin. "Ours will be the best, of course." Everyone knew I was joking. In fact, I'd be thrilled to have a little girl just like my niece Jesse, who would be serving as our flower girl today.

Bonnie eyed Nick pointedly. "So? When? I'm not getting any younger."

Nick chuckled. "Let me and Tara get down the aisle before we start talking kids."

I turned to my father. "Ready to give me away?"

"Heck, yeah!" he replied. "You've been nothing but trouble since the day you were born. You'll be Nick's problem now."

We all shared a laugh, but immediately afterward Mom's face clouded in concern. "Speaking of problems—"

I silenced her with a raised palm. "No need to worry. Detective Booth will be in a cruiser keeping watch out front, and all of the agents at the wedding will be armed and on the lookout."

Dad nodded. "I'm bringing my shotgun, just in case. So are the boys."

Of course by "boys" he meant my two older brothers, who were well into their thirties.

Bonnie put a hand on my mother's shoulder. "I've got Tara's shotgun, too."

Nick draped a protective arm over the back of my chair. "I'll have my Glock on my hip as well. Besides, there will be dozens of people around. Anybody who'd try to pull any crap today would have to be an idiot."

I glanced his way. His eyes said things to me that his mouth hadn't said to my anxious mother. *The world is full of idiots.*

Yep, my eyes said back to him. *And if those idiots show up, we'll make sure they're sorry they did.*

My mother nodded and said, "Sounds like things are under control," but her face still looked tight and she barely picked at her muffin, eating only a few crumbs. I wasn't sure how much of her anxiety was due to the fact that someone might be after me and how much was normal mother-of-the-bride nerves. Either way, there was nothing more I could do about it.

Though the wedding wouldn't start until four o'clock, we all headed to the church at one so that we could get ready there.

Our church was old, having served God and his people of the Baptist persuasion for several decades now. The parsonage out back was a mobile home. While it might not be anything to brag about, the relative modesty of the property was offset by the ornate stained-glass windows, financed by a wealthy parishioner looking to leave a lasting legacy while generating a big tax write-off.

We checked in with Detective Booth, who had parked her cruiser sideways across three parking spots near the entrance to the lot, in easy view of anyone approaching the church.

"How's everything out here?" I asked.

"Fine," she said. "Nothing's caught my eye."

"Good," Nick said, his hand tightening protectively around mine.

Eddie, who would be serving as Nick's best man, stood waiting outside the double front doors. Josh, Hana, and Will waited with him.

After we'd greeted each other, Nick stepped closer to our fellow agents and spoke under his breath. "Seen anything suspicious?"

"No," Eddie said. "We walked the full perimeter but everything looks clean."

Hana chimed in. "Josh and I will do a sweep inside once they get the doors open for us."

"I'll keep another pair of eyes on the parking lot," Will said.

"Looks like we've got everything covered," Nick said.

He and I exchanged appreciative fist bumps with the others.

The church secretary pulled up a moment later and came over to unlock the double front doors for us. My parents and Bonnie walked up as she pushed the right door open and reached up to release the bolt holding the left door in place. "There you go. Pastor Beasley will arrive around three-thirty. I'll be in the church office if y'all need anything."

I thanked her and the woman turned to go. As she did, my mom reflexively reached out a hand to stop her. "Has everything been okay around the church the last few days?"

"Okay?" The woman's brows formed a puzzled V. "What are you getting at?"

I exhaled a sharp breath. "I've received death threats."

The brows that had just pulled inward shot up now. "Death threats?" she shrieked. "My goodness!"

I raised a palm to calm her. "I can't imagine whoever it was would drive all the way out here from Dallas to try to hurt me, especially with a hundred and fifty potential witnesses around."

"Maybe not," my mother said. "But better safe than sorry."

The woman's gaze shifted between my mother and me. "Nothing out of the ordinary has happened. Just business as usual. Baptisms. Funerals. Couples booking for next summer's wedding season. We had a lovely couple out here on Wednesday for a tour, new parishioners who just moved to the area."

"So things have been normal?" My mother's face relaxed in relief. "That's good to hear."

I had to agree.

All of us headed inside.

Nick and I parted ways in the foyer. The next time he saw me, I'd be in my dress. He gave me a kiss on the forehead and a smile. "See you at the end of the aisle."

The men headed toward the Sunday-school classroom to the right while Mom and I headed to the one on the left. The classrooms doubled as dressing and waiting rooms for the bride, groom, and attendants.

We entered the room to find the chairs stacked and the tables pushed back against the walls to maximize the space for dressing. The curtains on the windows and exterior door, which opened to the building's side lot, were closed for privacy, but the overhead fixtures would provide ample lighting for us to do our hair and makeup.

Mom and I pulled a few chairs down from the stacks and situated them at the tables. Alicia and Christina arrived as we were unpacking my makeup and rollers. "Hey, you two!"

After exchanging hugs, Christina unpacked the extensive makeup collection she'd brought. I'd never seen so many different shades of blush, eye shadow, and lipstick outside of a department store's makeup counter. *Ouch.* The mere thought had me thinking of my bruised nether regions and crossing my legs in phantom pain.

We took seats at the table. Christina angled hers to face me. She'd agreed not only to serve as a bridesmaid, but also to serve as my makeup artist today. She was a magician with a mascara wand and could do some truly amazing things with lip liner and eyeliner. No doubt she'd make me look gorgeous and glamorous.

She cocked her head to one side then the other, looking my face over, and set to work on me, using a fancy makeup sponge to apply and smooth my foundation. "I brought my weapon," she said as she ran the sponge over my cheekbone. "Just in case."

I had to laugh. "There will be nearly as many guns as guests at this wedding."

Her chocolate-brown eyes met mine. "Good. We don't want anything to spoil your day. You know, like your death."

"That would be a bummer, wouldn't it?" I teased.

Alicia unpacked the stiletto heels she'd chosen to wear with her matron of honor dress and brandished one of them. "I don't have a gun, but these spiked heels could take out an eye."

Even my mother laughed at that. I was glad to see that she was finally relaxing. She and my father had spent a small fortune to give me the wedding day of my dreams, and I wanted her to enjoy the day, too, not spend it worrying about my safety.

Christina finished the foundation and retrieved an extensive palette of eye shadow. "Close your eyes," she ordered.

A moment later, a soft brush whisked across my lids and I reflexively scrunched my face. "That tickles!"

"Be still!" she insisted. "I can't put makeup on a moving target. You'll end up looking like a clown."

I sat as still as possible for the next fifteen minutes while Christina carefully painted my face as if she were Leonardo da Vinci and I were the Mona Lisa. She took occasional breaks between working on me to work on herself, too.

When she finished, she held up a hand mirror. I took a gander at myself. *Wow!* The purple-hued shadow and thick gray liner made my eyes pop and my lips look full and lush and lustrous.

Mom beamed. "You look beautiful, hon!"

Alicia nodded in agreement. "Great job, Christina."

Her work done, Christina packed her makeup back into the case.

Our faces done, we spent the next half hour on our hair. Alicia tackled this task for me, carefully combing out sections of my hair, using a curling iron to turn the locks into curlicues, and piling the curls on top of my head, allowing a few to fall free. The look would be the perfect complement for my fairy-tale wedding dress. When she was finished, I handed her a can of the contraband Chinese extra-hold hair spray Lu had introduced me to months ago. The stuff rivaled any industrial-strength adhesive. A few passes with the spray and my beautiful coif would be immobile.

Pssssh. Alicia waved the can over my head, using her other hand to wave the fumes out of our faces.

I stood and clasped my hands in glee. "Time to put on our dresses!"

The wedding colors were light blue and lavender. My mother's lavender taffeta dress had a fitted bodice, a ruffled peplum, and three-quarter-length sleeves. The neck and hemline were adorned with small purple beads.

I gushed when she put it on. "You look like a movie star, Mom!"

Christina and Alicia agreed. "You'd be right at home on the red carpet," Alicia said.

Christina looked like a bombshell in her light blue satin off-the-shoulder number, and Alicia was the consummate sophisticate in her lavender dress with its jabot collar and pencil-type skirt. Yep, I'd let the two choose the dresses, asking only that they pick ones that came in the wedding colors.

After I slid into a pair of silky, sheer white stockings, Mom, Christina, and Alicia helped me into my wedding gown. The beautiful garment featured cap sleeves and a handkerchief hemline, along with a lacy, beaded bodice. It was the perfect dress for me, a blend of traditional, sparkly, and fun.

My "something new" was my dress. My something old was a pearl bracelet my favorite aunt had given me for my sixteenth birthday. I'd lent it to Alicia to wear as her "something borrowed" at her wedding back in June. She helped me secure the clasp around my right wrist. My "something blue" would be my bridal bouquet. And speaking of the bouquet, where was the florist? I glanced at the clock.

The flowers had been due a few minutes ago. They must be running a little late. But it was too soon to panic. Surely the florist would arrive soon to deliver the bouquets for us women in the wedding party, a corsage for my mother, boutonnieres for Nick and his groomsmen, and an arrangement for the altar.

All that was left was the shoes. I slipped my feet into the lacy heels and glanced back at my mother. She was temporarily distracted, hanging up the clothes she'd worn to the church. I took advantage of her inattention to grab my holster from my bag. I was probably being paranoid, but there was no harm in being safe, was there?

Christina noticed what I was doing and stepped between me and my mother to shield me from view. I slid it on under my dress, pleased to see that the lace and beads hid it quite well. I'd carry my bouquet low and use my arms to further cover the bump under my dress.

Fully dressed and discreetly armed, I stepped over in front of the full-length mirror mounted on the back of the interior door. Alicia, Christina, and my mother had all seen me in the dress before, if not in real life at least in photos, but nonetheless they gushed like a rain spout after a thunderstorm.

Alicia smiled over my shoulder at my reflection. "You look like you stepped out of a magazine ad!"

Christina nodded in agreement. "Nick's eyes are going to fall out of his head."

And while we were on the subject of eyes, "I'm going to cry!" That last statement came from my mother, who was fanning her misty eyeballs with one of our wedding programs less a tear escape and leave a rivulet in her makeup.

Knock-knock! A rap on the exterior door drew our attention. I stepped over and pulled the curtain aside to see who was at the door. It was a man wearing sunglasses and a ball cap. Behind him was a white van painted with the logo BUDS & BLOOMS, the florist my mother had hired. The guy had backed the van up next to the door. It was probably easier to unload that way. Fewer steps. One of the two back doors was open, an abundance of flowers visible inside the cargo bay. Hana, who'd been standing guard at the corner of the building, walked up with her hand resting on her weapon. She gave the man a once-over. The delivery man greeted her with a smile and the two exchanged words I couldn't hear through the glass. Whatever he'd said seemed to relieve Hana's concerns. She nodded and stepped back a foot or two.

"Who is it?" my mother asked.

"The florist." I pushed the door open. "Hi, there."

The tall man gave me a smile and craned his neck to take a look into the room behind me. He raised his hand in a wave. "Hello, ladies. I have a quick question for the bride. Y'all don't mind if I borrow her for a second, do you?"

The three murmured in agreement.

I stepped outside and the door swung closed behind me. With well over an hour remaining until the ceremony, the side lot was void of cars and guests. Hana, the delivery man, and I were the only people out here. But he obviously didn't pose a threat. Better to send Hana back to the corner to keep a lookout for real danger.

"It's okay, Hana," I told her. "We're good."

"All right," she said. "You look really pretty, by the way."

"Thanks!" I couldn't help myself. I twirled around in my dress.

The delivery man chuckled while Hana groaned and turned to head back to the corner. The man gestured for me to follow him the few steps over to the van. As I did, he reached into the van and pulled out a gorgeous bouquet of blue hydrangeas accented with white roses and babies breath. "Doesn't your bouquet smell wonderful?"

I began to lean in and my nose picked up an odd smell, a medicinal, chemical smell. *Wait. Something's not right here.* Before I could retreat, the man shoved the bouquet into my face and clapped a hand to the back of my head so I couldn't pull it away.

Holy crap! What's that smell? Chloroform? Ether? Oh, my God! Is this the same nerve agent that killed Kim Jong-nam?

I reached out to push him back but he jerked aside to evade my hands. I held my breath and whipped my head side to side trying to free my nose from the bouquet, but it was too late. I'd already breathed in too much of the stuff.

My knees melted. The world went fuzzy. My brain went woozy.

That fortune cookie had been right. I should've lived like I was dying. Because this man was going to kill me.

chapter twenty-nine

When Things Went South

The man was going to kill me. I'd been right about that. But at least he hadn't done it yet, and he didn't seem to have a definitive plan formulated yet, either.

Little by little, the wooziness oozed out of my brain and I became slowly cognizant of several things. One, I was lying on the cold metal floor of the flower delivery van, which was in motion and contained the cloying scent of various flowers. Two, my wrists and ankles were secured with duct tape, while another strip had been fixed over my mouth. And three, a man and a woman—probably the ones I'd seen at the football stadium and at Neiman Marcus when I'd gone for my fitting—were discussing the options for offing me.

Turds.

The woman made a suggestion to her male counterpart. "She doesn't weigh much. You could tie her to some cinder blocks and toss her off a bridge. The map on my phone shows two reservoirs within an hour's drive."

Though my mind was still horribly foggy, I knew she was right. The Sam Rayburn and Toledo Bend Reservoirs were an easy drive from Nacogdoches. As a high school girl, I'd worked at Big Bob's Bait Bucket and sold all kinds of worms to anglers heading for the water with their boats and fishing poles. But I had no interest in ending up like a worm, as fish food. I also had no interest in drowning.

The man seemed to have no interest in drowning me. No, his preference was something quick and easy. "Let's just find a big rock, hit her in the head, and leave her body out in the woods. By the time anyone finds her we'll be long gone."

Blunt force trauma? Not particularly the cause of death I wanted listed on my death certificate. I'd much prefer it say I'd died of natural causes after reaching my hundredth birthday and being immortalized by Al Roker on the *Today* show.

"All right," the woman said. "As long as she's dead, I don't care how it happens."

"We can get on State Highway 94 in Lufkin," he said. "That'll take us out to the Davy Crockett National Forest."

I knew that forest. We'd detoured through it once on our way to a family vacation in Galveston. It was thickly wooded and rarely visited. I could lie there for years before being discovered, or animals could scatter my bones. I might never be found.

Never.

Be.

Found.

As my mind finally cleared from the chloroform or ether, it began to fuzz again with panic. *These people are really going to kill me!*

Instinct told me to gulp in air, but my law enforcement training told me to slow my breathing. If I panicked, I'd do something stupid and have no chance of escaping this situation. Hell, with my hands and feet bound, I probably had no chance of escaping the situation anyway. But the high chance of failure wasn't going to stop me from trying.

I could feel my gun on my inner thigh. *Good.* They hadn't thought to frisk me. Not that I could really blame them. Who would think a bride would be wearing a holstered gun under her gown?

Immobilized by the tape, I knew I had to be crafty if I'd have any chance of getting out of this situation alive. I also realized I had to be careful, not let them know I was coming around.

My eyelids spread into barely perceptible slits and my gaze followed the voices. I determined that I was lying behind the driver's seat. The woman was driving. The seatback blocked any view of her. The man who'd come to the door of the church disguised as the florist sat in the passenger seat, occasionally glancing at the driver.

He cut a look her way. "It would've been so much easier if we'd been able to get to her at the Cowboys game. With that huge crowd we could've disemboweled her and slipped out before she even hit the floor."

Aha! So I hadn't been paranoid or crazy. They had been trying to get at me at the stadium.

My eyes moved to the cargo bay. Across from me lay the real delivery driver, a twentyish boy with a light beard. He was also bound and silenced with duct tape. Unlike me, he appeared to still be totally out. Or maybe he was dead. *Yikes!*

His upper body was bare, my male kidnapper having evidently stolen the shirt of his uniform. I locked my gaze on his belly and thankfully noticed it going up and down. *He's still breathing. Thank God!* I would've felt horrible if he'd been killed on my account.

While the man in the passenger seat was a complete stranger to me, the woman's voice sounded vaguely familiar. Still, I couldn't quite place her. Where had I come across her before?

I wasn't sure, but determining her identity was the least of my problems right now. At the moment, priority one was getting to my gun, and I couldn't do that with my hands stuck together. I had to get them apart. Fortunately, the kidnappers had taped my hands in front of me rather than behind me. *Amateurs.* They seemed to be flying by the seat of their pants. They'd have no way of knowing for certain that they'd be able to lure me out alone to the van at the church. They'd gotten lucky. I could only hope that their luck wouldn't hold out. After all, they might be amateurs, but it didn't take much skill to kill someone. Hell, people did it all the time, sometimes even by accident.

I could only wonder how long I'd been gone and what was happening back at the church. No doubt my mother was beside herself with worry. Christina, Alicia, Bonnie, and my father, too. Nick would be fearful and furious, ready to beat my abductors within an inch of their lives. Surely they'd put two and two together and realize the man posing as the florist's delivery driver had snatched me. They must've called the police and sheriff's department and told them to be on the lookout for a van with a florist logo. In fact, was that a siren I heard right now?

Yep. Sure enough, a *woo-woo-woo* sounded off in the distance, growing closer.

"Dammit!" the man cried. "They're coming up beside us!"

Thank goodness! I'd be rescued!

"Duck down!" the woman hollered back at the man.

A moment later, the siren sound came from right next to us. But a few seconds later it turned off entirely. The woman laughed a nasty laugh. "You can sit back up now. The deputy just waved to me and drove off."

Drove off? What the hell?

Looked like I'd have to rescue myself.

Moving my head slowly to avoid detection, I scanned the immediate area looking for something—*anything!*—I could use to sever the thick tape.

There was an arrangement of long-stemmed roses in a clear glass vase. Unfortunately, the thorns had been clipped from the roses. The thorns probably wouldn't have been up to the task anyway, even if I'd been able to grab a rose without being spotted.

I could see the roll of duct tape and a pair of scissors on the console between the seats, but if I reached up to grab the scissors there was no doubt one of them would notice. *Argh!*

But then my eyes spotted something. An exposed bolt on the frame of the driver's seat, holding the seat to the floor.

That could work.

My eyes spotted something else, too. The driver's shoes, an expensive pair of Jimmy Choo mock Mary Jane pumps. I'd seen those shoes before. But where? On whose feet? It was hard to think in my anxious state. The one time I'd seen Leah Dodd in person she'd been barefoot. Had she been wearing these shoes in a photograph I'd seen?

Slowly, slowly, I rolled with the movements of the van, shifting position until my body was angled more sideways across the space and my hands were within reach of the bolt. Through my slitted eyes, I saw the man glance back at me and do a double take when he realized I'd moved. I closed my eyes and waited, but he said nothing. Luckily for me, the van was heading south and the afternoon sun was streaming through the window on his side of the van, his seat casting me in a slight shadow, making it more difficult from his vantage point to see that my eyes had been open, though barely.

When I dared to take another peek, he was again facing forward, apparently having satisfied himself that my movements had been caused by the movements of the van as it went around curves on the country road.

I reached my arms over to the bolt and brought the tape down on it, pressing with all my might, hoping the bolt would puncture the tape and give me a starting point for ripping through it. *Harder, Tara!* I silently encouraged myself. *Push harder!*

The tape wouldn't give. It was strong. But not stronger than my will to live.

I lifted my hands and brought the tape down on the bolt again. This time I felt the tape give way. *Hooray!*

The bolt had made a hole through the tape. Now I just needed to rip it all the way to each edge. I worked my hands back and forth, back and forth, back and forth, keeping an eye on the man and pausing each time he turned to look at the driver or glance back at me.

I had nearly ripped to the edge of the tape when the man gestured at the window. "Lufkin city limits. Ninety-four should be coming up soon."

"Is there a Starbucks in this town?" the woman asked. "If we're going to have to drag a body back into the woods I'm going to need some caffeine."

"I'll check." The man tapped some buttons on his cell phone screen. "There's one off Highway 59 in the south part of town. It's a little out of the way."

"I don't care," she said. "I need an espresso and I need it now."

Having relied on caffeine to get me through late-night study sessions in college, the CPA exam, and many a stakeout while at the IRS, I could relate to her need for the performance-enhancing drug. And while I thought it was stupid of her to drag out my murder, her detour for coffee would buy me more time to work through the tape.

A couple minutes and a couple inches of torn duct tape later, I felt the van turn into a parking lot and circle around to the drive-thru. My hands were nearly free.

"Can you believe this line?" the woman said. "Why are all these people going for coffee at three in the afternoon?"

"I don't know," the man said. "Maybe they've got people in their trunks that they plan to kill."

The two shared a laugh.

That'll be the last laugh they share.

My hands were free, the man had leaned over to look at the menu board, and I seized the opportunity. In a split second, I reached down, lifted the hem of my dress, and pulled my Glock from the holster. My ankles still bound, I rolled to my knees, crouching behind the seat.

"I'll have a tall flat white with an extra shot," said the woman.

"Give me a mocha," the guy said. "Grande size."

"Will that be all?" called the disembodied voice coming from the speaker.

I stretched up and put my gun to the back of the woman's head, using my left hand to rip the tape off my mouth. It took my carefully applied lip liner and lipstick with it, as well as my first two layers of skin. *Ow!* "Turn around and you're dead."

Like the woman's shoes, her hair seemed familiar. It hung over her shoulders in loose coppery curls. The dark hair in the security footage from Neiman Marcus must have been a wig. *Is it Leah Dodd?* Only one way to know.

My furious eyes met her startled ones in the rearview mirror. But this woman had no lip mole. She wasn't the pole dancer. She was Marissa Fischer, the ex-wife of disgraced former pastor Noah Fischer. *Holy cow.* Those social media pics must have been faked, her alleged month-long Mediterranean cruise a ruse to throw me off her trail. The double-Ds she'd sported at Neiman's must have been faked as well, an attempt to implicate her ex-husband's illicit lover. *Clever.*

"Sorry," came the voice through the speaker. "I couldn't make out what you were saying."

I leaned toward the open window. "Add a tall skinny no-whip latte to that order."

"Got it," the barista said. "That'll be $15.63."

The man in the passenger seat tossed off his seat belt and turned toward his door in an attempt to escape.

"Stay in your seat!" I demanded. "Or I'll shoot!"

When he ignored my demand and grabbed the door handle, I shot out the window. *BLAM!* He and Marissa screamed as the sound echoed painfully inside the van and glass rained down on the asphalt outside.

Marissa reflexively floored the gas pedal in an attempt to escape. A dumb move. After all, I was in the van with them. It wasn't like she could drive away from me.

The front bumper of the van rammed into the back end of the pickup in the drive-thru lane in front of us. *Bam!* The man at the wheel looked back and raised a palm in a "why the hell did you just do something so stupid?" gesture.

Totally flustered, Marissa threw the gearshift in reverse and slammed back into the car behind us. She then attempted to turn the wheel to the right to exit the drive-thru lane. But with the cars lined up bumper to bumper, there wasn't enough room to maneuver. She was stuck.

"Turn off the van!" I ordered, nudging her shoulder with the barrel of my gun. "Now! Or I'll blow your head off!"

I had half a mind to blow her head off, regardless. *Try to ruin my wedding day, will you?*

She turned the key off, sat still for a moment, then grabbed her door handle and threw the door open, turning to leap out. The joke was on her. In her haste she'd forgotten to undo her seatbelt and was jerked back into place, but not before the door bounced off the stucco wall and tried to shut on her leg. "Ouch!"

"Hands up!" I hollered. "Both of you! Now!"

Realizing I meant business and that I had no intention of letting either of them escape with their lives, they raised their hands.

"Who are you?" I asked the guy.

"Darryl Lundgren," he muttered.

"Marissa's new husband? The one from the *Do Over* TV show?"

"That's me," he said resignedly.

No wonder the two had seemed vaguely familiar when I'd seen them at the Cowboys game and Neiman's. I shook my head. "The things we do for love." *Sheesh*.

As if my words had given him an idea, he cried, "Marissa made me do this! It's all her fault!"

"That's a lie!" Marissa screeched back, spittle spewing from her lips. "This was all Darryl's idea!"

The young man lying beside me squirmed, issued a cough and sneeze, and looked up at me, his bleary eyes slowly widening.

"Don't worry," I told him. "I'm a federal agent. You're safe now."

He wriggled into a sitting position, leaning back against the side of the van, blinking and taking deep breaths, trying to clear his head.

I held up the scissors in my left hand. "Hold out your wrists."

When he reached his hands toward me, I snipped at the tape, having a bit of a hard time given that I was using my nondominant hand. But I wasn't about to take my gun off Marissa and her cohort. I didn't trust them one bit.

I eventually cut all the way through and the boy pulled the tape from his wrists, tossing it aside. He pulled the tape from his mouth, his mustache and part of his beard coming off with it. "Shit! That hurts!"

I gestured to Darryl and Marissa with my gun. "What happened with these two? How'd you end up back here?"

"I was on my way to make deliveries," the boy said. "I stopped at a red light and an SUV pulled up next to me." He pointed to Darryl. "He got out and came to my window, and when I rolled it down he told me he had a gun and that I better do what he said or he'd shoot me. He told me to let him in and next thing I knew he'd taken my shirt and hat and taped me up. Then he shoved a stinky towel in my face."

No doubt that towel had been doused with the same chemical agent Darryl had used in my bouquet.

I handed the boy the scissors. "Get the tape off my ankles," I told him.

When he'd cut the tape off my legs, I glanced down. Luckily, the tape hadn't snagged my pretty stockings.

I turned to Darryl. "Where's your gun?"

"In Marissa's purse."

I grabbed her purse off the console and unzipped it, taking a peek inside. Sure enough, there was a handgun lying inside. I retrieved the roll of duct tape. "Lean forward," I told Marissa. "And put your hands behind you." When she did so, I told the boy to tape her wrists together. *Let's see how you like it, bitch.* When he finished with Marissa, I directed him to do the same with the man in the passenger seat.

Marissa's and Darryl's hands now secured, I jerked my head to indicate the back of the van. "Open the doors, please."

"Okay." The delivery boy made his way to the back to open them.

Once the doors were open, I backed out, keeping my

eyes and gun trained on Marissa and her coconspirator. My appearance surprised the driver behind us, who screamed and ducked down behind her wheel for safety when she spotted my gun.

I hopped out of the back of the van. "It's all right!" I called to her. "I'm a cop!" It wasn't the exact truth, but it was close-enough shorthand. I didn't have time to explain that I was a criminal investigator for the IRS. All I knew is that with all of the concealed-carry permits and the state law allowing people to carry guns in their cars, I needed to make sure everyone in the vicinity realized I was the good guy before they whipped out their weapons and smoked me right here in the drive-thru lane.

I glanced down at the front end of her car. The bumper had been knocked in on one side and sat askew, but it could have been worse.

I motioned for the boy to step out of the cargo bay with me. Once he had, I told our two kidnappers to get their butts into the back of the van and lie facedown. Marissa struggled to release her seat belt but finally managed. When the two were finally ass-up among the flowers, I turned to the delivery boy again. "Tape their ankles and mouths."

He climbed into the van and did as he'd been told. The gleam in his eye told me he enjoyed giving our two captors a taste of their own medicine. Heck, so did I.

When he finished, I said, "Take the wheel. I'm late for my wedding."

chapter thirty

Wedding Bells

As I circled around the outside of the van, I noticed that the florist's logo had been covered with a large magnetic sign that read FIRST UNITED METHODIST CHURCH. No wonder the deputy had abandoned his pursuit. He'd thought he had the wrong van.

A glance ahead told me the pickup had driven off. I supposed I shouldn't have been surprised. Gunfire tends to make people scatter. Surely he'd contact the police and would be able to get Marissa's auto insurance information once everything was settled.

After I climbed into the passenger seat and clicked my seat belt into place, the boy drove forward to the window and turned to me. "You still want your drink, right?"

"Heck, yeah. And Marissa's buying."

I reached into her purse and removed her wallet, handing the boy a twenty-dollar bill to give to the barista. He exchanged the money for the drinks. When the barista held out the change, I told him to drop it in the tip jar. Marissa and her former husband had ripped enough people off. It was time she showed some generosity.

The barista gave us a big smile. "Thanks!"

"Did anyone inside call the cops?" I asked.

"About what?"

"About the gunshot."

His eyes went wide. "Someone shot a gun?"

"I did," I said.

His eyes went wider and he slowly shook his head. "We can't hear anything in here when the machine's going. It's too loud."

"All right." I raised a hand in good bye. "Take care." I wasn't sure if anyone else had notified local police yet, but I wasn't going to wait around to find out. I had a wedding to get to.

The delivery boy pulled away and I took a sip of my latte. *Yum.*

"Got a cell phone on you?" I asked.

"Sure." He pulled one out of his back pocket and handed it to me. I debated calling local law enforcement to take Marissa and her partner in crime off to jail, but the wedding should have begun ten minutes ago and I didn't want to keep my wedding guests waiting any longer or delay the event and end up having time for only a short reception. I wasn't going to let anything, not even a kidnapping and attempted murder, ruin my wedding day.

While the delivery boy aimed for Nacogdoches, I dialed Nick's number.

He answered right away. "Hello?" His voice sounded frantic and strained.

"It's me."

"Tara?!?" he cried into the phone.

"I'm okay," I told him. "I'm on my way to the church."

"Where are you? What happened?"

"Remember Marissa Fischer? Pastor Fischer's wife?"

"Yeah?"

"Let's just say she's been holding a grudge."

"Good Lord!"

"I've got Marissa and her new husband in the back of the van they used to kidnap me." I told him their hands and feet were taped and they no longer posed a threat. "I'm bringing them back with me."

"I'll get a marshal out here for transport."

"Is everyone still at the church?"

"Your parents and the guests who came in on the party bus," Nick said. "Everyone else is out looking for you."

"Round 'em up," I said. "You and I are getting hitched."

We ended the call and I dialed my mother's phone.

Like Nick, she answered immediately. "Hello?" she choked out.

"It's me, Mom," I said. "I'm fine. I'm on my way back to the church."

"It's Tara!" she cried aloud, presumably to my father. "She's okay!" She returned to the line. "Where are you?"

"Lufkin. I'll explain everything when I get back there. Tell Dad to have his shotgun ready."

Half an hour later, we pulled into the church parking lot. While all of the wedding guests were gathered on the asphalt, at the front stood Nick, my family, Bonnie, Detective Booth, Pastor Beasley, and my coworkers. All of the agents had their guns in their hands, including Lu, while my father and brothers had their shotguns. My six-year-old niece Jesse stood next to my father in her lavender flower-girl dress and pink cowgirl boots, her Daisy BB gun clutched in her hands.

Nick ran toward the van but I raised my hand. "Stop! You can't see me in my dress until the wedding! It's bad luck!"

"Bad luck?" He threw up his hands. "Hasn't that ship already sailed?"

Maybe, but I wasn't taking any chances. "Close your eyes."

He grunted, but nonetheless indulged me and closed his eyes.

When I opened the door of the van, everyone else rushed over, wanting details. I stood on the running board and addressed the crowd. "Last year Nick and I arrested an unscrupulous pastor and seized his assets. I was the lead on the case. His ex-wife and her new husband decided to even the score by kidnapping and planning to kill me." I hiked a thumb. "They're in the back of the van. I'd appreciate if y'all could help me keep an eye on them until we can get marshals out here to haul them off."

Eddie, now dressed in his best-man tuxedo, circled around to the back of the van and opened the doors. Will, Hana, and Josh joined him. They grabbed my prisoners and pulled them from the van.

Hana cut an anxious look my way. "You told me things were all right when this van showed up earlier."

"Sorry!" I replied. "I thought they were legit. If they'd murdered me, I would've taken full responsibility for the mistake."

She rolled her eyes, but her shoulders relaxed. Looked like she'd forgiven me for almost getting myself killed.

My father stepped over and held out a hand to help me down. I took it, but before stepping down, I looked out at the crowd. "Let's get inside and get us married!"

While everyone scrambled to their places, my mother, Jesse, and my bridesmaids met me back in the bridal room. Christina stood in front of me and quickly repaired my makeup, while Alicia took a place behind me to fix the curls tossed about by the wind coming through the shattered van window on the drive back. A few minutes later, I was ready.

My mother gave me a hug, fresh tears welling in her eyes as she stepped back and took my hands in hers. "You're a beautiful bride, hon. I'm so glad you found Nick. You two are going to have a wonderful life together."

I blinked back the tears forming in my eyes, too.

"Thanks, Mom. Now don't say anything else or I'll start bawling!"

She smiled and released me.

We stepped out into the foyer to begin the processional. Once Bonnie and my mother were seated, Christina tossed me a smile, took the arm of Nick's cousin, and headed down the aisle. Alicia and Eddie, the matron of honor and best man, joined together next. Alicia blinked back happy tears on my behalf, while Eddie gave me a thumbs-up. The two of them headed into the church.

The ring bearer was one of Nick's second cousins from his father's side, a cute boy of eight with amber eyes like Nick's. He looked up at me expectantly. My heart pounded in excitement as I bent down and put a hand on his shoulder. I looked from him to Jesse. "It's y'all's turn to go now." I gave her a kiss on the cheek to send her off.

Jesse clicked the heels of her pink boots together and skipped away with her basketful of rose petals from the bushes at my parents' house. The ring bearer trotted after her. Though I couldn't see far into the chapel from my vantage point in the wings, I was able to see the back row where Marissa and Darryl had been seated. While Booth sat between my two kidnappers, my brothers sat guard on either side of them, their shotguns on their laps. Jesse stopped at the back row, grabbed a handful of petals, and hurled them in Marissa's and Darryl's faces. She followed up by sticking her tongue out at them.

Standing next to me, Dad shook his head but smiled. "Your mother's right. That girl's got your spunk."

Having put my kidnappers in their place, Jesse continued down the aisle, offering the rest of the guests an adorable, gap-toothed smile as she and the ring bearer made their way to the front, leaving a trail of rose petals in their wake.

The organ music shifted, signifying my entry. My father

offered me his arm. "I never thought I'd be willing to give my little girl away," he said, "but I know I'm putting you in good hands, the hands of a man who loves you nearly as much as I do." His mouth turned up in a soft smile.

"Oh, Dad!" I said on a sigh as I slid my arm through his. "You and Mom are bound and determined to make me cry, aren't you?"

He chuckled and the two of us stepped into place at the end of the aisle.

The guests rose from the pews. Well, all but Marissa and Darryl, who couldn't stand with their ankles taped together and weren't invited guests anyway. As we headed up the aisle, I glanced left and right, meeting the happy gazes and supportive smiles of the people who meant the world to me.

My brothers who'd both tormented me and looked out for me, now watching over the man and woman who'd tried to end my life. My brothers and I might have driven each other crazy as kids, but I wouldn't trade the two of them for anything.

Neighbors, former classmates, and other assorted people from Nacogdoches, some of whom I hadn't seen in far too long but with whom I reconnected on special events like today. Clara Humphreys, a nice woman who shared a little too much information about her ailments but who'd always brought her car to the high school volleyball team's car wash fund-raisers and left us with a generous donation. Big Bob, my former boss from Big Bob's Bait Bucket, who'd ironed his jeans and shined his best boots for this fancy occasion. Miss Cecily, who ran the charm school my mother had sent me to so I'd learn manners and social graces and how to behave in polite company.

Next were the people I'd met working the various cases over the last year and a half. The Pokornys who ran the Czech bakery. Bernice and Merle from the dinner theater.

Madame Magnolia, the seer, who held up a crystal in each hand and softly murmured a chant as Dad and I walked past. My guess was the gesture was some sort of spiritual blessing or good-luck ritual. Benedetta Fabrizio and her three beautiful daughters. Judge Trumbull, U.S. Attorney Ross O'Donnell, and my former defense attorney, Anthony Giacomo, among others.

Then there were my coworkers, of course. My boss Lu, who'd teared up and was dabbing at her false eyelashes with a tissue. Next to her was her boyfriend Carl in his standard comb-over and leisure suit, along with his shiny white bucks. Hana, Will and his wife, Josh and Kira. Viola had come along in the party bus, too.

Sitting just before the rows reserved for family were Christina's husband Ajay and Alicia's husband Daniel. I was glad my two closest friends had found such wonderful men to share their lives with.

Finally, of course, came my family and Nick's. Well, other than my brothers, of course, being that they were on guard duty at the back of the chapel. My sisters-in-law smiled at me, as did my nieces and nephews. Bonnie gave me a warm smile from the groom's side of the aisle as we approached. My mother did her best to smile, too, though her lips wriggled with restrained emotion and her eyes were moist.

Eventually we reached the front of the church, where my dad shook Nick's hand, released me, and stepped back to take his place beside my mother on the front row. Nick looked down at me, his amber eyes aglow. He ran his gaze up and down, taking in me in the dress. "Wow," he whispered.

I ran my gaze over him in return. While I loved how Nick looked in his usual western shirts, jeans, belt buckles, and boots, he looked unbelievably handsome in his classic black tuxedo, too. "Wow, yourself," I whispered back.

Pastor Beasley, a short, stout man with thick salt-and-pepper hair, stepped up to the podium to begin the service. "Dear friends and family, we are so glad you all could gather here today to celebrate the marriage of Tara Holloway and Nicolas Pratt. While I've only recently had the pleasure of meeting Nick, I've known Tara since she was knee-high to a grasshopper and winning the biggest prizes at the shooting booth at the church carnival. Frankly, I was afraid she'd scare the boys off. I wasn't sure there was a man on this earth who could handle a girl like her." When the crowd finished laughing, he gestured to Nick. "I'm glad to see I was wrong."

Nick cut his eyes my way and slid me a grin. I slid him a grin right back.

The pastor launched into the usual niceties about what marriage meant, the union of two lives, etc., etc., blah-blah-blah. Already bored, the ring bearer started a subtle pillow fight with Jesse, gently swinging the small satin pillow and bopping her on the rear end. It was an unfair, one-sided fight given that she wasn't properly armed with a pillow of her own. But like me, the girl was resourceful. She upended her flower girl basket and pulled it down over his head like a hat. Fortunately, before things could get too out of hand, Alicia intervened, separating the two.

My niece Olivia, who was the star of her school choir, came to the front of the church with her guitar and sang a beautiful solo for me and Nick, her own special rendition of Shania Twain's "Forever and for Always". Before she left the altar, I waved her over to give her a hug. "That was perfect," I whispered. "Thank you." *Taylor Swift better stay on her toes.*

Finally, Pastor Beasley asked the million-dollar question. "If there's anyone who knows any reason why these two should not be wed, let them speak now or forever hold their peace."

A muffled sound came from the back row, an irate, red-faced Marissa making a last-ditch attempt to lambaste us but being thwarted by her duct tape. "Mmf! Mm-mmm-mumm-mf!" When my brother Trace nudged her thigh with the butt of his shotgun, she slumped back against the pew and went quiet.

It was now time for Nick and me to exchange vows and rings. We turned to each other, taking each other's hands and looking into each other's eyes. Nick shot me a wink, and I shot him one back.

Nick was the first on the hot seat. The pastor turned to him, reciting the vows, which Nick repeated. "I, Nick, take you, Tara, to be my wedded wife. To have and to hold, from this day forward, for better and for worse, for richer and for poorer, in sickness and in health, to love and cherish, forsaking all others, until death do us part."

I was up now, and reflected the same vows back to him.

Pastor Beasley turned to Eddie. "May we have the rings?" Nick had given them to his best man. A good idea since we obviously couldn't even trust the young ring bearer with a pillow.

Eddie stepped forward and handed the rings to the pastor, giving me a warm smile as he stepped back into place.

The pastor led us through the exchange of rings. When Nick slid the ring on my finger and looked into my eyes, it was all I could do not to burst into tears of joy. His voice was strong and full as he said, "With this ring, I thee wed and pledge my life to you. Wear it as a symbol of our love and commitment."

My ring now on my finger, the pastor handed Nick's ring to me. I slid it onto his finger and repeated the vow. "With this ring, I thee wed and pledge my life to you. Wear it as a symbol of our love and commitment."

We turned back to the pastor, who looked from one of us to the other. "Y'all want to seal this deal with a kiss?"

"Heck, yeah!" Nick grabbed me, bent me over backward, and planted a big warm kiss on my laughing lips. When he pulled me upright again, he gave me a nice, proper kiss. I wrapped my arms around him and pulled him close for a long, warm hug. *He's all mine now. I never want to let go.*

"Beloved guests," Pastor Beasley called out, sweeping his hands to indicate me and Nick, "May I present for the first time as husband and wife, Mr. and Mrs. Pratt!"

The crowd clapped, whooped, and whistled with congratulations.

Nick led me back down the aisle, but even though my feet hit the floor, it felt as if I were floating. *I'm Mrs. Tara Pratt!*

We walked outside the church to find marshals waiting by a squad car, ready to take Marissa and Darryl into custody.

"Congratulations," said one.

The other nodded and added, "Hope they didn't spoil your wedding."

"Nope," I replied. "Nothing could."

Nick hiked a thumb back at the church, where our guests were beginning to stream out. "A detective from Dallas and Tara's brothers are holding the two in the back row. Just so you're not surprised, her brothers are armed with shotguns."

The first marshal shook his head. "This gives new meaning to the term 'shotgun wedding.' "

He could say that again.

We continued on to Nick's truck, where he helped me in. He circled around to his side and climbed in. Though he slid the key into the ignition, he didn't start the engine. Instead, he turned to me. "An hour ago I feared I might never see you again. And now you're my wife."

"Crazy, huh?"

He smiled softly. "I don't know what life might throw

our way, but there's one thing I'm certain about. Life with you will never be boring."

I smiled back at him and leaned over for another kiss.

We headed out and, a few minutes later, turned off the county road and onto my parents' long drive, which Mom had marked with paper wedding bells and white streamers to make it easy for our guests to find. We parked in front of my parents' house and headed for the large tent that had been erected near the barn.

Everything looked perfect. The tables were covered with lavender and light blue tablecloths and featured centerpieces with cala lilies and purple asters. The caterers had set up a buffet along the back of the space and had the Southern supper spread ready to go. They'd made many of my mother's and Bonnie's best recipes. Chicken-fried steak. Fried okra. Cornbread. Even my latest favorite, sweet potato fries.

A well-stocked bar stood angled in the front corner, two bartenders ready to serve anything from wine to whiskey. An ice-cold keg was situated nearby for those who preferred a cold brew.

My parents and Bonnie arrived shortly after Nick and me, and the five of us formed a receiving line outside the tent to welcome the guests to the reception.

Eddie, his wife Sandra, and their adorable twin daughters were among the first to arrive. The girls squealed when they spotted the five-layer, four-feet-tall wedding cake towering on a table in the center of the tent.

"It's so big!" cried one.

"I want a cake like that when I get married!" exclaimed the other.

My mother and Bonnie, who'd baked and decorated the cake themselves, bent down to address the twins. "You just let us know the date," Mom said, "and we'll make you a cake exactly like that one."

The party bus pulled to a stop on the grass and the occupants disembarked one by one, beginning with Lu and Carl. They came over and Lu enveloped Nick and me in a group hug.

She stepped back, but held on to our hands. "I couldn't be happier for you two."

"Thanks!" We couldn't be happier, either.

Josh and Kira stepped up a moment later. While Josh wore a standard navy suit, Kira's wedding attire consisted of a pale pink minidress with black fishnet hose and black army boots. She'd changed her usual silver nose ring for a sparkly one for the event. The two made an odd but solid match.

I greeted them with a smile. "So glad you two could make it to the wedding!"

Kira shook her head. "So glad *you* made it. It would've sucked if the wedding had turned into a funeral."

Indeed.

Anthony Giacomo sauntered up, a red and white polka-dot pocket square peeking out of the pocket of his black suit. "That was quite a wedding," he said as he air-kissed both of my cheeks. "I've never been to one that involved a kidnapping, attempted murder, and shotguns before."

"I'm glad you were a witness to us driving up with Marissa and Darryl in the van," I teased. "That means you can't represent them." *Thank goodness. The guy could get just about anyone off the hook.*

He chuckled. "Oh, honey. I'd never represent anyone who tried to kill my all-time favorite client. Now where can I get my hands on that watermelon martini you promised me?"

Nick gestured to the bar. "Right over there, buddy."

He wagged his fingers. "See you later on the dance floor."

Bernice and Merle walked up next. Bernice, always

elegant, had worn a shimmery golden dress that showed off her well-preserved curves. Merle beamed, proud to be seen with the woman he'd pined over and finally landed after decades of being hopelessly in love with her. "Your wedding gave us an idea," Merle said. "We're going to host a murder-mystery dinner at the theater."

I couldn't help but laugh. "Glad my near-death experience could be of some use."

Our other guests swept by in a current of congratulations and best wishes and handshakes and hugs. Madame Magnolia was the last in line. She put a hand on my shoulder, her many bangle bracelets jingling. "I warned you that your wedding day would be chaos."

I dipped my head in acknowledgment. "That you did."

She waved a hand as if waving away any bad juju that might still be clinging to me. "Do you want to know what I see for the rest of your life?"

I glanced at Nick. With him by my side, I knew the rest of my life would be happy, no matter what. I turned back to the fortune-teller. "I think I'd rather be surprised."

She smiled and nodded knowingly. "As you wish."

The dinner was delicious. Afterward, we cut the cake. Each layer was a different flavor. Vanilla. Lemon. Strawberry. Italian cream. Hazelnut. Nick shoved a bite of hazelnut into my mouth, while I shoved a bite of Italian cream into his. We cut into the groom's cake next. It was chocolate both inside and out, and shaped like a football with a blue and silver Dallas Cowboys star in the middle.

Once everyone had a slice of cake and a glass of champagne, the toasts began, each more heartfelt than the next.

Eddie went first. Of course he seized the opportunity to razz me a bit. "I've been partners with both Nick and Tara on various cases over the years. Tara always seems to get her partners into trouble. Now she's dragged Nick into this mess." He shook his head in jest before grinning. "But it's a fine mess. A long and happy life to you two!"

We all clinked glasses and sipped our champagne in accord.

Alicia took the mic. "Tara and I have been best friends since our college days, and we've been through a lot together. When she first met Nick, she went on and on about how handsome he was, how ripped, how smart. She even said he was nearly as good a shot as she is. That's when I knew he was 'the one.'" Champagne flute in hand, she made air quotes with her fingers before turning to me and Nick. "Now you two have become one, no longer eligible for single filing status. I wish you many happy years of joint tax filing."

Clink! We took another sip of our champagne.

My father rounded things out, his arm around the shoulders of my mother, who stood beside him. "When Tara told her mother and me early last year that she was leaving the CPA firm to become a criminal investigator for the IRS, we had some reservations. We were worried about her safety, what kind of elements she'd be dealing with. Little did we know that she'd find her purpose in life at the agency, as well as a man so well suited for her. She followed her heart and it led to Nick. We couldn't ask for a better husband for our daughter, and we're proud to call Nick our son-in-law." He raised his glass. "To the happy couple!"

There were more clinks and more sips.

A few minutes later, when the champagne flutes were empty and the cake had been reduced to crumbs, we moved en masse to the nearby barn. A local band that played regularly at a honky-tonk down the road had set up and were ready to go. It was the very band that had been playing the night Nick and I stopped at the roadside bar, the band that played the first song we'd ever danced to.

And now they'd be playing the first song we danced to as husband and wife.

But first was the father-daughter dance. My father had chosen to have the band play "I Loved Her First" by Heartland. He led me out onto the floor while our guests gathered around the perimeter. We both got misty at the lyrics, which spoke of a father's love for his daughter, how even though he'd hoped she'd find a good man, it was still hard to give her away.

"Well, hell," Dad muttered, looking down at me as a tear ran down his cheek. "I'm crying right here in front of God and all these witnesses."

One ran down my cheek, too, and we reached out with our thumbs to sweep the other's away.

At the end of the song, Dad twirled me over to where Nick stood and gently handed me over. Nick grabbed my father in one of those manly half hugs. "Thank you, Harlan."

Dad made a choking sound and squeaked out, "I need a beer."

Everyone poured onto the dance floor, including Jesse and the ring bearer, their earlier playful spat forgotten. The band played some fun, raucous country songs intermingled with line dances, the Cotton Eyed Joe, the schottische, and the Chicken Dance. Nick requested they play their rendition of Luke Bryan's "Country Girl (Shake It for Me)," dedicating it to his bride, me. During the breaks, we played recorded pop hits. Everyone kicked up their heels and had a hell of a time. Nick and I had the time of our lives. I felt like a princess, twirling in his arms, and I never wanted tonight the end.

As midnight approached, the single women gathered around to see which of them would be next down the aisle, as predicted by my bouquet.

"Ready?" I called back over my shoulder.

"Ready!" they called back.

I tossed the flowers up and back, turning just in time to see Jesse leap into the air as high as her little pink boots would allow. Her tiny hand grabbed the stems and she pulled the bouquet out of the air.

My thirty-three-year-old cousin put her hands on her hips. "Darn it! When's it going to be my turn?"

Jesse, meanwhile, ran after the ring bearer, who'd taken off in fear that Jesse might force him into marriage right there on the spot.

Nick brought me a chair and I sat down so that he could ease the garter off my leg. He reached up under my dress. "Is that your holster I'm feeling?"

I'd forgotten I was still wearing the thing. "Yep."

His fingers felt around some more and he located the garter, pulling it down to my ankle. He slipped my foot out of my heel to remove it, then put my shoe back on my foot.

"Okay, fellas," he called as he stood. "Let's see which one of you bites the dust next."

He turned to face me while the single men gathered behind him. He tossed the garter over his shoulder. Josh snatched it out of the air and held up the prize, a big smile on his face as he turned to Kira. Would the two of them be the next couple down the aisle?

Later, Nick and I found our mothers at their table with their feet up. It was no wonder they were exhausted. They'd poured their hearts and souls and sweat and tears into this event, and it had come off without a hitch. Well, no hitches other than Marissa Fischer and her husband kidnapping me with the intent to end my life. But all's well that ends well. And once I'd returned to the church, the wedding and reception had been beautiful and wonderful and everything I'd always dreamed they would be.

I wrapped my arms around my mother while Nick did

the same with Bonnie. "Thanks for everything, you two. You really outdid yourselves."

Mom patted my shoulder. "Glad to do it, honey, though we could use a vacation about now."

"She's right," Bonnie agreed with a mischievous grin. "How about we go down to Mexico with you on your honeymoon?"

Nick stood bolt upright. *"¡Dios mio!"*

The band played one final song, Willie Nelson's "The Party's Over." Alicia, Christina, and various others who'd been recruited by my bridesmaids passed out confetti poppers to the guests and instructed them to line up outside. Once everyone was in place, Nick and I proceeded out of the tent and down the row, smiling and bidding good-bye to everyone who had helped make our wedding day so special. As we headed along, we were sent off by the *pop-pop-pop* of the strings being pulled on the poppers and a shower of confetti raining down on us.

Finally, we reached Nick's truck. Hearts had been drawn on both the driver's and passenger side windows, and the words JUST HITCHED! were scrawled across the back window in white shoe polish. Tied to the back bumper were a dozen empty Lone Star beer cans. If I had to hazard a guess, I'd say my two brothers had volunteered for the job of emptying those cans.

Nick opened my door and held out a hand to help me in. "Your chariot, Mrs. Pratt."

Once I was in, he closed my door and circled around to the driver's side, sliding into his seat. He started the truck and rolled down the windows. He beeped the horn and we waved out the windows while our guests hollered good-byes and final good wishes after us.

We spent the night at a romantic, secluded cabin just outside of town. Nick scooped me up and carried me over the threshold, not wasting a second before taking me to the bedroom to consummate our marriage.

The following morning we returned to my parents' house, where we opened our gifts. Many were things from our registry. Place settings. Silverware. Stem glasses. But a few of the gifts were more unusual.

Miss Cecily had given us the latest edition of the Emily Post primer on etiquette. Miss Cecily refused to give up on me, even though I repeatedly broke every rule of decorum she'd taught me in her charm school.

Big Bob had given us a gift certificate to the Bait Bucket. Nick threw a fist in the air. "Woo-hoo!" I would've preferred a picture frame or candlesticks, but the gift certificate was preferable to the bucket of worms I'd half expected my former boss to show up with.

Christina and Ajay had given us a fancy poker set, complete with chips and a green felt table cover. It was the perfect gift from the two of them. Christina and I had played Texas hold 'em with Ajay and the drug-dealing ice-cream man we'd been after on our first case together. I felt a tug at my heart. *They remembered.* Their card wished us well, the handwritten note appointing me and Nick as the official hosts of a monthly couples poker game.

Alicia and Daniel's gift was an elegant Waterford crystal clock that was sure to become a family heirloom. I made a mental note to put it someplace where Henry couldn't knock it down.

The gift from Bonnie and my mother brought tears to my eyes. They'd taken old clothes from my childhood and Nick's, cut pieces from them, and patched them together to make a quilt that represented the joining of our lives.

I ran my hand over a square. "This was my volleyball uniform in high school."

Nick pointed to another. "My peewee football jersey." And another. "High school football jersey."

We identified the other squares. The dress I'd worn to my graduation from Miss Cecily's charm school, complete with the grass stain from my wrangling with one of the barn dogs when we returned home afterward. A square from the curtains that hung in my bedroom back home. Pieces from our high school and college graduation gowns. A piece from the necktie Nick had worn on his first day of work after college. In the center was a small circle, a piece that had been trimmed from my wedding gown.

My throat was tight with emotion. "Mom must've made arrangements to get this from the seamstress at Neiman's."

Nick misted up a little, too, though he'd never admit it. He coughed to clear the lump in his throat and merely said, "Cool." But I knew better. He was as touched by this special gift as I was.

That afternoon we drove back to Dallas, where we said quick good-byes to the cats and Daffodil, reminded them to behave for Bonnie, who'd be babysitting them while we were gone, and grabbed our packed suitcases to head for the airport.

As we waited for our flight, I received a call from the marshals who'd arrested Marissa and Darryl yesterday. "An SUV had been left overnight in the parking lot of a women's boutique located only half a block away from the floral shop. The boutique's owner thought it was odd and phoned the local police. They discovered the license plates had been swapped out. They were able to identify the car by the VIN number. It belonged to a car rental agency in Dallas and had been rented by Darryl on Tuesday morning."

This information confirmed the story the delivery guy had told me.

"The church secretary identified Marissa and Darryl as the couple who'd toured the church on Wednesday. They'd scoped the place out under the guise of wanting to hold their wedding there. They both talked after they were arrested. Each tried to lay all of the blame on the other. Marissa claims the idea of commandeering the florist van and using it as a ruse to kidnap you was all Darryl's idea. He's saying the idea was hers. Either way, they're both guilty of kidnapping and conspiracy to murder a federal agent."

In other words, Darryl would soon be joining Marissa's ex-husband in prison while Marissa took a nice vacation at the women's correctional facility.

The marshal went on. "Beyond that, it looked like they were making things up as they went along. They were prepared to kill you any way they could. There were all kinds of things in the car. Binoculars. Rope. Rat poison. A pickaxe and a sledgehammer."

The two had evaded capture all this time through an odd mix of dumb luck and creative genius. Still, none of this told me their motive. "My investigation into Noah Fischer ended Marissa's marriage to the pastor, but she went right on to find another rich husband. By all accounts the two have been living high on the hog. Why come after me?"

"Because she had a good thing going until you came along. That 'other rich husband'? He filed for bankruptcy last month."

"Really?"

"Really. Marissa spent every cent he had and then some. He couldn't seem to tell her no. He had to borrow money from his family to hire a defense attorney."

"Sheesh." She had some nerve blaming me for her and her husbands' bad decisions. But I supposed it beat blaming herself. The profiler from Dallas PD had been right. My pending nuptials must have set Marissa off. Her marriages had been rocky, her life troubled, and the thought of me enjoying a happily-ever-after was too much for her. As far as her new husband was concerned, while he might not have been able to tell her no when it came to luxuries, he should have drawn the line at committing murder for her. That took devotion to a whole new level.

"With all this evidence," the marshal added, "those two won't be getting out of jail any time soon. You and Nick enjoy your honeymoon."

"We will. Thanks."

Soon my husband—*my husband!*—and I were in the skies over the Gulf of Mexico, plastic cups of wine in our hands as we soared toward Cancún.

Our honeymoon was both fun and romantic. We spent most of our time on the beautiful beaches, where we romped in the waves, snorkeled, and took a boat tour. We visited both Coba and Tulum, archaeological sites featuring ancient Mayan ruins. We ate *muy deliciosa* Mexican food and drank our body weight in margaritas. Nick showed me where he'd lived when he'd been in forced exile. It was a nice building in a gorgeous place, but knowing he was under constant surveillance by Marcos Mendoza's henchman—or hench*hombres*—Nick had essentially been imprisoned in paradise.

He looked wistfully up at the windows of his place. "I never knew when I woke in the mornings whether that day might be my last."

I encircled his waist with my arm. "I know the feeling."

He looked down at me. "We're crazy to do what we do, aren't we?"

There was no denying it. "Little bit. Yeah."

On our third night there, a hostess led us to a nice table on a patio overlooking the water. A moment later, a gorgeous Mexican woman with shiny black hair and doelike eyes approached our table with the menus. She handed one to me.

"Thanks," I said as I took it from her.

When she turned to hand one to Nick, she gasped in surprise. "Nicolás?"

He looked up and smiled. "Hola, Violeta." He stood and gave her a hug before gesturing to me. "Esta es mi esposa, Tara."

The woman smiled at me and said something *rápido* in Spanish, extending her hand.

I gave it a friendly shake. "Nice to meet you, Violeta."

When she left the table, I cut Nick a look over my menu. "Just when you had me feeling sorry for you, stuck down here in Mexico all alone."

He fought a grin. "Maybe it wasn't *all* bad."

"What did you tell her about me?"

"That you're my wife. *Mi esposa.*"

"Hmm. Well, you're not *esposa* hug women you used to date right in front of me."

Nick shrugged. "It's a friendly culture. It would have been rude not to."

He had a point. Besides, I'd noticed a wedding ring on her finger, too. Whatever the two might once have shared, they'd both moved on.

When Nick and I boarded our flight back to Dallas a week later, I was tempted to grab his hand and drag him back out onto the beach. I didn't want our romantic escape to ever end. But I knew it was time to get back home and get back to work. Uncle Sam and honest taxpayers needed us.

On the flight back, I fell into a dreamless sleep. There was no need for dreams anymore. Nick had made all of mine come true.

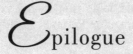

$\mathcal{E}$pilogue

Five years later, Nick scrambled around our house chasing our three-year-old daughter, who was running as fast as her tiny red cowgirl boots would take her. We'd named her Rebecca but called her Reba for short. Reba was a sassy little girl who looked exactly like me. Though she enjoyed her mommy time, she was a daddy's girl at heart, just like I'd always been.

Nick scooped her up in his arms. "Caught you, you little stinker!"

She tossed her head back and giggled with glee.

After Reba had joined our family, I'd gone part-time at the IRS, working half my usual caseload. The reduced work schedule allowed me to still enjoy the thrill and satisfaction of pursuing white-collar criminals, while also enjoying time with my children. Bonnie babysat them while I was at work, though my mother often drove in from east Texas to get in her granny time, too. And speaking of Bonnie and my mother, they'd finished putting out the food they'd prepared and were headed toward the door.

I followed them with my six-month-old son balanced on my hip, giving my left arm a workout. We'd named him

John Harlan after Nick's father and mine, though Hank became his nickname. He'd been big at birth, a nine-pound bowling ball of a baby, who looked just like Nick had at that age. He'd break a lot of hearts someday. But for now, he'd stolen mine.

I gave Bonnie a one-armed hug. "I don't know how we could have done this without you two."

"Glad we could help," Bonnie said, returning my hug. She turned her attention to Hank. "Ready to go to grandma's, little guy?"

He responded with a toothless grin and incoherent babble, waving his teething ring like a tambourine.

Mom gave me a kiss on the cheek and reached out to relieve me of my son. "Enjoy the shower."

"We will. Thanks."

As the two women headed next door to Bonnie's house with their grandson in tow, Alicia and Daniel pulled up to the curb. While they wouldn't be attending the baby shower, they'd offered to watch Reba for us during the event. Alicia and Daniel had one child, a girl who was an absolute sweetie despite being spoiled beyond belief. She and Reba had become virtually inseparable, best friends forever, just like their mothers.

Alicia's daughter sat up as tall as she could in her safety seat in the backseat of their car, straining to see out the window, her mouth breaking into a broad smile when Nick stepped up next to me with Reba in his arms. We walked outside together, rounded up Reba's child seat from my car, and buckled it in next to the other one.

"Hey, cutie," I greeted Alicia's daughter, reaching out to ruffle her hair.

"Hi, Aunt Tawa." She might not yet be able to pronounce my name correctly, but she sure knew how to dress. She was decked out in designer toddler duds, already a fashionista like her mother.

"Thanks for babysitting," I told Alicia and Daniel as I placed Reba in her seat and belted her into place. "We owe you one."

Alicia waved a dismissive hand. "You know we love having Reba over."

Her daughter threw her fists in the air. "Reba! Reba! Reba!"

We shared a laugh.

"Be a good girl," I told my daughter.

She nodded. "I will, Mommy."

Mommy. Was there any more wonderful word in the English language? I certainly didn't think so.

I gave her a kiss on the cheek and Nick planted one on her forehead. We closed the door and waved as they drove off.

Nick turned my way, a roguish gleam in his eyes. "We're alone. Think we've got time for a quickie?"

Before I could respond, the guests of honor, Josh and Kira, turned into the driveway.

"Darn," Nick said. "Rain check?"

I slid him a sexy smile. "You know it."

A few months after catching the garter at our wedding, Josh had proposed and Kira had accepted. They married eighteen months later, holding a destination wedding at a comic book convention in Austin. We all attended in costume. The ceremony was not at all traditional, but it was a heck of a lot of fun. Now here we were, holding a couples baby shower for the two of them. Kira was due to have their first child in four weeks.

We stepped over to the driveway. Josh climbed out of the car and beamed, a proud papa-to-be. Nick opened Kira's door and held out a hand to help her out. Pregnancy looked good on her, filling out her thin body and giving her porcelain skin a fresh, pink glow. She'd had to remove her belly button ring as she'd expanded, and she'd traded in her torn fishnet hose, leather miniskirts, and midriff tops for more conservative maternity clothes, but she had no qualms about making these sacrifices for the baby she'd soon bear.

"Hi, you two." I gave them a smile and stepped back, holding out an arm to direct them inside. "Come on in."

As Josh and Kira made their way to the door, Lu and Carl rolled up in their RV. They'd spent their retirement traveling around the United States. The postcards Lu had sent to the office from the Grand Canyon, Yellowstone, and the Everglades were tacked to the bulletin board in the break room.

When they climbed down from the camper, I called, "Where have you two been now?"

"Gatlinburg, Tennessee!" Carl called.

"The Smoky Mountains are beautiful," Lu added. "We saw a bear!"

Carl reached into the RV, pulled out a bottle filled with amber liquid, and carried it to our door, offering it to Nick. "Brought you a bottle of whiskey, straight from the distillery."

Nick took the bottle and offered a grin in return. "Beats the hell out of a souvenir backscratcher."

Lu and I wrapped each other in a hug. "So glad you could make it," I told her.

"Shoot," she replied, giving me an extra squeeze. "I wouldn't miss this for the world."

We made our way inside and I showed them to the table, fixing them glasses of punch and inviting them to indulge in the delicious spread our mothers had prepared.

Viola arrived next. After Lu retired, she'd stayed on at the IRS, working for Eddie and Nick and holding things together just like always.

"Hi, Vi," I said, taking the wrapped box from her at the door. "Come on in and have a glass of punch."

"Is it spiked?" she asked.

Nick held up the bottle of whiskey. "It can be."

"Add a dash," Viola said. "My bursitis is acting up."

Eddie and Sandra arrived soon thereafter. Eddie had settled into his job as codirector and found that he enjoyed it more than he'd expected. The regular hours allowed him to spend more time with his family.

After greeting Eddie, I turned to his wife. "Great to see you, Sandra. How are the twins?"

"The girls are great," she said. "Of course now that they're almost teenagers we get the occasional drama."

Eddie groaned. "That's when I hide in the closet."

Sandra cast him a look. "How can you be scared of your own girls? You've gone head-to-head with violent criminals."

"That's true," Eddie said. "But a man with a gun is nothing compared to a twelve-year-old having a bad hair day."

Nick put a hand on Eddie's shoulder. "I'll be calling you for advice in a few years, buddy."

Hana was the next one through the door. She was plugging along, still a star on the IRS softball league and my partner on an occasional investigation. She handed me an oversized pastel-striped gift bag. The handle of a plastic whiffle ball bat stuck out of the top. "Might as well start them young if they plan to make the major leagues."

It was far more likely Josh and Kira's child would become a computer geek like its parents rather than an athlete, but it couldn't hurt to give the kid a well-rounded childhood.

Christina and Ajay were the next to arrive, and hugs were again shared. "Great to see you!"

"You, too!" Christina had borne four rambunctious boys in rapid succession over the last few years, yet she somehow managed to maintain her bombshell figure.

Chasing so many boys around must burn a lot of calories. On a professional note, she'd recently teamed with the IRS on another major drug-and-tax-evasion case, this one against an organized ring that made deals online. Given that tech skills were needed to catch the culprits, Josh had been assigned the case. Though the two didn't do yoga on their stakeouts like Christina and I had, they'd made a surprisingly effective team and quickly brought the bad guys in, earning huge accolades from the higher-ups at both the DEA and IRS while also becoming friends.

Ajay cut a look my way. A year ago, Ajay had resigned from the minor emergency center to open his own medical practice with three buddies from medical school. "Haven't seen you in a while, Tara."

Since going part-time, I'd managed to avoid the constant injuries that had plagued me before. "That's good news, isn't it?"

"For you, maybe," he retorted. "But I've got my eye on a new EKG and I can't afford the machine if my best patient stays healthy. Can't you take another bullet or something? All I'm asking is for a small-caliber one in a nonvital organ."

I rolled my eyes. "You're going to have to find another way to finance your equipment."

"Damn, girl. I thought you were a team player."

Will and his wife rounded out the party, arriving with a long wrapped box topped with a gigantic bow.

"Welcome!" I called, inviting them inside. "Help yourself to some food."

Will took one look at the table and said, "Whoa! There's enough food there to feed an army."

"Our mothers live to cook," Nick said. "Everyone's going home with a doggie bag."

"Great!" Will's wife said. "It'll get me out of making dinner."

Over the years, Will had taken on bigger and bigger cases and proved to be a great asset to the office. He and Hana had picked up the slack I'd left when I'd gone part-time, though Eddie and Nick had recently put in a request to hire a rookie agent, too.

After feasting on the delicious dishes my mother and Bonnie had made, we gathered around the living room so Josh and Kira could open their presents. In addition to the whiffle ball set and baseball glove Hana had brought, the gifts included a portable playpen, unisex baby clothes, toys, alphabet blocks, and a veritable safari of stuffed animals. Nick and I had bought the baby an assortment of children's classic books, everything from Dr. Seuss to Curious George to Shel Silverstein. Snuggling up with my kids to read to them was one of our favorite things, and I knew Kira and Josh would enjoy it, too. I'd also borrowed my mother's BeDazzler and added silver studs to a baby-sized faux leather jacket.

Kira squealed when she pulled the jacket from the bag. "It's perfect!" she said, holding it up for all to see.

An hour later, Nick and I stood in the doorway, hands raised in good-bye as the last of the guests drove away. The shower had been a lot of fun, not only because it gave us an opportunity to celebrate Josh and Kira's upcoming addition to their family, but because it gave those of us from the IRS the chance to be together once again. These people were more than just coworkers—we were an extended family who'd strived, struggled, and succeeded together. Though our circumstances might change over time, the bond we shared could never be broken.

Yep, between my work family and my real family, I had it all. People I loved who loved me back. People I could count on, and who could count on me, too. Add in an interesting job, the comfort of a solid marriage, and the wonders of motherhood, and I couldn't ask for a fuller, richer life. I had no idea what I'd done to deserve all of this, but I was glad to have it, and I wished it for everyone else as well.

While the written tales of my exploits have come to an end, you can trust that I'm still out there, fighting for financial justice, bringing tax evaders to their knees. I hope you'll think of me when you receive your tax refunds.

Many happy returns.

**Don't miss a special E-original novella
with Tara on a nutty case to solve
a case of fraud at a county fair!**

Available now from St. Martin's Press